REGINA'S SONG

SHARLEEN COOPER COHEN

A Dell Book

Published by
Dell Publishing Co., Inc.
1 Dag Hammarskjold Plaza
New York, New York 10017

"Stars" by Janis Ian: © 1972 Mine Music Ltd.
Rights in the U.S.A. and Canada administered by
Mine Music Ltd. Used by permission. All rights reserved.

Copyright © 1980 by Sharleen Cooper Cohen

All rights reserved. No part of this book
may be reproduced or transmitted in any form
or by any means, electronic or mechanical, including
photocopying, recording, or by any information storage
and retrieval system, without the written permission
of the Publisher, except where permitted by law.

Dell ® TM 681510, Dell Publishing Co., Inc.

ISBN: 0-440-17414-7

Printed in the United States of America
First printing—June 1980

This book is dedicated to my loving parents,
Sam and Claretta White,
For all the wonders they have wrought
And to the memory of my sister,
Steffani,
Whose life was one of those wonders.

The characters in this book are all people who sprang full-blown from my imagination. Any similarity to people either living or dead is pure coincidence.

Stars, they come and go
They come fast or slow.
They go like the last light
of the sun, all in a blaze.
And all you see is glory.

"Stars"
by Janis Ian
Columbia Records
1974 C.B.S. Inc.
Mine Music Ltd./April Music Inc.
(ASCAP)

PART 1

REGINA

CHAPTER
1

Oh God, I'm hyperventilating! Regina gasped and tried to calm her wildly beating pulse. *Think quiet; think serene*, she commanded herself, but her breath was coming in huge pants, irregular gasps followed by giant ones; short, sick, scared roller coaster breaths in her stomach, plunging down again, screaming as they screeched through the tracts of her guts. Icy hands, sweating forehead; her back and her armpits dripped sweat onto her three thousand dollar dress from Bob Mackie.

"Florie," she managed to cry out, and Florie was there, soothing her back, smoothing her forehead.

"It's all right, darlin'," she crooned, "s'all right now; Florie's here."

Regina's huge blue eyes were filled with terror. Her pale skin looked colorless. Her lips were a gash of red; her cheek blush, painted on; and three sets of eyelashes weighed on her lids, a ton of beauty.

"Put your head down, now!" Florie commanded, pushing her into a chair, grabbing the back of her head, and shoving hard until the ground came up to meet her.

"Where's Mike?" Regina's voice was muffled by her thighs. She needed to see him. He was never here when she wanted him. No, that wasn't true. He was very devoted. Too devoted, smothering her with attention. The blackness threatened to take over, but she couldn't pass out now. She had to be on stage in a few minutes. She longed to let go and fall into that sweet black unconsciousness. A room full of people in her suite joked and laughed, waiting for her show to begin. She could hear them in the next room. She wanted to scream! Mike should have kicked them out long ago. She needed solitude before a performance. The house was packed tonight; it was always packed when she played Vegas. *Why do I panic like this? A seasoned performer?* She tried to sit up, but Florie was pressing her down. "Florie, let me up or I'll suffocate." She could smell the awful smell of her own beaded dress. Florie kept pressing.

How much time did she have left? Couldn't be much. The spurts of laughter from the audience were coming closer together; thunderclaps of applause rolled from large explosions to smaller ones. Those sounds meant that Buddy was coming to the end of his warmup. *Oh! A few more jokes,* please! she thought, *just a few more minutes, seconds, milliseconds. Anything!*

Her heart was quieter now. She couldn't hyperventilate while her chest was being pressed against her knees. Florie must have felt the tension ease because she let up on the pressure. Florie had magic hands. Regina took a normal breath. *Someday I'm going to tell them to make me up while I'm asleep; dress me, and comb me, and wheel me to the wings, bed and all. Then on cue someone will give me a very gentle shake, they'll elevate the electric bed to sitting position, and I'll wake up, step out of bed, and be ready to go right on stage and "knock 'em dead." There wouldn't be time to panic then, and I wouldn't have to go through this!*

Florie helped her to sit up so they could survey the damage. Regina could go through the ravages of hell and still look gorgeous. Florie smiled her soft, loving, brown-eyed smile, and Regina's eyes filled with tears.

"Still saving me from the bogey man, aren't you,

Florinda Mae Trainer!" She put her arms around the other woman's large waist and hugged her. Violets! Florie always smelled of violets. Regina had a sudden and clear picture of Florie's funeral. An ebony casket lined in pink satin ruffles with a black evangelist choir singing in the background and the scent of violets. There'd be blankets of violets for her Florie.

"Oh God," she whispered. "What would I do without you?" She and Florie had been devoted to one another from the first moment they met. Florie was working as a shampoo lady at Olivier's Salon on Fifty-seventh in New York when Regina discovered those magic hands. They'd talked for hours about Regina's career and Florie's problems. Florie was working two jobs at once, trying to make ends meet. And then that same night they'd run into each other at Regina's costumer's where Florie was working nights doing special handwork. Their meeting twice in one day had been quite a coincidence, and they'd struck up a friendship. Regina begged Florie for one solid year to come and work for her exclusively before Florie agreed. Florie hadn't wanted to leave New York. Her nephew lived there and she was keeping an eye on him. A lot of good that had done. He'd ended up nothing but trouble.

Florie pulled her up and out of the chair and propelled her into the sitting room. Regina saw Mike in the corner talking to Wilson from her PR firm. Wilson was a short plump man with pale skin, and by comparison Mike towered over him with his tall slimness, his gray temples, and his green eyes behind the green-tinted glasses. Mike was watching her to see if she was all right.

Jesus, there were Aunt Elva and Uncle Charles! She hadn't seen them in years. They waved to her and she waved back as she walked through the room toward the stage, and then her eyes caught another familiar face. Eddie Wakefield! What was he doing here? *He's aged,* she thought, noticing the way his thick brown hair wasn't as thick anymore and the laugh lines around his brown eyes had become creases; but his grin was still boyish and brought out the dimples in his cheeks.

"Knock 'em dead, sweetheart!" Eddie called to her and she winked at him.

He winked back, and at that moment she thought about Cord Crocker, and her heart lurched, and the smile froze on her face. But she kept walking towards the stage. *No heart twisters now,* she prayed. *Voice, stay open. Sinuses, stay clear.* She heard her name announced. She was standing in the wings. The air machine caught her chiffon sleeves, and she floated on stage to thunderous applause. At this moment how she loved it!

Just as Regina passed by Eddie felt an iron grip on his arm and someone whipped him around.

"You stupid asshole!" Mike Shaw shouted at him. "Don't you ever speak to my wife before an entrance again or I'll personally break you in two!"

Eddie wanted to slam his fist into Mike Shaw's red Irish face. In all those years on the road, all those early times of tours and hopes and wild success and incredible fame, he had always said to Regina before an entrance, "knock 'em dead, sweetheart," her favorite expression. Now her ex-boozer of a husband was humiliating him in front of all these people. It infuriated him. But he couldn't alienate Mike Shaw, not if he wanted a favor from Regina. Eddie yanked his arm away from Mike's grip.

"I didn't mean anything by it, Mike." The fake sincerity choked him.

Mike rocked back on his heels and relaxed his stance, straightening the sleeves of his tux. He always wore a tux with an open silk shirt when Regina was performing. Eddie thought it probably made him feel like a part of Regina's act. God knows he had never made it on his own. *But then neither have I,* Eddie realized.

"I didn't mean to jump on you like that," Mike said. "Regina's been awfully edgy lately."

Eddie held up his hands. "It's okay. I'll go catch the show and see her later."

"Sure," Mike agreed, "come on back then."

Eddie felt as though every eye was still on him as he ducked out of the dressing room.

Once past the stage door and down the green room corridor he felt better. He could hear Regina's voice from back stage, and then as he opened the door to the theater he got a full blast of her. The golden tones flowed around him like a soft caress. The auburn mane of hair shot fire around her face. A full mouth on a pixie face, and those incredible breasts above the tiny waist. She held the audience spellbound as she sang.

Eddie stood on the side aisle until her opening song ended, thinking about how it had been with Regina when she started out, a skinny kid from Montebello. She had no experience, just a gift for song and a stage presence that caught you and made you want to cry and laugh and fuck her all at the same time.

He'd never forget that night he'd taken her down to the Village where Cord Crocker and his younger brother Gene were appearing at some hole in the wall. They were forming a group with Don Drummond and they needed a fourth, someone who could sing. Regina had never sung with a group before, none of them had. *We were all so young and eager,* Eddie thought. And that's where the legend of Majesty had begun. The four of them were so right together, from the very first moment. He shook his head, remembering. That legend would still be going on if Gene Crocker hadn't overdosed.

The show lasted for an hour and forty-five minutes. By the time it was over the audience was screaming Regina's name.

* * *

The backstage area was pitch black. Only a dim light over the door to Regina's dressing room illuminated the snakelike cables that lay under his feet. Eddie wiped his sweating palms on his gabardine pants.

No noise escaped from the soundproofed room as he knocked and waited for admittance. Finally a door opened and a security guard asked his name. "Eddie Wakefield," he said. The man checked with someone inside and Eddie was ushered into the party. Smoky ambience floated around him, and Eddie saw Mike Shaw serving drinks behind the bar to a few guys from the orchestra who were still in their tuxedos. Eddie nodded to them as he walked by. Mike waved, all his earlier display of temper was gone now that the work day was over.

Regina came out of her dressing room dressed in a kaftan. She was still wearing her stage makeup and her jewels. Florie came over to her and unhooked the diamond necklace, took her earrings, and pulled the rings off her fingers, placing them into a velvet bag. Then she motioned to the security guard at the door to escort her out. Eddie remembered when Regina's jewelry consisted of a few silver and turquoise bracelets.

Regina made her way from group to group, accepting accolades, listening to the praises of the fortunate few who were invited into the inner sanctum. She gave them each a moment, then she spotted Eddie. She came straight over to him and threw her arms around him.

"God, it's good to see you," she said.

"You were incredible, gorgeous!" All the memories of the past came flooding back to him as he hugged her. It was as if his youth was in his arms again. When he pulled away he saw tears in her eyes.

She turned around and raised her voice above the

din of conversation. "Hey! Everybody! I want you to meet someone." Conversations quieted to a murmur. *Nothing like the star to demand the stage,* Eddie thought. "This is my friend, Eddie Wakefield, the songwriter. He's responsible for my getting into that old group of mine. What's its name?" Everyone laughed. "And he's a helluva musician!" A few people applauded, and Regina's bass player, who'd been with her for years, muttered, "A helluva songwriter!"

Eddie loved the attention, but he didn't want to irritate Mike Shaw in any way. He felt somehow embarrassed to be introduced as a songwriter when he hadn't written anything in a long time.

"I've got something I want to discuss with you. An idea I've been working on."

She nodded. "Shoot!"

"Not here. It will take some time to explain." He was aware that any minute she'd be interrupted and he wouldn't be able to give it the proper sell.

"Tonight's our last night here. I'll be back in L.A. tomorrow. Why don't you stop by the house. Things will be quieter there and we can talk."

"That's great," he said, elated by her reception.

"I'll look forward to it," she replied, kissing him goodby.

Regina watched him walk away, her curiosity intense. She was dying to ask if he'd seen Cord in the last few years, but she could never bring herself to do that.

She could feel it welling up inside again, the exhaustion that was always there just under the surface, a gray sluggish quicksand threatening to pull her down. She'd spent two grueling weeks of work followed by three more, two shows a night, three on weekends, never a break. But there were moments of extreme highs. This act was tough, and she fought the same fears every night, the same preperformance panic. And she never slept well on the road, because of so many things, but she wouldn't give up where she was until they carted her away in a wheelchair or a coffin.

Sleep. That's what she needed. A nonexistent experience for the nightclub performer. In another hour it would be two A.M. and all the company would be gone; then she would be able to eat dinner. She hadn't eaten all day (who could eat before a show or between shows?) and by two A.M. she'd be starving. She and Mike usually had dinner with fellow performers from other shows, and by then it would be four or five in the morning and she'd still be up, wired from her performance. Every night it was the same routine. After dinner she'd spend an hour or two unwinding, and then it would be five or six in the morning and the damned sun would be coming up. If she took a sleeping pill, she'd be puffy and groggy the next day. If she took a tranquilizer, it would only work for a few nights, and then she'd need another and another to relax her enough to go to sleep. She'd tried booze, but it gave her a hangover. And when she was lucky enough to finally relax and feel sleepy, the light from the brilliant desert sun would be creeping in around the blackout drapes. She had tried sleeping masks, but they made her feel as though she were drowning. So if Mike didn't want to make love, she would lie there and worry about the lyrics in the fourth song, or whether she could go on working with such an inadequate sound system, or how the children were doing at home without her. Just thinking about trying to fall asleep made her tired. Sometimes it was too damn much to take.

She wondered what Eddie Wakefield wanted to talk to her about. Well, she'd find out soon enough. Right now it was time for her to play celebrity.

CHAPTER 2

The approach to the house was between two stone pilasters and down a long driveway. Pine trees lined the roadway and scented the air like a Christmas forest. Eddie expected to see a fortress, but the house was ranchy, painted a dusty blue color, with white shutters. Fields of orange and yellow flowers were planted in sculptured areas; fern trees framed the front door. The little Dutch girl from Montebello had done all right.

Florie greeted him with her wide toothy smile and smoothed the front of her dress. Then she kept the Yorkies from leaping at his knees and pointed through the living room.

"They're in the family room, through there. I'll join you as soon as I put the dogs in the run."

No meeting with Mike and Regina was complete without Florie. She was their foil, their tape recorder, and their nursemaid rolled into one. She was a quiet woman who'd seen it all and who only spoke when she had something to say, but her opinion was obviously the most important one Mike and Regina heard. Especially Regina, who was devoted to Florie and trusted her completely.

Eddie made his way through a beautifully furnished formal living room complete with moiré sofas and a marble fireplace resplendent with silver-framed photos of the two daughters Mike and Regina doted on. The family room, which opened out to the pool, had used brick floors, a billiard table (circa 1860), a soda fountain and bar combination, and huge overstuffed sofas and chairs that dwarfed their inhabitants. Eddie listened for the sound of thwacking tennis rackets in the distance, but the court was silent today.

Regina looked pale and drawn from her stint in Vegas, though Mike sported his usual tan. She was curled up on the sofa with her hair flowing around her shoulders and no makeup. The cleavage of her famous chest peeked through the wheat-colored kaftan, and her blue eyes gazed at him from across the room.

"Come sit by me," she patted the down cushion next to her. But he took a suede straight-backed chair between her and Mike. "How are you, Eddie?" Regina asked.

"I feel great," he began. "I've started writing again."

"That's wonderful," Regina said, waiting for him to begin.

"But that's not what I came to talk to you about. It's something else. Something I think is very exciting."

The phone rang, and a buzzer on the instrument next to Mike buzzed three times. "I'll take it in the office," he said and got up to answer the call.

Eddie watched him go with disappointment. There were as many interruptions here as there had been in Vegas. He'd better ask her now, even without Mike and Florie, before he lost her attention. He took a deep breath and began again. All she could say was no, he thought. "I'm trying to get a deal going to do a reunion concert of Majesty, Regina. It would be a one-time event, large scale, very big promotion." He watched her carefully. "Before you say anything, please hear me out."

Various reactions fought for supremacy on her face. But the one he hadn't expected won out. She looked at him with utter disbelief, and then tears came to her eyes as she covered her face with her hands.

"Are you all right?" he asked nervously.

Tears were sliding down the outsides of her hands. She reached over to the antique table and took a Kleenex. "I'm sorry, Eddie. After Vegas I'm so wrung out that I shouldn't be expected to discuss anything. Nobody seems to understand that." The tears rolled down her cheeks and she tried unsuccessfully to smile. "I don't know why I'm crying." She was trying to compose herself. "My elder daughter, Jamie, has the flu. I was up with her all night. And my little one, Jana, sprained her finger yesterday. And Mike is pressing me to decide about our eastern tour which starts in three weeks. That means new songs, and new costumes, and constant work between now and then." She tottered on the brink of control while an image of Cord flashed in her mind. "And now you come here with an idea like this!" She started to laugh and to cry at the same time, but the tears won out, and then she cried quietly, too exhausted to sob. "I'm so tired."

"Regina," he said softly. "How much do you make a year? Seven hundred and fifty thousand, a million? Where does it all go? What have you got left after you kill yourself like this? Have you made good investments with your capital? Do you know that a reunion concert with one night of performance and a couple of weeks preparation would net you over three million dollars?"

Again Cord flashed across the surface of her mind—*never, never again!*

"Eddie. You're a sweet guy, but somebody's sold you a bill of goods. Some promoter who wants to sell books or magazines or Regina dolls talked you into approaching me, right?"

Mike came back into the room and sat down, watching her as she twisted her Kleenex and wiped her nose.

"Eddie wants me to do a reunion concert of Majesty."

The gold clock on the table ticked loudly. Mike's face was impassive.

Eddie would have preferred any reaction to the blank look on Mike's face. A child's voice called from the top of the stairs, "Mommy! Jamie is throwing up again."

Regina bolted out of the chair. "I'm coming, honey."

The phone rang again, and Mike answered it, this time without leaving the room. Regina was starting rehearsals for a TV special to be shot in London, and there was to be an album in conjunction with the show. Eddie half listened, not knowing what to do. He kept crossing and uncrossing his legs until Mike finished his conversation. It took a long time.

Finally Regina returned. She came into the room and stood staring at Mike as though they were having a silent conversation, and then in a quietly controlled voice she said, "I can't take it anymore. I don't care what he says about three million dollars. I wouldn't work with that bastard Don Drummond if my life depended on it!" A pale little girl with red hair and feet pajamas came into the room and climbed up on the sofa. Regina went to sit next to her, pulling the child into her lap.

"Three million? Regina." Mike raised his eyebrows.

She shot him a look.

He threw up his hands. "I'm sorry, Eddie, she won't consider it."

"You're damn right I won't, Mike Shaw. And I don't want you harping on it or mentioning it to me. I've said no! And that's final!"

Eddie was fighting a sick, dizzy feeling that kept erupting in his head. He couldn't believe it was all over this soon. Why was she so adamant? She hadn't even heard him out. He tried to interrupt her tirade, but she wouldn't let him.

"And don't tell me what an experience it would be to work with them all again," she said to Mike. Her voice quavered. "It would be an impossible experience, too damn much. That's what I've always said." Suddenly her shoulders sagged and she began to cry again. "Why doesn't anybody listen to me?"

Florie came into the room to find Regina hysterical on the sofa and Eddie white-faced and edging toward the door, while Mike's lips formed a grim determined line. Florie moved to Regina's side and put her arm around the bowed shoulders.

Mike showed Eddie to the front door. "I'm sorry this happened while you were here," Mike said. "We always have a couple of days of craziness after Vegas. But when she's had a few days of sleep and sun, she'll be itching to work again."

"Mike, about the reunion. . . ."

Mike cut him off. "She'll never say yes to a reunion of Majesty. There are too many old scars and some of the wounds never healed. I'm telling you because you need to know it's not you or your idea she's rejecting. It's the whole ballgame. She doesn't want to play and I don't want her to, either. I'd be crazy to throw her together with Cord again."

Eddie nodded, feeling as though he'd just been hit by a bat.

"Good seeing you, Eddie," Mike said and closed the white paneled front door.

Eddie stood there on the doorstep wondering what he should do now. *Find the nearest cliff and drive off.*

CHAPTER
3

Mike grabbed the phone on the first ring, before it woke Regina, and then he realized that Regina wasn't there. She'd gone to an early dance class. He could have sworn he hadn't slept all night, but he must have dozed off because he hadn't heard her leave.

"Good morning."

"What's good about it?" It was his accountant, Tony Darakjian.

"Why so early?" His tongue was sticking to the roof of his mouth.

"It's eight o'clock, Mike. I'm going to the office now. And I want you there by nine thirty."

"What's up."

"I'll tell you when I see you."

"Did you finish the books?"

"At four this morning."

"Well?"

"I'd rather not go into it on the phone."

"That bad?"

"That bad."

There was Muzak playing in the elevator of Tony's building as the doors closed in front of him. A serene version of Stephen Sondheim's "Everything's Coming Up Roses." Regina had sung it in an act once. The song did nothing for his spirits. If things were as bad as Tony intimated, Mike didn't know what he would do. He'd really climbed out on a limb this time. But he believed in this project. He'd covered all his bases, hadn't he? He just couldn't face the possibility of another bad investment, not again. Not this time. It was hard enough when he'd been in his twenties. But now he was pushing forty. How many more chances would he get in his life? He couldn't go on being "Mr. Regina Williams."

The lights in the elevator counted the floors as people got in and out. He envied Tony his office in this plush Beverly Hills building and always enjoyed coming here. But not today. He would have given anything to be somewhere else right now, rather than here in the elevator about to hear the news that Tony had for him.

"He'll be right with you, Mr. Shaw." Gloria, the receptionist, nodded for him to be seated on the Pace leather grouping. Each section of the sofa was curved for one body. *Not very cost efficient,* Mike thought, *especially for an accountant's sofa.*

Tony Darakjian was a shrewd businessman, which was why Mike had gone into partnership with him on this deal. Tony had been keeping tabs on things while Mike was away. But Tony was only an investor, not a producer. Mike was the one who knew the picture business. And he shouldn't have left town at such a crucial time in the production. He should have stayed where he could keep control of things. As it was Tony'd had to see the rough cut of the film without him. But he couldn't have let Regina go to Vegas alone. Never. She'd fall apart without him.

Gloria showed him into Tony's office.

"Coffee light?" she asked.

"That's fine," he told her and took a seat in front of the steel and oak desk. Mike perferred antiques himself, but he had to admit the desk was a knockout.

Tony looked up and sighed, then shook his head. Mike had prepared himself for the worst, but now his insides felt queasy, liquefied, jellied.

"They ran a rough cut for me two nights ago, and I've had every expert in the field in to look at it since then. It's no good, Mike. It's unusable. It stinks. It's shit. *We're* shit; all our money's gone."

There were tears in Tony's eyes. His expression said, "How could you do this to me. I trusted you, and you messed up."

"I don't understand. I saw the rushes. They weren't half bad. With dubbing, and scoring, and editing. . . ." Mike's voice trailed off. He should have stopped them months ago. But there was already so much money invested. He'd hoped they could pull it off. He'd hoped he was wrong when he saw rushes that didn't match the previous day's shooting. When he saw shots that were over- and underexposed; when he heard soundtrack that faded in and out.

"That was *my* money I lost, Mike. Three hundred thousand dollars. Those college kids didn't know the first thing about making a movie."

"They're graduates from USC for Christ's sake. I saw their student films; they were terrific. The script was terrific, too. You read it."

"The bank has called in our loans. I've had to give my house as collateral. Grace is having a fit. What did Regina say?"

"She doesn't know."

"Shit, Mike! What do you mean she doesn't know. How did you use your house as collateral without her signature?"

"I forged it," Mike said quietly.

"You what?" Tony yelled.

"Don't look so shocked. I've done it before. Regina doesn't like being bothered with financial details."

"But forgery. Lord, man, what got into you? They'll be serving you with a foreclosure notice. You and Regina will be kicked out on your asses."

Mike put his head in his hands. "Jesus, don't say that," he cried.

"Listen, I've set up a meeting with Browning at the bank. We'll see if we can stall them or see if we can resurrect the movie somehow."

Mike couldn't even meet Tony's gaze. This was the deal that was going to make his personal fortune. Never again would he have to ask Regina for anything. Never again would people call him "Mr. Williams." He'd be a producer. Someone who made five million on a film that cost six hundred thousand. What went wrong? What happened? If he'd stayed on their backs every day, would it have turned out any differently, or was he destined to keep making mistakes like this?

"You'll have to tell Regina, Mike. Ask her to bail you out."

"No!" he shouted, leaping out of his chair. "I can't do that."

"You mean you're going to let them take your house?"

"I'll think of something. But I don't want Regina to know. When I asked her for this money in the first place, she said no. No more speculative ventures."

"I don't blame her."

"This film was going to get me out from under her thumb."

Tony looked at him. "So where is Regina's money?"

"It's invested in oil stocks. Solid, well-protected. I was going to use the returns on the oil investment to pay back the bank."

"Then do it."

"I don't have it yet. It's taking longer than I figured. I'll have to have some money to tide me over."

"Don't look at me. I'm cleaned out. What about your father."

"Not much chance there. He's got it, but he won't give it to me."

"What about your "other" father?"

"Lubow?"

"Yes."

"I hate to get into him."

"You've done it before."

"But I didn't like it. He always expects a favor in return."

"But you're in trouble now, Mike."

Mike stared blankly ahead.

"So what are you going to do?"

"Something, I'll think of something." But right now he couldn't think at all. His brain was pickled in fear and dread and self-loathing. By sheer force of will he pulled himself out of the chair. He reached the door before Tony repeated the question again.

"Are you going to Lubow?"

"I don't know," he mumbled as he closed the door to the office. *I don't know,* he echoed into the black gaping hole that followed behind him, drawing in all the breathable air, sucking at his heels, as he tried to walk away from the truth. His guts ached from the thought of losing everything he'd worked for.

He walked in a daze out of the UCB Building, across Camden Drive, over Dayton Way to Rodeo. His feet carried him automatically on their favorite shopping route, but his eyes didn't see the window displays or the pretty shop girls. All he saw was his life in ruins. All he could hear was his own voice repeating over and over, *I don't know, I don't know, don't know, don't know.*

The house was quiet when he got home; the children were in school, Regina was at rehearsal. He walked straight through the parquet entry hall, through the coffee and beige living room, through the navy and rust family room, and into the upholstered leather bar. God, he couldn't let them take this house.

He poured himself a full shot of whiskey, but the liquor didn't take away the knowledge of his own failure. The feeling of desolation that had been growing in him all morning was choking him now. Even the whiskey didn't wash it away. Maybe it had always been there, ever since he was a kid. He had known in his heart that he was a failure, but he'd refused to see it for a long time. He was going to lose everything that was important to him again. Making a comeback after the first few times had taken all his energy, all his optimism. He was younger then. But there was no energy left now, no more optimism. He couldn't start all over again; the very thought was exhausting. He couldn't face the sneers, the jibes, the looks, the whispers. Loser Mike, down the tubes again; another foolish deal, trusted some kids who screwed him. Worse, worse than anything was the thought of hurting Regina.

Go on Mike, a little voice inside told him. *Have the final courage, take yourself off! At least she'll have the insurance. You've done everything in life worth doing, been at the top. What else is there but more of the same? Just more lies and more pointless effort and more failures ahead. Go on, do it!*

His gun was in his desk. He was very calm as he unlocked the drawer. His hands didn't even shake when they closed around the handle of the revolver. He even knew the exact spot to shoot himself, right behind the ear, no mistakes, no surviving as a vegetable, an instant end to problems. At least he wouldn't be an embarrassment to Regina anymore. The girls were young enough to forget him. That hurt him.

The box of ammunition was in the bottom desk drawer. He ran his hands over the polished wood. He used to love this antique Louis Quinze desk; had to have it. Now it meant nothing to him.

Should I write a note? he wondered. *Jack-off one last time?* But he knew he couldn't get it up. Hadn't been hard once in three weeks.

Regina deserves more than you can give her . . . the voice said.

His knees began to shake as he carried the gun into the bedroom. He wanted to pray, but there were no words. His heart wasn't even beating a protest. *See, you're half dead anyway. Go on. Go all the way.*

He released the catch and flipped the chamber away from the barrel. The bullet made a clicking sound as it entered the chamber. He thought about loading the revolver fully, but all he would need was one bullet. He peered down the inside of the barrel. The gun was clean. He took good care of it, the way he took care of all his possessions. Neat and clean. *Go on, do it already!* He rotated the chamber into position, and it snapped into place. Now his heart was pounding! He lay down on the bed. His hand with the gun lay beside him. The electric clock hummed next to his ear, and a siren sounded off in the hills. *Are these the last sounds I'll ever hear?* he wondered.

Slowly he raised the gun. He could see its black shape out of the side of his right eye. He was so tired, so weary, he might not have the strength to do it. *Just squeeze the trigger,* he remembered, *don't jerk it. Am I really doing this?*

Go on, the voice said. The gun seemed to weigh fifty pounds; he brought it up slowly toward his head. The barrel touched softly to the side of his skull, and a terrible chill of fear gripped him.

And something else. The thought of Regina; the way she looked standing on stage when the spotlight caressed her body and her wonderful voice filled the air. He remembered how much she'd needed him when he first met her, and how much he loved her. Everything he did, he did for her. If he killed himself, she would never live it down. She would blame herself. She would feel guilty again for another tragedy in her life. He couldn't do it to her. Not to Regina.

The first tragedy had nearly destroyed her. Then there had been Gene's death. She still couldn't talk about it to him. His suicide would finish her off for good.

Yes. Regina still needed him. Maybe he could go on, summon his courage once more. Find a new way. He could smell the metallic odor of the gun as his sweaty palm oiled the handle. Slowly he lowered it back to the bed, closed the hammer, and replaced the safety. His whole body was wet with perspiration, but he didn't care. He felt alive for the first time in months. This was the worst moment of his life, a time against which all else could be measured, and he'd survived it. He unloaded the gun, making sure all the chambers were empty. He replaced the shells in the box and locked the gun back in the desk. Then he lay down on the bed, turned over on his side and sobbed with relief. *I'll make it up to you, Regina,* he thought. *I'll make it up to you for everything.*

CHAPTER
4

Regina-Marie Togerson was Papa's girl. She lived for the weeks when Papa came home to Holland from his voyages as a merchant seaman. He told her wonderful stories about the places he'd been, New Zealand, the Orient, India, Australia, all the magic places in the world. Mama was happy too when Papa came home, and life was beautiful.

The three of them would go on picnics and outings to the zoo and the amusement park where Regina loved the ferris wheel and the sweet treats that Papa would buy for her. And then after several weeks when life was so wonderful that she was ready to burst with happiness, Mama and Papa would start fighting. Mama would begin to cry and Regina could hear them arguing in their room at night after she'd gone to bed. And then one morning she'd awaken to see Papa's gear packed and sitting in the front hall. The green duffle bag that struck fear in her soul; anguish wrapped in canvas.

Worst of all Papa would have on his traveling clothes, the navy pea jacket, the dark woolen cap pulled down over his red hair that made his green eyes bright and shiny, and on his feet would be his great scuffed boots. He'd lift her high above his head, so high that she touched the ceiling, so high that her stomach would be in her throat and it would feel like the ferris wheel. Then he'd drop her down to his chest and hug her hard and say, "Take care of your Mama now, Regina-Marie. You're a big girl, and Mama depends on you when I'm away."

Regina knew that if she looked Mama would have that sad expression on her face and her eyes would be all red from crying. So Regina would hug Papa very hard and say, "Please don't go. Stay home just this once. I'll be so good that you won't miss going to sea." But Mama had already tried saying all those things and it never did any good. Because Papa would go, wrenching himself out of her arms, and she would feel as though her heart had been crushed underneath his great boots.

"Regina, how much time did you practice today?" Mama's voice grated on her. *Not enough,* she knew. The piano waited like a silent accuser. Mama was choir director at the Dutch Reformed Church and a classicist as far as music was concerned. Bach, Mozart, Handel; they were her gods. But Regina loved the modern composers and, heaven help her, the popular songs. It wasn't that she didn't want to practice, but there were rehearsals for the Christmas pageant. She was playing the Virgin Mary, and she had to sew her own costume. And there was always choral practice, and homework to do. Besides she was running errands for Mrs. Wogen and Mrs. Tilhauser to try to earn enough money for new skates.

There was never enough money. The house was always cold in the winter. Coal was very expensive, and the portable electric heater they bought secondhand only worked half the time. Mitchell had been sick a lot this year, and Mama had to pay for the doctor and his medicine.

Mitchell. Ever since he was born he had been Regina's joy and her exasperation. An orange-headed four-year-old who depended on her for everything, especially his entertainment. She told him stories and acted out all the characters in different voices and she made up special songs for him. His favorite ones he wanted to hear over and over. Regina gave Mitchell so much love that Papa's comings and goings were not such a wrench for him. Yet each time Papa went back to sea, for Regina it still felt like needles in her heart.

But there was something wonderful to look forward to. The choral group from the primary school was going on a weekend trip by bus from Amsterdam to Brussels; they would be performing in an all-choral festival. Regina was going to sing two solos. For the first time in her eleven years she would be going away from home by herself.

And Mama had played on her desire to go, unfairly, Regina thought. She made Regina practice the piano for all the hours she would miss when she went to Brussels, and care for Mitchell every evening for the previous week while Mama led choir practice, and clean out all her drawers, every single one.

Regina was very tired the night before the excursion. When she finally got Mitchell to bed, after giving him his glass of water, reading him his stories, singing him his songs, she climbed under the down quilt across the room and fell instantly asleep.

That was why the loud noise awakened her with such a start. And then she heard Mama cry out. She bolted up out of bed and ran to the top of the stairs. Mama was sprawled at the bottom of the tiny hallway on her back. Her leg was twisted underneath her, and Mitchell's tinker toys were scattered all over the steep staircase. Regina had forgotten to put them away.

Regina flew to her mother's side. Mama was crying from the pain of her twisted foot. The first thing Regina thought when she saw that Mama was not dead was *now I cannot go to Brussels.*

* * *

The ankle was sprained, and it was her fault that Mama lay upstairs in pain, unable to handle her duties. And how mean of Papa to be away in the West Indies when they needed him so right here. If Papa were here, she would have been able to go. If Papa were here, she wouldn't have even wanted to go.

Regina came home from school on Friday utterly defeated. She could hear Mrs. Wogen upstairs talking to Mama. She knew they were talking about her, what a hateful girl she was, how badly she was behaving when Mama needed her so.

And then Mama called, "Regina-Marie, come here right away."

She scampered up the stairs and into Mama's room. How sweet Mama looked in her white lace bed jacket, the one from her trousseau that Grandmother had made. Her blond hair was tied up on top of her head with a ribbon, and she was smiling.

"Regina, how long would it take for you to get ready to go to Brussels with your group?"

Regina just stared, her mouth open.

"Mrs. Wogen has offered to help me with your brother and with my ice packs. She'll bring us over a picnic basket of food and look in on us every few hours. I think it will be all right if you go to the festival."

Regina couldn't speak.

"Well don't just stand there, child. Hurry!"

No one ever got ready so fast, actually her suitcase was still packed. Out it came from under the bed, and around her neck went her muffler; on went her knitted cap, and into her coat went her arms as she ran down the hall. She kissed Mama and hugged Mrs. Wogen and tore down the stairs, her suitcase bumping. "Thank you, thank you," she called. She could still hear Mitchell squealing and jumping up and down in the dormer window as she closed the front door and ran down Juiliana Straat toward the school.

If only she hadn't gone to Brussels, maybe they'd still be alive.

If only she hadn't gone, she would have been there to fill the coal bin, and Mama wouldn't have gotten so cold that night. So cold that she plugged the electric heater into her room, the one Papa always meant to fix. And if Regina had been home, maybe she would have smelled the smoke. And maybe she would have helped Mama down the stairs to safety and awakened the baby in time so that he wouldn't have suffocated in his bed. If only. . . .

They waited five days for Papa to come home and then they had the funeral. That tiny coffin next to Mama's tore her apart. Even Papa's presence by her side didn't take away the pain and the fear. *Oh God, why have you taken those angels? Never again to hear Mitchell laugh, and beg me for stories. Never again to hear my Mama say, "Have you practiced, Regina?" I'll practice, Mama, I'll be so good. Only please don't be dead. Please!*

Her scream of anguish filled the upper spirals of the church. "It's my fault," she screamed, "It's my fault."

Regina went to live with her Aunt Elva and Uncle Charles in Montebello, California. She didn't speak a word of English and she hated Montebello, a blighted area populated with minorities who knifed one another. The steel refineries, and industrial wastes, and hot, eye-burning smog, the cement yards, and the huge expanse of scarred desert land made it feel like another planet after the cool, green beauty of Holland. No snow, and no canals, and no ships, and no tulips, and no Mama and Papa and brother. For Papa hated his sister Elva, and she hated him, so he came to see Regina even less than he had before. And when he did, he was a different man, quiet and reserved and sad. There was no reason to come home anymore. There was no more home. And Regina knew that he blamed her.

They put her right into school. No one cared that she didn't understand what the teachers were saying. But she understood what the students were saying. "Muthafucker," and "white-cunt-bitch," and "squirrelly piece of ass," and "redheaded hole." The words were foreign to her, but the meaning was clear. She didn't belong. She was different, with her pale skin and her red hair that curled the way it wanted to. And she couldn't speak to them, couldn't answer back, couldn't find an area in which to relate to anyone.

No one she met in Montebello had ever heard of Mozart or Handel. The only music she heard morning and night was rock and roll or the Spanish-speaking station from East L.A. The noises, the unfamiliar sounds, the blight, all surrounded Regina like a haze of impenetrable dust. Regina withdrew into herself, like a larva in a cocoon. No one knew she was in there, watching and waiting until little by little she could learn the words, "Come-on-let's-go," or "What chew want?" or "Hey, what's happenin'." And slowly she began to understand that Montebello was a place to get out of.

Regina made a few friends in school, but she wasn't interested in her fellow students. In Holland she had been a star, the most popular, sought-after girl in her group. But California had different criteria for popularity than her native country. Here it was toughness that got you points. Here it was grossness or rebelliousness that got you accepted. Regina wanted none of it. She refused to participate and grew disdainful of the different groups that vied for supremacy. And they put her down as "stuck-up."

And then she grew breasts.

Her waist slimmed down to eighteen inches, and

her hips rounded to thirty-two, and her legs were long and shapely. And with her menstrual cycle her complexion cleared, and her few freckles faded. A touch of mascara on her long pale lashes made an enormous difference to her eyes. One day she was a child, unable to speak to others, and the next day she was a breathtaking young woman whose command of herself far surpassed her fellow students. Suddenly she was an extremely desirable commodity.

But any attempts by her fellow students to win her favors went unnoticed. It was too late by now. They were still gross and rebellious and unrefined. She just wasn't interested. She had a smile that infuriated them. It said everything she was too polite to say with words. "I'm better than you. I know more than you, and I'll get further in life than you!" But no matter what they did, they couldn't break her reserve.

"I don't understand you, Regina," Uncle Charles would say. "What's wrong with you, anyway? You're a good lookin' girl. Ain't you got feelings?"

Regina would smile that smile. "You mean why don't I go to parties and get drunk on beer and let some greaser feel me up? Is that what you think I should do, Uncle Charles? Well, don't make me laugh!"

No one in the Williamson family nor any of their friends went to college. Her cousins, Alfred and Peter, aspired to be auto mechanics. Peter would probably go into the army after high school, and Alfred would begin his adult life by pumping gas. After Regina's graduation from high school she was expected to get a job to help support the family who had given her so much. But she had other ideas.

She graduated on Thursday, June the eighteenth, and on Saturday morning at five A.M. she left Aunt Elva's and Uncle Charles' house for good. She took her guitar, one suitcase of clothes, and two hundred dollars. Her bank account had a thousand dollars in it.

The first job Regina got was at Denny's Restaurant on Santa Monica Boulevard in Hollywood. Hollywood was where you went if you were going to be a star. And that was her plan.

"Hey, Regina. Move your ass! Three orders waiting," Harry shouted at her from the kitchen. She grabbed the heavy, food-laden plates and carried them to their destination. She checked the tables for ketchup and condiments, refilled the coffees at all her tables, totalled a check, and wrote up a Master Charge bill. Her back ached today, period time again.

"Hi, Regina." It was that drummer who had a crush on her. A sweet kid who came in two or three times a week for coffee. He couldn't afford a piece of pie, but he'd smile at her, sip his coffee, and stare at her when she wasn't looking. She could feel his eyes on her back, but when she'd turn, he'd duck his head again shyly.

"How you doin'? Any gigs?" she asked.

"Naw. I went to an audition at P.J.'s, but it was packed when I got there so I left."

Regina shook her head. "That doesn't matter. You've got to stick it out anyway. Maybe your sound is exactly the sound they want. If you leave before they hear you, you'll never know."

He nodded seriously. "Guess so. How are you doing?"

"I've got an appointment with an agent after work today. At least he's agreed to see me. That's better than nothing." They stared at one another feeling the futility. It was so discouraging. Regina tossed her hair off her shoulders. "Hell, I'm gonna make it, babe. You'll see."

"I know you will," he said. "You've got something special."

Regina always gave him three refills, although the policy was only one refill per customer without a food order. Each time she passed the counter she could tell he was trying to work up courage to talk to her again. *Poor kid,* she thought. *They'll eat him alive out there.*

One day he came in all aglow. "Regina, I have to talk to you."

"What is it, Gene?"

"I'm thinking of taking off for New York. My brother's there." There was a long silence while she waited, coffee pot poised, aware of Harry's eyes on her. Harry would like to have more than his eyes on her. "I wanted to say good-bye."

New York. "How are you getting there, Gene? Bus?"

"No. I've got wheels. I'm trying to find someone to share expenses." His eyes were so hungry, large, and brown, staring out from light brown bangs, long shoulder-length hair, thin body. "Consumptive," Aunt Elva would have said.

"For how long?"

He shrugged. "Dunno. Depends."

"What would it cost?"

"Fifty to a hundred for half the gas. Sleep in the car." His eyes wouldn't meet hers and he bit his nails, she noticed. He was not the kind of guy you'd look at twice, but she'd heard him play. He was incredible. "Know anyone?" he asked.

She waited until he lifted his chin to gaze at her directly. His look was so naked that it hurt her.

She grinned at him. "Yeah, I know someone. Me."

The car was a Ford Pinto wagon. They bought sleeping bags and tacked curtains up over the windows at night. By Albuquerque they were singing duets. By Dallas he'd told her his life story; how he'd grown up in Wyoming, how he idolized his brother Cord, how their parents had died when he was fifteen, and how he'd been into drugs until just recently. Music was his life, the expression of his soul. But performing terrified him. If he could only be a recording artist he knew he'd do fine.

By Atlanta she invited him into her sleeping bag. It was her first time yet she was more excited than nervous. But the moment his nude body touched hers he ejaculated. And she held him while he wept. *What have I gotten into?* she wondered, listening to the sound of his shame and his pain. He was one fucked up kid.

And then they hit New York.

Regina remembered landing here with Papa; the customs, the immigration, the feeling of tragedy that was bottled up inside of her new traveling coat. She hadn't realized that seeing New York would bring back all those memories, fresh wounds to fester in her heart.

They found an apartment on West Twenty-third Street. Gene was in love with her, and she needed his companionship and his half of the rent.

And then she met his brother Cord.

Gene's friend Eddie took her by cab to the club in the Village. Andrew's On, it was called, a converted head shop on Bleecker Street. They had their wine and beer license and were trying for liquor. The place was jammed with bodies, overheated, smoking, sweating, and high.

Why isn't this man a star? she wondered as she watched Cord sing, mesmerized. He played lead guitar but that was only his way of getting across his talent and his material. He could have stood there and done nothing and she would have felt the excitement he generated. There was an equally good-looking man with him on the stage, shorter, stockier, with dark curling hair and green eyes, also very sexy. The combination of the two of them was electrifying, with their hips gyrating in tight-fitting pants and words that really reached inside of her. She felt a rush of joy flowing through her body, liquefying her everywhere. She'd hardly even noticed Gene. He was hunched over his drums, his hair falling in his face, his concentration intense. *The three of them are so good together,* she thought. But she couldn't take her eyes off of Cord.

When the first set was over, Gene brought his brother to meet her. Cord looked at her intently and then looked away. She felt the loss of his gaze as a sudden pain.

"Regina," Gene caught her attention. "This is Don Drummond." She smiled into green eyes and gave Don some of the glow she'd gotten from Cord. Don pushed a chair in between her and Eddie.

"Hello, luvlie," he grinned. He was all over her in a minute, but her antenna was tuned to the man across the table. She could feel Cord's stare, knew he'd be looking when she turned.

They talked about music for a while.

At the end of the break Cord got up to go back to the stage and motioned for her to follow. He was a blond, wiry beanpole with cocky assurance in every ounce of him and a challenge on his face. "I'm me," he seemed to say, "take me as I am or leave me alone." She couldn't leave him alone. Ever.

"What's your last name, Regina?" he asked.

"Williamson," she said.

But he didn't hear the last syllable and introduced her to the audience as Regina Williams.

It didn't matter. She was in total command of herself and the audience once she'd climbed up on that tiny stage. Something inside just opened up, flowered, and bloomed in that smoky room.

During the song she tried to smile at Gene, but his head was down. And then she saw him wipe the perspiration off his face. It wasn't until much later, after she and Cord had spent the night devouring each other so that she felt eaten and digested and reborn all at once, that she realized that Gene had been wiping away tears.

CHAPTER 5

Beau Morgan was very high. There were surges of wonder in his veins. His arms and hands extended to his drumsticks, beating out rhythms only he could create. Music was the voice of his soul and he was lost in the number.

The individual faces of the audiences blended together in the small club as they watched him in total concentration, but though they were beyond his consciousness, he sensed them with him. A sea of support pulsing with his pulse, beating with his beat. Cool blue lights filled his head; the heat of his body warmed him, and visions appeared in his eyes. He beat them into parts of him. This was his moment, his number, his night. He was on his way! *Gonna make it, man. . . . M-a-k-e it!* At times like these, even in a small dive in Downey, he felt loving. He loved the whole world, but most of all he loved the drums. He loved the brown plaster walls of the room, and the wires that hung from the lights, and the chairs that scraped against the sawdust floor. But there was no scraping right now. The audience knew they were hearing something good.

The set ended with enthusiastic applause. But he didn't want to come down. If only it was always like this! If only he didn't need smack to get him up there.

He knew Penny was sitting with some of their friends in the darkened area outside the stage lights, but he wasn't in the mood to talk to her right now. He wanted to keep these feelings to himself. Nor did he want Penny to know how he'd gotten so high. Hell, he couldn't let her know!

He walked out of the other side of the stage, down the narrow dingy back hall, and outside into the night air. There were two cops across the street making an arrest. Some poor kid was spread-legged, leaning against the black and white car. He shuddered at the thought of getting busted. The red light circled and flashed against the building. He crossed the parking lot, avoiding the cops but painfully aware of them, and glanced at the small marquee. The name of his group was set in orange letters. Purple Bubble. They were going places. They had a chance; he could feel it. They were better than Canned Heat or Iron Butterfly in their time, or his old group, Lord of Fare. And this time he wouldn't mess it up.

He made his way around the front of the building and pushed through the crowd waiting at the door. These fans were all waiting for him! It felt wonderful!

The bartender handed him a Coke, which he gulped. He noticed a few guys he'd seen here before. They hailed him and nodded their approval. The mood was different tonight. There was success in the air. He felt a tap on his shoulder.

"Hey Shorty." His manager, Neil Pearson, grabbed his arm. Neil was grinning down at him as though they had just been offered a contract with Warners. "I've been waiting for you at the table. I wanted to tell you that I finalized the tour arrangement."

"Hey, that's great!" This *was* his night. "Did you tell the other guys?"

"No. You're first. I thought you could smooth the way. You know, convince them what a good deal I got ya."

Neil was sweating more than usual. His thick neck

hung over the edge of his collar, and beads of perspiration grew like pustules on his balding forehead.

"What's the matter, Neil? Didn't you get a good deal?" Beau's heart beat a warning thump, but his high prevented him from panicking. What difference would it make what kind of tour it was; it was a tour! A chance. They could build their name on a national level!

"We-e-ll." Neil hesitated, running a finger around the inside of his collar to release the buildup of fluid at the edge. Beau expected steam to rise up from the inside of his shirt when the hot air was released.

"There's a couple of drawbacks."

"Like what?" He didn't want anything to change the good feeling he had.

"Like I had to commit us for a few towns that aren't worth the time and travel to play, but we couldn't get the deal unless we played them. And the whole tour will last four and a half months. . . ."

"Whoo!" Beau whistled. "That's a long time. What are the provisions?"

Neil avoided his eyes.

"No roadies and no families," Neil mumbled. "You travel by van with only space for instruments and band. Three guys to a room and no meals included."

The bubble popped, spewing purple smoke all over Beau's dreams. "That's for shit, man! What are you telling me? You want me to convince the guys to take this?" He didn't want to go on tour without Penny. He couldn't go without her.

Neil's voice changed from pleasant to hard. He pushed the words out from between white enamel crevices.

"Listen, Morgan. You can't afford to make any complaints. This tour will just about get you outta debt. You and your group are gonna do it. So don't act the big shot with me!"

Beau was sweating again, only this time it wasn't

a clean, work sweat. It was sour and uncomfortable. Neil's connections were no secret. If Neil said he'd made commitments already, then that meant Beau would go for sure. Of all the money Beau owed in the world, he owed Neil first. Everything had been going so great and now this! He tried to ignore the knot that was growing in his gut, tried to find the euphoria he'd paid so much for, but it had slipped away like his hopes.

Penny appeared out of the dimness of the café and wrapped her arms around him. How was he going to tell her?

"Hi, sugar. Did you hear the news?" she asked.

She seemed so happy for him he wanted to shake her, to tell her how rotten it was, but this night was still special to her. They'd tried so long to get back to where they'd been.

Penny looked like such a baby. She was small like he was with a tiny, freckled nose and large blue eyes. Her eyes were so blue he sometimes had the sensation he was drowning in them. She gazed at him while he reached his hand down and played with the ends of her long silky blond hair. It stopped just above her round ass. His dark hair seemed even darker next to hers.

"What's Neil been telling you?" he asked.

"Just that the tour is all set. Oh Beau, you're gonna be famous again. I know it! And this time you're gonna be ready for it and not let it get to you like before."

"Sounds nice!" He prayed that he was acting normal. If she knew he was using shit again it would pull her back too. She'd fall right over that edge again and start shooting, or dropping speed. Maybe it was for the best that they be apart for a while. Just until things were really set for him famewise. Then he wouldn't have to shoot up at all and he wouldn't have anything to hide from her. After the tour things would be fine! "Neil neglected to tell you a small detail." He shot Neil a look of disgust. "There's not going to be anybody but the group on this tour."

Her body flinched at the news. He wanted to cradle her in his arms to stop the shock waves.

"How long?" she asked.

"Not long," he replied.

"Couple a months, Penny, baby," Neil supplied, the humane friend. Beau could have sunk his fist in that soft belly.

Penny didn't say anything. She didn't have to. Beau knew what she was thinking. How was she going to make it without him? How was she going to stay off the stuff and off the streets?

He wished he knew the answer.

He left her with Neil and went back to join the group for the next set. But the bitter taste of fear was on his tongue. A metallic taste that conjured pictures of Penny hooking for a fix, her childhood innocence spoiled among filthy sheets while some prick jammed its way into her. Flashes of fury shot through him. He wasn't going to let that happen again. He'd call her every day while he was gone. He'd send her every dime he could spare. They'd get through it this time together. They had to.

CHAPTER 6

Waterskiing is a poor substitute for snow-skiing, Cord thought as he tilted his body to the right, parallel to the water. The outboard was pulling him in a large arc, and he slalomed into an opposite parallel, following the wake as it cut across the glassy smooth water. The boat pulled into a straightaway, and he bent his knees, flipping around backwards, balancing himself by hooking the rope handle between his knees. He watched the image of the lake recede behind him as the boat pulled from behind and then he bent his knees and flipped his body back again. He came down on the wake and faltered, almost wiping out! His heart leaped into his throat and he caught himself from slipping down into that black-green water. Suddenly he imagined nymphs and moss creatures cavorting there. No more fancy turns until he felt calmer, he decided. But that underwater image would make a good song.

The twins were watching him from shore; he waved to them and motioned to Freddie at the wheel to head the boat for the landing. Within minutes he skied to the ramp and released the rope. He fished his skis out of the water and climbed up the mossy bottom to the wooden plank, dancing as his bare feet touched the blistering surface of the cement. His sandals were at the top of the ramp where he left them and he squished in them all the way back to the trailer. The twin with the mole on her belly was sunning on a lounge chair, her body covered with oil. She looked like a sacrifice for the gods, anointed for him. Her sister stuck her head out of the trailer.

"You coulda broke your neck out there, Cord, doin' all that crazy stuff."

"I thought you'd like it."

"Shut up, Irene," the sunning sister said without moving a muscle. The mole on her belly was the only way Cord knew she was Elaine.

"When are we gettin' out of here, Cord?" Irene asked.

"Close the trailer door," Elaine insisted. "You're lettin' all the cold air out."

Jesus, he thought. "Hey, Irene, hand me my guitar!"

She bounced back up the stairs, her firm ass bare except for the string-bikini bottom she wore. She returned carrying the guitar cradled in her arms so that her nude breasts rested on the edge like two moons in orbit. She leaned over and kissed him, pressing the instrument into him. She tasted like peanut butter, and he had a sudden craving for the taste of jelly to go with it. Elaine sat up on her elbows to watch and then slid her hand between his legs to fondle him.

He pushed Irene away, disengaged his balls from Elaine's hand, and took the guitar. Freddie's trailer would be quiet. Freddie was out on the lake again with Janet, and Phil and Blake hadn't gotten up yet.

He could hear Irene trying to tune in the C.B.

"Breaker, Breaker, this is double trouble. . . ."

You can say that again, Cord thought as he climbed into Freddie's trailer. He slipped out of his wet trunks and flopped down on the bed. The bed was rumpled and smelled vaguely of unwashed underwear, but he soon forgot that as he began to strum and think about the vision of that underwater world he'd had while he was skiing.

The melody began to come to him. Melodies always came easier than lyrics. It had taken him a long time to learn to compose on his own after Majesty broke up. He and Regina had worked so closely together for so long. *Regina.* He hadn't thought about her for a while, at least not consciously. But her face had come to him as the water nymph in his song, her incredible blue-green eyes and that red hair, floating as she swam. Regina had loved to waterski. She loved everything he loved only more so. That had been part of the trouble; she loved it all more than she'd loved him. Well, he hoped she was happy now with Mike Shaw. He'd heard her husband gave her a rough time, but he doubted that. Nobody gave Regina a rough time. Nobody except him. He'd been very rough on her, when Gene died, blaming her, blaming himself, blaming all of them.

Irene's breasts preceded her through the doorway, or was it Elaine who was eyeing his limp penis. "Someone's calling you on the telephone. I think it's Chicago. Do you want to talk?"

"Hell no!" *How did they find him way out here?* he wondered. "Tell them you haven't seen me in months. Tell them I went summer skiing in the Andes!" She turned to go. "Wait a minute. Tell them I'll call them in a few days."

She bounced down the stairs to deliver her message, and called back to him, "Want some company?"

"No!" he shouted, rolling his eyes to heaven. "Later, okay?"

She would probably deliver that message and rub herself all over with that orange-flavored love-lube she thought he liked and be back in a minute. *What the hell's wrong with me,* he wondered, *you only live once.* But he knew what was wrong. He was tired of meaningless relationships. There'd been nobody since Regina except girls like Irene and Elaine. He couldn't let anyone mean enough to him to fire him the way

Regina had, so that he shot his come halfway around the world. Only music could do it now, and music was a lonely partner.

But not as lonely as death. What was it like to be dead? To be gone forever. Cord remembered standing on that hill watching them lower Gene's coffin into the ground. Twenty-five years old and gone forever. No more heartache for Gene, no more searching for completion, no more loving Regina, no more anything. Cord hadn't been able to cry at the funeral, but he cried later. God, how he cried. He hadn't wanted to give Regina the satisfaction of seeing his pain, that twisting of a knife in his guts; his brother was dead. Are you at peace, Gene? Have you forgiven me for taking your girl, your love, your Regina?

How he had hated Regina that day as she stood there in the sun, her hair flaming red against the green of the cemetery lawn, her dress clinging to her body as his mouth remembered it, soft and yielding to his kiss. She was so beautiful. He remembered their love, churned by sex and success. Seeing her face streaked with tears only made him hate her more. He'd wanted to scream across the grave at her, "It's too late to cry. You killed him, and now you have the nerve to cry?" After the funeral he wouldn't talk to her, hadn't since that day, since the morning they found Gene dead at the Beverly Wilshire Hotel in Los Angeles.

His hate was as passionate as his love had been. Only recently had he stopped hating her; it took too much energy to continue.

Face it, Crocker, he thought. *You were to blame, too.*

"Take care of Gene, Cord," his mother always said. "He's younger than you. Wait for him, Cord, he's more sensitive than you." No, Gene wasn't more sensitive; he was more protected. And when their parents died in that car crash, Cord had gone on protecting him until Gene met the most dangerous person of all —himself.

From the first night Cord met Regina, they were on a rocket that never came down until the night Gene died. Their love and their success rode that fiery tail. And Gene had stepped aside as soon as he saw the flames of their attraction. Gene loved Regina and he loved Cord. He wanted them to be happy together, but their happiness—at his expense—confirmed his own self-doubts and underscored his inadequacies. Gene wore his feelings as wounds on his body. He would watch Cord and Regina loving one another, and his sad eyes would be filled with pain. It drove Cord crazy sometimes. He almost understood why Don had lashed out at Gene so often. Don had his own self-doubts and worries, and Gene's presence frightened him. Gene was like a symbol of failure, of the star who was no longer desirable. And Don and Regina fought against that possibility with every living breath. Cord could take success or leave it alone. Oh sure, he wanted it then, still did, but for Regina and Don it was a matter of life or death. Well, they chose life, and Gene shot himself full of shit.

What would he do differently if he had it to do all over again? *Stay the fuck away from Regina*, he decided. *That's for damn sure.*

CHAPTER 7

"Twenty-eight, twenty-nine, thirty!" Don stared at the fuzzy fibers in the exercise mat underneath him. His broad shoulders strained against the force of gravity as his hands pushed his body away from the floor and his toes dug into the ground. His stomach was tightened into iron knots while he continued his push-ups. "Thirty-five, thirty-six," he counted. He would only have time for fifty today if he was going to jog before the meeting. He wanted to leave time enough to give Louise Carlin the grand tour. That was half the fun of owning a mansion, showing it off.

He didn't like doing business with a woman, but that's who Lubow was sending to discuss the terms of the new contract. Women should stay out of business; they were just something to fuck anyway. He imagined that's how Louise Carlin got where she was at CAMIL Records. Well, he'd make her squirm. In more ways than one.

He finished the fiftieth push-up and lay down on the floor to catch his breath. He was more winded than usual today, or was it his imagination? No, he was in perfect shape. Thirty-eight was the prime of life. To be in the prime of one's life meant that a plateau had been reached. The climb was no longer necessary; the struggle had been won. And that's where he was, on the glorious plateau at the top. Sure he had clawed and bit and stomped his way up, grinding his heels into the knuckles of anyone under his feet.

If they couldn't hold on against the force of his talent they didn't deserve a place.

Jerry Lubow, president of CAMIL, was heavy into film production, and that's where Don saw himself. A singer didn't have as many good years as a film star. Look at Chuck Bronson, or Clint Eastwood, even Duke Wayne before he died; timeless men. Their age was a tribute, not a drawback. All he needed was a start. But for a man in his position it was difficult to arrange. He couldn't ask them. They had to come to him, and that's what today's meeting was all about.

He took the lift to the basement, wrapped a towel around his neck, and stuffed it into his sweat shirt. The damp morning air gave him a crink in his neck. The door from the basement led through the garage and out behind the manor to the jogging path. He broke into a run as soon as he left the house, going over in his mind what he would say.

Movies, that's what he wanted. The two films he'd made when he was part of Majesty didn't count. Those were teen-age fantasy films. He wanted to star in something that would give him an Academy Award! That was more his style.

He noted with satisfaction that the grounds of the estate were in perfect order. The manicured acres of lawn pleased him, and the primrose and daffodil that lined the path stretched on ahead for miles. He felt a keen responsibility to the tradition of this land to keep it as it was meant to be. He would show them he wasn't the vulgar nouveau riche that the local critics labeled him when he bought Derbyshire Manor. How many manors in England were still privately owned and operated today as well as this one was? And not by Arabs, either. Hell, he employed a score of servants to keep up the stables and to polish the brasses and oil the paneling and sparkle up the leaded windows. Eight fireplaces had to be maintained plus his own dairy. And his servants were well paid too. In his garage was a collection of fine automobiles, a limo, sportster, buggy, truck and tractor, and five classic Rollses he hadn't been able to resist. His latest acquisition was a real live princess who was asleep right now in his bed.

The jogging path ran around the southern perimeter of the sloping lawn and meandered in and out of the forest that lined the edge of the estate. It turned past the tennis courts and just skirted the swimming pond. The red clay courts were deserted today, and he had a sudden urge to invite some friends down for a tournament. Perhaps Paul and Linda would be persuaded to come down from Wales. But he couldn't do it right away. He had the Palladium date only a few weeks off; rehearsals were already underway. He'd wait until after that. These concert performances paid him large amounts of steady money though they took a lot of hard work. As he jogged he punched the air to exercise his arms, punching at invisible foes who mocked the way he earned his living. "Gentleman Drummond," they called him behind his back. They didn't know that he didn't want to be a gentleman. It was tough enough to live like one; he didn't have to be one. He'd seen the way the aristocracy lived. Look at Princess Sonia. Her younger brother had cracked up his plane and his boat and his racing car, and he was only seventeen. And look at how mucked up she was. She'd swallow anything if it was small and round.

Frederic was waiting for him just outside the gym. "Steam today, suh?"

"No time, Fred. Just a quick shower. I'll call you for a massage after the rehearsal."

"Veddy good, suh," Frederic answered, holding the door open for him and following him into the bathroom. The room was moist and warm from the steam that had been turned on in case he wanted to use it. Camphor-scented moisture invaded every pore. Well, maybe he'd take just five minutes.

"My decorators have tried to find replicas of the exact furnishings used in this manor when it was built in the eighteenth century," Don explained to Louise Carlin as he escorted her through the west end reception room. Carlin was what he would consider a handsome woman, golden shoulder-length hair, beige chamois buckskin clothes and matching boots outlining her body, and a perfect American smile that lit her face when she used it. So far he'd only seen it once, and not turned on him. She was cool, this one.

"This room was originally done in red and gold with touches of blue, rather Federal, you might say."

"Very effective," she agreed, touching the panne velvet of a nearby chair.

"We found a damask in those colors, but we weren't able to have our own fabrics woven as they did with the restoration of Versailles. Nevertheless, we did well with stock fabrics from France."

"I'm impressed, Don," she admitted.

He smiled. "Of course, the furniture is 'of the period.' " Don ran his fingers over the surface of a magnificent Boule chest. "The English style of furnishing, aside from the Chippendale period, is more ponderous than the French. But it suits me better." He thrust his square chin forward and fluffed his dark curly hair.

Louise was about to comment when they were interrupted by a harsh voice. "Man, this is a fuckin' museum."

Don spun around to find Choo Choo Trainer standing there, his head nodding like a cork bobbing on water. Choo Choo moved toward them, his bouncing gait in syncopated rhythm, his hands jammed into his pockets, the fists clenched into knots that protruded out from his narrow hips. His legs seemed to extend directly from his thin chest encased in a leather-trimmed silk suit. And he wore his jet black hair oiled into a thick, bushy pompadour. None of that "natural" shit for him, he always said.

Princess Sonia followed closely behind wearing a nearly transparent kaftan. Her brown hair tumbled in waves down her back. Don disapproved when Sonia entertained anyone dressed like that, especially someone like Choo Choo. By Louise Carlin's expression she evidently agreed with him.

"What are you doing here?" Don asked.

Choo Choo grinned his wide toothy grin like a monkey who's about to get into mischief. "Ah'm just visitin' this little lady, here," he nodded to Sonia who avoided Don's eyes. "Got a present for her."

"Well, I'll see you later," Don exclaimed, taking Louise's arm and escorting her into his office. He wished the princess wouldn't use his house for her connections.

The office had been added to the house to contain all of Don's electronic equipment beyond what was built into his own rehearsal hall and studio in the converted ballroom. Phil Rostein, Drummond's manager, was already waiting for them, seated in Don's enormous desk chair. The desk was in a semicircular alcove of bay windows overlooking the west view of rolling lawn, swimming pond, and the Derbyshire Hills in the distance. Interspersed among the gold and platinum records and book shelves on the paneled walls were photos of Drummond framed in antique silver frames, of his appearances in Las Vegas and at the London Palladium, and of his presentation to the Queen.

Louise took it all in as she shook hands with Rostein. "It's good to see you, Phil."

"You two know each other?" Don was surprised.

This bird got around. Maybe she was doing something right.

"Louise and I go back a ways to when she discovered Fineline. I managed them, while she took them to the top and produced their first album with CAMIL."

"And Behemoth," Louise reminded him. "We worked together on that one, too."

"That's right," Rostein laughed. "The names these groups come up with."

"Okay, so you're old buddies. Let's get on with it," Don said.

Louise looked at him sharply, and he clamped his jaw shut. *That was a mistake. Never let them know when you're eager or tense or nervous. Big effing deal. So she is a vice president of A&R now. She still probably fucked her way to the top.*

Louise unzipped a Mark Cross case and removed two sets of contracts, passing one to each of them. "I've made all the changes you requested, Phil," she said. "And Lubow wanted me to convey his personal agreement with your suggestions over release dates and ad costs for your next album. We'll go all out for this one."

Don nodded. That's what he liked to hear. He caught Rostein's eye. Rostein had picked up on everything. *Smart man,* Don thought. *He's worth his exorbitant percentage.*

"We want Don's image streamlined," Rostein began. "We want him to appeal to a younger, record-buying audience. And we want a shot at a film."

Louise nodded. "There's no problem there."

"No offense," Don interupted. "But I want a starring role and I want Lubow's written okay."

She smiled. "You got it."

"One-year contract with an option for a five-year renewal, with renegotiation privileges," Rostein added.

Again she nodded. Lubow said to get Drummond tied up, and by God she'd do it. She made some initialed changes in the contracts and passed them back to Don and to Rostein to sign, then stood up to go.

"It's been a pleasure, gentlemen," she said, and Don grinned. He'd just staked his claim for another half a decade on the top of the plateau.

"Just one more thing." Louise turned, her thick lashes lowered over her blue eyes and her cheek dimpled slightly. She was about to let loose one of her special smiles. "You know the clause where you've agreed to participate in one event of our choosing to promote CAMIL Records?" Her long-awaited smile burst forth. "Well, Lubow is in the planning stages of promoting a reunion concert of Majesty. Just thought I'd let you know so you could think about it. Someone will be contacting you."

Don felt the color drain from his face. *The bitch! Look at her grinnning at him like that* Never. *NEVER!* "You tell Lubow for me. . . ." Don felt Rostein's grip on his arm, and Rostein interrupted him.

"Don wouldn't be interested in doing a reunion concert, Louise. He's past that point in his life. That's a dead issue. Better leave it that way. I'm sure Jerry can come up with a compromise way for Don to fulfill that stipulation."

"That's exactly what I told Lubow," Louise said. She put her hand sympathetically on Don's other arm. "I'm only conveying a message."

"It's a shit idea," Don said, aware of her touch. He put his hand on hers. *She's hot for me,* he thought. *But I wouldn't fuck her with Choo Choo's prick.* That idea made him smile. He leaned forward to kiss her, a kind of ambivalent peck on the lips. She tried to pull back but she was caught. So she stood there. *Nice tits,* he noticed.

She seemed flustered as she turned away, zipping her briefcase.

"A shit idea," Don repeated.

Frederic appeared to escort Louise out of the manor. As they reached the foyer they found the princess and Choo Choo waiting for them. The princess came and wound her arm through Don's, her childlike body perfectly visible to anyone who cared to look. But Don knew from her glassy-eyed expression that she was unaware of anyone else but herself at the moment.

"Choo Choo needs a ride to the city, dahling. Could Miss Carlin take him in her car?" the princess asked.

Don looked at Louise. There was nothing she could say but yes. She nodded. *Serves her right,* Don thought, with amusement. To be stuck with Choo Choo Trainer alone for any length of time was punishment enough for anyone.

He watched them get into her limousine. And then he closed the door behind them.

Don Drummond is worse than I'd thought he'd be, Louise Carlin realized as she settled into the deep cushions of the Daimler. She realized she'd prefer the company of a drug pusher like Choo Choo Trainer to a man like Don Drummond any day. At least with Choo Choo you knew where you stood.

CHAPTER 8

Mike was drunk again. Regina watched him leaning over her friend Corene as though he'd never seen breasts before and she wanted to cry. This was her special night; it was supposed to be perfect. She'd planned this party to the last detail, without Mike's help she might add, and Marcelle had made a wonderful dinner. All of their friends were dressed in their loveliest clothes, and the jewels sparkled, and the Taittinger flowed, and a string quartet sauntered through the house and gardens playing romantic music, to be followed by a disco band later in the evening . . . and Mike was drunk. Some birthday.

She remembered how she and Cord used to celebrate special occasions just by being together. They would try to please one another. *Don't think about that now,* she told herself.

Mike weaved his way toward her. "Hi, birthday girl. How's it feel to be thirty-two?"

She noticed Corene hurrying across the room, grateful to be free of Mike. Regina knew just how she felt.

"You're gonna catch up to me one of these days, yes you will. You're gettin' up there all right."

"Come on with me," she said, linking her arm through his and guiding him out onto the terrace. She smiled as she pulled him along, barely noticing the candles flickering in hurricane lamps along the brick wall. They cast floral shadows through their etched glass windows, while scented flowers and candles decorated the swimming pool and night blooming jasmine sprayed its enticing perfume on the air. But Regina wasn't enticed. How should she reproach him? she wondered. Be soft or be tough; tease him or shame him? She'd tried them all and nothing worked.

"It's a lovely party," someone called.

"Should be; costs enuf," Mike slurred.

Only nine thirty and he's already bombed, she thought. "Will you do something for me?" she asked. Perhaps she could appeal to his better nature.

"Everything I do is for you, baby. You know that." His eyes weren't focusing on her.

She took his hand and led him around the back by the service wing. "Will you come upstairs with me for a little while. I want to talk to you."

She felt him resist. "Aw baby, we can't leave the party. Everybody's here."

"That's all right, Mike. Come on." She led him firmly up the back stairs to the servants' entrance and through the long hallway into the main wing. "Shh," she cautioned him when he started to sing. "This is our secret."

He followed her into their bedroom and she turned to him, exasperation threatening to erupt. But he was so drunk, it wouldn't do any good. "Oh, Mike," she said. "Come on, sit here with me." She beckoned to him to come and sit beside her on the bed.

He looked perplexed by her new approach. She was usually screaming at him by this time when he drank. He knew he had let her down tonight and would hate himself in the morning for it. He sat down and she had to hold him from falling.

"You've been looking very tired lately," she said, smoothing the hair off his forehead. "Is anything bothering you?" She smoothed his cheeks, reached down and untied his bow tie. Lightly she rubbed his temples—something he always adored—while she forced him to close his eyes.

"Regina, what are you doing? We've got guests downstairs."

"Oh, they're all right, Mike. I want to be alone with my husband."

"I need another drink, Reg. Ring for Anson to bring me a Scotch on the rocks."

"Shh, Anson is busy with the other guests. Why don't you just lie down here and close your eyes, and I'll rub your temples. Then in a few minutes when you've rested, I'll go and get you a Scotch myself."

He smiled at her or was he smiling at the wall behind her. "You'd do that for me? You're really sweet, Reg. Really sweet. I'm sorry I'm not being a better host. I really am tired."

He lay back on the bed and was asleep in another minute. Regina covered him with the silk comforter and turned out the lights. He was better off here than downstairs. She couldn't stand to watch him ruin another evening for her. Something had to be done about him. He'd been on the wagon for a long time, and then tonight—no, for the past two weeks—he'd been hiting the bottle again. Damn it. What had she done to deserve this? she wondered. What in hell?

Barbara and Ron, Rickey and Len were the last couples to leave. She kissed them good night and ignored the looks in their eyes. She didn't want their pity tonight. Not tonight.

Mike awoke when she got into bed. He hadn't moved since she left him. "Do you want me to help you undress?" she asked.

"What time is it?" He smacked his lips together to relieve the dryness and then reached to the bedside carafe for water.

"Three thirty," she replied. "The disco band was terrific. We've got to use them again. You should have seen the way they got everyone going!" It came out like a reprimand. Mike was very subdued.

He went into the bathroom and urinated forever. When he came out he was nude. He threw his tux and shirt and underwear over a chair and stood before her sorrowfully. "I blew it, didn't I? Why didn't you wake me? Why didn't you send someone up to get me?"

"Because I didn't want you down there drunk or apologizing for being drunk."

He sat on the bed, his head in his hands.

"Please, Mike, I can't take one of your bouts of remorse tonight. Let's go to sleep, or let's make love, or let's get a divorce, but let's not go over it again."

He turned to her, and she saw how deep the lines in his face were getting. There was more gray in his temples too, but his smile was still flashy white, and his tan was still perfect, and she still needed him and depended on him for so many things. Why did it have to be like this? He let her down so often.

"I've had some things on my mind, Reg. That's all." He trailed his fingers up and down her arm. She hated that. The tentative foray, the indirect approach. If she removed her arm, he'd get into bed and go to sleep. Never would he say, "I need you. I want to fuck you for myself, whether *you* want to or not." Or "let me just please you whether *I* want to or not." She gritted her teeth and kept her arm where it was. She was thirty-two years old and the most desirable woman in the world according to a recent movie magazine poll. And most of the time she was absolutely miserable.

She leaned over and kissed him. Sour booze and the smell of unwashed mouth. Of all things that turned her on. She slipped her nightgown off her shoulders and wiggled out of it without breaking the kiss. Mike frustrated her when he kissed her, not knowing how, not knowing what to do with his lips and his tongue. There was a definite art to it, and he had never learned. She didn't let it bother her tonight.

Instead she climbed on top of him and lay the length of him, rubbing herself all over him, opening her legs, gliding herself up and down his hips and thighs, running her hands over his stomach, around his sex, under the silky hair of his underarms. He grabbed her ass and held her while his penis grew larger between her legs. And then she pushed up on her arms so that he could reach her breasts with his mouth. Again he frustrated her, attacking her nipples too soon, forgetting that there was more of her than these two buttons. Or else he'd stay on one nipple too long, until it lost its sensitivity. *Ignore it,* she commanded. *This is what you've got, so make the best of it.* She was already wet anyway.

He slipped inside of her and she pressed down on him, sitting up to ride him deep within. His eyes were closed, his head thrown back, while his hands kneaded her breasts. She could feel the tension building as she rocked and gripped his body with her knees. He was right where she wanted him to be. "Oh Mike. Oh baby," she whispered. And then suddenly he wasn't there inside of her anymore. She pressed and rode and held on, laying down the length of him, but he wasn't there. She could feel his penis slipping out of her. What was wrong? She stopped moving and waited, touching him, needing him. It had been like this every time for months. She'd thought it would be better this time. What should she do? What should she say?

"Are you all right?"

"I'm sorry," he sighed. "I guess I'm more tired than I thought."

She wanted to hit him. She needed him so much. What should she do with this feeling inside? She felt as though she were dying. The tears came quite suddenly. It was too much, too damned much. She sobbed so hard that she nearly passed out between breaths. And Mike patted her and soothed her, repeating over and over again, "I'm sorry, honey, I'm sorry. It'll be better next time, I promise. I promise. I'm so sorry."

"What's going to make it better?" she cried. "Stars don't have time for failed sex lives and inadequate hard-ons."

He pulled away from her, hurt by the remark. And then it was she who was sorry. But before she could tell him, one of the children awoke and started calling for her. She could hear it over the intercom.

"What timing," she sighed, wiping her eyes and pulling on her nightgown. Then she ran down the hall to help her child overcome a nightmare. If only there were someone who could help her overcome hers.

Florie looked up from her tea as Regina entered the breakfast room. "My poor baby," she said, noticing the dark circles under Regina's eyes. "You and Mike been at it again?"

Regina nodded, and helped herself to a cup of coffee. Then she sat down at the breakfast table. In spite of her resolve not to burden Florie, she sighed.

Florie reached out and took her hand. They sat there holding one another across the table, each gaining solace from the other.

"Have you heard from Choo Choo?" Regina asked.

Florie nodded.

"What's he up to?"

Florie looked down at her cup. "He's working."

"I can imagine," Regina said.

"I wish I could go see him, see for myself what's goin' on with Choo Choo. It hurts me to see what he's turned into."

Florie's nephew Lionel Trainer, known on the street as Choo Choo, was Florie's cross to bear. He was her sister's illegitimate son who she'd raised whenever she could get her hands on him. He had spent most of his youth in correctional institutions or on road gangs, until he ran away from his home in Alabama and ended up on the streets of Harlem. The boy had been no good as a kid and he'd grown into an adult criminal involved in rackets, drugs, and prostitution. But he did have a high class drug clientele. Regina knew many famous people who bought coke and pills from him, but his major dealings were in heroin.

If it weren't for Florie she would have turned him in to the police long ago. She knew enough about him to put him away for years. But Florie loved him and believed that all he needed was a chance. "That boy never had nuthin' good happen in his life," she'd say. And Regina would reply, "He had you, sweetheart, and that's more than I had."

Florie didn't believe that Choo Choo was bad, only misguided. But then Florie was an optimist.

"You know who I've been thinking about lately?" Regina asked.

Florie knew from her tone what she was going to say and she nodded. "We women is always thinkin' on those men who'se no good for us."

They smiled at one another. Florie had a Cord Crocker in her past. His name was Walter and if he walked in the door this minute, she'd disappear with him for however long he'd have her.

"It's just 'cause Mike is havin' some bad times is all."

Tears came to Regina's eyes. If only that were true. Mike was so good hearted. There were so many things about him that were dear. His admiration for her actually kept her going at times. When she faltered and doubted her talent, he would always give her encouragement. He was the one who convinced her to try new techniques, to stretch her talents, and not to settle into what she did easily. She'd do as he advised and always succeed even better than she dreamed. But he could never seem to apply that advice or those successful innovations to himself.

"Oh, Florie, I just don't know what to do anymore. Mike's so distant lately."

They both knew it was because he had been drinking again. "You just love him, Regina, and the good things will follow, baby. You'll see."

"But he disappoints me so. It's hard. . . ."

"Never said it was easy. Lionel's hard for me too. But I love him."

Regina shook her head. "You're one in a million, Florinda Mae. Maybe even a billion. Why don't you go see Choo Choo. Talk it out with him. I'll spring for the ticket."

Florie's dark face lit into a grin. "You'd do that?"

Regina shrugged.

"God bless you, baby! What I say!"

And they both laughed, feeling somehow lighter.

CHAPTER 9

Beau craned his neck to see the clock on the O'Keefe and Merritt range. The plastic face was broken, and he couldn't tell if he was looking at the crack in the face or the time.

"Penny!" You almost ready?" he called. She'd been in the bathroom for forty-five minutes. "The bus leaves in half an hour."

He carried his coffee cup to the sink and watched the light brown liquid pour down the drain. That sight always depressed him. There was something about cold coffee in the sink that he identified with poverty. Suddenly he felt nauseous. *I'm having sympathy morning sickness*, he thought. His hands were shaking and his forehead felt cold and damp. *How long since my last fix?* he wondered, knowing exactly how long it had been.

"Hurry up!" he called, more sharply this time.

The bathroom door opened and Penny came out. Her face was red and puffy from crying. She'd tried to cover it up with makeup. *Poor kid*, he thought.

She ran to him and threw her arms around him, letting go with renewed sobbing. He felt like crying with her. There was so much to cry about.

"It's not gonna be so bad, I promise you! I'll call you every day. I'll tell you all about what I'm doing, and you can tell me too. Won't you like seeing Timmy again?" The bones of her shoulder blades stuck out through the thin cotton blouse. "Your parents will fatten you up. The baby will be growing inside of you surrounded by that green Oregon country."

She sniffed and reached for a Kleenex. The box was empty so she went back into the bathroom to get some toilet paper. He could hear her blowing her nose, and when she came out she was carrying her makeup case. "We'd better get going," she said. "We'll miss the bus." Her voice sounded hollow and empty.

Separations. All of his life he'd had to face separations and he hated the shit out of them. Rich people traveled together. Successful people took whoever they wanted with them.

She lifted her suitcase with both hands, and he lunged for it. "Don't do that! I'll take it! You could hurt yourself lifting heavy things."

She made a face at him. "Don't be dumb. When I had Timmy I was working in a grocery store and lifting heavy cartons all the time. He was born perfectly healthy, in spite of all the things I did to try and lose him."

"But you were only fourteen then," he teased. "Now that you're an old lady of nineteen you've got to be careful!"

She followed him down the narrow staircase to the garage below the apartment and watched him put the suitcase in the van. "I don't wanna go, Beau," she said. "You don't know what it's like living with my parents. Sometimes I wake up at night with the feeling that I'm about to die! And then I realize I'm only having a nightmare of being back home. Poor Timmy. What a terrible life I've handed him by leaving him there with them."

He helped her into the van and went back upstairs to lock the apartment door. The only thing of value in the whole damn place was his hypo kit, which he hid under his side of the mattress. As long as his drums were safe in the van, there was nothing he cared about in that apartment. He wasn't sorry to leave it. He took a last look around and locked the door.

Penny sighed as he slid into the driver's side and put the key in the ignition. He backed out of the carport and into the alley. "Do you have a letter to the psychiatric clinic in Portland?" he asked.

"Yes."

"And you'll check in right away?"

"Yes."

"You promise to tell Timmy that I miss him and I can't wait until he comes to live with us."

"I'm not going to tell him that, Beau! I'm not going to raise his hopes unless we can deliver on our promises. He thinks I'm his sister, and that's that!" Her lips were drawn together in a tight determined line. At times she had some of her father's stiff-necked determination.

"Maybe you can join me later on if things are going well."

"There's no use in talking about it, Beau. It's impossible and we both know it. We can't afford it, and when you're on the road, there's nothing for me to do day after day but sit in the motel."

"When I get back from the tour, maybe we can get a house. Nothing fancy, just a pad in Laurel Canyon. One of the guys lucked onto one recently. It's not too expensive. He said he'd keep his eyes open for us."

"We could have a yard for the baby!" she said, a touch of hope softening her voice.

They pulled up to the bus station and he parked the van, reaching for her as she came into his arms. "I love you," she whispered.

"Me too!" he answered. "Me too."

As the bus pulled out and her tear-streaked face smiled at him bravely through the window, all he could feel was rage. He wanted to smash into the bus depot for being there. He wanted to ram the van into a pole. But most of all he wanted to wring her father's scrawny chicken-neck for all the punishment he would heap on her when she arrived in Portland.

CHAPTER 10

Choo Choo's feet hurt, and when his feet hurt he lost his temper fast. But he wouldn't admit that it might be his feet and not the shoes that were the problem. "A hundred and forty bucks for Gucci shoes, an' they's no different from the res'," he grumbled to Largo. But Largo was asleep in the Choo Choo's favorite chair. Choo Choo resented it when Largo slept in that chair. But he wouldn't dare wake him and kick him out. Largo was mean if you disturbed his sleep. In fact, Largo was mean most of the time.

Choo Choo wiped some lint off the ebony dining table being careful not to scratch it. And then he surveyed his domain. He was proud of his opulent penthouse. Maybe Ninety-eighth Street was a bit far uptown to be considered a classy address, but it wasn't bad either. And he had decorated it with the finest. Gold mirrors and marble tables and thick carpets. The carpets were what he liked the best after the filthy peeling floors he'd lived on all his life. Not that his Aunt Florie hadn't tried to give him better. But it had always been a struggle. Now he even had a special closet, booby-trapped with explosives, where he kept his drugs and payoff money.

His courier was late. He didn't like it when his people were late. Too many things could go wrong with his beautiful setup. Fassim had been telling him to find someone else to make deliveries and he was right. If Fassim got caught, Choo Choo would be in trouble! But who could he get? There was nobody else like Fassim. He worked right in that embassy. Carried all those airline flight bags, the white ones with the black Arabic writing on them. And when Choo Choo paid Fassim, those bags would be full of money, and he'd get Fassim's waist belt full of all that white shit! He thought about Fassim. A sharp black man wearing his sharp black suit and walking down those wide stone steps, and no one knew what he was carrying! Choo Choo smiled. The best part was that Fassim rode in a limousine right to the airport in Washington, D.C. That guy brought the shit in style!

When Fassim landed in New York, he'd take a cab into the city and get out somewhere near Gramercy Park. He'd go down to the subway cross town, then take another cab to midtown where he'd get out in front of a building, any building! And then he'd go through the front door and find another way out to the street, and then it'd be all right to take another cab uptown to Choo Choo's elegant pad. So far Fassim's caution had paid off. But there was always a chance that some cop was clever too.

The light for the private elevator flashed red. At last! Choo Choo heard the click of the cage as it got to the top. A loud buzzer jolted Largo out of his sleep, and he lumbered from his chair groggily. The big black man put his mouth up to the intercom and spoke into it.

"Wha's yo idenificashun?"

"I tole you a hun'red times not to spit inta the 'lectronic equipment," Choo Choo said. He didn't keep Largo around for his intelligence.

A tinny voice with a British accent answered back. "Ninety-five." Largo turned to Choo Choo.

"Put on the camera!" Choo Choo commanded, and Fassim's image came into view, dark skin, slicked back hair, black suit and tie against a white shirt. But he was not alone. There was a woman with him. A heavyset woman in her late fifties wearing a raincoat and a scarf. Choo Choo took a closer look. It was his Aunt Florie.

"Holy shit!" he yelled, plunging into furious activity, covering up the cocaine spread out in piles on the table. Checking to make sure his drug closet was locked. . . .

"Aunt Florie." Choo Choo was all smiles as he embraced his aunt. Actually he was glad to see her; but her timing was terrible. "Whatchew doin' here?" He turned to Fassim. "Yo late!" he said.

"I'm teddibly soddy," Fassim explained. "There was a brief power shortage in Washington, and all flights were delayed." Choo Choo crooked his head in the direction of the bedroom and Fassim took the hint.

"Why don't you set down, honey, and I'll take care of dis dude, and then we kin have a talk?" Choo Choo kissed his aunt on the forehead. "Be right back." He guided her into a chair and then ducked into the bedroom after Fassim, but Florie's eyes were on his back. He could feel her disapproval. Damn! He wiped his nose for any signs of his recent 'toot.'

"When we goin' to git our nex' deliv'ry?" he asked Fassim, once the door was closed.

"Not until the fifteenth of July."

"Why? Wha's wrong with a June shipmen'?"

"It was confiscated." Fassim's voice was deliberate. Dealing with American blacks was like dealing with spoiled children. "I thought you might have been informed about the fire."

Choo Choo stared at him blankly.

"Aboard our French freighter. The ship suffered extensive damage, and in the haste of the fire . . ."

"I don' wanna know from fires, man!" Choo Choo hissed. "I gots commitments! I gots respons'bilities, man. Don' fuck wit' me! 'Cause you gonna be daid!"

His face contorted with an instant rage that shot through him whenever his desires were thwarted. "You gets me mah stuff like yo' suppose to, you hear? Largo!" he bellowed.

Largo stepped into the room, leaving the door open, and flipped open Fassim's coat unceremoniously. Largo relished any excuse to irritate Fassim, and Choo Choo's attitude gave him license. But if Fassim was offended by the strong odor of the big man he didn't show it, only waited as Largo pulled his shirt out of his pants and relieved him of the double belts he wore about his middle. Largo handed the belts to Choo Choo, but Fassim never lost his composure or his affable expression.

"You fuckin' Africans thinks it's so easy keepin' ma people happy!" Choo Choo said. He opened the first section of the belt and pulled out one of the packets, tossing it to Largo, who went into the second bedroom to test it.

"This whol' damn shipmen' is promised to the coast. I'm takin' it myself! Dat leaves ma New York people waitin' on June shipment. You tells yo people we ain't waitin' till July. Or they'll see fireworks in June!"

Largo returned and nodded his approval of the goods. "S' almos' pure."

Choo Choo looked at Fassim, who was smiling. "That good, huh?"

Fassim nodded. "You can cut it enough to give you part of June's shipment. I shall get you more, don't worry."

Choo Choo was slightly pacified. He'd considered not paying for this shipment until the other one was in the bag, but that was dangerous. Fassim's people had their own organization, and he didn't want to get caught in the middle. He indicated to Largo to go to the closet. Largo shuffled forward, his huge body moving like a block of muscle. His hand reached for the doorknob without thinking. Choo Choo screamed "No!" grabbing the man before he opened the door. Choo Choo shook as he glared at his flunky. Dumb nigger! Largo smiled sheepishly and turned back to the doorknob. It had to be turned in a special combination or the whole damn building would be blown to hell.

Largo went into the false compartment at the back of the closet and returned with a white flight bag exactly like the one Fassim carried, only this one was filled with money.

Fassim opened it to make sure all the money was there. Only the perspiration on his upper lip and the rapid darting of his black eyes indicated any nervousness. Satisfied that it was complete, he leaned forward and embraced Choo Choo.

"Ariana has returned from California," he said. "It will be announced that she and James Fitzgerald will be married in June. The wedding will be held at our embassy."

"No shit!" Choo Choo grinned. "Then I'll see you at the weddin'!" He saw Fassim to the door and nodded to Largo to make himself scarce.

"Hey, Fassim," he asked as the man entered the elevator, "you ever buy Gucci shoes?"

Fassim shook his head.

"Well, don' 'cause they ain't worth shit!"

The elevator door closed and the red light went off. Choo Choo turned to his Aunt Florie, who was still sitting on the sofa in her raincoat and scarf the way he had left her.

He opened his arms and walked toward her. "So, darlin', how you been?" He worried for a moment about how much she might have heard.

"A lot you care how I been, Lionel. You never write to me; you never call. I had to come all the way to New York to see how you was. And now I know, don't I?"

Choo Choo ignored the pointed remark.

"That white bitch give you the time off?"

Florie's mouth tightened and she glared at her nephew. "Don't you talk about Regina like that. She's wonderful to me. And you're nothin' but a no-good, no'count."

"Hah!" Choo Choo pulled away from her. All his life she'd been telling him he was no good. He swept his arm to indicate the splendor of his surroundings. "What about dis? Is dis the place of a no'count. I gots friends *way* up there, Aunt Florie. I gots people who needs me, who pays me big money. I knows big stars and royal princesses, and they's always glad to see me."

"Sure, 'cause you give 'em that stuff." She spat out the word as though it was too filthy to be on her lips. "I knows what you are. Regina tole me. And Regina says you gonna end up in jail or worse."

"What does she know about it?"

Florie looked away. "Nuthin'," she said.

Choo Choo's eyes narrowed. So Regina Williams was passin' judgments on him, was she? Openin' her big mouth to his aunt about his dealin's. Who else was she gonna shoot off to besides Florie? He'd have to see about that. "Come on, Aunt Florie, stop fussin' and tell me all the news."

A slight smile began to play around Florie's eyes, and it worked its way down to her lips. Lionel was a rascal, but she loved him. *Lord, keep him safe,* she prayed.

"Help me with mah coat," she said, and he hurried to help her, anxious to appease the old woman. She meant well and she was the only person in his life who had ever cared about him.

"Why don't chew quit yo' job, Aunt Florie. You too old to work anymore. And ah gots plenty of money for the both of us. Whatchew need with that white lady for?"

Florie smiled and patted his hand. "I love her like my own daughter, baby. Like I loves you. Lord, how she can sing."

A rush of jealousy shot through Choo Choo at the expression of utter delight on his aunt's face when she talked about Regina. His aunt loved him, but she never approved of him the way she did that Regina. *We'll have to see 'bout that,* he thought. *We'll jes have to see.*

CHAPTER 11

Mike's taxi pulled up to the curb and he paid the tab. His hands were shaking. He'd been drinking too much lately, but he promised himself he'd stop as soon as he could get his life in order. Everything was riding on the next half hour. If only he felt better, but he was jangled from too much coffee and not enough sleep. The red-eye to New York afforded little rest, and getting Regina to go to the Golden Door for two days so he could come to New York had been some task. That woman was stubborn. But he'd done it, and now he was here with an appointment to see Lubow.

He stopped to straighten his tie and run his fingers through his hair before pushing through the revolving door of the building. CAMIL Records covered the entire twenty-second floor and part of the twenty-third. One of the largest privately owned record companies in the world, it handled both black and white artists. The elevator opened directly onto their suite; dim lights, dark paneling, and hardwood floors greeted him. A redhaired receptionist sat at an English-styled desk in the center of the reception area, smiling expectantly. From somewhere the muffled sound of work drifted lazily through the air, but this girl was the only one visible.

"Michael Shaw to see Mr. Jerry Lubow," he said.

"Won't you have a seat." She indicated a plush sofa in the corner and reached for her intercom panel, but he declined and went to study a work of art on one wall. It was lit by recessed lighting that gave it an air of importance, a huge assemblage of wool fabrics and yarns and pieces of steel worked into a pattern.

"It will be a few minutes, Mr. Shaw," the receptionist said. "He's finishing up a staff meeting."

Mike sat down to wait.

Jerry Lubow's gray eyes reflected his anger as he scanned the faces of the people who filled the chairs and sofas of his office. All of the muscles in his upper body were tense, and he wanted to smash somebody. His frustrations had to affect these people; his loyal confederates, his flock, his storm troopers, his lackeys. They hadn't been coming through for him. They just stared back at him like recalcitrant children. Most of these people he knew intimately, those who'd take it in the ass and those who'd give it. He was the best ass-fucker of them all.

"Anton," Lubow hissed through clenched teeth. "If you can't bring this film in on time, *and* within budget, I swear I'll take over the direction myself and do a better fucking job than you're doing any day." Anton sucked in his gut, but he kept quiet.

Lubow's private line buzzed and he picked up the phone, ignoring the redness that was creeping over Anton's face. *Serves the asshole Czech right,* Lubow thought.

"Yeah!" he answered.

"Can you talk?" It was Stylwickji.

"Wait a minute. I'll take it in another office." Lubow got up and crossed the room while fourteen pairs of eyes followed him. No one spoke.

Louise Carlin was hunched over her keyboard working out the rough spots on a song for one of their new albums. Her golden hair fell forward over her cheeks, revealing her shoulders and a pale and vulnerable neck. She was an excellent "song-doctor," a dynamic producer, and he'd give anything to get into her pants. But so far, no go. He wondered who she was saving it for. He thought he'd have a chance with her when he made her a VP of A and R. But she'd given him the best excuse of all. "I never shit where I eat, Jerry. But if I did, I'd certainly shit on you."

It was a classy letdown. She'd made him believe she wanted him without actually doing it. "I should fire you instead of promote you," he'd said. "Then we could get it on."

"But you need me, baby. I'm too good to fire."

And she was right, damn it, she was right.

Jerry reached over her shoulder and punched the last button on her call-phone, lifting the receiver. Louise started as he broke her concentration.

"What's happening?" he asked Stylwickji.

"Crowning Glory won't be giving you any trouble, Mr. Lubow. They fully realize their exact position in the company and their obligations to you."

Stylwickji always accomplished his assignments to perfection. Just one look at him was enough to get complaining artists into line, and his reputation for instant and final solutions preceded him among the trade. He was Lubow's most valuable asset. Lubow never asked how he got results; Stylwickji just got them.

"Where are you?" Lubow asked. He cradled the phone to his ear and kneaded Louise's shoulders. There were always knots there. She moved appreciatively against him and dropped her head forward to give him easier access.

"I'm right in the neighborhood," Stylwickji replied.

"How soon can you get back here? Mike Shaw is waiting for me."

"Ten minutes."

"We've located Cord Crocker. He's in Nevada. We've scheduled him to be in New York next week."

"Good—that's good," Stylwickji replied.

Louise looked up and their eyes met reflected in the plate glass window. Hers were almond-shaped and green, above a narrow chin and a generous mouth. He wished her mouth were around his prick this very moment. The skyline of Manhattan was a fitting backdrop for her youthful face. His face was deeply etched, capped with a helmet of curled silver hair, and bisected by heavy, graying eyebrows.

"You think Shaw is coming to you for money?" Stylwickji asked.

"Absolutely," Jerry replied. "And he's going to be very useful to me in getting my plans off the ground. You'd better get back here now."

"I'm on my way," Stylwickji replied.

Jerry hung up.

"You want me in there too?" Louise asked.

"Not now, baby." He headed back toward his office. "I'll send you a memo on what we discuss. Unless you want me to tell it to you over dinner?"

"Just send me the memo, Jer."

He closed the door to her office.

There were three secretaries in Lubow's outer office, and Mike stood aside as his staff filed out. He felt his heartbeat increase rapidly as he approached the man behind the desk. Enormous pictures of Majesty in their heyday dominated the walls, along with pictures of all the other stars and groups that Lubow had built from the bottom up. Mike hated coming here like this to beg for help.

Lubow extended his hand. "Mike! Good to see you. How's Regina?"

"She's fine," Mike replied, taking a chair in front of the ornately carved desk. Lubow's shirt was unbuttoned at the collar, his tie loosened. He was a jungle fighter, out of his element in a suit and tie. So was

Mike for that matter, who preferred tennis shorts to worsteds any day.

"How's the film going?" Mike asked. "I saw Anton Vaseleyvitch leave with that staff group."

"Anton sucks. I may have to take over the picture if he doesn't smooth things out with the cast. Especially Marlene."

"You're lucky you can do it. Not everyone has the ability to pinch hit for one of the world's greatest directors," Mike said.

Lubow leaned back in his swivel chair so that he was almost reclining. "You think directing a movie is any great shakes? Shit! Anybody who's got guts and a feel for emotions can do it easily!" Actually, Lubow was nervous about taking the director's reins. If he failed he would fail big, and a lot of people would be glad to see it happen. "I heard you were producing too."

Mike looked down at the creases in his trousers, held back from rubbing them. "Yes. But I ran into some problems with my film." He looked up at Lubow who was staring at him coldly. *He knows,* Mike thought. *The bastard knows. He wants to see me squirm.* "I suppose you know why I've come to see you. I was hoping to keep some semblance of secrecy. At least from Regina."

"Michael. What do you take me for?" Lubow sat up and leaned his elbows on his chair, his fingertips touching.

He reminded Mike of a huge spider waiting for a fly. Mike buzzed back and forth. But that spider's web was irresistible. He couldn't stay away.

"In this business people talk, but only to certain people. And I hear it all. The one thing I don't understand is why you didn't use OPM to finance your film?"

"I don't believe in risking other people's money on

certain investments," Mike replied. But he should never have used his own money in that venture. Both he and Lubow knew it. "Take this oil deal I'm into. It's an extremely rich field. I expect to triple my investment. The only reason I borrowed the money from a bank to produce the film is that I knew I could pay it back very soon. Of course I didn't expect to lose it."

"Of course," Lubow echoed.

"The oil investment will be maturing any day now. The area has been proven countless times. It's just that there's an extensive water table to contend with right now, but as soon as that's conquered, I'll have the money to pay my debts and then some. Maybe you've invested in this one yourself. Homestake Oil? A lot of big Hollywood names are in it."

"No. It's not one of mine." Lubow paused. "So, Mike. You're waiting for your well to come in, but in the meantime you're strapped, is that it?" He watched Mike's reaction carefully.

"Yes, I'm strapped," Mike acknowledged. He was certain that the vein pulsing in his temple was going to burst and he'd have a stroke right here on the handwoven carpet.

"What is your encumbrance?"

"Three hundred thousand. But I only need half right now and the rest in six weeks. I owe it all to one bank, and they've agreed to a lenient payment program."

"Six weeks to pay back the whole nut? That doesn't sound very lenient to me. You must have scared them badly. Where's all your liquidity, Mike? Regina must earn a million a year."

"A million a year is nothing. You've got no idea what our overhead is like. We employ six people full time at hefty salaries, plus we pay for our own orchestra when we perform on the road. And the cost of rehearsal time and music arranging is exorbitant, and then there's the costumes. Plus Regina supports her aunt and uncle in Montebello and contributes a fortune to charities. Everything else is invested. Either in condominiums or our own house or now this oil deal. I've got eight hundred thousand tied up there."

Lubow whistled. "That's a lot of cash. No wonder you're short."

Mike thought he saw a flicker of a smile. The bastard was playing with him.

"You're aware of my interest rates."

Mike nodded, holding his breath. Lubow charged usurious rates, but he had no choice.

"How long will your oil deal take, six weeks, two months?"

"No longer."

"All right, Michael. I'll help you out. Three hundred thousand at eighteen percent for two months and five points."

Mike flinched. He'd never expected it to be that much, but then he felt relief rush from his lungs as he reached across the desk and grabbed Lubow's hand. "You won't regret it!"

"I never regret my actions," Lubow replied. He pressed a button on his intercom and a side door in the walnut paneling opened electronically. Mike hadn't even noticed it concealed there. A man wearing a light-colored three-piece suit and shaded glasses came in, as though he had been waiting in that room for just such a summons. He had sandy hair and a square jaw like a sharp attorney in an ad for Heublein premixed cocktails. But when he turned his back, Mike noticed a large neck and a broad back that changed his image from studious to physical.

"Stylwickji, I want you to make out a draft for Mr. Shaw for this amount." He wrote a number on a paper and handed it to the man without a change in expression.

Stylwickji nodded and turned to go. Mike was jarred by the sight of a large purple scar that ran down the side of Stylwickji's face from under his dark glasses to somewhere inside the collar of his shirt. He looked as though he could carry out any difficult order and never even wrinkle his suit.

"This is to come out of Los Angeles," Lubow said.

Stylwickji nodded and stepped back through the panel which closed after him.

"I'm very grateful," Mike said.

"Good. Then you won't mind doing something for *me* in return."

"Anything," Mike offered, feeling that vein in his temple pulsing again. *Here it comes,* he thought.

"How well do you know Eddie Wakefield?"

"Well enough. He's a small-time, small-talent hanger-on."

"I understand he approached Regina with a proposal for a reunion concert of Majesty."

How did Lubow know these things? Mike wondered.

"Yes, but she turned him down."

"Good. Then there won't be any conflict of interest when she agrees to do CAMIL's reunion concert. And I'd say you're the perfect man to bring it off. Am I right?" Lubow stood and came around the desk. His eyes caught the light. Their charcoal gray color reflected his light gray shirt. But they turned to steel when he was determined. The man's power had certainly not been weakened by the murky enterprises at his fingertips. Lubow had a reputation for using every trick in the book to get his way, including force.

Mike could barely process what he was hearing. Only days ago Regina had insisted that she'd never do a reunion. And the last thing Mike wanted in the world was to bring Regina together with Cord. He tried to smile, but the muscles in his face felt as though they would crack. His marriage was shaky enough without inviting Cord Crocker in to mess things up. He didn't want to lose Regina.

"You know how much I want to help you, Jerry.

But that's a tough one. I know how my wife feels about. . . ." He stopped in midsentence.

Lubow's expression said it all without words. *Schmuck. I'm loaning you huge dollars, and you're turning down my request? I've had people hurt badly for less.*

This concert must be important to Lubow, Mike guessed. *And why not? It could be the biggest thing to ever hit the country.* "I'm sure I can get her to change her mind," Mike continued. His thoughts were racing. The reunion could save them both if she could only be convinced. . . . Afterwards she could take time off. They could go away—just the two of them. But should he convince her? *Have some faith in yourself, Shaw. Regina loves you. She won't stop loving you if she works with Crocker again. She had her chance with him, and it didn't work. That's all in the past now. If you could pull this off—a one-time reunion concert of the country's all-time favorite group—you'd have it made!* This could be the deal he was waiting for. It would be bigger than a reunion of the Beatles.

"You don't anticipate any major problems, do you?" Lubow asked.

"Naturally there'll be some. Regina's been asked many times before, you know, and always turned it down. But actually this is something I've toyed with myself."

"Have you?" Lubow seemed impressed.

"That's strictly between you and me of course. I'll tell Regina about it when the time is right. And Jerry. . . ." he paused. "If I put this thing together— I mean *when* I've put it together—I'm assuming that I'll be compensated."

"Well certainly."

"I don't mean just financially. I'd share with Regina as far as the profits go. But I'd like a title. That would mean a lot to me. And I'd like to be really involved in the production end, along with you of course."

Lubow shook his head in amazement. "You've got a helluva nerve, Shaw. I'll say that for you. Just don't take too long to do what I've asked, all right? And then we'll see what we can do. But I'm not making any promises."

"Oh, I understand," Mike said, trying to keep the excitement out of his voice.

"I've placed tentative reserves on four major arenas," Lubow continued. "Dallas, New Orleans, Los Angeles, and New York. So far my word will hold them for a short time without deposit. And naturally I want to keep this under wraps until everything is sewn up and we make an official announcement to the press."

This man didn't fuck around, Mike thought. Well, neither did he. "Perhaps I'll fly over and see Drummond in London as long as I'm halfway there." Maybe if Don commits. . . . And Cord—well, Regina would be more easily convinced." Lubow looked directly into Mike's eyes. They both knew Mike was thinking of Crocker. The affair between Regina and Cord was legendary.

"Good, I'm counting on you. In fact, I'd like to set an official date for Labor Day weekend. The closed circuit people will be ready to go when I give the word. We'll have simultaneous broadcasts in every major city in the country. And there are commitments from half a dozen separate countries for worldwide Telstar broadcast. All they know so far is that something big is in the planning, but they don't know what it is yet. They'll need six weeks to do the promotions and four weeks to prepare for it, so you'd better get all your people firmed up right away. CAMIL Records is renegotiating contracts with all three members of the group. That shouldn't take too long, so my attorneys inform me."

Labor Day? The news hit Mike with a jolt. He would need time to set this up. This wasn't some real estate deal where the property was sitting and waiting for the right offer. This would take delicate negotiations, and they couldn't be rushed until the parties were psychologically ready. Christ, until he was psychologically ready. He swallowed hard. He hoped he wasn't making a mistake.

"It may not be possible to get all three to agree so quickly! Their schedules are booked for months, even years in advance. And you know how opposed they've all been to this idea."

Lubow's expression grew in intensity. "Don't give me excuses, Shaw; I'm not playing games. Just get the commitments and everything will be fine." His smile was icy, baring white even teeth. Mike preferred the steel gray stare to an attempt at friendship.

"I'll get them. Believe me."

Lubow nodded and moved from the elaborately carved desk with its lions' heads and figures of Neptune. He escorted Mike across the leopard-patterned carpet. "Keep me closely informed, Mike," he said as they reached the door. "And Michael. We're assuming your oil well is going to come in. But if for some reason it doesn't, I'll have to collect my money no matter what it takes. And if that happens, I will only accept Regina's performance as repayment of your debt."

"But what if I can't convince her?"

"Just convince her, Mike. Because if you don't, I will."

But before Mike could ask him what he meant by that remark, Lubow closed the door between them and Mike found himself in the secretaries' office. *Was that a threat?* he wondered. No. He tried to dismiss it. But a terrible sense of dread grabbed him for a moment before he shook it off. Lubow wouldn't threaten him. And he'd never harm Regina. She was a meal ticket. She'd earned the company millions of dollars. Without her there wouldn't be a concert.

And then a horrible thought occurred to him. Maybe they needed Regina, but *he* was expendable, and so were the children. Jesus Christ!

Slowly he walked across the office wondering how he could have gotten in so deeply. The more he tried to fix things, the worse they became. How was he going to convince Regina to do something she absolutely refused to do?

He'd find a way.

He had to find a way!

CHAPTER 12

When Mike Shaw left, Lubow pressed the buzzer on his desk and the hidden door in the paneling opened again. Stylwickji came back into the room.

"I think Shaw will come through for us eventually," Lubow said. And then he noticed that Stylwickji was cleaning his dark glasses with a white linen handkerchief which he then folded carefully and placed in the outer pocket of his three-piece suit. Without his glasses the scar which nearly bisected his left eye was clearly visible. Lubow knew he only removed his glasses when he wanted to impress someone. Choo Choo Trainer followed Stylwickji into the room, glancing at the scar out of the corner of his eye.

Lubow was furious to see Choo Choo here against his explicit instructions. He held on to his temper.

"I thought I told you *never* to come here!"

"Hey." Choo Choo swung his lanky body across the remaining space between them and stood before Lubow with his head pivoting in its characteristic way. "I've brought you some good news, man!"

Lubow just stared at him. The people he dealt with had only one chance to step out of bounds, and Choo Choo had better learn that immediately. Any familiarity was intolerable. Especially between the owner of a company the size of CAMIL and the man who supplied its clients with an occasional fix.

Lubow's stare began to unnerve Choo Choo and he stopped bobbing his head.

"My new overseas contact is workin' smoo-ooth! I can deliver my quota eas'ly. In fact . . ." he hesitated for a fraction and Lubow's jaw tightened. "I wants an increase." By the time he had finished the sentence his voice had lost its bravado.

"You'll get an increase when I say! And not when you go against my express orders! I'm not accustomed to shouting my instructions, but I expect them to be obeyed. This office is for emergencies!" he stated. "Is that clear?"

Choo Choo tried to be ingratiating. "Hey, man! No sweat!"

Lubow took a step forward, forcing Choo Choo a step back into Stylwickji who had moved around behind him. Choo Choo's body began to shake, enough to show that he'd gotten the point.

"Do you know what you are to me?" Lubow asked him. "A bug! And I swat bugs when they pester me."

"You don' want me to sell my surplus elsewhere?" Choo Choo asked with a whine in his voice.

The man doesn't give up easily, Lubow thought. "When I do business, an increase is something you are awarded, not something you ask for!" Choo Choo was getting the point. He'd been caught trying to edge his way in where he wasn't wanted and the spot was too tight for comfort. *Damn black ingrate,* Lubow thought. These people thought their schemes were original, but he had invented every trick they ever thought of. Only he'd done them right!

"If you've overextended yourself, that's too bad!" he shouted.

"Whatever you say, man. You're the man!" He edged sideways to avoid Stylwickji and leave the office before Lubow's anger showed itself for real.

Lubow's supremacy had been validated by Choo Choo's fear. But fear wasn't enough. "You'll be hearing from me," Lubow said as Choo Choo reached the door. He didn't want to discourage him too much, just keep him in line. Dealing in drugs was a dirty business, but it was part of his world, just as occasional violence had to be. Every record company had its dopers. If he ignored that, he'd be at a disadvantage among his competitors. Besides he wasn't above an occasional snort of coke. But he abhorred dealing with people like Choo Choo Trainer.

"Wait until Mike Shaw is clear of the building before you leave," he instructed Choo Choo and pressed the buzzer on his desk to close the paneled door.

Lubow turned to Stylwickji. "Make sure that asshole is aware that I meant what I said!"

"He's got that Largo with him at all times," Stylwickji answered, more as a point of information than a reaction.

Lubow nodded. "Then be polite. But I want him handled. And mess up that pad of his on Ninety-eighth Street. The one he's always mouthing off about. Maybe a can of black spray paint on his marble tables and on his white fur bedspread."

When Stylwickji smiled only half of his face responded. He pressed the buzzer and left by the private entrance.

Lubow was certain that the next time they met Choo Choo Trainer would be more respectful.

CHAPTER 13

There were four other major celebrities and a United States senator in the greenroom at NBC when Regina walked through, but everybody stopped to stare at her. Even in a St. Laurent outfit, which she preferred over the more flamboyant gowns she wore for performances, she could stop traffic.

Freddie de Cordova, who had produced the *Tonight* show for eighteen years, came into her dressing room and kissed her. "You've been moved to the second spot, Regina. Senator Armstrong has to go on first. An emergency session's been called and he's due back in Washington tonight."

She nodded.

"Are you certain you don't want to sing?"

"Would Paul McCartney sing, Freddie?"

He shrugged. "It's great exposure." The standard come-on.

She looked down at her cleavage, which showed no matter what she wore. "I've got enough exposure, Freddie."

He laughed and went to find Senator Armstrong.

The Carson show was the first in a series of promotional appearances she would endure while she was between engagements. *Merv, Dinah!,* and *Mike Douglas* would all be taped in the next few days. As a visiting celebrity she'd push her new act, hype her new album, be cute and scintillating, talk about her marriage and her children. But most important of all, look gorgeous. It was easier than public speaking. Actually these shows were fun. She got to be a person for a change instead of a symbol, and on *Merv* and *Dinah!* she usually had a great time depending on who were her fellow guests. On those shows they'd sit around and visit on the air and then go out for dinner afterwards. It was the only way she got to meet certain celebrities. Contrary to what the public believed, not all famous people knew one another. But Johnny Carson was a good friend of hers and Mike's, and she enjoyed doing his show.

Once several years back one of the major talk show hosts had tried to book her and Cord and Don on the same show without informing them beforehand. It was someone's idea of an unauthorized reunion. But one of the host's staff members accidentally let it slip and all three of the ex-Majestys had cancelled, leaving the producer hustling at the last minute for a replacement. The staff member was fired, and Regina lost a week of sleep over what it would have been like if the three of them had come face to face with each other unprepared. What a nightmare!

For a while she refused to do any talk shows. And even now she insisted on seeing a list of the guests, signed by the producer, before she'd agree to do a show.

Florie was studying her for signs of anxiety, but Florie was the one who looked tired.

"I'm all right," Regina assured her, holding out steady hands to show to Florie who sat down next to her on the sofa. "Look, no fluttering of the fingers, no pains in the abdomen. My breathing is normal. I'm in terrific shape."

"I wish I were," Florie sighed, sinking back against the cushions. "My back aches and my left arm pains me. I picked up Jana this morning and I haven't been the same since. Lord that chile is growing."

"You know you shouldn't do that," Regina scolded.

She was always worried that Florie did too much. Florie was not getting any younger, and her extra fifty pounds of weight sapped her strength.

Florie smiled, that full-cheeked smile of hers that made her look both sheepish and defiant. "I know I shouldn't, but I love those girls so. Sometimes I just can't resist huggin' 'em."

Regina's eyes filled with tears threatening her carefully applied makeup. "They love you too, sweetheart," she said. There were so few people in her daughters' lives who really loved them the way Florie did, like a grandmother.

Mike came into the room. "Everything's set for the special. I just got word that we can have the rehearsal hall we wanted, and Dwight Hemion and Gary Smith have agreed to produce."

"What luck!" Regina exclaimed. "I adore their work, but every time I've asked them they've been committed to other projects. How'd you get them?"

"I moved the special up to October." He was almost out the door again, avoiding her. "I knew you'd be pleased."

"Wait a minute." She stopped him. "We can't do that. The special has to be in September because we've got Vegas again and then Atlantic City. October's impossible, Mike. Why do you do things like this?"

"We'll talk about it later, Regina."

"What do you mean, later? You're making commitments for me that I object to and I want it stopped. What are we supposed to do about Nevada and New Jersey?"

"I'll cancel them!"

"What?" She was incredulous. "Are you crazy?"

"That would leave you free in September."

"What for?"

"Well," he hesitated. "I realize this is a bad time to broach the subject, but if we hadn't just found out about getting Dwight and Gary, it wouldn't have come up." He came and sat down on the other side of her, taking her hand. "Honey, I know this might seem as though it's out of left field, but I've been thinking about it for a long time. Remember that suggestion of Ed Wakefield's? Well, I think you should do a reunion concert of Majesty in September."

She looked at him with enormous eyes. She couldn't believe what he had just said. It was times like these that she wondered why she stayed married to him. That he would even suggest such a thing—now of all times when she was about to go on national television —was incredible. Didn't he know what she went through?

Perhaps it was anger or sudden panic, but the room began to swim before her eyes.

"You're impossible," she managed to say. "And that's a ridiculous idea."

"Miss Williams," the assistant director called. "You're next."

It was as if someone had dumped a pitcher of ice cubes down her back. "I can't!" she wailed, reaching over to grab Florie. She was freezing from a sudden blast of arctic air.

Florie pushed her up out of the sofa. "Sure you can, honey. That's just Johnny out there. He came to dinner last week, remember?"

Mike reached to help her but she pushed him away. Then she turned on him, unleashing her panic into fury, melting the ice with her anger. "Sometimes you're so goddamned insensitive, I hate you! You ought to be glad I keep turning down a reunion concert, Michael," she said. "The day I ever agree to do one is the day I've given up on our marriage." And then she walked over to the entrance to the stage. But her whole body was trembling and she had to clench her teeth to keep them from chattering.

Florie looked at Mike. His face was contorted with

pain. "Michael Shaw," she scolded. "What have you got in your head for brains? For someone who loves someone, you sure don't act like it." She raised her hands for him to help her up.

"I didn't mean to upset her, Florie," he said. "But she'll get over it. I've got faith in Regina. And I think she should do the reunion and get it behind her once and for all. The two of us will be all right."

Florie's huge frame seemed to deflate, and she shook her head. "I don't think so. I think it's asking for trouble. Or is that something you already got?"

Mike smiled, but she didn't smile back.

She was a shrewd lady, he thought. And she knew more about their finances than Regina who was involved in so many other things. He put his arm around her and she winced. The pain she had been hiding all day was clearly visible now. "I've made an appointment with Dr. Simmons for you this afternoon at four thirty," he told her. "We'll take Regina home and then tell her we're going shopping."

Florie nodded; her breathing was heavy.

"You know you're crazy to be here right now. You should be in the hospital. You've got to lose some weight."

"Easy for skinny people to talk," she teased. "Besides Regina needs me here."

"She needs you alive and well, Florie," he said. Florie's hypertension worried them all. She was a woman you couldn't help but love.

Johnny Carson announced Regina's name and she stepped through the curtain. Florie was relieved to see her safely on the stage. Once she got that far Regina would be fine. But her relief was short lived when she thought about her appointment with Dr. Simmons today at four thirty. She didn't like doctors pokin' around on her body. Besides it was Choo Choo that was worryin' her heart. She just knew it. That boy was goin' to be the death of her.

Mike watched the monitor, waiting for the enthusiastic applause to die down after Regina's entrance. *Well, I blew that one,* he thought. *I'd better come up with a legitimate excuse the next time I approach her. Time is getting short.*

Regina walked over to the raised podium and kissed Johnny and Ed McMahon. Then she took the hotseat that Senator Armstrong had just vacated. It was still warm from his body heat. Carefully she crossed her legs. The audience was still applauding for her and Johnny made her take another bow. She could smell Johnny's cologne; he always smelled delicious.

"It's good to have you on our show again, Regina. I haven't seen you since last week." He turned to the audience. "I play tennis on Regina's court with her husband Mike. Mike's a fair player, but I usually win. When I'm not too busy looking at Regina." She laughed with the audience. And Johnny mugged looking at her body. She mugged looking at his. The audience loved it.

"You've just completed an engagement in Las Vegas," he said. "I understand it was impossible to get tickets for your show. Instead of chips at the crap tables winners were asking for reservations for the dinner show."

"I've been very lucky to have such loyal fans," she said.

"But you give them your all." He turned to the audience. "If you've ever seen her on stage, you know what an exciting performer she is."

There was an enthusiastic round of applause.

"How old are your little girls now?"

"Jamie is seven, Jana is five."

"Would you say they take after their mother?"

"Yes, they're both hams. They know just how to deliver a line. 'But Mommie, you promised!' " Regina made a pouting face just like Jana would make. Johnny laughed.

"Tell me, what is the single most frequent question people ask you? How you got started? What does it feel like to be Regina Williams?"

Here it comes, she thought. She could never escape it. "No. The most frequent question I'm asked is if Majesty will ever have a reunion."

"Funny that you should mention that. I was wondering the very same thing." The audience applauded enthusiastically. There were several whistles.

She forced herself to smile. "My answer is always the same. It would be impossible. Majesty does not exist any longer as a group. One of us is dead, and as far as the other three of us are concerned, we might as well be dead too." She shook her head emphatically. "I can't imagine a reunion ever happening."

Johnny turned to camera three and announced a commercial. The control booth took over and they relaxed a bit. Johnny patted her hand reassuringly, and she winked at him. He knew how she hated that question, and yet he had to ask it.

When the commercial break was over they continued the interview for four minutes more, and then it was over. Maybe someday the world would forget she was once part of Majesty, she thought, as she left the podium and went back stage again. God, she hoped so.

CHAPTER 14

Cord waited until the 747 had been emptied of all its passengers before he emerged from the first class section and followed the brunet flight attendant into the VIP lounge. He was exhausted and sleepy from the flight, and now it felt as though it was the middle of the night. The lounge was empty except for a striking blonde in her early thirties. She wore a pale rose-colored dress that moved nicely around her body and gold jewelry, and she smiled as she came toward him.

"I'm Louise Carlin, Mr. Crocker, with CAMIL Records in New York. I'm responsible for you while you're here." Her voice was efficient, her smile friendly. "Your baggage is being brought directly to the limousine. If you'll follow me I'll show you the way to avoid the crowds." He got a whiff of expensive perfume as she held the door open for him. Nice reception!

There was an exit from the building down a long corridor, and their footsteps echoed against the empty walls decorated with an occasional graphic. Louise Carlin stared at him, but if he looked at her she looked away.

"Are you tired?" she asked.

"Yes. I've had very little sleep in the past week. I did some waterskiing, but I've just come off a long tour."

"I know. I read all the reviews. They're very good!" He knew she meant it, but he wondered if her opinion held any weight with the company. "I'll get you right to your hotel," she promised.

They reached the end of the corridor and she pushed open the door. There were the car and driver waiting for them and soon they were on the expressway.

She settled back into the seat close by him though there was ample room in the huge car. And even as she gazed out of the window she seemed to be leaning toward him as though drawn magnetically, even though she was trying to hide it. It was the most indirect come-on he'd ever seen.

After a short time she opened her Fendi bag and took out a gold jeweled box, offering him a pinch of coke. He shook his head. "I really plan to sleep when I get to the hotel."

She closed it without using any herself.

"I understand. . . ."

"How long have you been . . ." They both began in unison.

"You first," he said.

"I understand while you're in New York you'll be meeting with David Merrick?" Her question was politely conversational but spoken with that same intensity of tone he'd noticed earlier, as though she was expecting something from him. He'd seen her at CAMIL before, but they'd never been introduced. He wasn't exactly sure of her function.

He smiled at her for the first time. "Can you feature me doing a Broadway musical? I told them it was ludicrous, but they insisted. Said the part was written with me in mind. This I've got to see."

"Would you enjoy appearing on the stage?"

"What do you think I do for a living? Pick my nose?"

She recoiled from his sarcasm. "I meant the legitimate theater."

He looked away, guilty for his remark.

"Mr. Crocker." She touched his arm.

"Call me Cord," he said. "Mr. Crocker was my father."

"All right, Cord. . . ." There was a slight tremble to her voice. "I've been an executive with CAMIL for some time. I handle celebrities every day as part of my job and I *never* go in person to meet them at the airport. I have assistants to do that. But meeting you was something special to me. I've been an admirer of yours for years."

He looked at her in surprise. The cool polished lady was human. She handled herself beautifully, and he was impressed to count her among his fans.

"Thank you," he said simply. "I started to ask you before how long you'd been in this business." He was feeling an interest in her; she was so straightforward.

"I worked my way up from the retail sales end, which is a fancy way of saying that I sold records over the counter when I was in high school. It was about the time that Majesty was on the rise. I became friends with the CAMIL sales rep for our territory. Then when I got out of college one thing led to another. I was lucky early in my career. I discovered two of our biggies, produced their first hit albums. I also doctor a bit." She wiped her hands on her dress nervously.

That was quite an impressive array of talent.

"Relax," he said, taking her hand in his. "You're doing fine." He expected her to bristle at his chauvinistic teasing, but she smiled instead.

"I needed that," she said and gave his fingers a squeeze. "I can't believe this. I haven't been as nervous in years."

"Where are you from?" he asked.

"New Joisey," she replied in an exaggerated accent. He laughed and laced his fingers through hers. It felt comfortable to be with her.

"Jerry Lubow wants us to discuss the details of your new contract," she said. They were caught in a traffic jam and the car was moving at a snail's pace.

"I haven't agreed to a renewal," he said, wary of her approach. Was this why she was being so friendly?

"I'm aware that you haven't renewed. I'm supposed to find out what would induce you to sign. We understand that ABC Dunhill has made you a great offer and A&M countered with an even better one." She stared at him as though his pores contained some knowledge she had to discover, some secret of the universe.

"You do get around," he said. "I only heard about A&M's offer this morning as I boarded the plane in L.A."

"I don't have to tell you about contract battles. You've won a few in your time." She was referring to his last contract when he'd considered forming his own company. The time wasn't right then, but now that he'd just completed a smashing tour he thought the time might be ripe to strike out. It had been a long time without the independence of his own subsidiary label. But after Majesty disbanded, their subsidiary label died with them and he'd signed on with CAMIL as a single performer. He'd been fairly content, but he wanted a challenge, needed a new risk.

Louise was staring at him, and he stared back, watching the gold flecks shimmer in her green eyes and feeling her intensity become his own. Nobody beat him at the eye game. It was dangerous to gaze so openly into someone else's eyes. He loved doing it, felt as though he could lose himself completely, but he never quite did. It was usually the woman who gave up and looked away, overcome by the suggestion he transmitted. Only Regina had ever matched him stare for stare, but now Louise was holding her own. By the time they reached the Plaza Hotel, he felt as though he knew her very well. "You're much better than my fantasy," she smiled, sliding across him to get out of the limousine. He wanted to pull her back into his lap, but he didn't. He watched her walk briskly up the steps, admiring her legs in the soft skirt.

She was waiting for him in the lobby by the elevator with his room key and his travel bag in her hand.

They were silent all the way up in the elevator while his mind toyed with the image of them making love. He was aware of her height as she stood next to him. He wanted to hold her hand, but instead he took the travel bag from her just to make contact.

His bags had been placed in his room, and he tipped the bellboy before she had a chance to reach into her purse.

"I've arranged theater tickets for you tonight if you wish," she said. "Or if you prefer, I'll be happy to order room service for you before I leave."

"You're leaving?" He was amazed.

She looked away embarrassed.

"Louise, I didn't think you came with the suite if that's what's on your mind." He waited, then started again, "If you're free for the evening, I'd be honored if you'd stay with me." He felt like a kid asking for a first date.

She was beginning to loosen up. She turned back to him. "You're not too tired?"

"Do I look tired?" He took a step toward her and unbuttoned her jacket, revealing the full-breasted figure he'd felt pressed against him in the car. His desire for sleep had been replaced by more immediate needs as he watched her remove her jacket and turn back to him. Her nipples were outlined by the pale silk of the dress that clung to her like soft rose petals.

"Would you like to order some food?" she asked.

He reached for the top button on her dress. "Later."

She stopped his hand and studied him while he waited, his anticipation growing. And then she began to unbutton the dress herself, never taking her eyes from his. She pulled the top out of her skirt to reveal her nude breasts through the opening, and he felt his pulse quicken. He slid his hand inside her clothes and cupped the soft firmness of her breast, heard the sharp intake of her breath. Her hand shook as she unbuttoned the top of her skirt.

She stepped up to him and pulled his shirt away from his body, opening it and touching his chest with her fingers, while she gazed into his eyes. She traced his muscles and body hair, brushing his nipples which hardened to her touch. Then she arched her back, still gazing at him, and wound her arms around him rubbing her breasts against his chest. He was overwhelmed by her sensuality. She reminded him of a white persian cat he'd once had who had fallen in love with his flokati rug and rubbed herself against it all the time.

He gazed back at her as he unzipped her skirt and slid his hands inside to cup her behind, pressing her against him, lifting her, straining her to fit his growing penis.

"You're really something," he whispered hoarsely. But as she closed her eyes and he kissed her, he had a sudden memory of Regina. The two women looked nothing alike, but there was a similarity between them. He forced Regina's face out of his memory and concentrated on the blonde in his arms. Regina had been like this, giving herself without reservation, without embarrassment, and in complete abandon. Maybe he'd finally met her equal; maybe there was finally someone who could make him forget Regina, who could surpass the comparison.

Louise was unbuttoning his jeans and he slid her skirt off her hips and let it fall. They each took a step to the side in an instinctual mating dance. And then they were on the bed, and he was pulling off his shirt and scraping off his boots, trying to keep the flow of motion going without stopping for incidentals like jewelry and socks. Her body was incredibly cool. She felt shimmery, like hand-formed aspic, and he could taste her under his tongue. Her hands touched him everywhere, and he lost himself in her, marveling at how long it had been since he'd made love like this. He wanted to prolong it, keep it from ending, because the end was usually bitter and empty. But his impatience and his desire urged him on. Her inner thighs were muscular and smooth. He stroked them with both hands, cupping her vagina, parting the lips and leaning down to dip his tongue, wetting the softness that didn't need more moisture.

He'd gotten so used to the pretense of young girls who thought that performance counted more than enjoyment that he'd forgotten how exciting it was to be desired for sensuality alone. She was urging him on, holding him to see if he was erect, placing him between her legs, reaching her hips up to meet him, so that he was carried away by her climax and came soon after he entered her. There was none of his usual strain toward culmination, none of the usual head trips he used to come. They lay in each other's arms, holding on, as though the wave that broke over them had not yet passed, had not tossed them around enough, had not even gotten them wet. He was surprised and pleased by his reaction and certainly not satiated. Just happy at the ease with which it had happened.

He wanted to make love again, slowly this time, leisurely touching the parts of her he'd only just met. But a second time meant he really liked her, and that was dangerous. That meant future dates and possible commitments and responsibility and getting hurt.

She reached down and touched him. He was still partially erect and she leaned up on her elbow to look at him. He couldn't help responding. She was so open and direct, so in control of herself and yet so giving that he grew hard in her hand. He felt the soft caress of her breasts as they brushed against him as she brought her lips down to his groin. She tasted him only long enough to excite him; there was no contest to make him come. She didn't insist that he ejaculate to prove she was doing a good job. When he was fully erect she sat up and swung her leg over him, moving her hips into place so that he could enter her again.

This time they took it slow, each one unwilling to let it end, touching and stroking, rocking and moving carefully, gently so as not to go over the edge. She watched his face for signs, and he studied her short nose and narrow jaw, pink-tipped breasts and slim waist ending with the shaft of his penis moist from their excretions. This time the wave broke fully when they could wait no longer, and she moaned in his ear as she clutched him, pumping against him and he into her.

Much later when they were finishing their dinner, she told him, "I've been wondering if we would ever do this again."

"I'll be here for a few days."

"I know exactly how long you'll be here; I booked your trip."

He smiled. "Do you have any free time in between my appointments?"

"Possibly," she said, smiling to soften her answer. "There was something else I was wondering about too."

He poured her another glass of Pouilly Fuissé. "How did I get to be such a good lover?"

"More personal than that."

He sipped his wine. "Oh?"

"What was the real reason for Majesty's breakup?"

"What did you hear?"

"The usual. An overabundance of vying egos, big bad stars who got too big for their own good. You know."

"Well, those are probably as good a set of reasons as any."

". . . And the death of your brother."

He nodded.

"What did happen?"

"He OD'd."

"Why?"

"He was on drugs."

"You're a man of many words."

"What do you want to know?"

"Was it suicide?"

"You writing an article?" He was only half kidding.

"No. Look, let's skip it."

Cord rubbed his forehead, grimacing from her directness. Anything to avoid that question. "I guess it was suicide in a way. Anyone who uses that shit must want to die. I know, 'cause I once used too. But I got off. My brother couldn't. Gene was a gentle guy. He was a talented musician, but he believed everybody else's opinion. Especially when Don told him he couldn't play worth a damn. Gene heard once too often that he had lumps on the end of his drumsticks." His jaw tightened as he talked. "And Regina would criticize him too. Her reasons were different—she was just blinded by her own perfectionism. But the words hurt worse from her, considering their . . ."

She cut him off. "Couldn't you tell him they were full of it?"

"I did! But he didn't believe me. I was so crazy about Regina, and Gene always looked up to me. He figured anyone I loved had to be right."

Louise reached across the table and took his hand. "I'm sorry. I shouldn't have asked."

"It happened a long time ago."

"But it still hurts," she commented. He nodded, surprised to find tears in his eyes.

She got up and came over to his side, putting her arms around him and hugging his head to her chest. He patted her behind and she moved away, gathering up her clothes and taking them into the bathroom.

When she came out, he was nearly asleep at the table. She steered him toward the bed. "I'll see you tomorrow at noon. We have a lunch date at Lutece with Lubow. Do you want me to pick you up?"

He shook his head groggily. "Don't bother. I'll take a cab."

She blew him a kiss and was gone before he realized he hadn't asked for her number. *I'll get it tomorrow,* he thought and was asleep in minutes.

CHAPTER 15

The bus ride up the California coastline and into Oregon was long and tedious. Penny used the bathroom more than any other passenger on the bus and she cried more than anyone else. So many emotions assailed her. She had very little hope that this trip would be pleasant, only that it would be over quickly. In spite of her fears the green forests, the hillsides, and the blue-green of the ocean were welcome sights. They were friends, steadfast sentinels to her errant life. The pine needles, the maple leaves, and the sweet meadow grass all beckoned to her, while the salt sea-air moistened the windows of the bus. But home meant other things besides the beauty of nature. It meant Clyde Burrows and Jane Whitbanks and Lucinda Morris and Finney. All the people she'd grown up with and gotten into trouble with. They had known her at the lowest moments of her life.

The first thing she saw as the bus pulled into the downtown station was her father's bald head above the heads of the other people. She remembered how his Adam's apple bobbed up and down when he shouted his hell-fire curses at her. Slowly she gathered together her possessions and the gift she'd brought for Timmy and made her way down the aisle, procrastinating until she was the only one left.

Her father's plaid shirt was open at the collar. There was never a shirt tight enough to fit his skinny neck. His wrists always hung out of the cuffs of his shirts, and his hips never met the inside edge of his baggy pants. He nodded to her as she descended the stairs and reached over, grabbing her by the shoulder.

"I came to git you myself 'cause I don't want the child to know nuthin'! You hear, Missy, nuthin' 'bout the past!" His teeth were yellow and he rasped when he talked. She'd forgotten that.

"Hello, Father," Penny said, shrinking inside her coat, trying to escape the feeling that she was returning to jail. Her coat slipped off her shoulders and he lost his grasp on her, but he grabbed her again digging his nails into her shoulder.

"Car's over yonder." He pointed to the weather-beaten Dart he'd driven for ten years.

"I have to get my suitcase," she said. He stood sideways with his shoulders hunched forward and his silhouette foreboding against the clouded sky as an ominous portent. She went into the building and claimed her luggage, carrying it heavily to the car. He opened the trunk and waited while she hefted it inside. She thought of Beau's concern for her and his gentleness when she tried to lift her bag. That seemed like ages ago.

The passenger seat in the Dart was so broken down that she felt as though she'd fallen into a hole. Her mother's bulk always ruined every mattress, chair, or sofa they owned inside of a few weeks. But her father's half of the seat was still normal, and he towered over her both in height and power.

She stared at the familiar landmarks, feeling no interest in the new seven-eleven store or the burger and pizza stands that had sprung up between the bus depot and home. It was all worse than she expected.

Doesn't he ever smile? she wondered. "How's Timmy doing in first grade?" she asked. From their occasional letters she knew that her son was a wonderful child, just as she'd been before she got started on drugs.

"School's not as important as his commitment to the Lord. And he's doin' passable there," he said. It was a long speech for him. *Timmy must be fabulous,* she thought.

"I'm doing very well myself, Father," she offered. "I'm married to a kind and gentle man. I'm a good wife to him and I do my praying every day." (*Beau, I miss you!*) She needed him so much at this moment. Seeing her father made her realize that Beau was the only person who'd ever loved her.

"He still workin' in nightclubs?" He said it as though he meant garbage dumps.

"Yes," she answered quietly.

"Cain't hear you, Missy, speak up!"

"Yes, Father, he still works in a nightclub. He's on tour right now; that's why I'm not with him. I thought it would be a good chance for a visit."

"We'll see," he replied. "We'll just see."

The first time she left Oregon at age fifteen, she vowed never to return again. And she'd only been home twice since then. This place haunted her with the memory of her life here. But she couldn't let those feelings envelop her again, or her need for drugs. Dr. Klein, the young resident psychiatrist at UCLA, had been helping her to understand herself, and to stay off of drugs. She had some tranquilizers to travel with. But she was no longer on methadone. She hadn't dropped any speed or Quaaludes for months. And best of all she was free from a lifestyle of drugs and the people who used them and sold them. That was the hardest part. Keeping away from her old connections. She didn't know how Beau could be so strong, but he still had a lot of his former friends. That's why she had to come to Oregon. There wasn't anybody they knew in Los Angeles who didn't use some kind of drug. And that was one of the things she feared about being here—being around her old temptations. But she had to test herself; Daniel in the lion's den.

The car turned up the tree-lined street. There were the sidewalks of her childhood, still dotted with tricycles and chalked in hopscotch squares on the white cement. The ash trees were just starting to leaf, and the maple leaves were still a miniature size. Spring was nearly here. She used to count the hours until the pansies opened, and the ranunculuses would paint the gardens with their cotton tufts of color. There was the walnut tree with its white painted trunk, and the mulberry tree in Mrs. Crowder's front lawn. The mulberries would ripen in August. She could almost taste them. They passed the empty lot where she'd gotten bit by a spider and they had thought it was a black widow.

The car pulled into their driveway, and she saw the green shingled roof and the white chipped paint on the old siding and the swing on the front porch where she'd first tried LSD, but before that her Grandma Parsons used to read her nursery rhymes there. *Where did it all go?* she wondered, seeing her blond, curly self hurling down the steps, dirty knees and faded dress, and then stopping at the bottom to walk ceremoniously to the car, eyes lowered, hands at her sides, to see who the visitor was in father's car. But this figure hurling toward her wasn't a blond, curly Penny; it was a reddish-haired Timmy wearing a football T-shirt and brown cords. She threw open the car door and ran around to greet her son, lifting the slender boy up in her arms, feeling incredible joy.

Timmy's arms wrapped around her neck it felt like three times, and Penny squeezed back the tears as she moaned, "Ohhhh, I missed you!"

Timmy was nearly six and could almost read Penny's letters. Even though Penny had only seen him twice since he was born, once when Timmy was two and then again at age four when she and Beau had gotten married, Penny felt she knew every freckle on that face.

She put her "brother" down and walked around the back of the car as her father unlocked the trunk. She and Timmy lugged the suitcase out and carried it between them to the house and up the steps. They giggled as though they were carrying a bucket of ice cream that they'd devour in private.

The scent of baking fruit pies assailed Penny at the front door, covering the mustiness of the house. Penny felt lighthearted for the first time since leaving Beau. Her mother was baking in her honor. At least someone would welcome her.

"That's enough!" her father barked at their backs. Giggling and happiness was intolerable to God. They both stopped immediately.

"How long you gonna stay?" Timmy whispered, anxious to pin down this wondrous fairy princess of a sister who stepped straight out of a picture book for his own delight.

"I don't know," Penny whispered back. "Beau's tour could be a long one unless he asks me to join him."

Timmy looked at her with huge brown eyes, and Penny felt a sudden chill course through her body as Finney's face stared back at her. It was uncanny. All these years she'd tried to figure out who Timmy's father had been, but there was no way to know. Not with the amount of men she'd been with. Finney was the first and she'd been with him during that time. She'd always wanted Timmy to be his, but there was no proof. And now, as clear as though there had never been anybody else, the unmistakable answer looked back at her. It made her heart constrict.

She looked up to see her mother's frame filling the doorway to the kitchen. She was wearing her butcher's apron over her shapeless body and she wiped her hands free of flour and shortening. Her face was softer and pudgier than Penny recalled, and her eyes were nearly lost in the folds of her cheeks. Her hennaed hair needed doing; the gray roots were at least three inches long. Her swollen feet in their oriental thongs flapped as she crossed the worn patterned carpet toward her daughter. Penny used to pretend the carpet was magic and she could fly away on it to beautiful countries where mothers and fathers hugged and kissed their daughters and never chastised them for not loving God.

"Hello, dear," her mother said, pushing her spongy cheek up to be kissed. Penny half expected her to taste like marshmallows.

"Something smells delicious." She tried to sound enthusiastic for Timmy's sake.

"Strawberry *and* apple!" Timmy exclaimed. "Mama says we're gonna do peach too as soon as they ripen." Timmy tugged at her hand. "I helped, Penny! I peeled the apples and I stemmed the strawberries and I even stirred the syrup and everything."

Penny put her arm around him. "Thank you, sweetheart."

"Myrna!" her father called, and her mother removed her apron guiltily.

"Yes, Fred, right away." She waddled across the entry hall to the dining room and took her place around the prayer table. That's where Penny's father sat studying his scriptures every waking moment when he wasn't at work.

"Lord, we praise Thee mightily and call upon Thy mercy in dealing with our sinful daughter, whose sins we well know. In Thy worldly bounty we beg Thy forgiveness while *she* is in this house of Godfearing Witnesses. Do not look too harshly on Thy humble servants for harboring her. We shall correct her for Thy sake! Amen."

Nothing had changed! Penny's neck still felt stiff

when she sat with her head bowed, as though it would snap like a piece of candy if she turned it. Candy! That's what they called shit; H, stuff, sweetener, mainline, smack, candy. She wanted to pray for strength, but in her father's house she was afraid of God. The God he spoke to was not a God she wanted any part of.

She reached over and touched Timmy's knee. Any touching during prayer was a punishable offense. She felt Timmy's leg quiver and withdrew her hand. It was probably still the same.

Her father was intoning all the wrath of the heavens down on the new sinner at their table, beseeching God Jehovah to protect them all from her evil influence and to guide her in straight paths. Didn't he realize that she wanted the same thing? All she wanted was to love God and Beau and to have a healthy, lovely baby. And someday be strong enough to take Timmy to live with her, away from this place and these people. She had a terrible sense of guilt about leaving Timmy with her parents, but she'd had no choice really. It was either run away or be sent to the juvenile home. Her father had frightened her with that threat so often that any alternative was preferable. So she left home at fifteen and hitched a ride to San Francisco where she latched on to other dopers and pimps and Johns to continue her race to hell. That's where Beau found her one day—at Tilden Park in Oakland. Some John had left her there the night before in her shorts and platform shoes. She had sores on her body from malnutrition, and dope tracks up and down her arms, and the perennial sniffle of the addict, besides a whining pathetic way about her that made her shudder to remember.

Beau let her sleep on the sofa in his place in Berkeley. He scored for her and found her a job to help pay for her habit. The sores healed and she moved into his bed. There wasn't any of the excitement she'd felt with Finney, but he was kind and sweet and he took care of her. Nobody had ever done that before. She promised to marry him the day they both were clean. That took two and a half more years while Beau recovered from what he called the biggest fuckup of his life, when his drug habit ruined his chances with his first musical group. But now this new group was going to do well, and she and Beau were clean, and things would get better for them. Maybe someday soon she'd be able to find a way to have Timmy live with her. But the idea made her throat tighten so that she couldn't breathe. She had talked about it with Dr. Klein.

"You can't expect to give love to a child and a husband when you need so much love yourself," Dr. Klein had said. "When you've learned to love yourself, you'll be ready to take the responsibility for Timmy."

But Penny didn't know what it meant to love herself. She still looked to others for approval and waited expectantly when she met someone new to see if there was admiration in their eyes or envy in their attitude.

Her father's voice interrupted her thoughts. "You goin' to work whiles your here? The Lord's work, I mean!"

"I'd like to see about finishing high school," she said quietly. She hadn't really thought about working. Coming home was enough of a trauma. If only there had been somewhere else she could have gone, but most of her friends used drugs of one kind or another. Dr. Klein advised her against staying with them.

"I could help Mama around the house."

"That don't pay fer your food."

"Oh. Then of course I'll get a job. I'll begin looking right away."

"Mama," Timmy said, and Penny responded.

"Yes," she and her mother both answered.

Timmy giggled at the mistake. "Can I take Penny up to my room for a few minutes?"

Myrna Constible nodded, and they pushed their chairs back from the table.

Penny could feel her father's eyes boring into her as she climbed the stairs, bumping the suitcase at every rise. *Don't think about him,* she told herself. *He can't hurt you anymore.* If only she could believe that.

She and Timmy were sharing her old room. The Sears and Roebuck maple furniture was still as shiny and lacquered as if it were new, and there were the funny little pegs dotting the screw holes here and there. She touched the faded quilts that Grandma Parsons had made long ago. Her old bulletin board was filled now with Timmy's memorabilia and schoolwork, his ID pictures, and a photo of a football player catching a pass in the endzone.

"I cleared out some drawer space and part of the closet for you."

"I'm sorry if I put you out," Penny said.

"Oh no. I don't have many things anyway; it was easy to make room."

Penny knew what he meant. "I brought you a present."

Timmy's face lit up with a smile, and Penny saw that familiar Finney charm again. But then the smile faded. "Pa won't let me have a present."

"I'll ask for his permission and we'll pray on it tonight," Penny promised. Even a diary had to be cleared by the Almighty.

Timmy kissed her and said, "I've been praying for you to come and visit."

Penny sighed and hugged her son. This wasn't going to be easy. None of it would be easy.

CHAPTER 16

"The Palladium," Mike shouted to the cabbie above the noise of the diesel engine. The driver nodded and made a U-turn in the middle of the road. *At home you'd get a ticket for that,* he thought. He shivered in his California suit. It was freezing for May, thirty-six degrees in London and cloudy. I should have brought an overcoat even for a few days! This was the first chance he'd had to get to London since his meeting with Lubow. He'd hoped to convince Regina to do the reunion before approaching Cord or Don. He was sure they would follow her lead once she was committed. But she wasn't committed yet. Far from it. Things were not going as he planned.

The cab let him off at the stage entrance of the London Palladium. Mike paid the driver and walked down the alley to the stage door. A guard passed him through for his appointment with Mr. Drummond.

There was an orchestra seated on the huge stage. Lighting technicians were going over light cues, and the musical director shouted to someone up in the lighting booth. "Up on numbers twelve and fourteen." And there was Don, standing on stage waiting for them to begin another number. Mike took it all in, the excitement of being back stage, of being part of the creative process. But his mind was torn by conflict. Lubow had placed his balls in a vise. It was proving impossible to get Cord and Don and Regina together again. But he had to do it; Lubow had made that perfectly clear.

"Ready down here," the musical director called.

Don, wearing an open shirt and black gabardines, stepped up to the mike. The conductor raised his baton and gave the downbeat. It was one of Don's golden oldies and he hadn't lost his touch. Even from the back Mike was struck by the way Don's muscular body moved; the stance, the pelvic thrusts, the voice, all designed to conjure up sexual fantasies in a female audience.

Mike joined in the applause with the rest of the crew and the few scattered friends in the cavernous auditorium. Don went right into the next four numbers. He was opening tomorrow night.

Finally he bowed and walked toward Mike. The sweat on his face glistened like oil and he was flushed from exertion, high on competence.

"Michael?" he exclaimed. "What the hell? I thought it was a mistake when I saw your name on the list."

Mike noticed up close the effect of the years. *It happens to all of us,* he thought.

"How's the coral cunt?" Don asked.

"Never better!" Mike laughed. "You're looking fabulous, Don! Country squiring agrees with you, I see."

"Have you heard the news about James Fitzgerald?"

"No, we haven't kept in touch."

"He's marrying a princess. A black diplomat's daughter." Don beckoned Mike to follow him to his dressing room right off the stage.

"So it's to be King James now," Mike retorted.

Don laughed. "Why not? He's king of the music scene, the longest-lasting career of any of us. Now he'll be complete."

Don's dressing room was filled with people, the usual entourage. Mike said hello to Phil Rostein, Don's manager, and several other musicians he'd met over the years. There was a beautiful girl sitting in the corner lazily contemplating the long-haired men and permanent-haired women. She had large brown eyes and pouty mouth and very pale skin.

"Got me own princess," Don boasted and waved to her. "Sonia, this is Mike Shaw. He just crawled out from somebody's hole somewhere."

Mike winced. "Cut the crap, Don, I think you keep this feud going with Regina just to keep the press interested. I'll bet you'd love to get together with the old group. Have a reunion." Mike's stomach felt empty and grabbed at the digestive juices to fill itself up. But he remained calm. The old master at work under pressure.

Sonia's thin body molded itself against Don's side and he put his arm around her. "I wouldn't set foot on a stage again with your wife for the Queen or the Cardinal."

Mike felt the acid burning in his guts. "Strange, Regina was absolutely thrilled about the idea! She said you'd both mellowed since the breakup, and it would be great kicks to do something together again. She sent me over to talk to you, said your career was incredible." Don stared at him in amazement. "She's always admired your talent," Mike went on. "She predicted that you'd be the biggest name of all three of you. Look how right she was."

Don was trying to detect a put-on. Mike kept his expression straight.

"Go on! Regina said that? After the way we used to fight?"

"She misses you and your mouth. Seven years is a long time."

Don shook his head. "It'd never work. After five minutes I'd want to kill her." He grinned at Mike. "You know how it is."

Mike laughed. "And there's the money, of course. You'd each get over three million for one concert."

Don whistled. "I'll bet Regina likes that. You wouldn't mind it either."

"What do you think, Don?"

"Are you serious? My God, the man's serious. A reunion?" He said it as though it had never occurred to him before. But Mike knew that wasn't true. *He's been thinking about this himself,* Mike realized—*and recently too.*

"Cord would never do it. And you'd really be a schmuck if you put Cord and Regina together."

"Don," Mike tilted his head and shrugged. "What do you take me for? Cord is no competition for me. Regina and I are happily married. This is a business deal. No problems."

"How could you get us three million?"

Mike's barometer exploded. Don was hooked! He pulled out Lubow's figures and led Don to a nearby desk. A tall thin man with stringy blond hair and stringy blue jeans clapped Don on the back. Don grabbed his hand. "Stay loose, Greg." Greg nodded gravely. "I'm tryin'. Good luck with the opening!" He ambled out and four other stringy types followed him.

Don's eyes followed Mike's finger down the list. "This is our projected gross." It was listed as thirty million, plus. "The concert alone should take in approximately ten million. The closed circuit broadcasts will contribute maybe four million. The show would play world wide by satellite; that's another ten million, and then the U.S. television rights should go for a million and a half. Plus we'll do a documentary of the rehearsals and the concert, like *Woodstock*, for international release. Not to mention the merchandising aspects of the album and souvenir items." He winked.

Drummond laughed. "You're forgetting one thing. Who needs three million?"

"I do!" Mike said, and they both laughed.

"But what about a drummer?"

"We'll find someone. There are lots of drummers."

"I don't know," Don said. "I'll think about it."

Mike grabbed his arm. "Good enough, Don!"

Don turned to Sonia and said, "What do you think of the idea?"

She had a soft throaty voice, reminiscent of Marilyn Monroe, only with an Austrian accent. "It is vhonderful," she said. But Don didn't really want her opinion. He bounced up out of his chair and went back to the stage to continue his rehearsal. The girl turned her head slowly to Mike, and he noticed how spaced out she was.

"You come from California?" she asked. "I vhould love to go there." She waved her chiffoned arm in a Dietrich-like gesture. Mike realized she wasn't seeing him at all. Well, if that's what turned Don on, why should he give a damn? At least she had the bread to keep herself in dope. She was a very well dressed addict, but screwed up nonetheless. California could do without her.

He said good-bye to her.

"Oh, good-bye. You're leaving? Tell your wife I think she's vhonderful."

He thanked her and turned away. The emptiness of her life depressed him and he quickly changed his thoughts to the discussion with Don. The old promoter trick still worked. Maybe it would work on Regina too. He had to do something to change her mind. Then he'd work on Cord. But Don's comment really bothered him. What would he do if that old flame between Regina and Cord was still burning?

CHAPTER 17

"Mommie, where did I come from?"

Regina paused halfway between securing the diamond earring in her ear and her five-year-old daughter's question. *Dear Lord. Not now,* she thought.

"Mommie's going to a party now, darling. And I'm late. I have to give a speech tonight, Jana. But when I come home we'll talk all about where you came from, okay?" *Was it all right to put it off,* she wondered. *All the books say to drop everything and tell your child the facts of life the moment she asks you. But I can't do it now. I'm late as usual. I could kill that Mrs. Grossman.* "Just a few words, Miss Williams, before you accept your award." *Asking me to give a speech is like asking me to pluck my underarm hairs and not flinch!*

Jana's lower lip quivered. "Jamie says I came from a different place than her, Mommie. She says hers is better. She's got everything better. She's got the big bed and the striped shade too."

"Jamie!" Regina shouted. "Come here!" she grabbed her evening bag and pulled her comb and cosmetics out of her regular purse to transfer them.

"Yes?" Jamie was standing in the doorway of the dressing room all innocence. Her expression was the same as the dog's when he had just made on the living room carpet.

"What kind of crap have you been telling Jana?" The top of one of her lipsticks had come off and smeared the inside of her new three-hundred-dollar bag. Now she had lipstick on her hand. Damn. She reached for a Kleenex.

"It's not crap, Mommie. Cedars-Sinai is a much better hospital than Beverly Glen. All my friends were born there! Nobody's born at Beverly Glen."

Regina suppressed a laugh of delight. So that's what Jana wanted to know, what *hospital* she was born in. "Jamie, your sister was born in a hurry and we couldn't make it to Cedars in time. The Beverly Glen Hospital saved her life, and mine I might add. It's a beautiful, wonderful, glorious hospital." She leaned down and kissed Jana's beaming face. "And I don't want to hear such ridiculous comparisons again! You did come from different hospitals, but they're equal! And as for the big bed, Jana, Jamie wanted a double bed and you wanted twins. You had your choice, remember? So don't tell me now that one is better than the other. If you want a double bed you could push the twin beds together." *Brilliant idea,* she thought. "Now about the shades; one is polka dot and the other is striped, but they're the same colors for God's sake!"

She swept by them trailing Bal à Versailles and sable down the staircase. Mike was waiting by the door, grim-faced in his lightly shaded glasses. *Why is he always so grouchy,* she wondered. *He's so insecure that he growls so as not to show it.* And then she remembered. "Oh God, I forgot my speech!" She turned forlornly to Jamie who was still halfway down the stairs.

"I'll get it." Jamie turned and ran up the rest of the way.

"It's on my dressing table," Regina called. "That stack of index cards." She glanced at Jana. Her face looked awfully pink. "Do you feel all right, sweetheart?"

Jana shook her head. "My tummy hurts."

I shouldn't have asked, Regina thought, feeling her forehead. It was warm.

Jana looked up at her with round eyes so like her own. "Why don't you call Florie and ask her to come over tonight? She takes such good care of me."

"Because Florie worked long hours today, darling, and she needs her evenings to herself. Mrs. Corbin is here, and we'll be home early."

Mike heard the end of the conversation and realized he hadn't checked back with Florie since his return from England to learn the results of her medical tests. But Florie must be all right. She'd been at work as usual. "Mommie's right, Jana. You don't need Florie tonight," he said. "Oh Daddy," Jana sighed.

Jamie came back without the cards. "I couldn't find them! They're just not there!"

She sounds just like Mike, Regina thought, lifting the hem of her jeweled gown to climb back up the stairs again.

"For Christ's sake! Regina!" Mike shouted. "You're the guest of honor. It's a slap in their faces if you're late."

She ran into her dressing room to get the cards for her speech. They really weren't there! Where had she left them? On the bed. They weren't there either! Oh God, it was bad enough to give a speech, but not to have her notes would be a disaster. She went to the top of the stairs and called down. "Have either of you girls seen my speech cards? They're small and white like this." She measured with her hand.

Jana looked up. Her adorable face was serious and guilty. "I made a house, Mommie. In my room!"

Regina tore down the hall to the children's wing. There in Jana's room was an elaborate construction of her five-by-seven cards right in the middle of the floor. Jana had even used her Fischer-Price people as part of the structure. A child's version of the Parthenon. She hated to ruin it before they took a picture of it.

This kid's going to be an architect, she thought, hurriedly gathering the cards and running back downstairs.

Her parting words to Jamie were, "You're beginning to sound a bit snotty about which hospital is better than which and which bed is better than which. It seems to me that Laura Winnick has been here today. Am I right?"

Jamie closed her mouth in that same determined line that her father got when he was "caught."

"If you're going to act like Laura Winnick and talk like Laura Winnick, then I won't allow you to play with her," Regina stated. "All I ever hear from that child is 'We just got this,' or 'My Dad just bought that,' or 'Ours is more complete than theirs.'" Regina did a perfect imitation of the child's nasal voice. "If they want to flaunt their money, we don't have to copy them!"

Jamie nodded solemnly and closed the front door. This wasn't the first time they'd had this discussion. Mike threw the Rolls into reverse and backed out of the garage, taking the driveway like it was a racetrack.

"Have you seen Dorothy Winnick's new emerald necklace?" Regina asked. "The Queen of England has one like it. Only smaller!"

It was only minutes to the Beverly Wilshire Hotel, but it was long enough for them to argue and for the strain between them to make her anxiety grow. She'd better not get upset tonight; she had a speech to give.

They pulled into the portico of the Beverly Wilshire with its tiny starlights all ablaze. A small crowd of celebrity followers were there, the same heavyset woman named Miranda and her anemic-looking son Morrie. They were at every function Regina ever attended. Regina waved at them and swept out of the car.

"At last! My, don't you look beautiful," Mrs. Grossman greeted her at the door. A woman in her fifties with dark, carefully coiffed hair and an ample bosom, she was a very dedicated lady who made a life's work out of putting together benefits. Regina knew how tirelessly she worked because they'd served on several of the same committees.

They made their way through crowds of people, some of whom they stopped to meet. Others embraced her. There was a lot of gratitude for the two hundred thousand dollars Regina had raised, and she was proud of that contribution.

Someone brought her a drink, which she drank too quickly, clutching her petitpoint bag with the white cards inside. And then it was time for dinner. She and Mike were seated at the head table looking down on fifteen hundred people dining on beef Wellington and baked Alaska.

On Regina's right was Dr. Marvin McCloud who was an OB-Gyn. at the hospital. He was young and sexy, and all she could think of was where he kept his hands all day. She refrained from asking him about it with great difficulty. Finally they began talking about children, and she recounted the discussion she'd had with Jana earlier and how she'd almost explained the facts of life to her before she wanted to know them. She was very nervous.

On her left was Mike, and sitting next to Mike was their good friend Harley Weinfield and his wife Evelyn. Harley was like a godfather to Mike who had never gotten along with his own family. Harley was president of the hospital and a member of the board of directors.

After the meal Harley got up and made a short speech to introduce Regina and suddenly her blood turned to ice. If there was any way she could have gotten out of giving a speech at the moment, she would have done it. *I ought to see a psychiatrist,* she thought. *This kind of panic is unreasonable.* She'd had it ever since she'd begun performing on her own after Majesty broke up. And it was getting worse. If only she could figure out why it happened.

Harley spoke her name. She heard it echoing hollowly over the electronic system across the tops of the teased and dyed and bleached and bewigged heads of Beverly Hills. She got up and walked slowly to the microphone to delay the final moment. Her knees were like butter melting on a warm piece of toast.

She reached the podium. "Good evening, ladies and gentlemen. It's a great pleasure to be here tonight." Her voice cracked on the word pleasure, and she clutched the edge of the lectern. Her cards! She'd forgotten to take them out of her purse. Stealthily she reached inside and withdrew them, only to find they were out of order. Jana's housebuilding session. Rising to the moment she smiled at the audience.

"I must confess I find it difficult to give a speech so I jotted down some notes on these efficient little cards. But my five-year-old daughter used them to build a marvelous structure." As she described Jana's building, she placed the cards in their proper order. There was a round of amused applause when she finished, and she relaxed a bit.

"The organization for the research in causes of bone diseases and other related diseases which is the beneficiary of our work in this organization has been close to my heart for many years. . ." she began. But just then there was a commotion to her left on the dais, and she looked over. A man in a dark suit had come on stage and was talking loudly to Mike and Harley. She tried to ignore him.

"When we began our program to raise funds for this project we considered many alternatives. . . ." The man was still talking loudly, gesturing and explaining. *Who the hell is he?* she wondered. *Why doesn't Mike shush him?*

"For those of you who worked on or attended our

first fledgling functions, you know how much effort goes into one of our drives. We have grown since those early days and now we are gloriously sophisticated. . . ." Mike pushed his chair back from the table and helped Harley to his feet, and then both of them followed the man off stage, hurrying as though to a fire. No one in the audience missed their exit, and everyone began to murmur. Regina waited a moment until it became quieter.

"Well, it looks as though one of my Mikes has deserted me. . . ." The sound of laughter rang through the ballroom. "But I still have this one." She leaned over and kissed the microphone, making a loud smacking sound throughout the room. Everyone laughed again, only harder. "Perhaps they've heard that the men's room gets very crowded after dinner? Standing room only," she joked, waiting until the laughter died down. "At this rate I could change professions and become a stand-up comic," she mugged a face, and they roared.

"But seriously, folks." More laughter. She turned to the wings and saw Mike gesticulating to speed it up and get off. Something was wrong! A surge of fear shot through her. What if something had happened to the children!

She hurried through the rest of her speech, shortening wherever she could and then she thanked the organization for honoring her. Evelyn Weinfield was not at her place at the head table, and neither was Dr. McCloud. She accepted her gold plaque mounted in plexiglass and hurried off stage.

Backstage everything was pandemonium. A huge crowd of people huddled around someone lying on the floor. And then Regina saw that it was Harley! Just then the paramedic rescue team arrived and began working on him, massaging his heart, administering oxygen!

Regina made her way over to Mike, who was holding Evelyn in his arms. Evelyn was shaking with fear. "What happened, Michael? My God, what's going on?"

"Harley collapsed. He may be having a heart attack." Mike motioned to Regina to come and take care of Evelyn. "He had some very shocking news and then he just fainted."

Regina led Evelyn to a nearby chair and sat her down. Harley had been in perfect health only minutes before. What had happened? Mike watched the paramedics working and then came over to stand with her. "Why did the two of you rush off the stage like that?" she asked.

Mike put his hand on her shoulder as though to brace her. "The Tulsa Homestake Oil Corporation has declared bankruptcy," he said gravely.

The news didn't register. Harley might be dying of a heart attack, and Mike talked of bankruptcies. She stared up at him.

"Harley has lost just about everything he has!"

Some horrible premonition of dread hit her. "The failure of one company could wipe him out?"

Mike nodded.

"That's not our company, is it?" Mike would laugh at her for being so ridiculous. But he didn't laugh. He nodded!

"Oh, my God!" It was then that she noticed the color of Mike's skin. It was almost the same whiteness as his shirt.

The paramedics picked Harley up and put him on a stretcher, hurrying out of the side entrance with him. Evelyn jumped up to follow. "We'll meet you at the hospital," Mike told her. "Go with the ambulance."

Regina and Mike hurried out to their car through the side lobby. Regina's brain couldn't register what he'd just told her. Had they lost everything too? Halfway to their car she stopped and turned to him. "You only invested with Tulsa Homestead once, didn't you?"

He shook his head, his voice dry, the words coughed out. "The second investment went through while we were in Vegas. You were so tied up with the show I didn't want to bother you."

"Bother me? Bother me?" she yelled. "How much, Michael?" She was scared to hear.

"Eight hundred thousand."

All the strength in her body deserted her and she sank to the ground unable to hold herself up. "All gone?" A tanker truck had just run over her, and she hadn't even seen it coming.

Mike sank down beside her, and with a groan he buried his head in her lap. The sight of him repelled her. She couldn't comfort him. Had she signed anything? She couldn't remember. Yes. She thought she was signing a loan for the addition to the house. Was it the loan or a guarantee of losses? Her rage began to build. All she could think of was the pain she suffered when she had to appear, the strain of being good at all times—flu or colds or loneliness were never allowed! The tremendous responsibility to her audience, to her overhead, to her contracts, to her talent.

She never had time to enjoy life.

The fury began to build. "If you weren't my husband, I'd fire you! I'd sue you for mismanagement. I work my ass off! I *kill* myself, and you lose eight hundred thousand dollars. That's a fortune, Michael! My fortune! I earned it; I sweated for it. I did it! Over the years I've made millions and you've blown it!" she screamed at the top of her voice. Mike pulled away from her and stood up, shaken by the truth of what she was saying. "Please, Regina," he said.

She didn't hear him. "I can't be all things to all people. I'm an artist. I have a great talent. I can't be expected to be a financial expert," she screamed again. Several people stopped to stare at her, but she didn't give a flying shit. "How long do you think I can go on being on top? My albums aren't selling anymore. Not like they used to. It's all up to me. My guts, my sweat. I'm not going to be young forever." She was on the verge of tears. "And you go and lose eight hundred thousand dollars!"

"It was a swindle, Reg," he pleaded. "We're not the only ones who got taken. You wouldn't believe the list. Everyone's on it." She'd never seen him so scared. She looked at him and realized with a great jolt to her heart that he'd lost much more than money. He was worried about Harley and worse, probably, he was worried about what kind of man he was. She felt pity overtake her. How cruel could she be?

"I'm going to the hospital," she said. "Are you coming with me?"

He nodded.

"And there's one last thing I want you to do for me." He tried to take her arm, but involuntarily she pulled away.

"What is it?"

"Call whoever you need to call in the morning and tell them I've changed my mind. I'm going to do the reunion concert."

Mike watched her walk away not knowing whether to feel miserable or relieved.

CHAPTER 18

After a short time of being in Oregon Penny was sunk into a misery of despair. Her father's repeated denouncements had taken root, and she felt she was as sinful and despicable as he said. Only for Timmy's sake did she pretend to be happy.

Beau's calls were her lifeline to a normal world, and she was famished for his news, questioning him for every detail of his life. His words of love over the phone were like a balm on a burning hand. She never told him how bad things were for her because she knew it would affect his playing, but she begged him to call her only in the morning when her father was certain to be at work. The verbal abuse she suffered when her father knew Beau had called made her almost wish he hadn't. Her pregnancy made her tired all the time so she couldn't resist her father's tirades. She had no appetite and she was losing weight. *I should be joyous,* she told herself, *that I'm having a baby who will live with me, who will know its own father.* But that knowledge just didn't lift her spirits.

She went job hunting, but the responsibility of working for someone else and not being able to make a mistake gave her a choking feeling. She'd never worked at real jobs except as a box girl at a market, and that hadn't lasted for long. Finally she got a job working in a theater as an usherette. That meant working evenings and walking up and down aisles. She was scared to death to tell her father what she was doing. Movie houses were the spawn of the devil, houses of sin and pornography. She told her father she was a library assistant.

She longed to study for a real profession as a stenographer or dental assistant, but those courses cost money, much more than she had. If she weren't pregnant and so tired all the time, she could have gone to school during the day. Perhaps her salary could have gone to pay for a secretarial course. But she gave half of her salary to her parents for her room and board, and the other half she saved for the baby. At least this job left her free in the daytime to be with Timmy after school.

She had been working at the theater for five days when it came her turn to clean out the candy counter after closing and prepare the machines for the next day's business. She tried to hurry, but she was unfamiliar with the routine and it took her an extra twenty-five minutes. The library closed at ten-thirty and she always got home before eleven. But now it was eleven fifteen, and she was afraid of what her father would say.

She prayed he was asleep as she tiptoed up the front porch recalling all those times she'd tried to sneak into the house when she was high on drugs or exhausted after turning three or four tricks. She hadn't cared then what her father thought. His religious ravings couldn't hurt her when she was spaced out. She'd gotten revenge on him in the arms of strange men and would secretly gloat while he screamed at her, his body so taut and rigid she thought he'd turn to stone.

But tonight was different. She didn't want to give him any reasons to denounce her in front of Timmy. She was trying hard to be a model for the child, a loving sister, who could easily slip into the role of parent when the time was right.

The house was dark as she creaked open the door,

shoes in hand, heart pounding in her ears. So far so good! She was safe inside when suddenly a light flooded her eyes, blinding her for a moment, and she gasped. Before she could cry out, a blow to the head sent her crashing to the hardwood floor. Her father's voice bellowed at her.

"Grovel in the dirt and in the disgust of your vileness, you filthy slut!" Her temple was throbbing where he'd hit her, and an icy fear clutched her as she thought of the baby. *Oh, my God, don't let him hurt the baby!* She was so stunned that her father had hit her that she couldn't think, couldn't react beyond covering herself with her arms and turning her back to him. In all the years she'd lived with him, he'd never struck her before. It was so against his beliefs that she was awed at his fury. Think how he must hate her to go beyond the bounds of his religion! And now that he had lost his control, what would he do? She lay there shaking, feeling the floor beneath her cheek. A hard blow landed at the back of her legs! He'd kicked her! And then again and again. The shame of it; to be treated like an animal was worse than the pain shooting up her back. She moaned and cried out.

"Don't, Father. Please, God, don't hurt me!"

"You call upon God?" he raged.

She heard Timmy's moaning, and in spite of her fear she lifted her head. Her mother, huge and stoic, was sitting on the stairs holding Timmy's head between her hands like a vise, forcing the child to watch this degradation.

"This is what sluts and whores and fornicators deserve," her father said, and then he spat in her face.

Timmy wrenched his head away with a loud cry and threw himself between his father and Penny.

Penny felt the nausea assail her and she knew she wouldn't make it to the bathroom. There was a small satisfaction in knowing she'd vomited on her father's shoes. She crawled to the small bathroom behind the kitchen. Timmy was trying to help her up, but she was too stunned and weak to do anything but crawl. All the time her father's voice shouted behind her, "Burn in hell! The eternal fires of damnation will sear thy flesh, woman of sin! And all thy tears will never wash away thy transgressions!"

In that moment, spewing the rest of her guts into the toilet, hearing Timmy's tortured sighs echoing in the small bathroom, her fear of her father turned to hate. She was suddenly filled with it. A burning, searing, white-hot hatred that manifested itself in a desire to hurt him that was so strong she had to hold on to the edge of the toilet to keep from leaping at his scrawny throat or grabbing a kitchen knife and plunging it into his heartless chest. Finally the bile found its way out of her, and the heat of her hatred subsided. She breathed deeply to give herself strength. Timmy came and sat on the tile floor next to her and hugged her tightly.

"It's my fault that he spanked you like that." His words were shortened by hiccoughs. "I told my friend Gary that you were an usherette for King Kong and Father . . . overheard me."

Penny stroked his reddish brown hair, shaking with rage at the injustice the child was suffering. Her father was standing right outside the door. She could hear his raspy breathing, but he stayed out of sight, listening, waiting for information to use against her in the trial for her soul.

"It's not your fault, darling. I was going to tell him myself because it's wrong to deceive others. He may not approve of my work, but he accepts the money I make."

"But he thought you were working at the library . . ." Timmy excused him.

"It doesn't matter," Penny assured him, "everything

is going to be all right." What was it about that phrase, about the dependency of a child in her arms, that gave her courage? Maybe it wouldn't last, but she had it now. Slowly, she pulled herself up off the floor and rinsed her mouth and washed her face. There was a large red mark across her cheek and she knew it would be a bruise. But she didn't care. She hoped it would last and last. She'd be sure to turn it toward her father whenever he preached to her. He had no right to preach to her anymore, not after what he'd done. Someday God would punish him!

By morning her temporary bravado had deserted her, and she was desperate for Beau's call. She waited all morning for him, but today of all days the phone didn't ring. Finally she had to leave for the psychiatric clinic. She stood among the group of ex-addicts, most of whom were unkempt and unmotivated to better themselves. A lot of them were still using drugs and selling drugs, and they talked about it as though they were fooling everyone. They understood one another, these lost, blue-jeaned legions of the devil, and they assumed she was one of them. She didn't want to be.

On the way home from the clinic she couldn't get the thought of Finney out of her mind. *Maybe I could just see him from far away,* she thought. *Nothing bad would happen. I wonder if he's still in Oregon? I wonder what he'd say if he saw me.* She knew what he'd say—"Hi, sugar"—in that way he had of making her feel all funny inside. Finney could have been a movie star. He always told her that, but he preferred to stay in a small city and be a big cheese, as he put it. Hollywood was full of fruits who screwed you in the ass. It was funny the way he put that down because he was always doing it to her.

The bus route passed right by the neighborhood where Finney used to live, and on an impulse she got off and found herself standing on his corner. She looked up the street to where his apartment was and wondered why she was standing there. *I can't do it,* she thought. But another bus passed by and then another, and she was still standing there. *I'll just walk up the block and see if his car is there. But he wouldn't have the same car after all this time.* She walked a little closer. *He probably doesn't live here anymore.* She imagined what would happen if she knocked on the door and he opened it. His hair would be the way Warren Beatty wore his, not so slicked down. And he'd smile at her. She wondered if he wore open shirts and gold jewelry like some of the movie stars did. He was always up on the latest things. How would he feel about her being married, and what would he say about Timmy? She wouldn't tell tell him about Timmy. "How do I look?" she'd ask. Her skin was clear and the pregnancy made her breasts swell, but she didn't show yet.

Just walking up the path to his duplex gave her the shivers, and she felt her nipples harden as she thought about him. Beau was so far away, and her father had been so mean to her. But neither thought kept her from ringing that bell. She pressed the white round button and held her breath as the door opened slowly. It wasn't Finney.

An old man in his sixties stood there looking at her.

"I'm trying to find Finney Rourke."

"What's that?" he asked.

"He used to live here. About four or five years ago. Do you know where he is?"

"Young fella? Reddish hair?"

"Yes! That's him!"

"He died! Took drugs or got shot, something like that. Why'd you want to know?"

She backed away from his stare. Finney dead?

"You all right, young lady?" he asked.

Finney. With his carrot-red hair and crooked grin.

He was so alive to her. She'd expected to see him standing here, and now he was dead. A half a block away the tears broke and she cried. Never mind that Finney Rourke had seduced her and used her and hooked her on drugs and pimped for her. She'd loved him. And he was the father of her child.

All of her own anguish came bursting forth. She was so helpless and dependent on others, so thwarted from ever achieving what she wanted for herself. And then she realized how close she'd come to ending up like Finney. Somehow she'd have to stick it out in Oregon until Beau sent for her; at least she was alive. But someday she'd figure a way out of all this. Somehow she'd find a way to get herself the kind of life she'd always wanted.

CHAPTER 19

Louise opened the door of her apartment wearing skin-tight jeans tucked into leather boots, Cord's favorite look. Her breasts swung freely beneath the loose silk of her shirt. He stepped into the foyer of her apartment and reached to kiss her. She melted to him, tasting familiar and smelling faintly of food which made his stomach react with hunger. She pulled away and smiled at him.

"Welcome to my home." She took his hand and led him into a small elegant living room, cluttered with expensive-looking accessories that would keep any housekeeper busy for days. On one table was a collection of crystal animals; on another, hundreds of small antique boxes; and on another, a grouping of jade objects.

"Do you take inventory in this place?" he teased, sinking into a puffed-up chair covered in some kind of flowery material. The fabrics in the room were all light shades of spring colors, but the walls were a deep, dark green. It made him feel as though he were in a forest glade where shafts of sunlight reflected off pools of water, only in this case the sun reflected on glasstop tables. He smiled approvingly as she studied him. His eyes went past her to the patio which was bathed in sunlight and offered a view of the west side of Central Park. There was a table on the patio set for lunch, and he could see the top of a bottle of wine in a silver cooler. The scene looked like something out of a movie. He turned to her.

"Best way to a man's heart?"

His banter lightened her expression. "I don't know about you, but I find it frustrating when we play with each other under tablecloths and waiters hover around trying to see what we're doing there." She leaned forward and planted a kiss on his forehead. "In privacy we can finish what we start." She went back into the kitchen. "Open the champagne if you're thirsty," she called.

Champagne, he thought, getting up to follow her instructions. He didn't care much for labels on wine —he preferred liquor—but the bottle said Crystal Roederer and it was imported. He opened it and poured it into the etched stemmed glasses at each of their places, replaced the bottle and took the glasses into the kitchen.

The kitchen was minuscule with pots hanging from the ceiling and a blue and white tile covering every available inch from floor to walls to ceiling. Louise was adding the finishing touches to some green and pink culinary concoction. It looked like shrimp.

"You lived here long?"

She nodded. "Friends of mine used to have this apartment, and I would dream about what I'd do to it if I ever got my hands on it. Finally he got a job in a series and they moved to West L.A. So I've lived here three years in absentia and four years in reality." She picked up her wine glass and raised it, staring at him. He felt that same stirring inside when he looked at her. The more he knew this woman, the more she impressed him.

"To reality," she said, and they drank.

"That was as noncommittal a toast as any," he said.

"You know why I've always loved your music? Because your style evokes a promise of a better life.

Your songs have that sort of theme, as if you were saying 'Things may not be so good right now, but with patience and hope and perseverance we can make it.' That's unusual for a man. I'd call it a kind of hopeful determinism."

She put their lunches on a glass tray along with her champagne glass, a silver bowl with some white sauce in it, and a basket of steaming french bread she retrieved from a container on the stove. She took his glass and handed him the tray. "After you." She inclined her head toward the patio. "You do agree with me, don't you?"

"I hadn't thought of myself as an optimist," he said, enjoying her enlightened praise. He also enjoyed the way she commandeered his assistance without asking him. It was part of her command of self. She didn't even have to think about her equality. He placed the tray on the sideboard by her seat at the table.

The food was delicious. He told her so.

"I learned to be a gourmet cook when I was married," she said. "In my youth."

"How long were you married?" There was so much about her as yet unshared.

"Three years. He was a stockbroker, very intense and successful and confining."

He understood. "This is really . . ." he began.

"You know, there's something . . ." she said at the same time, and they both laughed. "We seem to do that a lot. It's a sign of awkwardness, I'm afraid."

"I don't feel awkward with you." He sipped the wine. It was dry and delicate; even he could tell that. "I'd say I feel more comfortable with you than anyone in a long time."

"That's why I haven't invited you here before." She had an appealing way of raising her eyebrow when she was serious. "I didn't want to have memories of you in my home. I wanted to keep the impersonality of hotels and restaurants between us. Put you at a safe distance."

"Then why am I here?"

She shrugged. "I couldn't keep it up."

It was what he wanted to hear, but it bothered him. That old clutching feeling again. What if she started to turn him off? Or what if she didn't? He concentrated on his lunch.

"Have you come to a decision about doing the play?" she asked.

Again he was impressed. She had told him she cared without pressing, although he already knew. Her sexual intimacies shouted it, but hearing her say it meant it was official.

"I'm reserving my decision until after I complete my new album. Right now music is all I can think about."

She smiled suggestively. "That's all?"

"Well, almost," he laughed. "You know, the play idea does intrigue me. A musical version of *Midnight Cowboy*. I'd be more interested, though, if they wanted me to write the score."

"Did you tell them that?"

"I don't like it when people laugh at me."

She was astonished. "Why would they laugh? You'd write a wonderful score. Maybe they were waiting for you to offer."

He shook his head skeptically.

She got up from the table and went directly to the phone, pushing a number rapidly.

"Annette, it's me. Get me David Merrick's number." She waited a minute and then wrote it on a piece of paper. "So Jerry Lubow wants me," she said patiently. "I'm not in the office right now, am I?" She listened to Annette. "I *am* working. I'll call him later; the promotion can wait. This is priority! Tell him I'll be in this afternoon." She hung up and pushed the new number.

"Mr. Merrick, please. Louise Carlin calling." She waited with her back to Cord, one hip pushed out higher than the other, pencil tapping on the desk.

"David? It's Louise. I've got an important question to ask you." She laughed. "You know I can't stop for amenities when I'm excited. Yes, I'm fine thank you. You?" She laughed again. "I wanted to know if you've signed someone to do the score on the *Midnight Cowboy* project or whatever you're calling the musical version?" She turned to Cord. "I see. . . . And it wasn't working out? That's too bad. . . . Yes, he's wonderful! Those were exactly my thoughts. Yes, I think he'd be interested. Of course I'll speak to him, first chance I get. . . . I'll let you know. . . . No, he won't come cheap. Fine, David. Oh, and it's been lovely talking to you," she teased as she hung up.

She threw both her hands in the air with a flourish. *"Voila!* He'd love to have you do a score. They're without a composer due to a problem of temperament and they didn't mention it to you because the role of the cowboy was more important to them."

He hadn't realized her job carried as much weight as it did. She wasn't just some errand girl they'd sent to pick him up at the airport. He studied her face, animated with the excitement of the transaction and flushed with the expertise she displayed, and he was plunged into a darkened mood. He got up from the table and came toward her. So many things were running through his mind. He wanted to thank her, to tell her how wonderful the idea was, but mostly just to hold her before she flew away with plans and commitments and dates for beginning. He put his hands on her shoulders and pulled her to him. She came against him quietly and let him hold her, sensitive to his mood.

"It's not going to work," he said into her hair.

"Why not?" Her voice was muffled against his chest.

"You could write a fabulous score." He wasn't referring to the score.

"You and me. In the back of my mind I've been thinking about you being with me in Colorado or on tour or in the recording studio. You just couldn't be a record business widow; it would never work. You're a dynamite lady who's got to stay exactly where she is." Was he being entirely honest, he wondered, or did his own feelings for her have to be stopped before he got in too deeply?

She had tears in her eyes as she looked at him. "It doesn't have to be all or nothing."

"It does with me. That's what went wrong last time. Two strong people pulling on each other for the spotlight."

"Things could change," she said wistfully. "In our lives, in our attitudes."

"Maybe." He looked skeptical.

She was trying to be brave. Her strength might have just cost her a lover. "Do you want to finish your lunch?"

"I've lost my appetite. And I think they need you at your office."

"The hell with the office," she said, wiping her eyes. "They'll live without me for the afternoon. You and I are going to finish our wine and make love, and I'm going with you to the airport."

"You don't have to do that," he said, putting his arm around her and walking back to the table.

She hugged him. "I've always wanted to see the Antelope Jet." She picked up her glass and forced a smile, but she was still tearful. "Friends?" she questioned.

"Friends," he nodded.

CHAPTER 20

Jerry Lubow awoke at 3:00 A.M. cursing the time difference between L.A. and New York. He'd read three newspapers and two contracts by the time the catering office opened and then he made a luncheon reservation in the Polo Lounge. He didn't have to be at MGM until ten-thirty, so he had plenty of time for a manicure and a walk down Rodeo Drive. His lunch date with Mike Shaw and Regina Williams had been made through his secretary. It wouldn't do to let Mike think he was getting in too tight with the big boss. Mike must have some good news for him or he wouldn't have called. He'd better have; time was getting short.

The meeting at MGM went very well. CAMIL Records was co-venturing a three-picture deal with the studio, and Lubow would be the executive producer. *Lots of bucks*, he thought, but mostly it was the power he wanted. One of the films would be perfect for Don Drummond. *I'll use him if he comes through for me*, Lubow thought. Don hadn't said yes about the reunion yet.

He dropped Craig Ziegler, president of CAMIL's West Coast division, at the office and told him that today's lunch was private. Then he headed back to the hotel.

The Polo Lounge was crowded, but his favorite booth was reserved for him, right in the center of the green room facing the door. He'd wait till

Mike and Regina got here before taking his seat.

Parson McAdams, his New York counsel, waved to him and got up from his table to say hello. He was sitting with network executives from NBC. Lubow knew their faces, but not their titles. It didn't matter; next week they wouldn't have the same jobs anyway.

"Did you hear?" McAdams asked, leaning in toward Lubow's ear.

"What?"

"Tulsa Homestake Oil turned out to be a swindle. Everyone in Hollywood is crying poverty, according to *Time* magazine. A lot of money was dropped. Andy Williams, Bob Dylan, Barbra Streisand, Alan Alda, even the former president of General Electric. And Regina Williams was one of the hardest hit."

Lubow kept his face impassive. So his three hundred thousand dollar loan to Mike Shaw was now unsecured. Shaw had better have an answer from Regina today to do the reunion or he would be up shit's creek.

McAdams nodded his head toward the door as he went back to his table, and Lubow turned. Mike and Regina were entering the Polo Lounge.

All eyes stared at Regina as she sauntered across the room, her red hair a luxury of curls down her back. She wore an off-the-shoulder white dress sprinkled with violets.

"I decided to be flamboyant," she said, kissing Lubow on the lips and sliding into the booth. "I've been in hiding since . . . Vegas and I thought today would be a good time to show the world I'm still fighting."

And that you haven't been knocked out by your huge financial loss, Lubow thought. He'd never seen Mike so subdued; his usual copper-colored tan looked yellow.

Regina ordered a frozen Daiquiri, and Mike a Vermouth Cassis. Lubow stuck to Perrier. He decided not to mention the oil deal gossip unless they brought it up; no sense in rubbing their noses in it. But knowing about it gave him an edge.

"You were in London?" she said.

"Yes. Finalized some new talent contracts. I even caught Don's show at the Palladium. He said to send you his love."

Mike coughed nervously.

"Don sent me his love? That'll be the day!" Regina laughed.

"No, really. He raved about you. He'd seen a videotape of one of your TV specials and couldn't say enough about your beauty and talent. He was very nostalgic about the old days. He told me he regretted the way he'd acted back then. He said a thing like that could never happen again. He's really changed!"

Regina stared in obvious amazement. "Don said that?"

Lubow had been rather surprised himself by Don's attitude. "He admitted he used to be jealous of your talent and your relationship with Cord. But that was only childishness. He even admitted you were a superior performer and he only wished you well. . . ."

"What else did he say?"

"He said he'd love to see you again sometime. When you come to England, he wants you to call him. He's got quite an estate, you know."

"Yes, I've heard," she said enviously. "Did you mention the idea of a reunion concert?"

"We discussed it. He said he'd love to do something like a reunion, but he never thought Cord would agree. Not after Gene's death."

"But Don's been saying for years that he'd never do one."

"People can change their minds you know."

"Yes, I know." She looked away.

"I don't think Cord would have too many objections, do you?" Mike asked.

Lubow was sure he would, but he wasn't about to admit it to them. The waiter interrupted. Regina and Mike ordered the cracked crab, and Lubow asked for an omelette, promising himself the apple pancake for dessert if the luncheon went the way he wanted it to.

"So what do *you* think about Cord?" he asked Regina, enjoying her discomfort.

"I have no idea," she said. "I haven't seen him in years."

"Jerry," Mike spoke up, "Regina's considering your proposal. I thought we ought to let you know." He shot his wife a look.

Lubow smiled. "That's good. What can I say to convince you?"

Mike didn't smile back. "The money is what we're interested in, not friendships or who wants to work with whom. Regina's schedule is tight. Have you a definite date when this thing would take place?" He sounded as though it were all within his control, but he was actually trying to hang on to his position. Lubow wanted to brush him off like an unwanted fly. He was an insect, with his green shades, rubbing his hands over and over at the idea of that three million (less three hundred thousand plus points and interest).

"My backers are talking about this Labor Day. That means you'll have to hustle to get everything done over the next two months."

"Why that's practically tomorrow," Regina exclaimed.

"The sooner the better, I feel. Why prolong it? You're all seasoned performers. You've worked together before. It shouldn't take that long to whip up a show."

"You'd be surprised how long it takes these days to whip up anything," she said with a glance at Mike.

Lubow caught her sarcasm. He realized suddenly just how explosive it would be to put her together again with Cord. "I have some figures on the payment schedule. Perhaps they'd interest you." He passed them his preliminary budget and began eating his eggs.

Regina studied them, passing each page to Mike. Mike barely glanced at them. Regina had a few questions. Mike answered them quietly.

Lubow's eggs tasted like ambrosia.

Regina finished reading the proposal and began eating her crab. Finally she looked up. "All right! I'll do it!"

Lubow squeezed her hand. "That's great!" Even Mike seemed pleased and reached across the table to shake his hand. Lubow didn't know what kind of game Mike was playing, but he wouldn't embarrass him. They all beamed at each other. "I'm sure Cord will agree now that you and Don are in."

"If he doesn't, then old Don and I will carry the show on our own."

"Don't ever call him 'old Don' to his face. He's matured, but he's still as vain as ever."

"Don't worry," Regina pinched Lubow's cheek. "I'll be very proper. I'll rave about him."

The waiter, Abe, who was cleaning away their dishes, leaned forward and whispered to Lubow, "Congratulations, sir."

Lubow winked back and ordered his apple pancakes.

Mike and Regina were silent all the way home in the Rolls. The soft brown carpeting and the tender leather seats didn't give her the usual thrill today. She loved this car although she seldom got to ride in it. Mike's profile was rock hard. She wondered what he was thinking about.

She hoped he was scared about her doing the reunion with Cord. It served him right. God, how he'd changed. Had she changed too? Or was she the same as when they met, all brave exterior covering a childhood fear that at any moment her whole life could fall apart from some disaster?

It was a disaster when her family was killed. It was a disaster when Majesty broke up. It was a disaster when Cord stopped loving her and started hating her.

"Are you going to talk or keep on punishing me?" she asked.

"Aren't you punishing me?"

"You're so perfectly cast in the role of the martyr," she snapped. "Poor Mike, lost a fortune and now Regina's determined to get back at him." But that's exactly what she was doing and she'd gotten what she wanted. Why provoke him? It was just that he was so docile.

"I'm *glad* you're going to do the reunion, Reg. You can't go through your whole life being blind to an important part of your past. Once and for all you've got to exorcise those Majesty ghosts. I'm sure as hell tired of living with them."

"You never felt that way before. How come you've changed your mind? Aren't you worried about me anymore?"

He didn't look at her. "Sure I'm worried. Especially because of . . . because of my problem. But I know you'll be fair. With all your faults you've never been crass enough to dirty your own back yard."

"Mike, what's happened to us?" She could see his knuckles whiten where they gripped the steering wheel.

"Don't start this again, Regina. You know what happened. When I married you, you needed me for important functions, like love and stability and marriage and fatherhood. You snorted coke too much and you only came alive on the stage. Cord had fucked your brains over by his blaming you for Gene's death. You were a child then. But you're a woman now."

So he'd noticed.

"I didn't mind being Mike 'Williams' because we both knew how important I was to you, how important we were to each other."

She remembered how it had been when she'd first met Mike. He was managing the Forum in L.A. and each time Majesty appeared there they renewed their friendship. If she and Cord were fighting, Mike always offered a sympathetic shoulder. He said it was part of his job, that he listened to everyone's troubles. But he was very good to her. And he treated her like an ordinary woman, not some untouchable superstar. It got so that whenever they worked L.A. she stayed away from pills and coke, because Mike didn't approve. When Gene died, he sent her flowers, a gesture that showed how sensitive he was to her need. Shortly after that when the group broke up, he flew to New York to be with her, and never left her side again. Even when she was terrible to him. And she had been terrible. She took out on him all the pain of losing Cord, and all the fear of being on her own, and all the guilt over Gene's death. But the more she dished out, the more he took. He won her trust by default, and the love came after. It was only after they were married that she noticed his flaws. Or was it that he finally let her see them? She didn't know. How was it that he could be so strong for her and not for himself?

"I don't know if it was I who helped you make a comeback," he continued, "but it sure as hell didn't take long before you were on top of the world again with a platinum album of your own and bookings worth a fortune. God, each time you quit work to have a baby it cost us a bundle. Oh hell, you know all this."

"You *did* help me, Mike," she said. And then she thought of all his failures. If only he could stand on his own.

"But not anymore, is that it? What good am I now except as your lackey."

"You're not a lackey. I need you very much. Who else would do for me what you do?"

"A well paid servant, Regina. That's who. That's why I keep trying to pull something together on my own."

"But you don't have to prove anything to me."

"Yes I do!" he shouted. "I have to prove I'm a man. A man's got to have more to do in life than check on dinner reservations and find that they've already been made, and argue with sound technicians when they've already been instructed, and order a limousine for a performance and then find that you don't want one."

He pulled into the driveway and waited for the electric gates to open.

And then with a sudden rage he leaned forward and slammed his forehead against the wheel again and again, as if he could make the pain go away on the inside by hurting himself on the outside. "I'm sorry, Reg. I'm sorry, I'm sorry, I'm sorry!" he cried.

"Mike! Stop it!" she screamed. She was scared and angry and full of hurt for him, for herself. She pulled at him to stop.

"Stop it, Mike—stop—you're acting like a child."

He caught himself up short, then reached across the seat and threw open her door, pushing her from the car. "Go on, get out. I can't stand the sight of you! You goddamn blame me for a mistake that anybody could have made. Well, I've done things wrong in my life, plenty of things, on my own, and this isn't one of them."

Did she blame him unfairly? She didn't know. And then she decided no! It was *his* fault. She jumped from the car and slammed the door, wincing at the rattle she was causing to her beautiful car. "What are you going to do now," she yelled as the car backed wildly out of the drive, knocking through a patch of newly planted daffodils, "go get smashed *again*? Come home with a limp prick *again*? Lose some more of my money *again*?" She started after him, but the car was already in the street. She could hear the rubber he laid as he took off, flooring the gas pedal into the beautiful brown carpeting.

The girls' school bus pulled up just then, and the young bus driver looked at her curiously. What was Regina Williams doing? Having a fight with her husband? A Grayline tour bus drove up and Regina could hear the driver announce her name over the loudspeaker. God, how she hated those tours. People from the bus would come back later with binoculars and look into her windows. They'd camp in her driveway and block her coming and going. They'd leave hamburger wrappers and Coke cans on the lawn; they'd even try to climb the fences. And if they were hurt, she was liable.

"Quick!" she yelled to the children, who ducked their heads down and ran toward the hedge to hide from the curious sightseers. The girls had been well trained because Regina had a terrible fear of kidnaping. Any one of those idiots on that bus could be a potential criminal. You didn't have to have a faulty electric heater in your house to lose the ones you loved.

"Mommie, why was Daddy so mad?" Jamie asked. "We waved to him and he didn't even smile."

Regina held their hands and led the girls along the inside of the hedge to the side door by the billiard room where they waited for someone from the house to open the door.

"He'll be all right, baby," she said, putting her arm around her daughter. "Tell me about the book fair. Did you buy the ones you wanted?"

"No, she didn't," Jana interrupted. "All the Judy Blume ones were sold. It's not fair!"

"Let me tell it, Jana!" Jamie said, pushing her sister.

"All right, all right," Regina stopped her. "We'll go to Brentano's and get you what you want."

"But I wanted to buy them at school. It's not the same buying at the book store," Jamie wailed.

Nothing in life is ever the way you want it, Regina thought. *Absolutely nothing.*

Regina fixed the girls a snack and then went into the office. Her secretary Bertie was typing in the outer office, so Regina walked directly through to Florie's office needing to talk to her. Florie would know what she should do about Mike. But Florie wasn't there. She looked at the time. It was after three. Florie should be back by now.

She crossed to the desk, not really seeing the familiar objects, the Bible open on the side table, the photo of Choo Choo in one of his wide-brimmed hats and white suits (his pimp duds), the autographed photos of Alex Haley, Martin Luther King, and Bobby Kennedy. Florie had few heroes, but the ones she had were the best. She opened Florie's daybook calendar and ran her finger down the list of appointments.

Florie had a lunch date with Cassie Barnes, one of the producers of the *A.M.* show. She was picking up costumes at two, wigs at three and had to make a stop at the jeweler in between, and then . . . Regina's red tapered fingernail stopped at a three-thirty appointment. Dr. Simmons? Simmons was the cardiologist who took care of Harley.

"Bertie!" she called. Bertie was there in an instant. Bertie always looked startled when Regina called her. Maybe it was the thin face and those round glasses.

"Why is Florie seeing Dr. Simmons?"

Bertie's face slowly turned from a pale hue to

flushed pink, the world's worst liar. "I don't know," she tried.

Regina was going to yell, and that would unnerve Bertie even more. "What's wrong with her?"

"Nothing. Just some tests. She's getting the results today. Mr. Shaw is meeting her there."

Regina sat down hard in Florie's chair. "How long has this been going on?"

"Only a week!" Bertie insisted. "She's been feeling much better. The doctor's just watching her to be sure."

"You're positive?" How she wanted to believe that.

"Positive," Bertie assured her, backing out of the room.

Regina hated the effect she had on that woman, but she was so timid it couldn't be helped. So Mike would be with Florie and they hadn't even told her. She felt ashamed of the way she'd acted with him. He was sparing her worry and she was adding to his. Florie had had health problems before. But she'd always been all right. Nothing to worry about. She couldn't let herself get frantic over a doctor's visit. She should probably have a checkup herself.

But still . . .

Don't think about it now, she told herself. *Think of something pleasant. Think of the reunion.* But that only made her stomach tighten.

Her eye fell on a letter tucked into Florie's daybook. Regina recognized Choo Choo's childish script. And then her own name caught her eye. She pulled the letter up so she could read the sentence. "And you can tell that white bitch for me to keep her mouf shut or I'll stop her cole." Cold was spelled c-o-l-e. If it wasn't so pathetic, she would have laughed. *That rotten little turd,* she thought. *Writing to Florie like that, upsetting her with his crazy rantings.* This didn't help Florie's condition at all. God how she hated him.

But as long as Florie was alive his crummy little secrets were safe with her. She pushed the letter back into the book, closed it, and went upstairs to lie down and wait for Mike and Florie to return. When they got back, she'd give Florie a big hug and kiss and find out exactly what Dr. Simmons had to say. And then she'd apologize to Mike. She needed him to be on her side, in her corner. There were tough times ahead, and this was no way to head into them.

CHAPTER 21

A damp mist blanketed the Monterey airport as Cord stepped off the Antelope *Gulf Stream*. The airport was deserted at this hour except for one other plane at its loading port.

"Will you be unloading my instruments now?" he called to the steward.

"Yessir, Mr. Crocker. Would you care to supervise?" Most entertainers and musicians were quite particular about their equipment.

Cord went to stand by the hold. Within minutes the metallic door opened above him, and a conveyor belt lowered his equipment to the waiting baggage cart. Two airport attendants arrived just at that moment with another baggage cart filled with musical equipment marked "James Fitzgerald." Cord smiled. He hadn't seen James in a long time.

He watched the Antelope minibus until it was loaded with his gear and then he climbed into the limousine to enjoy the ride down the coast to Big Sur. The verdant countryside of the Monterey Peninsula was restful to his eyes, but not to his brain. He was still dwelling on Louise, regretting their different lives. He needed to immerse himself in the new album now. Get his mind off of her. She might even lend a poignancy to the songs he had to compose. There was nothing like an impossible love to fire one's imagination. Though he didn't love her yet, there was that possibility. She was so levelly nonneurotic. It took the craziness out of the relationship. Not like with Regina.

He forced himself to concentrate on the gray misty clouds that hung over the edge of the highway obscuring the sea from time to time. He wouldn't think about Regina; that was a dead issue. He'd have to be a stupid masochist to continue fantasizing about Regina. They'd eaten each other alive, and both of them had needed years to heal from the wounds.

The lobby of Antelope Inn was pine-scented and inviting. There was a large fire glowing in the Franklin fireplace. The scent of cinnamon coffee filled the room and led him directly to the pot.

Fideo embraced him, beaming his pink-cheeked cherubic smile. Cord pulled away too abruptly, spilling his newly poured coffee, and Fideo chided him. "I never corrupt straights, Cord." And then he winked as if to indicate that's exactly what he did do.

Cord laughed in spite of his aversion. "You know that kind of talk makes me uncomfortable," he replied, not really intimidated by Fideo. Fideo's newest friend was standing nearby, a young boy with a beautiful Latin face, black eyes rimmed with dark lashes, and straight black hair sculpted over his head. His slender childish body seemed vulnerable. Cord could never meet a gay man without immediately picturing him making it. He tightened his ass against the painful idea.

As though Fideo knew what he was thinking, he laughed and patted Cord on the behind.

Cord stepped out of his reach and walked around the room admiring the décor. Sofas were upholstered in nubby handwoven fabrics; huge chairs were made out of logs of bleached pine, and end tables were chunks of a tree trunk, cut and bleached and polished. The lamps in the room were made from baskets, and the floor was a mosaic of polished woods, while the ceiling high above his head was crisscrossed with rough exposed beams. The room looked like an affluent ski lodge except that beyond the windows was the gorgeous view of the meadows and pine forests above the sea. Cord took his steaming cup of coffee and stepped out on the patio that ran the length of the lobby. James Fitzgerald was sitting there.

"Well, if it isn't the old Crock!"

Cord grinned. "You been warming the toilet seats around here?"

"If you mean have I been shittin' around, it's not so!" James patted his lap which contained several tape containers.

"New album?" Cord acknowledged, envious that James had already finished when he hadn't yet begun.

"A present for me bride." He rolled his rr's in a heightened brogue.

"You planning to drive her crazy?" Cord teased.

"Go on," James laughed. "Aren't you goin' to congratulate me?"

"I'm as envious as hell," Cord said seriously. "I hope you'll be happy together for a long time." That was as close as he could come to forever.

"Thanks," James said simply. "How long will you be here?"

"Long enough. I'm booked indefinitely. I've hired Craig Mulaney and Dorn Stevenson."

"Good boys." James acknowledged the expertise of that backup. "Got a theme?"

Cord smiled more to himself. "Unrequited love. Seems I'm an expert."

"Hah!" James exclaimed. "No more scenes?"

"Now and then," Cord admitted. They both laughed, remembering the time in Dallas with six teenyboppers and a pile of whipped cream.

"God, we were sick after that," Cord said. "Tell me about Ariana. I'd really like to know what finally brought you to the forbidden zone."

"She intrigues me," James said, trying to put Ariana into words. "She's hard to get. Oh, not in bed, but I don't own her. She's not on this earth for my pleasure alone, and I've never met a woman I could say that about. She's the first one who's loved *me*. Her work fires her. And that fires me. I watch her manipulating heads of state and governments to get what she needs for her people, and it makes what I do look like what it is sometimes, playing with myself."

"You've had the longest career of any rock or pop singer in the business. Don't you like what you're doing? Do you think our music has such little value?"

"I never thought about it before Ariana," James said. "That's why she's such an influence on me. I know I'm good. But it's not the same as feeding starving black children, now is it?"

Cord didn't answer.

"I don't want her to know she has the upper hand, but she does anyway. I need her more than she needs me, and that's a fact." He seemed surprised by the discovery. "It's going to work, Cord."

Cord stared off into the gray sky, listening to him talk, and saw a pair of green eyes begin to form among the strata of various hues. The eyes stared back at him, mocking him as James talked. Ariana's independence with James was the exact element that had kept Cord solitary, unable to form a commitment to someone like Regina or someone like Louise. Cord believed that marriage was supposed to be a husband and wife and family. Not two warriors pitching spears across the veldt, each one throwing farther and farther, straining every muscle, sweating against the accomplishments of their mate, until at a certain moment they turn against each other and hurl their spears. A direct hit! He could still feel the piercing tip of that thrust. When had it come? he wondered. When had they ceased competing and began murdering? How ironic it was that Regina married someone and was living a domestic life, the kind he'd always envisioned for them. But then Mike Shaw was not a spear thrower, he was a sword swallower. Cord's stomach tightened at the idea of Regina and Mike.

He patted James on the back. "Best of luck, buddy," he said and turned toward his cabin.

"Cord," James called out. "I want you to stand up with me at my wedding."

Cord was touched by this offer of friendship. "Sure I will. You know I'll be there. Is it soon?"

"End of the month."

"May I bring a guest?"

James smiled. "Of course. It's not going to be an intimate affair. More like an international circus."

"See you then." Cord waved and walked down the path toward his cottage. He hadn't had such a feeling of loneliness in a long time. Funny, he realized, that his first thought had been to invite Louise, as if the atmosphere of being at a wedding might rub off on both of them. Or was it to protect himself against the possibility of running into Regina, who was sure to be there?

He unlocked the cabin door and went directly to the phone. Louise answered on the second ring.

"Hi," she sounded warm and cuddly. He told her so.

"The plane landed safely?"

"I'm calling, aren't I?"

"I miss you."

"Yeah," he said. "So what's new in New York since this afternoon."

She hesitated. "Well, there is something I meant to ask you about."

"What?"

"Would you be amenable to a reunion concert of Majesty?"

The question hit him like a thunderbolt. He had

the feeling someone wanted to crucify him and he'd just walked up to the cross and spread his arms. "What the hell are you talking about? You just remembered this? I told you that pompous, prick-wagging Don Drummond killed my brother, as easily as if he'd filled the hypodermic with poison. And Regina was there to push the plunger. How can you ask me a question like that? You of all people?"

"Calm down, Cord. I didn't mean to upset you so. And it's not my idea. I promised Lubow and Mike Shaw I'd talk to you. But never mind, just forget I mentioned it."

The wind had been knocked out of him. He was embarrassed by his outburst. "I didn't mean to yell like that."

"You're carrying a heavy grudge, Cord. It can only fester and decay. You've got to get rid of it. I know. I hated my ex-husband. Spent a lot of time wishing he'd bloat up and turn green. Funny thing. When we finally got together and talked, just recently in fact, I found that I'd been the cause of a great deal of the ill feeling between us. You're carrying the guilt of your own contribution to Gene's death, but you're blaming Regina and Don for it. You couldn't have saved your brother, you know. We can only save ourselves."

"Gene was naive, and Regina and Don rode right over him."

"That was wrong of them, Cord. Terribly wrong. But Gene's character, his dependency on drugs, his naiveté, *and* the circumstances all contributed to his tragic death. There are many people who, given the same circumstances, would not have done what Gene did. Certainly others can hurt us, but it's up to each of us to overcome that hurt. No one else can do that for us."

He was silent for a moment, hearing the truth in her words, wanting to believe her, but at the same time aware of the distance between them. A distance not only of miles.

"What has Mike Shaw got to do with this reunion?"

"He's one of the promoters."

"Why didn't he ask me?"

"He figured you'd say no to him."

"He was goddamn right." There were fresh wounds bleeding inside of him. He felt actual physical pain at the idea of a reunion, and what a betrayal it would be to Gene's memory. "It's unbelievable. After all the time you and I have spent together, this has been going on behind my back and you didn't tell me. I don't like that!" *What would it be like to face Regina and Don again,* he wondered.

"Nothing's been going on. Lubow just called from the coast and asked me to speak to you. That's all."

Cord was trying to figure out if this was the truth or some bizarre story she made up. But why? It was like discussing his own death with a great deal of dispassion. He sighed. "Hey, I called you to invite you to a wedding, the end of the month."

"Oh Cord, how wonderful. I wish I could."

"But . . . ?" This sure as hell wasn't his day.

"I'm taking a Greek cruise with a group of friends. We'll be on Crete at the end of the month."

"How dandy."

"I'm so sorry, Cord."

He didn't reply.

"Cord? Look, I've got to get to work. I'll call you sometime." And he hung up. What the fuck! She was no different from all the rest. She had used him, used his attraction to her like a string to tie him up and leave him vulnerable. They could all come begging to him, Louise included, especially that prick Mike Shaw. Let them just think there was a possibility of a reunion, and then watch their faces when he shoved them in their own shit, even Louise. Stuck-up lady.

"I'll be in Crete." Damn her. He wished he didn't miss her.

He went over to the fireplace, igniting the crumpled newspaper and smoke-chips prepared for his convenience. But he couldn't get warm. The chill of the place had gotten into his blood, and he was suddenly dreading the thought of working here. He wondered what it was like in Crete.

He took out a joint and stretched out on the king-size bed. It felt big and empty. He lit up and drew in the smoke deeply. Mellow. That's what he wanted right now, anything to ease the knot in his chest and the tightness in his neck.

He picked up the phone again and asked for Fideo. "What's happening around here, man? Place is too quiet."

"Anything your heart desires." Fideo sounded clipped and efficient over the phone. "Boys, girls, stuff, you name it."

None of it appealed. "Have you heard from my backup?"

"They're arriving now."

Cord heaved himself up from the bed. The grass was beginning to numb his forehead, his thighs, his fingers and toes. "Might as well get to work. I'll be in the studio if they want me." He hung up the phone. *I'm too damned sensitive,* he thought. *Let it go. Do like Louise did. Let it go.*

But he couldn't let go, and he couldn't forget Gene's face, so young and peaceful in death, those soft brown eyes closed forever. Forever! The idea made him sick to his stomach. Work. That's what he needed. And soon he was immersed in his sound, hearing the notes in his head come alive through his hands on the strings.

PART 2

THE REUNION

CHAPTER 22

The humid Washington night enveloped them as they walked from the hotel lobby and settled into the air-conditioned limousine. Regina welcomed the warm air; her hands were like ice. This was almost worse than before a performance. What would Cord say to her; how would he look? He might refuse to speak to her; what would she do then? God, she had really let herself in for it. Mike seemed nervous too. But he had stayed off the booze at least for today. Her Charmeuse handpainted dress billowed around her into a soft green cloud. It was the perfect color for her hair and eyes. She'd sprayed herself with Mistigris, the perfume Cord had always loved. *Oh Cord,* she thought.

A line of limos ran double around the block as they approached the embassy. The wedding ceremony was due to start promptly at eight and it was already that now, but the crush at the entrance was overwhelming.

"Quite a shindig!" she commented as security guards hovered around her, escorting them up a red carpet emblazoned with the crest of the government. The guards tried to keep the noisy excited crowd from grabbing their clothes, tearing her dress. Flash bulbs were blinding and she almost tripped, but Mike had her firmly by the arm. The embassy was a stone structure complete with pillars and sculpted topiary trees lining the stairway entrance. The red carpet ran from the curb all the way up to the entrance which was ablaze with lights and flanked by uniformed guards. She could hear her fans screaming her name over and over, "Regina! Regina!" She smiled and waved right and then left.

The embassy itself was jammed with people of every kind and description, and multitudes more spilled out onto the back patios and terraces and overflowed the rows of chairs set up to view the ceremony. Mike spotted two places near the back and edged them into a row.

"They should do this wedding in shifts," Regina said, "to give everyone a chance to see it." The crush was incredible, and everyone turned to look at her. She smiled and nodded, then took her seat, grateful to be hidden from view by the row of people in front of them. Mike looked nervous too.

The garden was in bloom, force-fed by several different florists. And a full orchestra was seated behind a flowered arbor to the right of a raised ceremonial platform. The music was by James Fitzgerald, played as if it had been written by Lawrence Welk. Regina smiled at the way it sounded, "anna one, anna two."

A trumpeted fanfare quieted the guests, and a plaintive primitive song floated out from behind a green, leafy screen. And then a procession of black musicians wearing ceremonial dress wound their way down a side aisle to take their places around the platform. An appreciative murmur went up from the guests who realized that this ceremony would be like nothing they'd ever seen before.

When the strange music ended, there was a hush of expectant silence broken by a collective "Ahhh" as James and Ariana stepped out from behind the flowered arbor and stood on the ceremonial platform. They each wore magnificent robes, hers was white and gold, embroidered with a shower of shimmering stones, sapphires and diamonds, woven into floral bouquets. Her head was turbaned with a white silk fabric and festooned with feathers and jewels. James's robe was multicolored and richly embroidered in silk threads fashioned into figures of animals and serpents interweaving on a background of trees and mountains. Green and red jewels flashed from the eyes of the animals on his robe.

"Those costumes must be the country's treasury," Regina said.

"You know how much money James is worth," Mike whispered.

"She's gorgeous," Regina decided.

Ariana was one of the most striking women Regina had ever seen. And she seemed radiant tonight.

And then Regina saw Cord.

He was standing next to James on the platform, wearing a white tuxedo. The combination of his blond hair and light clothing gave him a look of purity. Her cheeks began to burn. And her heart had leaped to her throat, beating there as though it belonged, as though she were supposed to be choking like this.

James and Ariana drank from five cups of liquid during the long ceremony, each cup made of a different precious metal and decorated with a different theme. The bride and groom were fed from several dishes of food, and then each presented the other with a lighted candle fashioned in the shape of a bird.

When the ceremony was over, The Fitzgeralds, husband and wife, smiled at the crowd and embraced to enthusiastic applause, while the guests filed out of the aisles to congratulate the bride and groom as they made their way down from the platform. Regina was hemmed in by a happy, jostling crowd and she lost sight of Cord.

Mike moved close to her. "It's all right, gorgeous,"

he told her, guessing her mood. "Everyone's on our side."

"I didn't know it would be this difficult," she managed to say.

"I did." He grinned. The two of them were like Hansel and Gretel about to be discovered by the witch.

"There's Don," Mike said, spotting him. Don's curly hair fell nonchalantly over his forehead. He was wearing a black tux, a white ruffled shirt, and there was a crowd of women surrounding him as he held court. The Princess Sonia was tucked under one arm. Sonia too was gowned and curled, but Mike noticed she wore her usual glassy-eyed expression.

Again Regina's heart did strange things to her throat. She wished the ground would open up and swallow her while she smiled and nodded to admirers and acquaintances.

Don took a step in their direction and then turned back to help the Princess, whose spiked heels were sunk into the grass. She was pulling on them like a dead weight, while Don tried to help her. Regina could feel perspiration gathering under her arms, and the scent of her perfume grew suddenly stronger. Don looked over at them and shrugged like any helpless idiot whose girl had gotten stuck in the mud, and with that look Regina's nervousness broke and she smiled.

"Come on," she commanded and took Mike by the hand to where Don and the Princess were stranded. Her heart sank back down to where it belonged, and in its place a laugh bubbled forth; it was her sensual, star laugh. When she reached Don, she threw her arms around him, captivated by the moment. God, she couldn't believe it. It felt like steel bands reuniting; bands that had been severed long ago in a horrible melee that was told and retold in every scandal sheet in the world. But now the words were old, and the feelings long forgotten. It was amazing how the broken pieces fit together perfectly. She pulled away.

"You old bastard." He looked so good to her, so dear.

"You magnificent coral-cunt!" he chuckled. "Was this your idea?"

"It's all his." She nodded toward Mike. "Boy wonder. And faithful hubby." She tried not to sound brittle. Mike and Don shook hands.

"What do you say?" Mike asked Don. "Have you given the reunion more thought since London?"

Regina looked at him in surprise. So that was the mysterious business that had side-tracked Mike to London. And Lubow had told them Don was already committed. Damn them, they'd hooked her first. She was the only one who had agreed for certain. Damn them all.

"Have *you* said yes?" Don asked, touching her cheek with his finger, tracing a remembered line down her face to her chin. The same old seducer. She felt herself respond. What the hell, why not? She said she'd do it and she would.

"Yes, I have. I think it will pump some new blood into the old veins. Even I suffer occasionally from 'stale-style.' "

Don stiffened at the jibe, but Mike interrupted. "What Regina means is that she loves the whole idea, Don. We both do."

Princess Sonia swayed on her feet as though she might collapse, and Don grabbed her under the arm and held her up, continuing his conversation. "Anybody talked to Cord yet?"

"He's playing hard to get. We thought you might change his mind," Mike said.

Don laughed. "You were all chicken, weren't you?"

No one laughed with him. "Well," he continued, "I wouldn't take part in a reunion that tried to recapture our youth. None of us are the same as we used to be. We've grown and changed. And I won't be a carbon copy of the past. It would be a washout anyway. But there could be something new."

"Why don't we shake on it?" Mike asked.

Regina looked into Don's eyes and saw only amusement and interest and friendship with a touch of greed. She leaned forward and kissed him on the mouth.

"Vell!" Princess Sonia exclaimed, and the three of them laughed as Regina and Don hugged one another.

Don turned and looked around. "Shall I find Cord and talk to him?"

Just then Regina spotted Cord's blond head protruding above a group of people. She put her hand on Don's arm. "I think I'd like to do it," she said. She squeezed Mike's hand and left the three of them standing there.

What had gotten into her? she wondered, stepping across the grass. *What will he say to me?* But she had pictured this moment for so long that she couldn't put it off one second longer. She knew every one of his arguments better than he did. She was prepared. The only thing she wouldn't be able to take would be his hostility.

The crowd on the lawn had thinned out somewhat, and she had a clear line view of Cord. At that moment he turned and saw her coming toward him. It was as though someone had shut off all the sound; she lost awareness of everyone around her. With each step she felt as though she were walking back in time. They stared at one another for what seemed like forever, and she prayed that she was passing his inspection. *It's been so long,* she thought.

He watched her approach and she saw different expressions cross his face. He was remembering his anger, and then he controlled the anger, which was replaced by curiosity and a touch of defiance. And then something else seeped in; she saw a look of tenderness.

Regina stood in front of Cord and gazed at him without words, but the question in her eyes asked, *Can we be friends?* He started to smile and there was an ache inside of her that threatened to break away from its chains. *Only friends* she promised him, aware of Mike's eyes on her back.

Cord took both her hands in his and leaned forward, kissing her lightly on the mouth. She'd forgotten the fullness of his lips. So much she'd forgotten.

"Hello, Princess," he whispered. "What's this I hear about a reunion?"

Regina could hardly breathe; only this time it was passion and not panic that erupted inside of her. "Oh, Cord," she whispered. "Would it be too crazy? Do you still hate me so much?"

He looked at her sadly. "I couldn't help it then. But I think I can now. God," he shook his head in wonderment. "Look at you."

She smiled at him. "And you."

"But why would you want to do something like this? Take this chance? And why should I?"

"How could Don and I do it without you?"

"Have you both agreed?"

She nodded.

Cord waited for the old familiar pain to shoot through him again, even tried to dredge it up, but for some reason it didn't come. He felt almost naked without it, lighter, tons lighter. Was he finally free? Just like that? Or had Regina entered his bloodstream again, blotting out everything else, carving out her own place within the structure of his cells, fitting herself there as an antigen to his allergy, curing him with one massive dose of herself. He remembered Louise's conciliatory words. How ironic if they had paved the way for this. He opened his arms, pulling her toward him, holding her.

Regina came into Cord's embrace feeling that place of safety she hadn't been to in a very long time.

"Is the reunion what you want?" he asked.

She nodded.

"You're sure?"

She nodded again, overwhelmed by his touch and his voice.

"I'm not going to let you tear my guts out this time, Regina."

And then Mike was there, shaking Cord's hand; Don was clapping them both on the back. Even Mike looked pleased, and then Don hugged her again, and Cord kissed her cheek, and everything was settled.

Mike left them and pushed his way through the remaining crowd. He climbed the stage and commandeered the microphone.

"May I have your attention, please!" His voice quavered slightly as it echoed through the loudspeakers. "I'd like to take this opportunity to make an historic announcement. And there could be no more fitting time than at the wedding of James Fitzgerald, one of the world's greatest entertainers. But I'm talking about another star of equal magnitude. A star that has burned brightly in the entertainment world ever since its phenomenal success more than a decade ago."

The audience began to murmur. Mike held up his hands.

"Wait! I'm here to tell you it's true. The long awaited, greatly anticipated, most desired concert in the country's history is going to happen. That's right! It's official. There's going to be a reunion of MAJESTY!"

The roar of the crowd was deafening.

Mike had never been so excited in his life. And this was only a preliminary to what it would be to stand on the stage of an international forum and announce to the world, "Ladies and gentlemen, here is Majesty!"

Well, it's here, Regina thought. *The biggest entertainment event of the century.* She prayed it wouldn't kill her.

CHAPTER 23

Penny grabbed a Kleenex just in time to catch her sneeze. Either she'd caught Beau's cold, or her sinuses were working overtime. The same thing had happened to her the last time she was pregnant, but this rainy New Hampshire weather wasn't helping. Look at Beau. His nose ran constantly. Pregnant women were supposed to be immune to infection, or was it nursing infants who were immune? This baby growing inside of her made her realize how fortunate it was that Timmy hadn't been born with any defects or addictions, considering all the stuff she had taken during that pregnancy. What if the new baby was born with short little arms of cerebral palsy like the child of one girl she'd met at the psychiatric clinic in Oregon? After seeing that poor little thing she'd given up cigarettes and alcohol. She even stayed out of the club at night while Beau was performing because she'd heard that inhaling cigarette smoke from other smokers was as bad as smoking yourself. It kept her apart from Beau, but she didn't mind. Anything was better than being in her parents' house.

But tonight she had to be here because they were meeting Regina Williams's husband who was coming to see Beau perform. Beau had asked her to keep him entertained.

He was already seated at Beau's table when Penny got there; he helped her to a chair. She liked his looks; he had kind eyes and he reminded her of Finney. Finney's face had appeared again in the person of her son. She really missed the child. How broken-hearted Timmy had been when Beau sent the plane ticket for her to join him. They had formed a very close relationship while she was in Oregon, but still she wasn't ready to have Timmy with her full-time. First she'd have the new baby and learn how to take care of it as her therapist suggested before she'd be ready to take on the responsibility of an older child.

If only Timmy wasn't growing up so fast.

When the first set was over, Beau came down from the stage, wiping his forehead with a towel. Penny blew her nose again, dimpling with pleasure at the idea that someone so important in the music world had come all this way to see Beau's group. It might even mean an album. But she was nervous too that Beau wouldn't say or do the right thing.

They shook hands and Beau seemed confident enough. She began to relax. They'd been through all this before. The promises and the hopes and the letdown.

Louis and French and Corky followed Beau down to the table to take their customary places during the intermission, but Beau gave them a look so they excused themselves with a friendly pat on Beau's back or his arm. They all liked him.

"They're a great bunch of guys," Mike commented when they left.

"Yeah. We've been living together on the road for weeks and there's been no hassles. It helps when you've got something going with the people you work with."

"I like their sound, Beau. It's good."

Beau smiled and winked at Penny, taking her hand under the table.

"Do you know how good you are?" Mike asked. He

was supposed to play it cool with Morgan and not stroke the kid, but when someone was that talented, it was a crime not to tell him.

Beau shrugged modestly.

"No, I mean it! Hell, you're as good as Billy Cobham and Bobby Caldwell. And I know them both. I've sat in on their sessions. You've got golden hands, Beau. I'm impressed."

"You mean that?" Beau couldn't hide his pleasure.

"I wouldn't say it if I didn't. But your talent is lost in these hick towns."

"You have a better idea, Mr. Williams?" Penny interrupted.

"Call me Mike," he told her, wincing at her mistake.

"Quiet, baby," Beau cautioned. "Let him alone."

"But I just thought . . ."

She saw Beau's expression and stopped in midsentence.

"She wants me to be famous," Beau smiled shyly.

"And you? What do you want?"

"I think this group can make it."

"Don't hype me, Beau. I heard the music. You're the talent here. You're the one who shines."

Beau caught his meaning. "But you haven't heard the rest of our stuff yet. Stick around for the next show; we've got numbers all worked out. Some good ones. We work on new material all the time." Beau was beginning to get that crawly feeling all over. The group was good. Damn good! Why did the man come if he didn't want to hear them?

"And whose songs are they?" Mike asked.

"Louie's mostly. Corky sometimes."

"And you?"

"That's not my thing. I just interpret."

"My point exactly. You've brought that stuff to life. Without you it would be what it is, second-rate."

"You mean you came all this way just to see Beau?" Penny felt her excitement build.

"Yes. I wanted to talk to him about something important." He had their attention now. Penny leaned forward and Beau was on the edge of his chair. "Have you heard about the reunion?"

Beau shook his head.

"You mean about Majesty?" Penny asked. She listened to the news. Read magazines.

"That's right. The reunion is my baby. I'm putting it together."

"Do you know Don Drummond?" Penny asked in awe. "I've been in love with him since I was a kid!"

"Sure I know him. He's a great guy. You'll probably meet him." He turned to Beau. "That's why I'm here. Majesty needs a drummer, and you're my choice. If you want the spot and if the group approves, you've got it."

"Me?" Beau was amazed. "With Majesty? Man, you gotta be kidding."

"Hell, no. I'm serious. What do you say?"

Beau stared at him in wonder. "When is it taking place?"

"We're pushing for early September."

Beau felt his throat tighten so that he could hardly swallow. It choked his breath and drained all the color from his face. A chance of a lifetime! But he'd never be able to handle the pressure. He'd been shooting more shit lately since Penny got here. Things seemed to be getting tighter and tighter, and for some damned reason he couldn't loosen them up. Whenever things went well for him he started to choke on the idea of losing it. What's wrong with me, he'd ask himself over and over. He couldn't take it when things were bad and he couldn't take it when they were good. How could he say yes to this offer when he was using?

"You understand that it isn't definite until Majesty

approves, but I wanted to alert you to the possibility so you could join us at Antelope Inn for rehearsals right away. They'd need to know if you're available so they can make their decision."

It was time to go back again and play the next set. Beau stood up, his eyes still downcast. He could feel Mike staring at him. "It's just my obligations are important. I've got a contract . . ."

"We'll buy out your contract if we decide on you," Mike assured him.

"Oh, Beau," Penny sighed. "What's the matter with you? This is the chance you need."

He glared at her and turned to climb back on stage. Penny kept her eyes glued to his back. He got to the platform, then abruptly turned to Corky.

"I'll be back in a minute," he said and went to find his stash. *Just a little bit to tide me over,* he thought, *until my throat loosens up. My God, Majesty wants me. Too fucking incredible!*

Penny was amazed at Beau. She'd never seen him like this. "I think he's in shock, Mike. But he'll do it! I promise he'll do it. He's just too modest. He doesn't think he's good enough, but he is. And he doesn't want to hurt the other guys. But they can replace him, can't they? They'll just have to. He owes this to our unborn baby even if he doesn't want to do it for me."

Mike looked at her lap and she blushed. "It's very early," she admitted.

"As long as we're being personal, Penny, have there been any more problems with drugs?"

"Beau?"

He nodded.

"Oh, no. Beau's clean. He did it all himself too. I needed help; but he's been off a long time. You don't have to worry about that. When he makes up his mind to do something, he does it. That's why I know he'll do the concert. You'll see." And she promised herself to keep at him until he agreed. Don Drummond! She could hardly wait to meet him.

CHAPTER 24

Almost everyone was there when Mike and Regina arrived at Lubow's office. Regina had worn a butter yellow dress with not too much cleavage showing, but the skirt was split to the knee. Mike had on a raw silk sport coat over navy slacks, and Cord was in jeans, sprawled half out of his chair. Kikky Hunt, Lubow's personal secretary, a woman in her forties and slightly overweight, was all efficiency, seated next to a rather uptight Jerry Lubow. Lubow sat behind his carved desk, dominating the room, letting them all know who owned them no matter what they each believed. Mike and Regina shook hands with the others and took their seats just as Don arrived with Phil Rostein, followed by the attorney representing CAMIL Enterprises.

The attorney, Parson McAdams, one of the new killer lawyers out of Harvard Law School who practiced with one of the most prestigious New York firms, assumed control of the meeting. His watery brown eyes peered through rimless glasses, and his thinning blond hair was combed over a shiny scalp. He had the look of prosperity.

"So that there is a sharing of knowledge between the parties, CAMIL Enterprises has awarded CAMIL Records the recording rights and worldwide distribution of the concert album to be recorded partially in session and partially live." He nodded to Jerry Lubow to explain.

"We'll probably do four sides, and because of the historic nature of this event we'll include an anthology, either sold separately or as part of the album. The package will retail for around twenty-five dollars," Jerry said.

Cord let out a long low whistle. "You gonna choose the producer of the album yourself, Jerry?" He knew full well that Jerry had to have his finger in every pie, and this gooey one was no exception.

"I've been giving it some thought."

"Any suggestions, Cord?" Mike asked.

"Well, it's a crucial decision," Cord replied. "The artistic ability of the producer is essential to a successful sound. We have to find someone we'll all admire and be compatible with."

Lubow looked at him slyly. "I was going to suggest Louise Carlin."

"The lady is tops," Cord conceded.

Don shrugged. "I've liked her work."

"Then that's settled." Lubow turned to Kikky. "Make a note to discuss it with Louise when she calls."

"Just a minute," Regina interrupted. "I don't know anything about her."

Lubow handed her Louise's credit sheet and her resume. It was very impressive. A B.F.A. from New York University, a master's in music from Columbia, a list of enormously successful albums, and a title as VP of Artists and Repertoire. "I guess she's acceptable," Regina agreed.

"Fine," Lubow said. It was a favorable decision. He would still have his say as to the material played at the concert, and since he owned the publishing to most of Majesty's music anyway, he could maintain control and determine policy at the same time.

Kikky made a note as per Lubow's instructions, her contoured face furrowed with concentration.

"Is Louise still in Greece?" Cord asked.

"Yes," Lubow replied. "But she checks in regularly."

Regina glanced at Cord, wondering why he seemed so interested in this Carlin woman.

Cord noticed her watching him. He felt Regina's presence strongly, and it worried him. He realized that having Louise as album producer was the best protection he could have to keep him away from Regina. That wasn't going to be as easy as he'd thought it would be.

"The major financing and all contracts with Telstar and the national closed circuit coverage will go through this office," McAdams announced, in case anyone had any doubts.

"I understand the independent theater owners are clamoring to get aboard," Don said.

McAdams smiled. "Clamoring is putting it mildly." He turned to Mike. "Mr. Shaw can coordinate the national promotional plans in conjunction with CAMIL's publicity staff. And Jerry will make the arrangements for the concert itself at the Superdome."

"Is that the location we've decided on?" Mike questioned. "I thought Houston was still in the running. I spoke to Gus Falcette this morning, and he gave me the impression you were going to Houston."

"If anybody had asked *us*, we'd have preferred Montreal," Phil Rostein interrupted. Don held up his hand in a cautionary gesture. "I'm sure they know what they're doing, Phil."

McAdams turned around to look at Jerry Lubow, who nodded. He turned back. "It's the Superdome, ladies and gentlemen."

"But I promised Gus I'd put in a word for him," Mike insisted.

"And you have, Mike," Lubow said. "It's still the Superdome."

Mike sat back in his chair, but his fingers gripped the arms tightly.

McAdams turned to Lubow. "Along with her duties as acting producer of the album will Miss Carlin be able to assume the position of creative liaison between Majesty and CAMIL?"

"You mean can she handle our complaints?" Cord said, crossing one leg over the other.

Lubow laughed. "She's great at that."

Louise Carlin is probably fat and middle-aged, Regina thought.

"I have a question about the official title of producer for the concert . . ." Mike said.

McAdams cut him off. "Jerry, the film crews that will be shooting footage for the documentary about the reunion will be quartered at Antelope. Will you be able to control them, or do you want to assign a line producer for the film?"

Lubow shook his head. "One of my assistant producers can handle it. It's one of those millions of footage projects that's made in the editing booth. I'll take over myself a full week before the concert when the group moves to New Orleans."

"Which brings us to the subject of a drummer," McAdams said, glancing at his notes. "Since each of you has a separate musician with your respective acts, we feel an outsider would be preferable. Someone with no previous loyalties or prejudices who could bring his own special touch to the sound."

"I have something to say about that." Mike stood up. "I've just been to New Hampshire where I talked with Beau Morgan. If any of you haven't heard him, he's very good. Those of us who know his work can vouch for his talent." He glanced around the circle and noted interest in several faces. "He is available."

"He's wonderful," Regina exclaimed. "I saw him perform years ago and I never forgot him. What's he been doing all this time?"

"Didn't he have a problem with drugs?" Cord asked.

"Yes, he did. But I saw him and talked to him. He's clean. And married now. His wife is expecting.

He's making a comeback with a new group named Purple Bubble. They're having a respectable showing on the road. Average sound. But Beau is reliable and conscientious. I led him to believe we might use him."

"You had no right to do that," Don insisted.

"Yes, I did. Jerry asked me to scout a drummer. This kid's fantastic."

"An ex-addict is always an addict," Don said. He had counted on forcing them to use his own drummer, John Lawson, as the fourth member of the group. With Lawson Don would have a majority voice whenever things got out of hand or if any decisions had to be made. He knew what it was like before when Gene and Cord stood together and Regina sided with Cord against him. This time it was going to be different. "John Lawson may be my drummer, but he's one talented man. I want him to be *our* drummer. He deserves this break. Neither Regina nor Cord have a regular man they work with."

"I certainly do," Cord insisted. "And I wouldn't nominate my man because I agree that the fourth member should be someone new, someone none of us can manipulate."

"You're overly sensitive," Don said.

"I have a right to be," Cord replied.

"I agree. The fourth member should be neutral," Regina said.

"Well, let's use someone else then," Don insisted. "Using an ex-addict is insane."

"He should have a chance like anyone else to make up for his past," Cord told him.

"That's right," Mike added, knowing too well how difficult it could be to come back after one mistake.

"Then we'll have John Lawson as a backup drummer. I insist," Don said. "Just in case there's any problem."

Regina looked at Cord, and he shrugged. Cord noticed that Mike Shaw was annoyed every time Regina looked to him for a decision.

"I'll agree to that," Cord conceded.

"So will I," Regina added.

"Then that's settled," McAdams declared. "Mr. Shaw, we'll leave it to you to inform Mr. Morgan."

"You know, I remember Beau Morgan," Kikky said to Cord. "I always thought he played a lot like your brother Gene."

There was an embarrassed silence while McAdams shuffled his papers.

"The date for the concert is next on the agenda," Lubow said.

"Oh, yes," McAdams cleared his throat. "We've chosen Labor Day as the best time for the largest turnout. Many countries throughout the world have holidays on or about the same date as our Labor Day, and it will be easier to coordinate the satellite transmissions at that time."

Cord nearly jumped out of his chair. "This is June twenty-sixth! September is two months away. That's not nearly enough time to compose a whole album. We'd need at least six months."

"*Six months*," Regina protested. "Are you crazy, Cord? I can't spare that much time. I have commitments and contracts up to my ears to fulfill."

"So do I," Don added. "We'll just have to do the work within the time we have between now and September."

"Isn't it possible, Cord?" Mike asked.

"I'm not thinking of what's possible. I'm thinking of the logistics of learning to work together after all this time, of turning out an album that the whole world has been waiting for. And frankly, I don't want to be murdered for selling out our fans or ourselves. If we don't give every phase of this concert the proper time, we'll end up with something that stinks. I don't want to leave a legacy like that."

"Cord, it's all the time Don and I can spare," Regina insisted.

"She's right. Leisurely preparations are an indulgence I haven't allowed myself in years," Don added.

"You two are still chasing the same pot of gold you always chased, aren't you?" Cord asked disgustedly. "When are you going to learn that grabbing for something is the surest way to lose it. You've got to let it come to you. I would never allow my commitments to rule my life."

"You always had a strong philosophical base, Cord. But your rhetoric hasn't improved with time," Don told him. Damn his arrogance.

"Then we're agreed on Labor Day?" McAdams asked.

Mike and Regina and Don all answered, "Yes," at once. Cord said, "Oh shit."

"I'd like to offer a suggestion," Mike said. All eyes turned. "It's just a suggestion," he stressed. "But everyone knows that the fans don't want all new material. They want to hear Majesty doing the songs that made them famous. So why not split the program and the album? Half new and half old. That way you won't have so many new compositions to worry about."

Regina gave Mike's hand a squeeze. "Very smart!"

Even Cord was a lot happier at the suggestion. Filling a three-hour concert with all new material written in two months' time sounded like a nightmare. It would be hard enough to write half that, but maybe it could be done. Hell, it had to be done.

"I second the suggestion." Cord raised his hand and the meeting adjourned on a high note. It wasn't until Mike and Regina were on the plane back to California that Mike remembered no one had answered his question about whose name was to appear on the marquee as producer of the reunion.

CHAPTER 25

Penny pulled her clear plastic umbrella down over her head and stepped onto the tarmac, juggling the umbrella handle between her makeup case and her stack of magazines. Beau followed along with the baggage cart filled with his instruments.

"Come on, honey," she urged. She waited for him to catch up to her. "The attendant will take care of your things." But Beau kept looking around as though he was expecting trouble.

Ahead of them was the plane, all white and shiny and shimmery on the wet runway with its red and white stripes on the side and the black letters that spelled out Antelope Inn. A private jet! Such exciting things were happening, and this was only the beginning. What if Beau really became famous? What would her father say then? She had a pretty good idea.

"Be careful of the wet pavement," Beau cautioned her. A steward stood at the top of the portable staircase waiting for them, silhouetted by the light from the open door. To Penny it was the stairway to paradise.

And then she looked around the plane. Inside it was like a real living room with chairs and tables and a sofa. A TV stood in one corner next to an electronic game table, and at the other end was a bar and kitchen. "Can you believe this?" she asked in a voice filled with reverence.

Beau was glad for her excitement, but he didn't share it. He was too worried about what lay ahead for him with his new associates and what they would expect of him. He was overwhelmed by their expertise in the field of music. They were giants in the industry, while he was a nobody. How could they have possibly chosen him? And how would they judge him?

"I'd better go down and see that all the instruments are loaded properly," he told Penny, wishing that he could just run down the stairs and out across the rain-soaked field and disappear forever. What if he failed? He didn't know how he was ever going to make it. He stood at the top of the stairs clutching the staircase railing.

Penny flopped onto the sofa, sinking into the luxurious cushions.

The steward approached her. "May I take your coat?"

Immediately she realized that she shouldn't have sat down in a wet coat. She gave him the coat with embarrassment, then put all her magazines on the coffee table and tucked her makeup case under one of the chairs.

She called out to Beau, "Hurry up, honey."

Her voice startled Beau out of his frozen state, and he turned around and came back into the plane.

Penny watched him curiously. "What is it, Beau?" He was shaking all over.

"Nothing," he told her through chattering teeth. "I must have gotten chilled by the rain."

"Well, come warm up, silly. You've got to take care of yourself now. You're going to be famous."

It seemed like a long time later that he lay on the sofa listening to the drone of the engines. The ache inside was still with him, but he couldn't risk another dose. A feeling of despair dragged at him, pulled him down. The dark night around him was his personal hell, as though the plane were plunging into a noxious vortex. He turned his face away to hide the tears in his eyes.

Penny noticed. She closed her magazine and came to sit on the floor next to him. "What's wrong, honey?" She touched his cheek.

"Nothing. I'm a little motion sick," he mumbled.

"I wish you felt better. I'm so happy inside I'm likely to burst." She touched his face, tracing the bump on his nose and the outline of his lips with her fingers. She touched the dark eyebrows, and the place where his hair grew in a point on his forehead.

His body flinched at her touch, hating it. "Aren't you worried?" he asked her. His skin was so sensitive it felt like her fingers were covered with needles. He tried to move away without offending her.

"What is there to worry about?"

"You know."

"Oh. Yes, I worry sometimes. But not as much as I did when I was in Oregon. It was terrible there. So many times I wanted to get high. I was so lonely for you. I hated it there. But I kept remembering what it was like before, when I was using three or four times a day. I'd almost die until my next pill, or snort or fix. I was always so afraid until I knew I had a supply for the next day."

"Shhh," he pleaded. He didn't want to cry, not now.

"I'm learning so much, Beau. I'm learning from you. How to take one day at a time." She tried to stretch out next to him on the sofa, but he wouldn't move over to make room for her. She sat back down and ran her hands over his body, touching his chest and stomach and making circular motions over his muscular thighs. He took her hand and held it still.

"It won't hurt the baby for us to make love."

"The steward might come back here."

"I could ask him not to."

"Not now, Penny."

"You haven't wanted to for such a long time, Beau."

He put his arm across his face and turned his body away. There was no way he could make love. He hadn't had a hard on in months. Heroin took away all his desire for sex. He wouldn't even think about it if Penny weren't around. Her presence reminded him that he was letting her down.

She went back to her chair and picked up a magazine. There was a picture of Cheryl Ladd on the cover. *I'm as pretty as she is,* Penny thought. *Why doesn't he want to make love to me anymore? Why is there always something wrong? Even in the midst of all this good fortune, God is punishing me. My father was right. I'll never be able to get away from my sins.*

CHAPTER 26

Regina closed the cabin door quietly so as not to awaken Mike and stepped out onto the porch, delighting in the atmosphere. The chill of the morning crept between the folds of her terry-cloth robe and she pulled it around her leotard more tightly. There was a mist from the ocean which spread a piney scent over the fresh green meadow, and her breath made white puffs against the crisp air. As she walked down the path toward the main building, a squirrel dashed in front of her and up a nearby tree. "Whisk your bushy tail!" she said, remembering a line from one of Jana's first nursery songs. Fingers of sunlight filtered through the redwood trees on her right. But the early sun wasn't strong enough yet to dry off the wet grass.

The Antelope lobby was deserted, but the aroma of cinnamon coffee filled the large room and mixed with the scent of burning pine cones in the fireplace. *Paradise can be such a simple place,* she thought, sinking into the rough, textured sofa and sipping the hot delicious liquid from a huge china mug.

A pile of instruments sat in one corner waiting to be taken into the recording studio. *Beau Morgan must have arrived last night,* Regina thought. She was anxious to meet him. She finished her coffee, wishing she could stay here all day, curled up in this corner just watching the world go by. But that wouldn't do. No break in the routine was allowed.

The gym too was deserted as she began her morning workout. The most difficult part of exercising was getting to the gym. Once she was there, she worked very hard. Today it had been easier to get going because she knew that Cord was somewhere nearby, and that thought was enough to make her blood race and her energy level zoom.

She raised her hands above her head and stretched, bending forward to touch the floor, loosening up the tight muscles after a night in a strange bed, even though the down quilts and pillows had felt wonderful. And then she did her jumps to get the circulation going, followed by a couple of jogs around the room, before she began the real work. Pliés, twenty-five in each position, then back lifts and side stretches, followed by the arm series (*concentrate on the back of the arm*). Her facial muscles, breast, and diaphragm were worked, and then down on the floor for the hardest part.

Cord's feet beat an even rhythm on the hard pack of the trail beneath his feet. *First a jog and then a workout in the gym. Exhaust yourself, Crocker; get her out of your mind, out of your dreams, out of your thoughts. Don't think about her . . . don't think about her . . . don't think about her . . .* His breath pounded in rhythm with his feet, but even in syncopated two-four time he couldn't stop himself. Her face danced in front of his eyes; her arms beckoned to him from among the trees, curling, winding around the trunks as he wished she were wound around him. It was like trying not to think of a pink elephant. Once someone mentioned it to you, it was there in your mind, smiling and winking and blowing pink champagne bubbles into the air. Regina had been with him like that, filling his mind with her presence, stretching her arms through his awareness, smiling into the canyons of his memories, ever since he'd seen her at James's wedding.

Damn!

No matter what he did to forget, it didn't work. He thought about Louise, but she was a long way away; and she wasn't Regina, who was here, wearing that perfume again. He remembered the odor of her, the saltiness, the powdered sugar sweetness of her. This morning he'd awakened with an erection, and it still hadn't gone away. All he need do was think of her and the blood filled his loins with a hot rush. *Don't think about her. . . .*

One more turn around the path and he'd have a workout in the gym. Where was she right now? What was she doing?

Don't . . . think . . . about . . . her.

Regina was pushed up onto her shoulders with her legs in the air above her doing scissor kicks when the door opened, letting in a blast of cool air.

It was Cord.

Wouldn't you know? she thought. Here I am with no makeup, sweating, out of breath, and he walks in. Perfect timing! She kept on counting, "And twenty-one, and twenty-two . . ."

"I see you're as disciplined as ever," he commented, watching her for a moment before he removed his jogging suit. He was wearing gym shorts underneath. When he'd opened the door to the gym and seen her there, he'd thought she was a figment of his imagination.

"We've got to stop meeting like this," she laughed between breaths and scissor kicks. Finally she lowered her torso to the floor, but kept her knees up and began her hip rotations.

Cord went over to the leg press in the opposite corner and began working the weights, turning his back to her. My God, what was she trying to do to him? He attacked the weights with such fury that he realized he might strain himself. *Slow down, Crocker. Take it easy. Don't think about her . . .*

Regina loved the way Cord's muscles were defined, the taut skin stretched over his angular sparseness. There was nothing excessive about Cord, never had been, except in his lovemaking. He was succinct in his looks, in his music, and in his words. And when he made love, there was great control until they both reached the point of wild abandon.

"Where's Mike?" he asked. The weights clanged up and down as he moved them.

"He never gets up this early."

"I'm surprised that you do."

They continued their physical routine, the silence punctuated by panting and breathing and counting. Up down, two and three and; up down, five and six and . . . Regina's heart, starved for oxygen, was racing from excitement and exertion. The more she strained her muscles, the more acutely aware she became of Cord. She knew he was bothered by her presence too because he avoided looking at her. Their grunting and straining gradually assumed a reciprocal sensuality. Regina couldn't help but think about the satiation lovemaking brought, though she tried not to.

With Mike's "problem" lately exercise was the only satiation she'd had in a long time. And now here was Cord. She could work her body to its fullest, but there was a more important part of her hungry for fulfillment. *I'm never going to get through this summer. It's much more difficult than I imagined.* The man in the corner, his muscles straining, his body gleaming, was someone she couldn't forget. His was a body she knew intimately, whose image had appeared again and again over the years, which still haunted her with memories of passion. She had given up so much when she left Cord. No! Face it! Admit the truth! Cord had left her.

She lay on the floor completely spent, fighting the reality of the man in the room with her. She didn't want Cord to know how vulnerable she was. Somehow she would have to control her need for him. She couldn't risk everything she'd built. *Oh, why did I agree to come here?* she wondered.

The exercise machine had stopped and the room was quiet. She thought Cord had gone, but when she turned, she saw him staring at her. Her heart leaped to her throat. She longed for an invisible cover she could pull over herself to hide the blatant desire she felt for him.

Slowly he came toward her, never taking his eyes from hers. He pulled the towel from around his neck and let it fall to the floor. Then he reached out his hand to help her up.

Her hand was wet in his and nearly slipped from his grasp, but he held on tight, pulling her up to him in one swift movement. They stared at each other for only a moment, and then his mouth was pressed against hers, and his hands were in her hair, grinding her lips against his, tasting her, sucking the juices from her body as she clung to him with all her might. She felt him hot and wet and slippery against her. She was kissing his mouth, his cheeks, his neck, his hair, his eyes, his mouth again, trying in this moment to fill herself with him, to feed on him and assuage the hunger that had been starving in her guts for so long, so long.

"It's been so long," she sighed, rediscovering him. Oh God, how he felt. It was Cord. Every part of him familiar; his feet under hers, the back of his legs as she wrapped herself around him, his waist, his height, the way her neck felt as she strained to become part of him, how he hunched his shoulders over her, enfolding her into him, wanting her to be part of him too.

Finally she caught her breath enough to pull away and stare at him. She felt stricken. Never in her life had she wanted anything as much as she wanted him right now. "I can't let you complicate my life, Cord."

His expression was as desperate as hers; her words told him one thing while her eyes begged him not to listen.

"You always did talk too much," he said. And he reached down, sliding the leotard off of her shoulders, pulling her bra along with it, until her breasts were free. And with an agonized sound he buried his mouth in her chest, lifting her off the floor until she wrapped her legs around his waist. Then he carried her into the shower, locking the door behind them.

Regina felt fused with Cord; and confused about what would happen now. They were sitting on the patio outside the restaurant and the sun was so brilliant that she couldn't look at his white robe. Hers must be blinding him too. But if they moved into the shade it would be too cold. Besides she needed the public setting and the bright sunlight to keep from grabbing him again.

She shifted her weight on the bench, feeling the soreness between her legs. She hadn't been sore like this in years, and neither had she felt the hunger that Cord awakened in her. She sighed and smiled at him. She could have made love all day.

He was silent across from her, staring into his coffee. Now and then he'd turn and look off toward the blue of the ocean barely visible between the haze on the horizon and the edge of the cliffs in front of them.

"It's so peaceful," she said. The tranquillity enveloped her. She unwrapped the towel from around her hair and fluffed it out to dry. It would look terrible without setting, but she didn't care. She used to wear it this way when they'd met and she wanted to recapture the girl she'd been. The girl who had attracted him wildly; the girl who didn't give a damn about when or where they made love or how her hair looked or that her white skin would turn pink if she stayed out here in the sun much longer. Fused and confused.

"Why haven't you ever gotten married?" It popped out before she could stop it.

He smiled slightly. "Do you want the truth or an answer that will flatter your ego?"

She blushed, a preview of her sunburn. He could still see through her. "I guess I'll never hear it often enough. The things you whispered to me in the shower were like echoes of my dreams. I didn't know who was saying them, you or I. But it was stupid of me to bring it up. I always want things spelled out. So there can be no mistakes. But there're always mistakes. Stupid, huh?"

"Regina, you are never stupid," he laughed.

She smiled back. "I was to let you go."

He took her hand across the table. "I'm back," he said.

She heard the screen door slam behind her and pulled her hand away from his, jamming it into the pocket of her robe. Something about the way the door sounded told her who it was.

"So there you are!" Mike called out. She turned around to see his outline coming toward her and shaded her eyes from the light. She squinted and smiled at him. She was in a state of suspension going through the motions; her body was moving, her head was turning, while all the while she was still inside that shower and Cord was still inside of her.

Mike wore a three-piece suit and carried a briefcase. She'd forgotten he was going back to L.A. He slid onto the redwood bench next to her and kissed her lightly on the mouth. Knives of guilt stabbed her insides.

"Don't stay out in the sun too long," he cautioned. "You know what it does to your skin."

"We're going in soon," Cord promised. "Got to get started this morning."

"Have you met Beau Morgan?" Mike asked.

"No," they both answered. And then Cord said, "He's sleeping in this morning. Flew in during the night." Cord's voice sounded tense. "You think he'll work out?"

Mike nodded. "I'm sure we won't have any problems." He turned to Regina. "I'll let you know what happens." He was going home to take care of business, her business. There was a deposition concerning their lawsuit against the Homestake Oil Company, and somebody had to keep track of the children, and the house, and her career so she could be free to commit adultery. And right now all she wanted was for him to go and let her get on with it.

Mike reached across the table and shook hands with Cord.

"Don't get up."

"How long will you be gone?"

So civilized, Regina thought. They asked one cordial question after another.

"No more than a week, maybe sooner," Mike replied.

Cord nodded.

Mike turned back and kissed her again.

"Give the girls my love," she said. "And tell them to call me when they get home from school every day. That's the best time for them, and the best time for me. Oh, and Mike, watch out for Florie, I've been worried about her."

Mike nodded. He had decided to keep to himself what the cardiologist had said about Florie. Regina didn't need that pressure now. But Mike was concerned, too, that Florie take care of herself. He patted Regina on the shoulder and stood up, glancing at Cord and back at her with a quizzical expression. "I'll take care of it," he said, but he had a strange look on his face.

He knows! Regina thought. *What if he knows!* She thought about how it would be for him alone in the house without her, alone with the children, and her business details, and his feelings of failure, and his resentments. She watched him walk away until he was out of sight, and a feeling of despair began to crawl up from her toes to attack her stomach with vile little pincers. She turned to Cord.

"Jamie—that's my elder—is getting very popular."

"I know who the hell she is, Regina!" he snapped.

Tears sprang to her eyes. "We've really started out with a bang, haven't we?" And then she realized what she'd said, and they both laughed.

"Come on," he said, pulling her up from the bench and draping his arm around her shoulder. "Let's go knock 'em dead."

She put her arm around his waist, and they walked back into the restaurant.

CHAPTER 27

Beau awoke in a strange bed and immediately realized that he had to make a connection. He opened his eyes and stared up at the ceiling, tall and peaked with natural-hewn siding and huge carved beams. The walls were pecan color, and the sun shone through calico curtains onto a brilliant blue carpet. He pushed himself up on his elbows to look around. It was a beautiful room. Penny came out of the bathroom wearing a blue terrycloth robe that matched the rich blue carpet and framed her straw-colored hair like a sunflower against the sky.

"There's one of these robes for each of us in the bathroom," she said. "And Beau, there's a meadow in front with miles of grass, and there's a huge forest of trees out back. I just can't believe this place." Her eyes were the same bright blue as the robe she wore.

He swung his legs out of the covers. The carpet curled between his toes. Penny smiled at him and he smiled back.

She handed him a note. "This was under the door. They want to see you in rehearsal when you get up."

His heart fell into his empty stomach. Not yet. Not Majesty. God, he should never have accepted this offer.

"What are you going to do today?" he asked her.

"I'm going to take a walk in the forest and then

sit by the pool soaking up the rays. I've got magazines to read, don't worry about me."

"Why don't you go ahead then and leave me alone so I can get my head together."

"All right, grumpy," she laughed and slipped into a pair of espadrilles. She put on her dark glasses and left the cabin, her magazines tucked under her arm.

Beau locked the door after her and then reached under the mattress to pull out his stash. He was low. He had to connect soon. His last connection had told him that Fideo, the owner of Antelope, was cool. Carefully he lit the match, holding it under the spoon, watching the white powder turn to liquid. He would have to find a place to bury his disposable hypodermics. He'd do it on the way to rehearsal. He wouldn't dose himself too much this morning, just enough to take the edge off his panic, keep him mellow and on top of it. . . .

When Beau opened the door to the rehearsal hall everyone looked at him. He smiled shyly and said, "There's sure a lot of famous people in here."

That broke the ice, but he was still perspiring even though the air conditioning in the room blasted him. It was very low to keep the instruments in tune. He glanced around, noticing the different kinds of instruments they were using. A Les Paul, a new set of Tama Octabans. How he wanted to try those! Cord Crocker came over and extended his hand.

"How ya doin'?" he asked.

Cord seemed like a regular guy. "Fine," he acknowledged.

One by one they came up to him. Regina first, wearing a robe like Penny had on only white, and then Don Drummond with his dark curly hair. Don motioned to a short stocky man to join them. He looked like he had some negro blood in him. "This is John Lawson, my regular drummer. He'll be sitting in on the sessions just to keep us all honest."

Regina shot Don a look that he ignored. But Beau felt nervous about it. Why another drummer? "That's cool, man," he said.

Beau's own drums were set up on the platform. The mike was in position, everything exactly the way he liked it. What a pleasure to have roadies again. Nobody had set up his instruments for him in a long time.

"Shall we get to work?" Regina asked. She sat down at the keyboard and wiped her hands on her terry robe. She felt that unreasonable fear begin to ascend from her toes to her legs, grabbing her stomach, and she stiffened. But then she looked at Cord and he smiled, and like a bad dream the feeling faded away. She was amazed. Was that all it took, Cord's presence? *Is that what I've been missing all this time?* she thought.

"Why don't we run through some of our earlier numbers," Cord said. "None of us have done them together in years, so we'll all be in the same place." He was trying to make Beau feel comfortable, Regina realized, but it was helping her too.

"I don't mind telling all of you I'm a bit scared myself," she offered. She looked at the music in front of her. They were Gene's original arrangements of "Any Old Time." A grip of sadness clutched at her. She could imagine how Beau Morgan must feel. He was taking the place of a ghost, appearing for a dead man. This classic song had sold millions of copies; could any of them do it justice anymore? *Well, let's give it a try,* she thought.

They were all awkward at first. The song started slowly with a long offbeat introduction. Regina kept her eyes averted and hummed the first five bars, and then she heard Cord and Don support her on the vocal. It was like coming home again after being lost for a very long time.

> Any old time you think you want me,
> Any old time you think you care,
> You're the lover who still haunts me,
> If you need me I'll be there.

Beau's sound was very much like Gene's on this number; it gave her chills, though he was a little too stiff. But he'd loosen up. And then she forgot about him as they reached the middle of the song and the lyric swelled and the three of them were one incredible unit. Their voices blended better than ever. She was back on that stage again, that first night, and the magic was happening. She looked at Cord with tears in her eyes.

> Any old time that you have chosen,
> A love like mine that sets you free,
> Any old one who makes you happy,
> Someone I could never be.

When the final chord faded away, Regina went over to Don and put her arms around him, hugging him tightly. She could tell he was moved by the experience of singing with her and Cord again. And then she went over and hugged Cord. Only this time when his arms folded around her, she broke into sobs. The very thing she feared most had happened. She still loved him. And now she knew that she needed him for her very sanity.

The sound of Regina's crying made Beau feel helpless and embarrassed. The technicians stood around waiting, with their long hair and their short hair and their T-shirts that read Antelope Inn or I'm a Recordomaniac. They all wore headphones and held sheet music, and everybody stared at Regina, wanting to comfort her, wanting to say it's all right, but they were choked up too. Finally she broke away from Cord and ran out of the hall.

"Take ten," somebody decided. And the studio emptied out.

Beau felt battered by a wave of sentiment he couldn't control. He'd never thought the group might find it difficult to work together again or that their emotions might overwhelm him too.

Fideo was a man in his forties, slightly balding with fair skin and blue eyes. He looked nothing like the Italian name he bore as he smiled benignly at Beau and extended a pudgy hand. "How do you like your accommodations? Is there anything more we can do for you?" He had a slight accent; Beau couldn't place it.

Beau had to be extremely careful in what he said. He couldn't come right out and ask the man if he was a dealer. "My wife is expecting a baby in about seven months," he began. "And both of us are into proper nutrition. I was wondering, if I wrote out some special instructions for her diet, could you provide these things for her?"

"Of course. Our kitchen uses only natural foods. We have our own garden. No processed breads or flours, only the purest ingredients. We pride ourselves on it, I assure you."

Beau nodded.

"And vitamins. I understand you each require your own special brand?"

Beau looked at him in surprise. His last connection had called "shit" vitamins. "My wife has her own. She goes to a clinic for it."

He watched Fideo running his hands back and forth along the natural oak desk, caressing the edge of the blotter as though it were an object of sensuality. Suddenly Beau recalled hearing that Fideo was gay. The way Fideo was looking at him made him feel acutely uncomfortable. So far he'd never had to grant any favors to anyone in that way to get his "shit." He prayed he wouldn't have to start now.

"A friend of yours, Sandy Aldonatta, called me from New York. He said you might need something special." Fideo had a round soft-looking mouth. Beau tried not to stare at it, but it fascinated him. Just the thought of where that mouth had been. He nodded to the question, greatly relieved.

"We can arrange that too."

Through the window Beau could see Regina and Cord, arm in arm, walking back toward the rehearsal hall. He'd better get back.

"How do I pay you?" Beau asked.

"If you think I extend credit, you're dumber than I was told."

Beau blushed red, but he kept quiet. Dealers and pushers often enjoyed insulting a buyer when they knew they could get away with it. But even if Beau hadn't needed Fideo's "shit," he wouldn't have answered back anyway. His lack of choice in the matter shamed him. "I've got to get back to rehearsal," he mumbled.

"Then go ahead." Fideo's round mouth turned up at the corners, but his pale blue eyes remained cold.

Beau walked slowly toward the door. There was no comment from Fideo. He turned back. "Look, what do you want? I'll pay your price. I've got money. But I'm a little low on stash right now and I need something pretty soon."

"Not quite low enough." This time the smile reached Fideo's eyes, and they narrowed as his round cheeks pushed up. His meaning was clear. The vitamins had a special price.

Beau felt nausea begin to pour from his stomach up to his throat. His face took on an expression of pleading in spite of his resolve not to beg.

Fideo's small pink tongue came out of his mouth and ran a circle around his asshole of a mouth. "Don't worry, gorgeous. I'll take care of you."

And with a trembling hand Beau opened the door and closed it behind him. The blinding sunlight enveloped him. But it did nothing to warm the icy dread inside.

Fideo watched with great interest as the "stretched limo" snaked its way toward him, appearing and disappearing among the grass-covered slopes that curved from the highway up to the complex of buildings that was Antelope. Fideo's office was on the second story of the main building which housed the lobby and the registration facilities. It also overlooked the entire complex, the approach road, and a good part of the highway both north and south, not to mention the enormous and everchanging view of the Pacific ocean beyond. Today the ocean was a brilliant blue, and the day was so clear that the horizon appeared as a crystal cut midpoint across the sky. But the breathtaking view could not stop the swinging of Fideo's mood from a week's anticipation of an encounter with "virgin" Beau Morgan to apprehension over who might be approaching in that long, gray Cadillac.

The car drew closer, its squared television antennae aimed at him like fingers of doom. It had to be Lubow, checking up on the chickens he'd left to roost in Fideo's luxurious coop. *If Beau mentions to him that I'm on the make, I'm in trouble,* Fideo thought, and then his eyes creased again as a smile began. *Beau can't tell Lubow anything. If Lubow finds out he's using, he'll kick his ass out of the group with lightning speed. No,* Fideo thought, *I've got Morgan exactly where I want him.* He hurried down the handhewn staircase through the lobby and out to the porch that ran the length of the building.

By the time the Cadillac arrived he was there to greet it, his arms folded across his short, full body, his face beaming, his scalp showing pink through his blond thinning hair. The driver opened the back door of the car, but it wasn't Lubow who got out. Choo Choo Trainer's long skinny legs extended themselves to the road, followed by his long narrow hips and chest, and then his even narrower head.

"What's happenin', baby?" He reached out for a "brother" handshake.

"What the fuck are you doing here?" Fideo demanded, pushing away his hand in alarm, looking around quickly to see if anyone had noticed Choo Choo's arrival. Arrival, Christ. It was like waving a banner, "Pusher is here. Come and get it—pills, smack, speed fresh off the boat!"

"I was in L.A. so I figured I'd drop in on my old buddy. The bees likes to visit the hive now and then. Likes to see where all the honey goes."

Fideo gripped Choo Choo's arm, thin and bony beneath his hand, and Choo Choo stopped suddenly. "Mustn't touch, baby," he drawled and snapped the fingers of his other hand. And from the inner reaches of the limousine Fideo heard a growl almost like a bear awakening from hibernation, and then Largo's low forehead appeared in the light: the wide pushed-in nose, the small eyes and the full lips over a pitiful array of broken and rotting teeth.

Fideo dropped Choo Choo's arm quickly while Choo Choo straightened the sleeve of his leather jacket and Largo sank back into his seat.

"Just get this car out of sight," Fideo pleaded, pointing to a clump of trees by the side of the cabin. Then he beckoned for Choo Choo to follow him up to his office.

The left side of Choo Choo's face was swollen, and his cheek and lip had recently been stitched. "What happened to you?" Fideo asked, closing the door to the office. With a man like Largo around someone had to be pretty bad to get to Choo Choo.

"I gots me a score to settle!" Choo Choo's black eyes shot angry looks at Fideo.

Fideo dropped the subject. "So?" he said, leaning against the desk. He didn't invite Choo Choo to sit down; the sooner he got rid of him the better.

"Hear they's some mighty fine birds singin' in yo' trees," Choo Choo commented. "The place is doin' real fine."

That proprietary air of his maddened Fideo to the edge of his control. But more than Choo Choo's air, he was furious about the fact that he'd had to give Choo Choo a small percentage of the ownership of Antelope a few years back when he couldn't meet a drug payment. It was imperative that he keep his customers supplied with their poisons, and business had fallen off. He had been over a barrel at the time. "Everything is under control," he said.

"So. Who you got?"

"Majesty is here right now, rehearsing for the reunion. They've been here about ten days." In spite of his jaded opinion of entertainers Fideo was excited to have the legendary group here. He was a fan of theirs from the early days and secretly hoped they might dedicate a song to him as other artists had; the way Elton John had entitled an entire album to the Caribou ranch in Colorado.

Choo Choo's grin was lopsided due to the swelling of one cheek. "So the big mouf, redheaded bitch is here."

"Doesn't your aunt still work for her?" Fideo asked.

"So what!" Choo Choo was obviously displeased by that arrangement.

"You two are practically family."

"Like hell we is. She's a cooz and no good to my aunt, no how. But my aunt don't see it. I don't care what Regina Williams thinks she knows; she don't know nuthin'. In my business talk is cheap. I ain't afraid of *her*, that's for shit sure. But man, I'd like to get her. I'd like to get her somehow and cut her. I'd slice her good."

The look of sheer hatred on Choo Choo's pinched features and his lust for blood amused Fideo. He knew about the baser instincts and responded to them. Once they were unleashed, once they were allowed to happen, they were impossible to contain. He thought about Morgan, and his mouth filled with saliva and he swallowed hard.

"One of the group is using." He said it softly, watching Choo Choo receive the news, his head tilted in contemplation, listening, calculating.

"No shit? Not Williams?"

"No. It's the new guy. The drummer."

Choo Choo laughed, but it hurt his mouth and he winced. "Lubow would surely come blood if he knew that. Maybe we ought to tell him?" Choo Choo's eyes were glazed as he thought of what it would be like to see Lubow's face when he learned his fabulous reunion was threatened by a man who was using shit. Anything could go wrong when you depended on a junkie. "Or maybe we should keep that little bit of news to ourselves." He smiled his half smile, the white, capped teeth bared for a moment in a kind of sneer. If only there was some way he could get Stylwickji back with this one too for beating him and ruining his beautiful pad.

Fideo was swept along with Choo Choo's plotting, enjoying the possibilities. Beau Morgan was a delicious enticement.

"It sure could screw up Miss Cunt's big show, too. I been lookin' for a way to git her for years." Choo Choo looked directly at Fideo. "Dis jes might do it. Do 'em all real good. You keep that drummer happy, hear? And when you needs anythin' for him, it's on the house." And he danced down the back stairway and climbed into the limousine, stopping to give a jaunty wave.

CHAPTER 28

"Do you realize how many good people have died since we first started?" Regina asked. She didn't notice the sudden look of pain on Cord's face. "Jimi and Janis."

"And Mama Cass, and the singer from Chicago, what's his name?" Don asked.

"Jerry Kath," somebody answered.

"Let's not forget Elvis."

"How could we?" Penny said and then blushed when everyone laughed. But it didn't matter. She still felt like she was sitting on Mount Olympus.

They'd finished their first meal together—freshly caught trout amandine, organic salad, steamed vegetables with herb cheese sauce, and a superb French wine.

Waiters in T-shirts brought out an enormous fresh fruit tarte prepared by the chef.

"How will I ever diet around here?" Regina echoed everyone's fears.

"What you should be worrying about is whether we can form a new sound out of the bones and sinews of the old. The three of us have grown apart musically over the past decade. I felt it happening before we broke up. Gene's death merely clouded the issue, but we weren't seeing eye to eye about the basics. Look at Don." Cord gestured to Don who was in deep conversation with the princess. Nobody had known she was here until she appeared at dinner.

"Don hasn't written anything of consequence since we split."

Penny sat at the table listening to them talk and felt as though her entire body were alight with thousands of silvery fireflies. This was the most wonderful night of her life. At least it would be wonderful if only Beau would say the right thing. But so far he only seemed to antagonize them. She put her hand on his knee and gave it a squeeze, but he moved her away. Don Drummond was sitting only three seats away from her, and it made her heart pound in her chest. But she couldn't bring herself to look at him. He had been her all-time favorite for as long as she could remember. She wished someone would introduce them.

"How did you get started in your career?" Penny asked Regina.

Regina was startled by the question, but she smiled graciously. "I've always loved music. It's been part of my life since I was a child. I used it to escape reality. And to become somebody."

Penny nodded. "Weren't you happy at home?"

Regina's face stiffened. "No," she replied, noticing that Penny's eager understanding seemed deeper than surface.

"I knew it," Penny whispered. "It's sad for you, but lucky for the world."

"Life is tough all over," Cord said. But his eyes, too, clouded with a strange expression. The three of them looked at one another and then down at the table. There was an awkward silence, while Penny prayed she hadn't offended these two great people.

"I'm going to have a baby!" she blurted and then blushed.

Regina smiled. "How wonderful. Is it your first?"

Penny's eyes were sad. "No," she said.

But Regina couldn't pursue the subject with Cord sitting there. He realized it too and excused himself.

"I'm going out for a walk in the meadow," he told Regina. "Want to join me?"

"In a little while," she said. She sensed that Penny needed to talk. And talking to someone wouldn't hurt her either. She missed Florie's company. Suddenly she realized how lonely her life really was. There were so few women she had ever been close to. The only close companions she'd ever had were men. And their views of life differed from hers in many ways.

After Cord left, she leaned in toward Penny. "Did you have a miscarriage?" she asked.

"No." Penny's eyes were incredibly clear. "My son was born when I was fourteen. He's living with my parents now, and someday I hope to have him come and live with me. Perhaps when Beau is more established in his career and I've had the baby."

Regina nodded. "You must miss him. I know how I miss my girls. Everything they do every moment of their lives that I'm not there, is gone forever, and I'm jealous of their nurses and their sitters, and their father because he's with them more than I."

Penny glanced down at the table and reached for the sugar bowl which contained colored crystals. She lifted the spoon and let the crystals fall back into the bowl in a soft pastel rainbow. "My son thinks I'm his sister," Penny admitted quietly so no one else would hear. "His name is Timmy."

Regina was moved. "How you must ache to tell him the truth."

Penny looked up at her, overwhelmed by Regina's compassion. "You know," she stammered, "you're not at all the way I expected you to be."

Regina smiled. The next thing Penny would say was, "You're just like a real person." She made a move to leave the table, but Penny looked so stricken, so bewildered at the possibility of having offended, that Regina eased back down in her chair again.

"What's it like to be a star?" Penny asked. "To

be Regina Williams." Her eyes glowed with lights of wonder and envy and absolute adoration.

Regina knew she ought to laugh and launch into an extravagant account of life at its zenith, but suddenly she felt overwhelmed with sadness. The reality of the question hit her harder than a clenched fist in her guts. She didn't know; she really didn't know what it was like to be *Regina Williams*. Not in the sense that Penny meant, a beautiful woman in the prime of life with fame and family and fortune. Everything she ought to say caught in her throat, and she fought for control. "It's not what you might imagine," she admitted. Perhaps she was admitting it to herself for the very first time. "The work is tiring and so difficult, so interminably difficult that I cannot describe it. And yet it's wonderful. Just wonderful. There are moments of pure, absolute joy." Just to think of those moments when everything came together into one miraculous blend made her radiate with excitement. "But to achieve those joyous moments," she shook her head, remembering the hours of work, of aching frustration, of disappointment, and of fear. Oh yes, don't leave out the fear. "And yet I have this unquenchable need to feel every part of life. I'm so moved, I'm so touched; I'm so overwhelmed. I have to let it pour out in song, in lyric, in voice. Thank God I have a voice to use. And I want to be loved. By the whole goddamned world."

"Oh, but you are," Penny said. But Regina didn't hear her. She was lost in her thoughts.

"When the excitement is high and the energy is surging through my veins like volts of electric charge, I feel on fire with a kind of cold heat, a fire of the damned. For that's what we are, we entertainers, just crazy damned fools, every one of us. That peak, that pinnacle lasts for such a short time. And it's so *hard* to achieve. If only *I* could make it, you think before it happens. For me it would be different. For me it would last forever. And you try, and you dream, and you reach; God, how you try. With every bone and sinew and ounce of energy you've got. And if it happens, if you get it, the spotlight, the frenzy, the adulation, you'll do anything to stay there. Sell your grandmother; sell your youth; sell your soul to keep it. Yes, some of us have even done that.

"And if you start to slide, to age, you still hang on, never letting go. You'll let them change your image, your sound, your anything! You'll adjust to new demands, lesser demands, but still you've got to stay there. Even if it means Podunk or Sacramento or Lincoln, Nebraska, instead of the big time, the big places. You need that applause and those lights and that place in the sun more than food or drink or love. Well, almost more than love."

Penny was regarding her with rapt attention, and there was something more on that smooth young face, more than the touch of freckles across her small-shaped nose, more than the deep clarity of her gray-flecked blue eyes, or the beginning of a dimple in her cheek; there was a look under all that admiration of complete and total understanding. "I know what you mean," she said. "I've almost been there myself."

"Are you in the arts?" Regina asked, suddenly wary that she'd given too much away, told secrets to someone who might use them against her, who'd begin to push up from the bottom of her ladder; a new young face ready to topple her off of her peak, a new young talent with sharper claws, deeper desires, and firmer breasts and more determination than her own. *The enemy.*

"Oh, no," Penny assured her. "I'm not an entertainer. But I've had another kind of high. One that's even harder to give."

Something in Penny's expression told Regina what

she meant. "That's tough," she said. "How are you doing now?"

Penny's smile was dazzling. "Just fine," she said.

"I'm glad," Regina offered. But her gladness for Penny's state of health was overshadowed by relief that the girl was not any competition for her. She needed supporters around her now, not threats. Life was complicated enough. And she wouldn't go into a description of the domestic sludge that could slow down a performer's life. It was hard enough to push through it herself, without describing it.

She stood up and took Penny's hand. "It's been lovely talking with you," she said. "I look forward to our next conversation when you can tell me what it's like to be Penny Morgan, expectant mother," and she winked before she went out to join Cord.

"Isn't she wonderful?" Penny asked Beau when Regina had gone. Beau had been staring out into space, not listening to their conversation. Penny wished he had. Regina was so inspiring.

"Cord is the one with the musical integrity," Beau said. "You should hear him improvise. He's a master. I hope I can live up to him."

"Oh, you will, honey," she assured him. After her talk with Regina she felt fired with hope. Anything was possible if you wanted it badly enough.

"Come on," she said, pulling him up. "Let's go take a walk."

He went with her reluctantly. "What about Don Drummond?" she asked. "Don't you admire him too?"

"He's all right, I guess." Beau knew how she felt about Drummond, but there was no comparison between Cord's music and Don's.

They walked across the moonlit lawn toward their condominium and off to the right Penny saw Regina and Cord silhouetted in the moonlight. They were kissing.

At first she was shocked. But then she felt it was

right that they should be together. Right and very romantic. If only Beau would kiss her like that. Maybe soon he would feel more comfortable with the group. He had no reasons to fear them that she could see. And tomorrow she'd try and talk to Regina again.

CHAPTER 29

Mike was already awake and stretching when the eight o'clock wakeup call rang. He dialed for room service and ordered fresh orange juice, poached eggs, and those sensational French croissants. Then he jumped into the shower to wash away the effects of last night's high living. *Michael Shaw, New York is your town.* Even without Regina these ten days had been spectacular. He'd been accepted here and entertained royally. He was so seldom apart from Regina that he'd forgotten he was still an attractive man in his own right, desirable to women even younger and more beautiful than Regina. Of course those women weren't stars, but they made him feel like a king.

Breakfast was waiting when he came out of the bathroom. The waiter had turned on the TV to Donohue; all that bright enthusiasm so early in the morning.

He watched for a while, but it was still too early to call the coast. Neither Regina at Antelope nor the children at home would be up yet. He'd call them both from Lubow's office about ten.

The orange juice was sweet, as sweet as the whole day would be. As sweet as his meeting with Lubow this morning to firm up the final details of the concert. Regina sounded relaxed and happy when they spoke yesterday. He was relieved to hear how well the group was working together, and mostly he was relieved to hear that the old attraction between her and Cord had not been revived. He could tell there was nothing between them when he'd seen them together, but it was good to hear it from her.

He'd been working with CAMIL's PR firm for two days now. The documentary crew wouldn't be moving into Antelope for a few more days, but he had done some fantastic preliminary work with them. And his major plans were going to shake up the whole country when the big publicity push began. All he needed now was the nod to go ahead.

But the best part of all would be to get the title of Producer of the reunion. His name was going to be above all of the other names on the marquee. "Mike Shaw and CAMIL Records present, Majesty!" Regina would have to take notice of that! And he *should* have it! After all he was the one who'd pulled this thing together, who'd put his marriage on the line. But sometimes these deals got away from you. He'd seen it happen. You created something out of your sweat and your experience and your connections that no one else could do; you pushed it, and prayed for it, and nurtured it until it was finally sold. Success and recognition were yours. But then everybody started to change it, to stick their fingers into the pie, to use your creative talent for their own ego fulfillment. Everybody's got an ego or an idea to contribute, and they all want to be the ones to have done what you've done. Shit. Ideas are cheap. And suddenly you've got a corporate product that hardly resembles your original creation. Now it belongs to the world and you have no more say about it. It's like raising a child, as soon as they start dressing themselves it's good-bye Dad. Even his own children at their young age were becoming independent.

He was halfway out the door when the phone caught him.

It was Gordon, the PR man assigned to the reunion. The two of them had closed Studio 54 last night.

"Listen, Gordo, I'm just on my way to Lubow's office. I'll get back to you."

"I know where you're going for Chrissake. But I've got something to tell you before the meeting."

"Shoot."

"You're expecting to be the producer of name, right?"

"Right!"

"And you're supposed to have the authority to make the decisions, right?"

"Subject to approval . . . you know how these things work."

"I don't mean big things. I mean little pisspot decisions. Like the color of the crepe paper or who's selling the popcorn. You know?"

"So?"

"So, I just got word this morning that no decision coming from you is valid. I'm supposed to check everything through Jerry Lubow first or Louise Carlin or, now get this, Parson McAdams."

"Their lawyer? What kind of crap is that?" Mike exploded.

"That's the word, buddy. I thought you should know. There's a memo on my desk right now that says Lubow and McAdams are in charge. Their names are on the contract for the giant video screens at the Superdome. I saw the papers myself. I thought maybe one of them owned stock in the company or something, but they're not even listed in the roster. What gives, Mike? What do you want me to do?"

Mike felt a shot of insecurity course through him. There had to be a good reason. Lubow wouldn't undermine him like this without a reason. But what could he do about it? *Don't worry,* he told himself. *Lubow won't screw me!* Or would he? The feeling of insecurity began to chomp bigger bits of his guts. He'd been screwed by friends before! Royally.

"You still there?" Gordon asked.

"Yeah. I'm thinking."

"You want to call me after the meeting and let me know what they say?"

"Okay, Gordon. And thanks."

The people from Telstar were just completing their discussion when Mike arrived at Lubow's office and was shown in by the secretary. Kikky Hunt and Louise Carlin nodded to him; Parson McAdams shook his hand. But nobody offered to introduce him to the Telstar people, three youngish long-haired types. *Don't be paranoid,* he thought.

"You have to understand our position, Mr. Lubow," the spokesman for the group was saying. "We need exactness. We work on precision. There are hundreds of difficult considerations when televising an event such as this by satellite. This is the tenth of July. We've got to have a definite schedule within two or three days from now or we'll miss out on half our receiving countries. Do you have any idea what kind of figures we're talking about? Millions of people."

"I understand, Frank," Lubow replied. "The purpose of today's meeting is to settle that question. You'll have your schedule before you need it."

Frank nodded. He needed this information a month ago, but he shook hands all around, nodded to Mike, and left, followed by his two assistants.

"Jerry," Parson McAdams said to Lubow as the three engineers left, "this concert is going to be bigger than the Bicentennial."

"It could be, McAdams," Lubow answered. "But unfortunately I have a company to run, and so do you. And we don't have the resources available to us that the United States government had, so we shall have to settle for something a bit less grandiose than the Bicentennial. Even though the concert will be just as exciting."

"It's as though we are recreating an era," Louise

said. "The past and future coming together. But there's a lot of work to do."

Mike cleared his throat. "You know, I'm expecting to help with some of this responsibility. As producer of the reunion it should be my job to settle problems as they arise. I could assist the Telstar people. After all I've got a direct line to every aspect of this event and I'm informed." Lubow nodded, and Mike felt more courageous. "You know, Jerry, it's been bothering me that I haven't had more authority. You can all use my help." He included Carlin and McAdams in his speech.

Lubow ran his fingers through his thick hair, looking thoughtful, as though he was considering what Mike had said. Louise seemed agreeable too. Only McAdams stared at Mike with no reaction. Mike could feel Louise was on his side.

"One of the items on our agenda today is the nature of your duties, Mike," Lubow said. "It's been brought to my attention that you've been making promotional decisions with Gordon Wilson and the other advertising people, but you were never authorized to do that, were you?"

"What do you mean? You said yourself that I was in charge of promotion along with CAMIL's staff." Mike didn't like Lubow's tone; it was silky smooth with a hidden barb underneath. Exactly the way his father always baited him. He cursed himself for not getting something in writing that defined his exact duties. "Look Jerry, I've been functioning as a producer. Naturally I've supervised the advertising and promotion. You and I discussed my title when this whole idea was conceived, remember? Well, I've been producing. I've had daily reports from Antelope. You've seen them; I've sent you copies of everything."

"I didn't say you weren't efficient," Lubow soothed. "I appreciate your contributions, but you're missing my point. Wouldn't you agree that everything connected with this concert should be bigger than life?"

Mike nodded.

"And wouldn't you also agree that the name Mike Shaw is not exactly a household word. Except as Regina's husband."

"What's that got to do with anything?"

"Your name isn't big enough or famous enough to be listed as producer of the reunion. Maybe mine isn't even big enough for that matter," he added with a smile, "but if we use yours it smacks of nepotism and chauvinism. And that's why we've decided to use only my name as producer, along with CAMIL Records."

This was the first Louise had heard of this. She turned to Jerry in surprise and he shot her a "stay out of this" look.

"Yours alone?" Mike repeated. His head felt like it was being squeezed by a vise. This decision was crucial. If he lost the title, then the power would go. Everything would slip away again, right through his ineffective fingers. How far could he push? How much could he insist? "Jerry, you know this concert is so big anyone's name can be on the marquee and it wouldn't make any difference. It's not the promoter's name that matters; it's the stars. The public doesn't know Jerry Lubow from Adam and they don't care. They want their favorites, and as long as the music is sweet and the show is exciting, that's all that counts. I brought this reunion off. No offense," he said to Louise. "You might think you contributed, but it was I. I've been the only one who could make the members of Majesty want to work together again."

"What are you talking about, Shaw?" Lubow asked.

"Who does he think he is?" McAdams said to Louise.

"Hear me out," Mike insisted. "What I did wasn't easy. I went to Don before any of you got there, and I convinced him to agree." He ignored the look Lubow gave Louise Carlin. "I was the one who got Regina to agree too. And she was dead set against it."

Lubow stared at him and then nodded slightly. That part was true. He knew of course that Eddie Wakefield had tried to get Regina to agree. In fact he was so worried about Wakefield pushing himself into the production demanding a finder's fee or an active participation that Stylwickji had "convinced" Wakefield to leave the country for a while.

"It was my guts and my sweat and my know-how that went into this," Mike continued. Some of the color was coming back to his face. He felt as though he were pleading for his life against a prejudiced jury. And Lubow seemed to be listening. He'd be damned if he'd let them get away with his title. He had to be on that marquee!

"Now cool down, Mike," Lubow soothed. "Remember where you are. We all know how much you've done." Lubow's face was passive but his tone was accusatory again. "But I'm afraid we still can't agree with your request." He looked to McAdams for corroboration. McAdams nodded.

Mike was up and out of his chair, leaning over Lubow's desk. "I'll call the whole thing off, Jerry," he threatened. "I'll tell them not to go ahead. They'll listen to me."

"No one can call it off now, Shaw." McAdams's voice came at Mike from behind and he spun around. "Each member of the group has signed an agreement with CAMIL. I wrote those agreements myself. They would stand to lose over three million apiece if they backed out now."

Mike stuffed his shaking hands into his pockets and turned to Lubow, trying to calm his voice. "What if I accepted co-producer title. Jerry Lubow, Mike Shaw, and CAMIL Records Presents?"

Lubow was unmoved. "No one's asking what you'll

accept. Your name is not going to be on the marquee."

Mike burned with hatred for Lubow. Those cold steel-gray eyes, unfeeling. Everyone kowtowed to him and he was nothing but a lowlife.

"You'll still work behind the scenes. You'll still get your cut," Lubow said. "But it will be without marquee credit. Might as well understand that right now."

"Just what is my cut?"

"You'll get a percentage of the gate after we deduct what you owe me," Lubow replied.

"The three hundred thousand I owe you is a piss in the bucket compared to the one and a half million I'm entitled to as Regina's husband," Mike said. "It wouldn't do to underestimate me, Jerry. I know all about how you work, including some of your more underhanded dealings." Mike was furious. He didn't care who heard what he had to say. "Like Choo Choo Trainer. His aunt works for us, and Regina's told me all about Choo Choo's dealings. Exactly where he makes his buys and just who he sells his poison to." Mike loved the look of dismay on Lubow's face until the look turned to fury.

Lubow's eyes narrowed, and he rose to his feet. "Don't—ever—threaten—me—Shaw!" His body was flushed with anger, and he controlled himself with great effort. "That would be extremely foolish."

Louise reached over in alarm and placed her hand on Jerry's cautiously. He brushed her aside.

McAdams grabbed Mike's elbow. "You'd better leave now," he said firmly, pulling Mike toward the door. "I'm sure you don't mean to threaten Mr. Lubow, now do you?" He waited for Mike's reassurance.

Mike was startled by the reaction he'd stirred. He'd only meant to frighten them into giving him his way. He'd never really do anything with what he knew. Didn't they know that? He wanted to say, "Hey, it's just a joke." But it was too late for that. In another moment he found himself through the door and in the outer office.

McAdams closed the door after Mike and turned to his client. What a damn fool thing to do. Mike would be the loser in any showdown with Lubow. Any of them would if it came to that. Lubow had a mean streak when he was pressed. "He's a bit eager, Jer. He just got a little hot under the collar. You can't blame him."

"He's a cocksucker and a fool! Nobody threatens me! I thought Stylwickji took care of that Choo Choo Trainer," he mumbled. "Now I've got to worry about what Regina knows. Shit!" He pushed the buzzer on his panel and the door to his private entrance opened. Stylwickji entered, wearing his usual three-piece suit and dark glasses. The scar under his left eye was strikingly visible below the rim of the dark lenses.

"I want Mike Shaw to be taught some respect," Lubow told him. "Let me know exactly what he does, where he goes, and who he talks to. Make sure that Regina Williams keeps her mouth shut too!"

Stylwickji nodded and disappeared into the private office again, closing the panel after him.

Louise couldn't contain herself. Mike Shaw was a desperate man who had spoken out of turn. She couldn't let Lubow turn Stylwickji lose on him or his wife. "Jerry," she pleaded, "call him back. Mike is just upset. He'd never do anything against you. Neither would Regina, no matter what she knows. Or else she'd have done it long before now. Everyone in Majesty is Mike's friend. They all trust him to keep things going smoothly. It wouldn't do to upset the delicate balance. This reunion could run into difficulties any time. We need Mike as a troubleshooter. He can smooth egos and tempers; he's valuable."

"Don't tell me my business, baby. I know what I'm doing. I know Mike's strengths and his weaknesses.

Believe me, nobody is indispensable, least of all him! But at this point we'll just keep our eye on him."

She exchanged looks with McAdams. Just keep an eye on him? Terrific. Unless that eye has a scar running through it.

Penny lay on the pool deck trailing her hand in the water. In spite of her concern about Beau she was happy. It was so beautiful here, living in all this luxury. She tried to picture the baby growing inside of her. What would he or she look like? (Her abdomen was still smooth.) This baby would be born with every advantage, but that wasn't as important as having happy parents. One of the main reasons Penny wanted Beau to be more content with himself was for the baby's sake. Unborn infants could sense things, and Beau was so worried all the time. But she couldn't understand why. There was nothing to worry about. His music was good. Everybody said so. But he was still so unsure of himself. He was afraid that he wasn't doing his part, that his contributions were less than everyone else's. But that wasn't true. Couldn't he see the obvious? The others just found it easier to work together than they did with him. "Give it time," she'd told him, but he was impatient. And moody! She'd never seen him so moody. One minute he'd be up and the next shot down into such a deep hole that even she couldn't reach him. And when he wasn't working he was preoccupied with something else. Always running off to see someone, though nobody else around here was in any hurry about anything. *Least of all me,* she thought.

The sun felt so good on her body. She was getting tan from lying out every day, and her skin was turning a golden color everywhere the bikini didn't cover. Soon her nipples would turn brown and her stomach would swell in preparation for the baby. But so far nothing had changed except the size of her breasts and a feeling of well-being that held her in protective tenderness.

If only she could get Beau to start enjoying his success. He had to realize how talented he was. Look at the way Fideo, the owner of Antelope, was being kind to them. There were fresh flowers in their room every day, and the kitchen prepared special health foods for her. Everyone was so thoughtful. If only Beau would ease up on himself, maybe they could get back to lovemaking. He hadn't touched her in ages. Of course he'd been under a lot of pressure, but she couldn't go without sex for nine months. She was sure that her pregnancy was the problem. She'd read in a magazine that some men were frightened to have sex with their wives during pregnancy as though it would hurt the baby. But the article said there was no danger unless the pregnancy wasn't secure. And her pregnancy was perfect. Not a single problem since the moment she missed her first period.

She turned herself over on her stomach and pressed herself against the mat. Its soft terry cover caressed her warm skin, and she couldn't resist rubbing herself against it. Her nipples hardened and she felt an immediate response to the sensual movement. It had been a long time. Maybe tonight Beau would be more like himself. Maybe tonight she would tell him to read that article about sex during pregnancy, and he'd stop being so withdrawn.

The sound of music that floated to her through the warm summer air reminded her of what she was doing here, and she drifted into her favorite daydream. Beau was on stage dressed in a white satin suit with glittering lapels, only he had curly hair like Don Drummond and a build more like Don's. A huge crowd of people were chanting his name, screaming for him to play his music. He bowed and smiled at her. She was standing backstage holding their newborn child in her arms. (Her figure was better than it had ever been.) And then Beau began to play and sing just the way Don Drummond did, only he dedicated his song to her. Penny sighed and stretched. Oh, life was so wonderful!

CHAPTER 30

Beau was trying to hang on to the beat, but the sticks felt like wet spaghetti in his hands. The sight of Fideo standing in the sound booth watching him through the glass made him sick. The sickness was with him all the time now. Sweat dripped down his back, poured from under his arms, ran down his face; he had to keep wiping the back of his hand across his forehead. Jesus, he was off count! How could he be off count? Don shot him a look of disgust. *Does he know about me?* Beau wondered. *If Don knows, he'll get rid of me!* He closed his eyes and tried to get into the number, grabbing at the music to blot out his consciousness. When he opened his eyes again, Fideo was gone. *What am I going to do,* he wondered. There was a shooting pain in his rectum that ached all the time. *Don't think about it,* he told himself. He shifted his weight to his right cheek and bit down on the inside of his mouth to keep from crying out. *Concentrate, concentrate! Oh God, please help me.*

The skin between his toes itched, sending shivers of fire up his legs. A sign that his last dose was wearing off. Soon it would be time for more. Time to use. Time for peace. All he needed was peace, sweet peace. His life was so unreal. He forced himself to block out the sexual encounters with Fideo and think only about the reward that came afterwards. The first few times he allowed Fideo to use him, he had been physically sick and vomited into the toilet. Every vile name he could think of, he called himself. Until a kind of resignation occurred. And then the most horrible thing of all; he'd lost his ability to play music. It was gone somewhere along with his self-respect. He had to find it again! What if he never got it back? Then he couldn't go on. The music coming out of him now was nothing but dirt and filth. Sounds unfit for anyone. *I ought to quit,* he thought. *Go somewhere until I get my head straight. I'm no good for anybody here.*

Regina stopped singing in the middle of the song and turned to look at him, then she sighed and laid her head down on the keyboard. "Good God!" she whispered.

Don gave a smirk to his backup drummer, and Beau wanted to smash them both. Regina's disappointment reached right into him. It was all his fault. He wiped his wet hands on his jeans and shifted his weight to the other cheek. A picture of Fideo's evil pudgy face flashed to him, and immediately the sickness rose again. If he could just concentrate on Penny, think of her sweetness and her trust, he'd get through this somehow. She was the only reason he stuck it out. He couldn't bear what it would do to her if he quit. And if he walked out on Majesty, he'd probably never work again. Back to the dives and the crummy tours and sweating out his connections. *I've got to get straight,* he thought. *If only Cord were here right now.* When Cord was around, Beau felt more secure, as though he was protected from Regina's temper which could lash out at any moment and from Don's scorn which was more obvious all the time.

Regina sat up and called out, "One more time."

Beau gave her the beat. She played two intro chords and stopped. "Give me that again, Beau."

He beat the accompanying sound to the second three bars, and she hummed a slightly different tune than the one she'd been singing before, stopping now and then to jot down the melody.

"I don't like that variation, Regina," Don said sharply.

"I think it's an improvement."

"It's not! And the beat's not the same either. Morgan threw you off. He throws everything off!"

"I thought it might be better this way," Beau mumbled.

"You're not here to think. You're here to play what we tell you to play," Don shouted.

"Shut up, Don," Regina said, glaring at him. "This is my number. You can do your thing on your own songs, but let me handle mine!"

"What's that supposed to mean?"

"Your last lyrics were a bunch of crap!"

"Listen, you bitch, *I* can write music. *You* can't write your name."

Everyone in the studio had stopped to watch them. Their tempers were as legendary as their fame, and this explosion had been coming for weeks.

Beau was shaking. He couldn't let the whole concert blow because of him. "Wait, please! Don. Regina. It's all my fault. I shouldn't have improvised." The terror in his voice reached them and they both stopped yelling and glared at him, glad to blame him. He shrank into himself, into a puddle of his own sweat. Finally, Don turned and yanked off his earphones, threw them down and stomped out of the room, nearly colliding with Cord, who was coming in.

"Well, good morning," Cord said sarcastically. Don didn't pause.

Regina barely looked at Cord. "Give me that opening the way you improvised it, Beau," she asked. Don had really upset her. He was up to his old tricks again. How dare he say those things to her. God, he was infuriating. He hadn't changed one hair in all the years she'd known him.

Beau tried to recapture the improvisational beat

he'd done before. Regina nodded and closed her eyes, playing the new variation.

"Listen to this," she said to Cord. She really felt the song this time. It was working.

Cord came over to stand behind her, listening as she played it through. "That's very good," he said, dropping his hands to her shoulders for a moment. And then she wrote the notes on the music sheet while Cord tuned up his guitar.

Beau felt the awful tension of the past few minutes subside and a semblance of normalcy return. "Is it okay if I take five?" he asked.

But Regina jumped at him. "Your 'fives' always turn into 'twenty-fives,' Beau. I'd rather you didn't leave just at the moment."

Cord looked up, alerted by her tone, but he didn't interfere. And Beau realized things were still too tense for him to insist on taking a break. He looked at the clock. Still two hours till lunch. By then he'd be totally strung out. *I'll give it another half hour,* he thought, *and then insist on a break.* Regina was a dynamo when she was working.

Don was furious. It galled the hell out of him to let that bitch get the last word. Beau Morgan was an incompetent. He had to find a way to get rid of him. But he only had one vote in the matter. As usual Cord and Regina were in tight, just like the last time. He'd been a bloody fool to fall for that line, "Regina's dying to work with you again." All she had wanted to do was get hold of Cord's cock! He couldn't wait until Louise Carlin got here. She'd see how shitty Morgan was, contract or no contract. Then maybe they could get rid of that creepy bugger. Weasels like Morgan made you ache to step on them. They were always asking for it. Well, he'd be damned if Beau Morgan was going to achieve fame on his coattails. The dummy had hamhocks for hands!

As his eyes grew accustomed to the bright sunlight, he could see the blue of the ocean off to the left. Too bad England didn't have weather like this, all this gloriousness was wasted on the Californians. He stretched out on a lounge chair and closed his eyes when a woman's voice called to him.

"Hello."

It was Morgan's adoring little wife waving to him from across the pool. She was a cute little cunt with a nice body. She beckoned. *Why not?* he thought and stripped off his clothes down to his briefs and dove into the pool. He bobbed up right next to where she was sitting and gave her his famous grin. She giggled.

"Good morning, loverly lady," he drawled.

Penny twinkled her smile. "In all the time we've been here we haven't been properly introduced. I'm Penny Morgan and I've loved you for years." It wasn't what she'd meant to say, and she blushed.

He pulled himself out of the pool on straight arms and turned to sit on the edge, his body dripping water onto her pad.

"'ave you now?" he replied. "And you 'ardly look old enough to remember me from way back then." He always dropped his *h*'s when he flirted with a bit of fluff.

"Oh, I'm not as young as I look. I mean, I'm not very old, but I've been around."

"'ave you now?" he said again and they both laughed.

She reminded him of a box of pink and white taffy, all wrapped up in twisted paper and begging to be unwrapped. He could almost taste the flavor as he'd sink his teeth into the soft chewy confection. Taffy was his weakness, but candy was fattening.

"I can't tell you how thrilled my husband is to be working with you," she offered. "He admires you so much. You're all he talks about."

Beau Morgan couldn't stand him. Beau Morgan was

afraid of him, so it was obviously not her husband's admiration of which she spoke. "What exactly does he say?" he grinned, taking a wet hand from the pool and dripping water from his fingertips onto her shoulder where it made lazy trails down her arm to her hand.

Penny never took her eyes from his, barely able to speak. To have Don Drummond sitting here so close like this with his underwear clinging to him. She dared not look down or she'd never stop staring. Her heart was pounding so loudly she thought he must be able to hear it.

"He says you're an incredible musician and he wants so much to be an asset to the group." Her voice shook with emotion.

Don dipped his hand in the water again; only this time he dripped the water further up her shoulder so that the moisture made tiny trails down her chest and across her firm round breasts. He followed the trail with his eyes as the droplets were absorbed by the fabric of her bathing suit. Her nipples came erect through the cloth, and she shivered.

"Don't you think Beau's going to be an asset?" she whispered.

"Oh yes," he smiled and leaned forward to kiss her small upturned nose. "He has wonderful taste in music and even better taste in women." He kissed her cheek and the side of her face with soft breathy kisses.

Penny swallowed hard and turned away. She couldn't breathe. What was he doing? God help her, she didn't want him to stop. She felt just like Regina must have felt when Cord kissed her.

Don reached over and took her chin in his hand, turning her face to his. "You're a very sweet luv, you know that?" And then he leaned forward, touching his lips to hers, lightly, gently. Pieces of taffy were better if eaten one by one, not all at once. *Wouldn't want to get sick, now would we?* he thought. He could feel her trembling beneath his hand. *Very nice!*

He stood up then, dripping water on her while his erection poked out of his briefs, but he made no move to cover it. *Let her see,* he thought. "Will you be around later?" he asked with a voice full of meaning.

"Oh yes! I'll be here."

And he winked before he walked away, knowing he had a delicious afternoon interlude ahead of him, and knowing also that it might be just the wedge he needed to get rid of Beau Morgan.

CHAPTER 31

Mike had to get Lubow to understand how important the title of producer was to him. It could mean a whole career, a chance to pull himself out of the hole he'd been in for years. And even if people thought he was riding Regina's coattails, he didn't care. He knew how much work he'd done and damn the opinions of the world. If only he hadn't said those things to Lubow. He might have ruined his chances. *Jesus, that was dumb of me,* he thought. *Why do I say things I'm sorry for when it's too late to call them back?*

Louise Carlin's phone call didn't make him feel any better.

"I'm terribly worried about you, Mike," she said. "You should never have spoken to Jerry that way." An edge of fear underscored her words, and Mike heard it in her tone. This was serious. He'd really done it this time!

"But I didn't mean what I said. I was sorry one minute afterwards."

"I knew you were, but he's still very angry. I think you should get out of New York immediately. And make it very clear to Regina that she must never reveal anything she knows about the man you mentioned or about our mutual friend Lubow."

"Regina wouldn't say anything."

"But you've got to be careful. Does Regina have any personal protection at Antelope?"

"Why?" he asked. His heart gave an unauthorized leap.

"Because, I think she might need it." Louise's voice sounded desperate.

Mike was shocked—but only for a moment. He'd been around music people long enough to know how dangerous some of them could be. He knew—oh how well he knew—who he was toying with. He pulled himself together quickly, not wanting Louise to know how frightened he was.

"I'm leaving for L.A. first thing in the morning," he told her.

"Now, Mike. Leave now!"

But when he called to change his reservations, there was an airline strike and seats were at a premium. He was one of the fortunate ones to be getting out in the morning.

He started drinking right after Louise's call, sobered up by five, then started again at dinner. At midnight he staggered into his room at the Waldorf and fell across the bed. The summer humidity of New York was stifling. Piece by piece he peeled his clothes off and then passed out.

An hour later the operator woke him with a confirmation on his L.A. flight in the morning. He went to the toilet and peed a quart of water, drank another quart from the tap, and fell back into bed with the air conditioning blasting. It was several hours later when something woke him.

Stillness.

The room was pitch black and it was hot. The air conditioning had gone off, and he was perspiring. And then he heard a floorboard creak. A sudden feeling of fear clutched him. For a moment he couldn't orient himself or find the reason for his fear. And then a bright light flashed in his eyes blinding him, and something cold and sharp stuck into his neck. A knife!

"Not a word out of you, you hear?" a voice rasped in the darkness.

Hands yanked him off the bed, and the light blazed in his eyes. This had to be a nightmare! But no, he was awake. He could feel the carpet beneath his feet and another sharp pain as someone grabbed his wrist from behind and twisted his arm, nearly dislocating it.

In spite of the knife at his throat he cried out. "Who are you? I don't have any money."

"Shut up!" the raspy voice ordered, slapping him across the face. Hands pushed him forward, and a dull pain shot up his shoulder as the man behind pressed hard, twisting the socket.

"Don't please!" he gasped, feeling the sharp point of the knife pressing under his chin.

"When I say quiet, I mean quiet!" The voice again.

Outside the rim of light Mike saw a tall man in front of him. He was wearing glasses and he had light hair. There was the glimpse of a white shirt and the darkness of a suit. The man holding him from behind smelled like tobacco and liquor and something else he couldn't place. And then he knew what it was. Hatred. The man pressing his arm up out of its sockets would kill him with pleasure. His knees almost gave way under him, but he held on. *Am I going to die?* he wondered. *Is this it? In this crazy moment?* He would never see the concert. He would never prove himself to anyone. Who would care if he died? He would! Dammit! He would care.

"I have a message from Mr. Lubow," the voice said.

Mike could hear the sound of his own heart pounding. Lubow? Did he say Lubow? The man behind gave him another twist, and hot pain burned his shoulder. He wanted to scream.

"Mr. Lubow doesn't like your mouth. He asked me to shut it for you."

Here it comes, Mike thought as he heard the click

of another switchblade. *Oh God, there's got to be a way out of this!* Raspy Voice stepped up to him, and he clenched his stomach muscles as the cold steel of the knife slid inside the elastic of his trunks. With a swift movement the elastic was cut, and his trunks fell to the floor leaving him exposed and vulnerable. The tip of the knife pressed into his left ball.

"Oh Jesus," he whispered.

"If it's so important to show you've got balls, Shaw, be sure you can hang onto them," the voice said, giving the knife a push. "One word out of you about Mr. Lubow or any of his dealings and this one right here will be the first to go." The knife turned sideways, giving his ball a slight bounce.

Mike had never known such fear. But he didn't utter a sound. He could almost hear himself sweat as his senses filled with the stink of the man behind him. Raspy Voice smelled like expensive cologne. Mike's brain churned and plotted. Could he possibly overpower both men? Would he live long enough to try?

He sensed rather than saw the signal Raspy Voice gave to the man behind him, and the sharp knife pressing into his throat was removed along with the one sticking into his groin. But just as the sweetness of reprieve flooded him, Raspy Voice let go with a fist into his gut.

"Ohhh!" he gasped and doubled over. There was no breath in him at all. Nothing but pain. And then before he could breathe again, another fist to his jaw sent him backwards onto the bed. He felt as though he was falling into a black hole. The filaments from the flashlight burned round hot circle into his retina, and his head and his body exploded with throbbing pain. He heard the door to the room open, letting in a whiff of hotel air. He turned to look, saw the face of the tall blond man, the horrible scar on his cheek, a fitting punctuation for this terror.

"Tell your wife to keep her mouth shut too, Shaw.

Or we'll be glad to pay her a visit at that fancy ranch and shut it for her."

And then he was alone.

He curled up on the bed, pulling his knees up to his chest, while he fought the feeling of fear and invasion. He shoved the pillow against his mouth to muffle the hatred burning inside. Those bastards! Those stinking bastards! My God, Regina! He had to get her away from Antelope. Keep her safe with him. They had no right! And then he realized that he was alive, and he almost wept for the joy of it. Maybe he ought to quit right now. Right this minute! Is that what they wanted him to do? No. Lubow was just trying to scare him into keeping quiet about Choo Choo. Well, he was damned scared all right. He wouldn't say a word about anything. He'd be absolutely silent if only he could finish what he'd started. He'd speak to Regina. She'd never say anything either.

His shoulder and his stomach and his jaw ached, and the images of round filaments still burned into his eyes, reminding him of how close he'd come. He'd been a fool to shoot off his mouth like that. Nobody threatened Lubow and got away with it. What good had it done? He'd only put Regina in danger.

There was no use in trying to go back to sleep, so the rest of the night he waited depressed and fearful, for morning.

CHAPTER 32

The minute Regina stepped into the shower the phone rang. She threw on her terrycloth robe and ran wet and dripping to answer it.

"Hello, Mommy?" It was Jamie. "I'm sick, Mommy." A loud croupy cough underscored her claim. "I want you to come home!"

Oh God, not again, Regina thought. She had prayed Jamie's health would improve over the summer. Poor Jamie.

"What does the doctor say?" Regina asked.

"I have an ear'n'fecshun, and he gave me the cherry medicine again. My ear really hurts, Mommy. Are you coming home now?"

Regina sank down on the edge of the bed. The tears that she had held back all week were very close to the surface. "Let me talk to Daddy," she said.

"Reg? How's it going?"

"All right, I guess. When did you get back from New York?"

"Yesterday," he said

"What's wrong with Jamie?"

"She's pretty sick, poor baby." Regina could just see them. Mike was probably sitting on their bed with his arm around Jamie, her face flushed with the redness of fever and her eyes having that glazed look. Regina used to take Jamie into bed with her when she was sick, and just by putting her hands on the small feverish body, the fever would be lowered. She had such a bond with those two children. And through them to Mike. But she couldn't stay married to Mike now that Cord had come back into her life. For the first time in years she felt really alive.

"What does Dr. Weston say?" she asked.

Mike put his hand over the receiver, but she could hear what he said. "Jamie, why don't you go and get back into bed. I want to talk to Mommy by myself. Go on now." He waited a moment. "Reg?"

"Yes, I'm here."

"The doctor is afraid of a mastoid infection. I think it's serious. There's talk of hospitalizing her. You'd better come home." He hesitated. "Besides that there's something I want to discuss with you."

Regina's knuckles ached as she gripped the receiver. "I can't come home now!" she cried. "I'm right in the middle of composing and rehearsing. They're bringing movie cameras in here tomorrow which means makeup and hairdos every day. Do you have any idea what it's like here? The tension? The nerves? And what do you have to talk about that's so important? Can't you take care of anything?"

"I am taking care of things. But your child may go to the hospital, Regina. I think you should be with her. And I need you too. I need to talk to you." He paused a moment and then suddenly as though the thought had just occurred to him he said. "I know why you're reluctant to come home. It's Cord, isn't it? You can't tear yourself away from him, can you?"

A heavy silence hung between them in the miles that separated them while she fought for a reply.

"Am I right, Regina? he asked. His voice sounded wild, cornered, as though he knew precisely what she'd been doing every minute since he'd been away. *Oh Michael,* she thought, *what's happened to us?* She felt split in two. The heartless bitch mother. Where were her loyalties? Which were her most important obligations? What did men do in these situations? Or did these things only happen to her? She reached for a cigarette, put it down, picked it up again, and lit it, taking a deep drag. It was the worst possible thing for her voice. She'd promised Cord she'd stop smoking. So far she'd quit four times. "Michael."

"Yes, Regina," he answered sarcastically.

"Keep me informed moment by moment. If Jamie's fever doesn't come down or if she goes to the hospital, I want to know about it. But if I come home now, she'll know she can get me to run every time she's sick. And whatever else you want to talk about will have to wait."

"Dammit, Regina!" There was that touch of hysteria again, of a child lost in a dark forest, the hideous sounds of unnamed fears and nightmares. She knew those sounds well. "Please come home," he begged.

She turned to the open door. Cord was standing there staring at her. "All right, Michael," she sighed. "All right."

When she hung up the phone, she realized that she was still wet from the shower, but she ran to Cord and threw herself into his arms, shaking from pent-up fury and frustration. She was filled to the brim with all the anger she wanted to unload on Mike and from something else she had detected in his voice. What was that sound?

Cord felt her shivering and closed the door. "Shhh," he soothed. "Tell me what happened?"

"Oh God, he's infuriating," she said.

"I could have told you that before you married him." Cord took her into the bathroom to get a dry robe. He turned on the heater and stood her in front of it, rubbing her arms in the dry robe until she stopped shivering.

She told him about Jamie.

"Shouldn't you be there?" Cord asked quietly.

"I don't know where I'm supposed to be," she cried. "I'm so torn. Who wrote the commandment that says, 'Thou shalt sacrifice thy career for the sake of thy children'?"

He just looked at her, offering her no solace, no answer. She went back into the bedroom and grabbed the receiver, jiggling the button to get the operator's attention. "This is Regina Williams. Please have the plane ready for me to go to Los Angeles, and if it's not available, book me on the next flight out of Monterey." She turned to him. "There. Is that what you wanted?"

"Don't be childish," he snapped.

"Oh, leave me alone," she shoufed, "and get out of here!"

"Regina, there's no reason to lose your temper."

"I'll lose my temper if I want!" she yelled, pushing him out the door. "Ohhh, damn!" she shouted, stamping around the cabin, throwing a few things together she'd need at home.

Jamie would be fine! The doctor had it under control. This was something Mike and Jamie had cooked up to get her to come home. Well, she'd call their bluff. She'd go home; she'd take the chance of ruining the rehearsals; and she'd soothe everybody's ego. She'd do it all, as usual. Wife, mother, performer, lover. "Shit, shit, shit!" she cried as the operator called to tell her the plane would be ready to leave in forty-five minutes.

Cord was standing on the porch of the cabin as she stormed by. "Tell them I'll be back in a day or two; and tell them I'll finish my new songs at home; and tell them that whatever I write will be better than anything *any* of you can do. And tell them to go FUCK themselves!"

Cord followed her down the stairs as the cart arrived to take her to the Antelope van which would whisk her to the airport. Just as she reached the cart, he called out to her. "Hurry back, Regina. Please."

His words caught her, and she stopped and turned.

He looked so beautiful standing there, the sun highlighting his gold hair, his hands plunged into his pockets. He was a parenthesis encasing her future. What would it hold? The look on his face was both vulnerable and determined. He was revealing himself this once, perhaps he never would again. For a moment that insight grabbed her, and she almost went back. But the moment passed. "I have to go, darling," she said and climbed into the van. "But I'll be back soon." *Mike needs me,* she thought. And as the cart drove away, she was struck with a sudden memory of what that sound in Mike's voice meant. It was the way he sounded when he had made some colossal screwup.

Her house always looked wonderful to her when she came home after being away. It was a beautiful haven, safe from the world until the world intruded. Bertie organized her business activities, and Florie took care of all her personal requirements, but still there were many demands made on her, scripts to read for TV appearances, movie offers (she was always looking for a good script). And the decorators had finally secured the architect and builder she and Mike wanted so they could begin the addition to the house. It would have a sauna and a gym for Mike, and a rehearsal hall for her, complete with recording equipment. Again the tedious details drained her. But once it was completed, she'd love it.

Mike helped her out of the limousine and put his arms around her. She stiffened. It felt wrong to be here after Cord's embrace. She missed Cord already, resented this interruption of their idyll. Infidelity was as difficult as being unhappily married.

"How's Jamie?" she asked.

"The antibiotics are working. She's going back to school tomorrow."

Regina looked at him in amazement. "I came all

the way home for this? That's typical, Michael, really typical." She pushed past him and entered the house, detecting a faint odor of dust. No one ever opened a window unless she was home, and all the plants would have puddles of water in their drainage dishes from being overwatered. But someone was cooking; delicious scents of saffron and garlic permeated the air. Florie. God bless her. She knew Regina would need something pleasant to come home to.

Mike followed her up the stairs. "How was the flight?"

"Short and bumpy." Her bathroom was spotless. Even though she'd showered only hours ago, she turned on the water in the tub. Mike hovered, and her anger toward him exuded through every pore; the air was soggy with it. He watched her undress and step into the water. "Close the door," she said. "It's chilly in here."

He closed the door, but stayed in the bathroom. She didn't look at him as she soaped herself. *Oh, Cord!* she thought, missing him.

"How long can you stay at home?"

"I should get back right away, but as long as I'm here, I'm going to get some work done. The distractions at Antelope are not conducive to concentration or creative thought."

"I'll bet."

"Cut the sarcasm, Mike. There's a lot of tension between Beau Morgan and the rest of us. I'm not so sure it's working with him, and it's too late to find anyone else. I'm very concerned. I don't want to end up looking like a fool."

He held up his hands. "I'm sorry."

She lay back in the water and closed her eyes. Outwardly she looked relaxed; inwardly her nerve endings were raw. She wanted Mike to leave her alone with her thoughts, yet she was afraid to ask him to go. He was needy too. Whatever it was he had brought her home to say lay between them, floated on the surface of her bath like globules of oil that refused to emulsify.

He sat on the john and leaned on his knees. "Can we talk?"

Here it comes, she thought and opened her eyes. His face looked strained and thoughtful. "Okay."

He shifted on the seat. "I ran into some trouble in New York."

Her nerve endings jumped again. "What is it going to cost me?"

"It's not money. And it's nothing I can't handle."

"I'll bet."

"Will you listen?"

She nodded. The water was lukewarm so she stood up and reached for her robe. He helped her out of the tub and into the fleecy garment. His hand lingered on her back. Again she felt guilty as she moved away.

"I may have done something foolish, Regina."

Her senses were suddenly wary. *Don't say anything,* she thought, *just listen.* "Go on."

"I threatened to expose Jerry Lubow's drug connections."

"Everybody knows about that."

"Not the authorities."

"You didn't threaten to tell *them,* did you?"

"Well, not really, but I lost my temper."

"That wasn't very bright! Lubow can be dangerous."

"Don't you think I know that?"

"What made you lose your temper?"

"He refused to put my name up as producer of the reunion. It means a great deal to me."

They went into the bedroom and sat on the lounge chairs by the window. This wasn't such terrible news, she thought, feeling slightly relieved. "Why would you expect to be named producer of the reunion? Lubow never gives anything away."

"I'm entitled to it, Regina. I was instrumental in

bringing off the reunion. I've been working behind the scenes as unofficial producer."

"You?" This was the first she'd heard of this.

He nodded. "I was going to surprise you."

"I'm surprised all right. Very surprised." She looked at him with new interest. "How have you managed to do all this? I thought Jerry Lubow was the one."

"Well, he asked me to help him, and I've been organizing all the independent theaters who've subscribed to the closed circuit broadcast. I've worked with the design people on the album covers; I've had half a dozen meetings with the Superdome group; and as for ticket sales, that's been my responsibility too. Of course, the ad campaign is what I'm most proud of."

"I'm impressed." And she was, she realized. She began to relax a little.

"I've worked damn hard on this project, and I'll continue to work no matter what happens with the marquee credit because this could be a whole new career for me. But damn that Lubow. He's taken all the desire out of me."

"Do you want me to say anything to Jerry? I could insist that he give you what you want."

"No! I'll do this on my own." He paused. "There's something else." His eyes took on that look he got when he was trying to con her. She hated that look. She felt a heavy weight descend on her shoulders as she waited to hear what he was going to say.

"Lubow sent a couple of goons after me. Two nights ago they broke into my hotel room in New York and roughed me up." He was still scared and it showed. "They wanted to make sure that I kept my mouth shut about what you and I know about Choo Choo, and they threatened to do the same thing to you." He swallowed to stop the quaver in his voice. "They were going to hurt you. That's why I wanted you to come home from Antelope."

She stared at him for a moment while the realization of what he was saying hit her. Her husband, beaten by hoodlums, criminals! "Oh, Michael." She moved over to him and put her arms around him. He held on to her. "Are you all right? Did they hurt you badly?" There it was again. Those unnamed terrors always lurking. They could leap out and ruin your life at any moment! She clung to him, shaking.

Mike was talking. "What really scared the shit out of me was their knives. They said they'd cut off my balls if I didn't keep my mouth shut. They'd do it, too. You know what I was thinking while that that steel knife was pressed against my testicles? That this sure as hell wouldn't help our sex life. It's funny what you think at a time like that."

"Oh, Michael. That Lubow is a bastard! He can't do that to you! He owes me! What right does he have to treat us this way! I'd like to cut off *his* balls! If anybody tried to come near me, I'd kill them. I swear I would. I'll get the gun. I'll take it back with me to Antelope. Where is it?" She looked around as though she expected it to be on her nightstand.

Mike laughed and a bit of his tension eased. "You're some fighter when you're angry. You'd really do it, wouldn't you?"

"You're damned right. Nobody can hurt the people I love and get away with it." She was shocked at her own feelings. She cared. Dammit, she really cared. And she would kill to protect them all if she had to.

"It's been a long time since you've said you loved me," he said softly.

"Of course I love you, Michael. I'm married to you, aren't I?"

"Yes. But I've been expecting you to tell me any day you didn't want to be married anymore. And after this I wouldn't blame you. Hell, there have been plenty of times I wouldn't have blamed you. But you've stuck it out. You're still here."

She looked down at her hands.

"I know I've made some enormous mistakes, Regina, but they're all in the past now. I'm going to make you proud of me; I swear I will."

"I am proud of you, Michael." She smiled at him. "I know how you try. Maybe you just shouldn't try so hard. Maybe things would be better between us."

He nodded.

"How's Florie been?"

"I've been wanting to tell you that I took her to a doctor—a cardiologist—"

"I know," she said—nothing else needed to be said. They both knew what it meant.

"She's terribly upset. When I arrived home yesterday, I just couldn't pretend in front of her, and then she saw the doctor checking me for any injuries. She feels responsible because of Choo Choo's part in all this. She's ready to kill somebody too."

"Oh, Mike, I wish you hadn't told her. She worries so, and it's not good for her. I hate that weasel Choo Choo!"

"Florie will be all right. It's you I'm concerned about. Perhaps we should hire a bodyguard."

"Michael, have you told me all of it?"

"What do you mean?"

She noticed a tightening around his mouth. "Is there any more? Because if you haven't told me everything, I want to hear it now. I can't take any more surprises, Mike. Please. Tell me. Is there any more?"

He stared at her for the briefest moment and then he said, "That's all of it, sweetheart. That's all." And he reached for her.

She let him hold her, surprised that she felt like crying. He was her husband after all. She didn't want anything to happen to him. Divided loyalties pulled at her. If only she could feel about him the way she felt about Cord. Hadn't she once? Long ago? She remembered the way he'd made her feel, loved and secure and safe. And there was passion too. They could recapture it again, couldn't they? It had to be there, buried under all his mistakes and her anger.

Mike kissed her cheek and her hair and held her tightly against him. She could feel his erection. *I owe him this, God knows I owe him his self-respect.*

He opened her robe and bent down to kiss her neck, moving softly to her shoulders and her breasts. His breath was warm against her skin, and he was trembling. She was too. This would be a renewal, an affirmation of life.

He took her hand and led her to the bed and then he removed her robe. Suddenly she saw him as he really was. Imperfect, but so dear to her. And as he lay beside her, she felt him come alive beneath her hands. The lover she'd wanted him to be, he now was, urging her, loving her, devouring her, fiercely, gently. What had happened? Had she stopped expecting this of him, and so now he was able? Had her concern for him proven her love? Was that what he needed, the one element she'd unconsciously withheld for so long, out of disappointment? But what about Cord? What did she feel for him? The confusion almost suffocated her. But then she stopped thinking and gave herself to the enjoyment of their lovemaking.

Afterwards Regina couldn't believe the irony; for so long she had prayed this would happen, and now it had happened when she least wanted it.

She reached over and took a cigarette.

Mike didn't flinch. In fact he lit it for her. She knew he wouldn't spoil this reconciliation with a reprimand about her smoking. "Do you remember the night Jana was born?" he asked.

She smiled as she exhaled. "What an event that was. I nearly didn't make it."

Mike stroked her arm and laid his hand on the inside of her thigh. It was a possessive move, both tender and claiming. "I was more frightened at the thought of losing you that night than I was when those men broke into my room. I figured if I died, well, that would be that. But if I lost you, I don't think I could go on."

She stared at him in the dimness of their room, her cigarette a glow of light between them. "You'd go on. You'd have to. The children would need you."

"No," he said. And then again, "No."

She knew he wasn't saying it out of weakness, but out of strength. He wanted her to know how much she meant to him and he'd never been able to tell her before, not like this. She thought at that moment that he knew about Cord and was trying to say to her, "Get it out of your system and come back to me. When you do, this is what it will be like."

She snuffed out her cigarette and reached for him again, feeling that deep sadness from her past threatening to build up and wash over her in one great wave of misery. But she fought it and clung to him.

"Thank you," Mike whispered in her ear. "I love you so much." And for the first time in her marriage she felt ashamed.

CHAPTER
33

Cord sat at one of the redwood tables around the large patio warming his hands on a cup of steaming coffee. He watched as the van unloaded the Shaw entourage. They were all here. He could hear the excited cries of the children as they pulled on their father's hand. Mike was followed by Florie; Regina brought up the rear. He saw her look around for him and he gave a slight wave. He didn't realize how much he'd missed her until this moment, and that same old longing assailed him. Why had she brought Mike back with her?

Florie saw him and waved, "Cord! You ol' devil! There you are." And she came waddling toward him all the way from the parking lot down the path past the cottages and up to the main building.

He met her halfway with a grin and a hug. "How are you, lady?" He squeezed her hugeness against him, remembering all the solace she'd given him when Gene died. What a wonderful woman she was. "You been feeling all right?" he asked.

She shrugged. "Off an' on."

Mike was ignoring the exchange between Cord and Florie. "But you're a sight! Skinny as ever. Don't you never eat?" she teased. Regina stood watching them, her body framed by the morning fog, hands on her hips, and the rest of her poured into her jeans and a white cotton shirt that hugged her breasts provocatively. She came toward him and he blinked to moisten his eyes, which were dry from staring at her.

"You look delicious," he said over Florie's head, and Regina shot him a look of caution.

Florie heard the tone in his voice and pulled away to study him. "Lord, Lord!" she exclaimed, surmising the truth from Cord's expression.

"Florie, would you please see that the children are organized for me. I imagine Cord has a lot to tell me."

Florie shook her head at them both and left.

"That's a formidable woman," he commented. "I've never known anyone like her . . . except you." He wanted to take her in his arms, claim her again after her absence. Images of her in Mike's bed, in Mike's house, had tortured him for the eight days she'd been gone. It wasn't going to be easy with Mike and the children here.

"How's Jamie?"

"Fully recovered. Her fever was down when I got home, and she went to school the next day. She's still taking the antibiotics, though."

"Why didn't you come right back?" he asked, remembering the lonely nights without her.

She seemed embarrassed. "Oh, you know how it is at home. There were some finish cuts to do on my last album, and the decorator kept me busy for days running around for fabrics for the new addition. Besides I did some composing for the concert."

"You're adding on to the house?"

She looked at him guiltily. "The plans were started last year. We've been waiting for the contractor to finish three other jobs, and now he's finally ours."

"Do you think it's wise to start a project like that now?"

She smiled sheepishly. "Probably not. But I didn't know what to say to Mike. It would have taken too much explaining to back out now. You know how

I am. I get involved in things. Can't stop once the wheels are in motion."

"Is that how it is with me?" His temper was beginning to boil. He'd been so sentimental about her, mooning around while she was gone, and she couldn't have cared less. The Beverly Hills matron, ad nauseam. He pushed past her angrily, tossing the remains of his coffee in the bushes.

"I'll see you in rehearsal," he shot back. "If you're not too involved elsewhere."

"Cord!" she called out.

But he kept walking. He didn't know who he was angrier with, her or himself. *I'm letting her do it to me again,* he thought. *Goddammit! She's doing it again.*

Regina felt the bottom slip out from under her. What could she do? She couldn't tell him the real reason Mike had called her home. And she had other obligations! A marriage, a family, a household, a career. She felt disloyal to both Mike and Cord. Well, at least she had used the time at home to write the music she'd been unable to write while she was here. And the songs she'd finished were good. She'd been looking forward to playing them for him, but now she'd lost her desire. Did he resent her bringing the children? No. It was having Mike here. Well, that couldn't be helped. Mike was making an effort to change. They'd had one of the best weeks of their marriage. She couldn't be insensitive to Mike now, not after what he'd been through. She'd settle things with Cord after the concert. But for now they would have to remain apart. And what would she decide then? To tell Cord good-bye or to divorce Mike? She couldn't imagine a divorce. How could she get along without Mike? All the years they'd spent together had been meaningful ones; they depended on one another, and his devotion to the children was total. She abhorred the thought of taking them away from him as a divorce would necessitate. And she didn't know what kind of father Cord would be. He was good with children, but he didn't even know hers yet. Well, this would be a perfect opportunity for Jamie and Jana to get acquainted with him. Cord had never said anything about getting married, but she was sure he was thinking about it. What if bringing Mike and the girls back here made him change his mind? Well, that couldn't be helped. She wanted her loved ones with her now, safe, where she could keep an eye on all of them. But her cavalier attitude about the results of her action belied the constricting of her heart when she thought about losing Cord.

"You're back!" Don was walking toward her, his arm draped possessively around Penny's shoulders. *When did this happen?* Regina wondered. A more unlikely pair she'd never seen. How did he juggle Penny with the princess? *I should talk,* she thought.

"Yes, did you miss me?" Obviously he hadn't.

"Well of course, luv." He grinned with satisfaction. The seat of Penny's pants were grass-stained, and so were the knees of Don's slacks. *That's what we need around here, a little hanky-panky among the children.*

"See you in rehearsal," Don called back. His right hand rubbed the nape of Penny's neck.

"How's Beau doing?" Regina called. Penny's back stiffened. She stopped and turned.

"He's been sleeping a lot lately. But then he's been working so hard." She sounded desperate, as though she were trying to explain.

Poor Little Red Riding Hood, Regina thought. *Her Woodsman is too sleepy to save her from the Wolf. Well, maybe this Grandma ought to give it a try.* "I'll join you." She put her arm around the other side of Don's waist. "Mmmm. You smell good. Is that the scent of Deceit by Fabergé?"

"Oh, no," Penny offered. "He wears Royal Briar by Atkinson. I just love it, don't you?"

"Oh, to be sure," Regina said, winking at Don, who took his arm from around Penny's shoulders. "Don has always 'smelled' . . . very nice."

Don threw his head back and laughed. "Regina, you're too much. The prize bitch of the century!"

"Takes one to know one, darling. Just wait until you hear what I've written."

"Been a busy girl in Los Angeles, hey?" His sense of competition was heightened.

"Ah, Don, I love to toy with you. You're so predictable."

They had arrived at the recording studio, and Regina pulled open the door for Don to follow her. Penny stopped at the entrance.

"Will I see you later?"

"Yes, sure," Don said, waving her away. "Later." And he followed Regina into the rehearsal hall.

CHAPTER 34

"Who's the blonde in the sound booth?" Regina asked Beau.

"I don't know," he replied.

The woman seemed to be staring at her with a judgmental attitude, and she didn't like it at all. Neither did she like the way Beau looked with his perennial runny nose. In the two weeks since she'd been back from Los Angeles Beau seemed to be worse than ever, as though he were suffering from some constant ailment. When Regina was impatient with him, he was so obsequious that she had to fight the temptation to be even rougher. He almost asked to be punished.

The blonde kept staring.

"Who is that woman?" she asked Don. He was working on a section of music and didn't answer her.

"Give me the beat on 'As We Like It,' Beau," Don barked. Beau's delicate condition didn't deter Don's animosity toward him. Sometimes Regina found Don's attitude catching; she found herself using Beau to ease her own frustrations. It was unkind of her, but he was so usable.

Beau started to play and got five beats into the song when Don yelled at him, "I said 'As We Like It,' stupid, not 'Brothers Three'!" He glared at Beau, who seemed to sink into his chair. The songs were basically a similar rhythm; it was an easy mistake. "You are one stupid man!" Don insisted.

Regina clapped her hands to her ears. "Will you two stop it!" she yelled. "All I ever hear from you is that he's stupid. He's not stupid!" She turned to Beau who sat there looking forlorn. But there wasn't anything positive she could find to say about him.

She turned back to the sound booth and saw Cord standing next to the blonde. There was fury in his eyes. He burst into the recording studio.

"What's going on here?" he demanded of the startled group. "What were you saying about him!" He shoved through the equipment to get to Don.

"It's none of your business, Cord!" Don retorted.

Cord grabbed him by the shirt. "And I say it is! You were giving him crap! Weren't you? Just like you did with Gene. You never know when to quit, you bully. Let the kid alone! He's sensitive, Don. Something you wouldn't know if you fell over it!" Cord's face was red, and the veins stuck out from his neck. He pulled Don toward him by the fabric of his shirt.

Don glared back and with a swift motion knocked Cord's hands away. "What are you defending, lover boy? Your sweetheart? Are you the one he's taking it in the ass for?"

Regina gasped. "Don!"

Cord uttered a wild sound and shoved Don, pushing him backwards against the amplifiers. Music stands, instruments, and equipment went flying. "You dirty bastard, you filthy, dirty bastard," Cord yelled. He was in a murderous rage. Regina had never seen him like this. Regina grabbed his arm, coming between him and Don.

"Stop it!" she said. "Cord!" He looked at her without seeing her.

"You can't defend the world, Cord. Beau can take care of himself. He's not Gene!"

The look Cord gave her sent knives into her.

Don scrambled up from the pile of instruments and

shoved Regina aside. He was shorter than Cord but more muscular. He let go with his left fist into Cord's abdomen, followed by his right to Cord's chest. One blow came right after the other, so that Cord was barely able to defend himself. He backed away hunched over from the blows and finally managed to let go with a right cross, catching Don on the chin and knocking him backwards again; only this time Don fell into Beau's drums with a loud boom.

Beau was shaking so, he could hardly see what was happening. All the other musicians had backed off and were keeping out of the way except for Regina.

"John!" she shouted to John Lawson. "Do something. Stop them!"

Lawson moved away from the wall into the melee and grabbed Don just as he was about to charge Cord again. Regina kept holding onto Cord, insisting, "Stop it! Stop it!" until finally Cord backed off. Both men were panting from exertion. Don pushed his drummer away and glared at Cord.

"You so much as touch me again, nursemaid, and this whole fuckin' fiasco is off! I won't walk on a stage with either of you!" He jerked his head toward Beau and disgustedly stomped out of the studio.

Regina was close to tears. "Are you all right?"

Cord was holding his battered side and breathing heavily. He pushed her hand away. "Leave me alone, will you."

Flushing with embarrassment she turned and went after Don, but a backwards glance told her the blonde in the booth had seen the whole thing.

Regina felt as though she was losing control. Cord was so unreasonably angry, so volatile, and still identifying with the underdog. They hadn't been alone once since she and Mike came back from Los Angeles, and he hadn't even asked to see her. At first she had been grateful for his restraint, but now it was beginning to weigh on her. Everything was so unsettled, though she and Mike had been getting along very well. The mutual threat against them both had brought them closer together. If it weren't for Cord her life would be very smooth right now. But she missed him, still wanted him. And today's blowup only made matters worse.

A subdued atmosphere hung over the restaurant at lunch. Don stayed away, and Regina wondered if Cord would too. But he turned up with the blonde from the sound booth hanging on his arm. The concert would never come off if he and Don continued like this, Regina thought.

"Louise Carlin," Cord said. "I don't think you've met Regina Williams, and this is Beau and his wife Penny Morgan." He went around the table. "Mike Shaw." Mike smiled at Louise.

"We've met of course. How are you?" He took her hand.

Regina raised an eyebrow. Mike was full of surprises lately. So *this* was the illustrious Louise Carlin. *Damn! She's beautiful.*

"I'm glad to be here," Louise was replying, "and anxious to get to work. Cord's been bringing me up to date on all that you've been doing."

"You can talk to Don later," Cord said. "What did you think of his form in action this morning?"

"I'd say you were both in rare form," Louise commented, and Cord laughed.

There was an electric current between these two that sent stabs of uneasiness through Regina. "Will you be here long?" Regina asked, her curiosity leaping out.

"That depends," Louise replied, glancing at Cord meaningfully, "on how quickly we make decisions and agree on arrangements. We're so pressed for time. But I'll be here as long as I'm needed, until all the tracks are mixed, and then I'll go on to New Orleans.

By the way I'd like you to know I've listened to everything that's been done so far and I love it. I've made some notes, but I have only a few suggestions."

"Only a few?" Regina commented. "How nice. I can't wait to hear them." She couldn't stop the resentment from showing. What could a woman like Louise Carlin possibly know about her music?

Mike was studying Regina's reaction to the competition with interest, and she knew he was enjoying her discomfort. She was trying not to let Louise Carlin bother her, but since they were seated opposite one another at the table, that was difficult. Louise was not only extremely attractive, but she was self-possessed as well and she had an intimacy with Cord that shocked Regina to the core. Regina's ravenous appetite which had been demanding attention only moments before suddenly departed, leaving her empty inside. And to make matters worse Jamie and Jana were coming to have lunch with her today for a much promised meal with Mommy. Just then she saw the girls enter the restaurant and she waved to them. Might as well make the best of it.

"Over here, sweethearts," she called.

And proudly they came forward in their matching shorts outfits with their double sets of ponytails. They kissed all the adults at the table, and Regina beamed.

"Will you all excuse me," she said, standing up. "I'm going to dine with my daughters today. Are you joining us, darling?" she asked Mike, who picked up her cue.

"Wouldn't miss lunching with my ladies."

For a moment she felt triumphant at the look of pain on Cord's face when he heard Mike's announcement, then she saw Louise looking at him too, taking it all in.

The four of them took a table by the window, leaving the others to dine on grown-up talk. But Regina's ears burned with the laughter of her rival, and the soft throaty way she talked, and the way she looked at Cord! Damn her! Why did she have to come here and ruin things?

"You're not eating your lunch, Mommy!" Jana reminded her as she played with her salad. "If I have to finish my samwich, then you have to eat too."

"That's right," Jamie chimed in. "Eat your vegchables like a good girl." Jamie could imitate Florie to a T.

Regina laughed and shared a moment of intimacy with Mike. The girls were an adorable consolation, and she was shamed into eating her vegchables.

Louise drove skillfully as she maneuvered one of Antelope's Mercedes around the mountain curves and turned right into the parking lot of Nepenthe.

She shut off the engine and turned to Cord, watching him with a tentative expression. Then she leaned over and kissed him. He smelled her perfume, remembering New York and how much he had wanted her. It wasn't fair of him to lead her on. He was using her. And judging from Regina's reaction at lunch today it was working too. At the same time he was struck by how much he cared about Louise.

She lingered with her head on his shoulder, the gear shift between them reminding him of his high school days.

"I wouldn't have thought of you as a home wrecker. But I don't blame you. Regina's an exciting woman."

"So are you," he said, kissing her hair. "Shall we go in?"

She nodded, and they both got out of the car.

He took her hand, and they climbed the long stairway to the restaurant. It was a gorgeous night. A canopy of brilliant stars shone overhead, and the air was warm and balmy. Inside the restaurant couples huddled together over candlelit tables, and waitresses with long hair and jeans served platters of huge hamburgers in the smoky room. Outside the huge glass windows was a dense blackness that could not obscure the presence of the immense ocean. It made the atmosphere inside all the more cozy.

Cord put his arm around Louise and drew her toward him sadly, as if protecting her from himself.

There was the usual flurry of head-turning, eyes craning to see him as he stood tall and conspicuous by the door. A table was hurriedly cleared in a private corner, and they made their way through the crowded room. Only a few people called his name. Happily, he didn't know anyone.

They ordered iced-coffees with Kahlúas. "I've missed you," she said. "Masochistic, aren't I?"

"Louise," he began.

"I know," she said. "Timing's terrible. You should have warned me when I called from L.A. I didn't know I'd be interrupting anything."

Cord avoided her comment. "You know, I see red when a big, strong, famous bully picks on a little defenseless guy."

"Sounds familiar."

"That's exactly what I thought. Don never knows when to leave well enough alone! And Regina didn't help either."

"It's called self-preservation."

"You know about that?"

"I invented it," she smiled. "I also know why Regina resents me. It only took her one look to see that there had been something between us. And only a woman with proprietary interests would react as swiftly as she did."

"You said, 'had been'; I'm not putting us into that category."

Louise studied him. There were gold flecks in her green eyes, and she looked at him with a total understanding he found unsettling. "Cord, let's agree on one thing. No games between us. I'm not that kind of player. And I'm here to work. There's an album to produce and a concert to perform, and it's my job to get them done. We'll have tonight together, you and I. And then we'll both go into training. When I'm working, I don't have time for anything else, and I don't believe in mixing activities. It clouds the issues."

"Are you just using tonight to establish your beachhead, or is it that Lubow will be here tomorrow?"

Louise appraised him. "Regina must have hurt you very much for you to be so nasty."

He sat back in his chair and ran his hands through his hair. "I'm sorry, baby. I guess I mistook your candor for another kind of game. You're right. I am hurt. When Regina brought her husband and her children back here with her, I was tempted to quit the whole thing." His eyes showed his pain. "I'll never understand her," he said. "Her motivations elude me."

"That's because she doesn't understand herself."

He felt the truth of what she said, but it didn't comfort him. "And you do?" he asked.

"You're damn right I do!" she grinned. "You know what?" She reached across the table and took his hands. "Let's finish these fattening concoctions and go back to your cabin and make love all night. Tomorrow morning you're going to look so satisfied that your lady friend will bust a gut. And then I'll give you one one long lingering kiss as we part, standing in some propitious position so that no one will have any doubts about what we've been doing."

He smiled at her; she was some lady. "I don't know if I can play my part," he said. "I'm rather preoccupied at the moment."

She stared into his eyes searching for something and then smiled as she saw what there was for her. Admiration, respect, affection, and a touch of lust.

"Don't worry about a thing," she said. "Leave it all to me!"

Regina hadn't slept all night, not one single wink. She tossed and turned, envying Mike asleep beside her. And then she began to pace. The peaked ceiling of the pine-paneled cottage with filled with stale smoke from her cigarettes. Twice she had made the trip to the cigarette machine. Both times she walked past Cord's cabin and saw candlelight flickering inside. *Oh, Cord,* she cried, clutching her arms to her stomach as though to ward off the pain. But the pain slipped through her protective coating and twisted hot acid in her entrails.

Finally Mike sat up in bed and switched on the light, studying her ravished face. "For chrissakes, Regina, what's going on? You know I've got an early plane to catch." He was going to New Orleans in the morning. Something to do with the Superdome arrangements.

"Nothing's going on," she said. "Go back to sleep. I'm just nervous tonight. That fight between Cord and Don upset me. I should have taken a walk earlier to clear my head, and now it's too late."

He started to fall back to sleep. "Do you want me to take a walk with you?"

"Oh no! You need your rest.". Sarcasm seeped through, added to anger and rage. Nobody should be able to sleep when she was feeling like this. Why did he have to go to New Orleans anyway after what Lubow had done to him? She was a tight coil ready to spring, a tigress protecting her lair; only who was the hunter? Where was the danger? It was all around her! All the nameless fears, the pressures, the obligations, and the guilts; God, the guilts! "Go back to sleep, Mike."

He sat up. "I'm awake now. What's wrong?"

"Oh, nothing," she began. "This is one big camp of orgies, that's all. Don is screwing two different women, and Fideo is screwing all the waiters, and Cord . . ."

He raised one eyebrow. "That's what's bugging you, isn't it? Your ex-loverboy has found a new hole!"

Why was he being so terrible? Things had been good between them lately. "Don't be crude, Mike."

"What do you think I am? Blind? I've got eyes. The minute I leave here, I can just imagine what will go on."

So that's what was really worrying him, she realized. He was afraid to leave her alone, not because of the threat to her, but because of Cord. "There's nothing going on with Cord," she said. "He's with Louise Carlin."

"And that's just eating you up, isn't it?"

"You don't understand, Mike. I'm scared!" She grabbed his arms like a life raft in a stormy sea. "There are people out there who want to hurt me. I don't know if my music is any good anymore. I don't know if I'm going to be the laughing stock of the whole world on intercontinental television. What if the critics crucify me? They could, you know. I'm nearing middle age and still trying to appeal to teeny-boppers. Don's act is passé; Cord's music is too soft. I'm geared to middle-of-the-roaders. You have no idea what it's like to be the focus, the brunt, the body they'll all pick clean! And to be afraid that any minute someone horrible is going to break into my room and hurt me or the ones I love." It was true that these feelings were torturing her . . . but they always tortured her. It was Cord and Louise who were making everything else unbearable. "What if the whole reunion is a colossal failure! I'll never work again. Oh, Mike!"

He put his arms around her. Every muscle in her body was tensed. She was shaking, and her shoulders were hunched as though she expected blows to rain down on her. She smelled from tobacco and fear.

"I'm sure we're safe now, darling. Lubow has made his point." She moaned in his arms. "I've never seen you like this before, Regina," he said, trying to soothe her. "Do you want me to call the doctor? Shall I cancel my trip?"

"No!" Her teeth were chattering.

He went into the bathroom and brought her two ten-milligram Valiums and a glass of water. "Here! Take these."

"I don't want them," she insisted wildly, preferring her dramatic suffering to medication. "I won't be able to work tomorrow."

"You won't be able to work if you go on like this."

Finally she took the pills. They hit her like a huge hammer, and within an hour she was as far down as she had been up.

"You're going to be wonderful in the concert," he told her as she began to relax. He stroked her hand, watching her eyelids begin to droop. "You're a beautiful, talented woman; this concert is going to be your crowning glory. And afterwards we're going on a vacation, just you and I. Maybe a cruise. How would you like that? Our own yacht in the Greek Islands. We'll talk about it in a few days when I get back."

His words were so comforting. He could always make her feel better. Was that why she loved him? She could feel herself floating on the Aegean, or was it the Ionian Sea. Warm blue waters. A cruise. Just the two of them. "That's lovely," she sighed. "You'll be a tall Greek god." And she fell asleep with her head on Mike's shoulder.

He held her for a while longer before she became too heavy and then he eased her back against the pillows. *My beautiful Regina,* he thought, watching her sleep. Her eyelashes rested on her creamy cheeks, her hair curled in a coppery frame around her head just like his children's. They were going to be all right; he knew it. She had called him a tall Greek god. That's what he wanted to be for her. Perhaps he didn't have to worry about leaving her alone with Cord after all.

CHAPTER 35

Two occurrences surprised the hell out of Lubow as he alighted from the helicopter accompanied by his secretary Kikky Hunt. First of all Cord Crocker was kissing Louise Carlin on the front porch of his bungalow as though they were two lovers departing for a war zone. And Regina, who had evidently witnessed this tender scene, came barreling toward Lubow and threw her arms around his neck.

"Oh, I'm so glad to see you!" she cried as he stood dumbfounded. "It's been impossible around here lately. Mike has gone and we've needed you so much!" She reached out to grasp Kikky's hand. "Now I know things will become sane again! You two are going to save this concert!" she exclaimed.

Louise and Cord joined them on the lawn, and Lubow glanced at Louise with a dubious expression. "Does the concert need saving?" he asked.

"Oh, you wouldn't believe what's been going on," Regina answered with a look at Cord.

Lubow saw the look and put his arm around Regina's shoulders and walked her toward the recording studio. "What's the matter?"

"Everything!" Regina insisted. "Don and Cord have been at each other like a couple of male cats. Don says the recording console they have here is obsolete! That it's so outdated we can't get the sounds we're striving for. He has better equipment in his own home than they've got here. That Fideo is so cheap.

He should have known computer recording was around the corner. Everybody else has a computer system now."

"What's wrong between Don and Cord?"

"Who knows; they're not speaking."

"How is the music going, aside from the electronic problems?" Lubow was amazed to see her so overwrought. The last report he'd gotten, things were going well. He beckoned to Louise to follow them.

"You can judge the music yourself," Regina said, noticing that Cord was walking behind them. "I've completed my songs, but nobody's even asked to hear them yet!"

"But why?" he asked. "I thought you three were composing together."

She answered loudly enough for Cord to hear. "Some people aren't interested in hard work and creative excellence. They're too wrapped up in their *own* pleasures to do their job."

"Well, I want to hear them!" he told her. "And I'm sure Louise does too. Will you play them for us now?"

"Please do, Regina," Louise added, falling into step with the two of them. She seemed sincere.

"All right," Regina agreed, still holding on to Lubow's arm, but talking to the space behind her. "But only for you two, no one else."

They entered the recording studio and Lubow turned to Cord as Regina and Louise went inside. "What's with her?" he asked.

"It's a long story," Cord answered.

"Well, it better be good," Lubow snapped. "I'll send for you when we're through in here."

Cord nodded and turned away.

Lubow figured he had some smoothing of egos to perform. Maybe he'd pressed too hard on Regina and Mike. But he had his own concerns to worry about and he came first. Regina would straighten out. He'd see to it.

But Lubow needn't have worried. Regina was a pro, and all her tensions seemed to pass as she played for them. He was transfixed by her music. It was like listening to a ghost from the past. How she had grown musically! He almost felt a twinge of jealousy at her talent. Her new music had a depth and a stature that overshadowed her earlier more facile tunes, even though that music had found a wildly enthusiastic audience. Those were children's songs compared to these. *What was it about her music?* he wondered. Not just pathos came through; it was her very soul she was expressing. He looked at Louise. She recognized it too, and there was no envy there, only admiration. For the first time Lubow realized how important this reunion concert would be, what an impact it would make on the music world. Something lasting was being created!

Regina's third song ended quietly; she seemed proud of her accomplishments. Lubow put his arms around her and kissed her on the cheek. He felt her stiffen a bit.

"Do you know how good they are?"

"I hoped so. I really prayed they would be. Those are my guts in every note! Every word is part of me."

"Thank you for sharing them with us," he said, using his most sincere tone.

"They're wonderful, Regina," Louise murmured, as moved as her boss. She recognized Regina's spectacular talent, and she was thankful that Regina was so emotionally volatile. At least that gave her a fighting chance with Cord.

"I wrote these songs at home over an eight-day period. I just couldn't work with all the tension around here." Regina reached for her cigarettes and lit one. "Louise, tell me, do you really like my music?"

"It's superb, Regina. They're the most moving songs I've heard in a long time. And I won't allowed Jerry to put his commercially minded fingers on one of them. Not one note will be altered to add to the commercial appeal. I promise you."

"Don't you think they have commercial appeal?" Regina demanded.

"Of course!" Louise stated.

Lubow changed the subject, aware of Regina's insecurity. "How are Cord's and Don's songs coming?"

Regina weighed her answer. "Don's songs are predictable. Same old stuff. Frankly, we're going to have to lean heavily on arrangement to resurrect them and keep the audience and the critics from berating him. Cord's work is another matter. I think he's improved in some ways, but in other ways he's never grown. A childlike quality comes through, a kind of petulant spoiledness that I can recognize now that I have children of my own. I used to think it was his individuality."

Lubow remembered Cord saying almost the same thing about Regina many times in the past. Louise remembered too, judging from her expression.

"On the other hand," Regina continued, "some of Cord's work is wonderful! I'd say it inspired me to go as far as I did with my songs."

"Maybe it was Cord himself and not his songs that inspired you," Lubow commented.

Regina didn't answer, and neither did Louise.

"What about Beau?" Lubow asked. "I was hoping he would contribute something original to the concert. Have you heard him?"

"Beau is very strange," Regina replied.

"Why?" Lubow prodded.

"He just doesn't fit in. I have no idea what kind

of a musician he is because in all these weeks I've never heard him play anything original. He accompanies us and sits there like a zombie. I thought eventually he'd come out of his shell, but no such luck. He's weird!"

She was interrupted by Don, entering through the sound booth.

"Who's weird?" he asked. "Hello, Jer." They shook hands. He kissed Louise on both cheeks. "Did anybody tell you what bloody miserable equipment they've got here. Take a look at this!" He pulled Lubow into the adjoining sound booth and contemptuously pointed to the dazzling array of electronic equipment. Lubow studied the setup. It was excellent as far as he could see.

"This stuff is obsolete! I wouldn't have it in my pissoir!"

"The equipment has nothing to do with the quality of work!" Regina called from the studio. "It's the songs that count!"

"You wouldn't know a thing about quality, now would you, sweetheart?" Don shot back.

Beau chose just that minute to walk in, and Don said under his breath, "Speaking of no talent."

By the flinch of Beau's shoulder Lubow could tell he'd heard Don's remark.

"Hello," he whispered to Louise. He had dark circles under his eyes. "I've got laryngitis today," he shrugged apologetically.

Louise took his hand. "Regina's been telling us what a help you've been."

"She has?" he smiled, glancing at Regina from under lowered eyebrows.

"Sure," Regina said sarcastically.

Cord pushed open the outer door letting in a wave of moist air. There was a fog rolling in from the ocean. Regina ignored him.

"We've just been singing your praises, Beau, haven't we, Don? We're just one complimentary group around here!"

Lubow looked from one to the other, noting the highly explosive nature of the atmosphere. Don and Cord were avoiding one another. Regina avoided Cord.

"What do you say we get to work!" Louise suggested.

Don finally looked at Cord, mounting anger etched on his face. "I'd love to get to work! I've been here all this time, ready to work, willing to work. I haven't been off entertaining pussy from New York or running home to spruce up my kitchen with calico curtains!"

"Lacking any ability, it didn't make any difference, did it?" Regina shot at him.

They were like children in a playground. Louise sat down at the keyboard and began to play the melody of one of Regina's new songs. It sounded flat and empty without Regina's special interpretation.

"Let me do that," she said, pushing her aside. Then she sang the new song, keeping her eyes on the keys, but it was obvious she was playing it for Cord. When she finished Cord was smiling.

Lubow saw tears in both of their eyes. Beau stared at Regina with a mixture of wariness and admiration.

"Do you like it?" she asked Cord. It was her first civil word to him in days. He was beaming at her.

Don interrupted. "It's nice, Regina. But not for Majesty."

She recoiled as though she'd been struck. Don didn't even notice. "You've always tried to foist those kinds of numbers on us, and this one doesn't belong either. It's perfect for Barry Manilow!" He laughed at his own joke. "I can just hear what Jimmy Page would say, or Mick, or Bowie for that matter. Make way for Linda Ronstadt."

"Shut up, Don," Cord told him.

Don glared back, fists clenched, instantly ready for another go around. "You gonna fight Regina's battles now, Crocker? It's not enough to stick up for snot-nose over there?" He jerked his thumb toward Beau, who cringed.

Cord took a menacing step toward Don. "You never quit, do you?"

"Aw shit!" Don exclaimed. "I'll be back later." And he pushed past Cord, almost knocking Beau over on his way out.

Lubow watched him go.

"How are we going to get anything done if he keeps acting like that?" Regina asked Louise.

She shook her head.

Don was sure as hell on a short fuse. He'd have to talk to him, Lubow thought. He'd have to talk to all of them.

But even a week of talks with Lubow and Louise's soothing presence didn't really change anything. Don was thoroughly fed up with everybody. Especially that prick Beau Morgan. Why did he always find himself surrounded by the idiots of the world? He finally decided it was time for drastic action.

When he located Penny on the patio of the restaurant reading a magazine, he was so furious with everyone it took all his control just to appear civil to her. She had gotten boring lately, but he'd wait a trifle longer before throwing her over. Just until he got rid of Morgan. Jesus, what a bleedin' freak he was.

Penny looked solemn today; no big smile greeted him. Well, he had been a touch stiff with her lately.

"Hi sugar. How about a cozy little stroll through these green gardens with me?" He leaned over her shoulder and nuzzled her ear, peering down her white cotton dress. Those fresh pink mounds with the dark nipples never failed to excite him. Engorged they were, and gorgeous. She was like a little ripe peach, all fuzzy and new, he thought as he tongued her neck.

"Don. Not in public." She looked around fearfully and closed the gap of her dress. But he caught her wrist and plunged his hand inside, cupping her firm roundness and rubbing the tip until it popped out right between his fingers. He squatted beside her chair and ran his hand up her skirt, delighting in the silkiness of her skin, running his fingers around the edge of her panties, across the dampness of her crotch. Her eyes had a glazed look, and she moistened her lips, wanting him to stop and wanting him to go on.

"Come with me," he said.

"No." She gripped the arms of the director chair. "We can't. I can't. Please, I've got to talk to you!"

"Later!" he insisted, pulling the chair away from the table and stepping in front of her. He put his arms around her waist and lifted her up, pressing her against his chest. She was not giving in to him; there was none of her usual eagerness.

"You're not miffed at me, are you?" he asked. "Have I been a bad sort lately? Said some nasties? Well, luv, you've got to understand how mucky it's been around here."

She looked down at his chest. "It's not that," she hesitated and then looked up at him. *Oh, to be so young,* he thought. *So clear, so free of tightness around the eyes and sourness of the expression.*

"I don't think we should see each other any more. I've tried and tried to tell you this, ever since the first time, but it's been so hard."

"Don't be a ninny. Come on, walk with me back to my place." Then he remembered the princess was there. "No, maybe we'd better go to yours."

"I can't do that, Don. Not anymore. You don't know what it's been like for me, sleeping in the same bed with my husband where you and I . . . where we . . !" Her voice trailed off.

He jerked her around to face him. "Don't give me that sorry crap, lambie! I know all about you. You've been a genuine whore! Don't try and go sterling on me. I'm not taking any plug nickels today."

She pushed away from him and took off across the meadow. He caught her easily, pinching her arm. This kind of shit he didn't need. "Now just a minute. Nobody dumps on Don Drummond. Especially not you, buttercups."

She was crying now. "You've got to understand, Don. I can't keep cheating on my husband. I love him. And this is hurting him. More than you know. He's not himself. I've been so wrapped up in us I've let him fend for himself, and it's been very destructive."

"My! What a grownup word. Didn't think Little Miss Illiterate understood it."

"I understand a great deal," she said. "I can tell a bastard when I see one!" She wiped her cheeks with her hand, and he handed her a handkerchief.

"All right. I'm sorry. But all this talk has made me mean. Now what do you say? Let's kiss and make up, huh?"

"No, Don. I'm serious. I'm not going to see you anymore."

She was very determined. He wondered how far he could go by force. And then he decided against that. He had enough troubles as it was. But no two-legged bitch was going to throw him over. He would stop fucking her when *he* decided, and now was not the time.

"Penny, shiny Penny," he pleaded, changing his tactic. "You know what you mean to me. I need you! Look, darling," he put her hand on his erect penis. "What am I going to do with this? I understand how you feel," he said, rubbing her hand up and down. "I respect what you're trying to do. It's all right. Really it is." He let her withdraw her hand. "But I came looking for you with nothing but love in my heart. I imagined your beautiful body pressed against mine, your wonderful breasts in my mouth, your lips on my prick." He smiled at her winningly. "I promise, sweetheart, we'll make love only this once, and then no more. This will be our last time. Let's make it something to remember. Oh sweetness, you don't know what you do to me." He pulled her close, kissing her hair, feeling his own ardor pulsing in his veins. He'd really talked himself into a fine state. She'd better say yes.

"Do you mean it?" she asked. "This is the last time?"

"Cross my heart," he smiled.

And she nodded her assent.

The morning session was over and it had not gone well. Beau leaned against the wall outside the sound booth trying to ease the misery he felt inside. He would never get used to their hatred. It came at him in waves of searing pain. The plaster was cool through his cotton shirt and jeans, but it couldn't cool the half of him that burned with need, the need for compassion and acceptance, and the need to shoot up again. One of his worst fears was that Fideo would grow tired of him and not want him anymore. Then his drug supply would be cut off. He forced himself to think of new ways to entice Fideo's desires and he was getting more bold in his display of sensuality, born of desperation. But he still hated the act violently and fought bouts of nausea before each time. If only he didn't need drugs so badly. If only he wasn't captive in this place. His immediate supply would only last for a few more days and then he'd have to approach Fideo again.

He walked to his cabin trying to look normal, trying to forget about the pain in his rectum, and the ache inside, and the itch that was down between his toes at the moment but would soon be up to his crotch and then to his belly and then to his elbows and armpits until it burned right into his brain.

He hoped no one would tell Penny he was in their cabin, so she wouldn't come looking for him. He needed to be alone, to prepare his beautiful oblivion, to take that metal phallus with the tiny point and gently prick the vein until all the itches were soothed away. His drug was the sweetest thing in his life; what would he do without it? He'd die, that's what he'd do. He didn't want to die; he wanted to live with this sweet beauty in his veins, this balm that kept him alive, kept him playing his drums, helped him avoid the words and opinions others threw at him. The drug kept him able to let the notes and the beat come from his sticks and onto the drums, kettle, boom, tighter skin, percussion, cymbal, back and forth.

He headed back behind the building through the trees to his cabin, and once there it didn't take long before he felt the kiss of life again. Death had been foiled, besieged by the forces of alchemy; begone you dark voices, you blackened faces.

He headed back toward the studio, only slightly unsteady. The forest smelled damp and cold from the fog that was still rolling in. It curled around the trees like spun sugar around a toasted cone. He heard a noise next to him, a pleasant sound, the murmur of voices and movement, breathing, rustling, magnified by the fog. He was having a wonderful "buzz," and the sounds blended with his glow. He would have a good time on the drums before it wore off. The trees sighed as a breeze passed through the leaves, and a woman sighed almost next to him. He turned and saw her leaning with her back against a nearby tree. Her dress was up around her waist, and her white buttocks were bissected by the dark brown bark of the slender trunk. The man standing in front of her was pushing her against the tree in a hard rhythm so that her buttocks were flattened again and again against the trunk. Her blond hair spilled down her back just the way it had the day Beau met her, and the man's face was pressed into her shoulder as his body shuddered and he released his fluid into her.

Beau was so close to them he could hear Don's words as he whispered, "Oh, baby, yes, yes, that's fine." And then Don looked up and saw Beau watching him fucking Penny, and he winked.

Quicksand sucked at Beau's feet as he retreated back to his cabin. Fideo said those same words to him when he came. "Oh, baby, yes, yes, that's fine." He could taste Fideo on his tongue, feel him inside his intestines. At this moment it was the thought of Fideo that made him retch his bowels into the toilet, and suddenly his beautiful high was plummeted down into the quicksand with him. Penny! He cried from somewhere deep inside where there were no tears.

He was sitting on the floor unable to move when the cabin door opened. He expected to see Don's face leering at him, but it was Louise Carlin. She came over to him and helped him to the bed.

"Aren't you feeling well, Beau? You said you'd be back in a few minutes and it's been nearly an hour. I rang the phone several times. Why didn't you answer?"

"Would you get me a glass of water?" Beau asked. It was as if he were asking for part of his soul.

Louise looked at him strangely, noticing the sickening sweet odor of vomit in the room. But she brought him the cup of water.

Beau took a sip and then dipped his fingers into the cup. Birthing fluid, amniotic cushion. He dabbed a bit on his eyes to see better, and on his ears to hear better,, and he poured a speck on his tongue, letting it fill his mouth. "Rebirth!" he said, stifling the cries that begged to be released. *Mustn't cry in front of strangers.* Finally he got up from the bed. "Let's go," he said. "I've got to have music in me today." His face was wet, but it wasn't from the water.

CHAPTER 36

When Don got back to his cabin after leaving Penny, Princess Sonia was sitting in the middle of the floor right where he'd left her that morning. She was still wearing the white chiffon negligée she hadn't taken off for days and trying to put together a jigsaw puzzle she'd bought in an art gallery in New York for two hundred and fifty dollars. The pieces were handcut in the form of figures, but she'd never had her head straight long enough to finish it. She'd pick up the pieces and study them for hours before trying to find where they fit. How could she stay here like this, he wondered, day after day?

"Nirvana," she said to him as though he'd only been gone a few minutes. "They call it nirvana."

"Sure." He took off his shirt and slacks.

"Do you want to make luf?" she asked with a pleased expression. She almost never wanted sex, but she was using some new kind of drug that Fideo gave her. Yesterday it made her violent, and she'd torn up all the curtains in the room and the bedspread into little pieces. Today she seemed more mellow. She got up slowly and came over to him, stepping up close she ran her tongue over his lips. "Achh! No!" She shoved him. "You are terrible! You smell!"

Don saw red! Nobody else was going to push him around. "Goddamn slut!" he shouted, blindly striking out. He hit her across the face, and she fell backward, sprawling into her puzzle. Her nose started to bleed, and she burst into sobs. Now he'd done it. She'd probably be on a crying jag that would last for hours, even days.

"You are a monster!" she sobbed.

Her tears did not move him. If she weren't beautiful and a princess, he wouldn't keep her around. And she wasn't so beautiful right now. In fact she was a mess. He couldn't stand the sight of her. When he came out of the shower she was still crying. "I'm going for a drive to Carmel," he told her. "When I get back tonight, I want you gone. Out of here!"

She kept on crying.

"Did you hear me?" he shouted. "I want you out. Go back to Austria!"

The sound of the door slamming echoed across the fields and into the fog-shrouded ravines behind the meadow. That woman belonged in a bleedin' looney bin. He should have gotten rid of her before when she wasn't in such an emotional state. But what the hell, she was always in an emotional state.

He stopped by the office to pick up a set of keys to one of the cars. And as he was driving up the mist-enveloped coast, he thought about the look on Morgan's face when he'd seen his wife gettin' boffed. *Serves the bleedin' mucker right,* Don thought. *He shouldn't have been where he wasn't wanted. Now he'll have to leave Antelope to take Miss Muffet away from the Spider.* And that was exactly what Don wanted. He was sure Penny wouldn't stick to her resolve about not seeing him anymore. She was crazy about him.

He dined at Phillipe's in Carmel on squab and soufflé, went to a film, and drove back to Antelope rested and ready to begin another day. The princess was gone, though she'd left all her clothes and the jigsaw puzzle behind. The last thing he thought about before he fell asleep was that he'd been too rough on her.

Except for the howling of coyotes in the night he slept very well.

He discovered at breakfast that the sound of the coyotes had unnerved everyone. Regina was more quiet than usual, but at least Cord said hello to him. That was a switch. Don guessed that Cord was sorry for his outburst yesterday.

Louise finally approached him and sat down, placing her coffee mug on the table. "I've heard everybody's songs but yours. How about a session this morning?"

Don shrugged and started to get up. "Why not? I'll go warm up and tell John Lawson to come along."

"No, Don." Louise held him back. "I'd like Morgan to sit in. It's about time he worked directly with you. He *is* the drummer for the group, you know."

Don's jaw tightened, and he pulled his arm away from her, ready to fight again.

But she smiled. Those dimples always got him. "Hey, there's a concert to perform, remember? And you've got contracts that bind you. Right?"

Don's temper began to subside. No point in starting the day off wrong. "Okay with me," he said. It should be interesting to see if Morgan could even face him now, much less accompany him.

The session went smoothly, and the man played better than Don had ever heard him play before. "I didn't know you had it in you, Morgan," Don couldn't resist.

When they finished Louise called a break and came up to him. "Your songs are good, Don! I especially liked 'Tiny Little Girl.'"

Don nodded. "Thanks. I like that one too!"

"I've asked Beau to show us some of his work this afternoon. Cord and Regina are reading it over right now. I thought the four of you could try it after lunch."

Jesus, Don thought, Morgan was really making inroads. It was time for a bit of strategy.

Everyone was seated in the dining room when Don came in for lunch. The cliques that had formed during the time they had worked together at Antelope were obvious at mealtime. Don came over and pulled up an empty chair next to Penny. Morgan didn't look up from his salad.

"Hi, gorgeous," Don said, loud enough for Beau to hear. "I missed you last evening. I drove into Carmel for a bit of supper. I'm tired of this health crap. Maybe we ought to go there sometime."

Penny grew pale, and her eyes darted to Beau to see if he was aware of Don's behavior. But Beau didn't seem to notice.

"How's the princess?" Penny asked.

"She's gone. Back to Austria." Don ran his fingertips up and down Penny's arm. She shivered.

"Please Don!" she whispered, pushing his hand away. He gave her a mock hurt look.

"But you've got such soft skin."

Regina was watching them with annoyance, but Don didn't give a damn.

Penny pushed her chair away from the table and stood up. "I don't think I'll eat right now; I'm not very hungry."

Everyone at the table turned to look at her, and she backed away in embarrassment, aware of the awful silence. Finally Beau nodded to her. "See you later," he said.

From the look on Beau's face Don knew that Beau would not be able to remain in this situation much longer.

Regina watched Don in action and couldn't believe his nerve. The little sexcapade between him and Penny was getting out of hand. To be so blatant; even she could see how much Beau was hurting. She excused herself and followed Penny out of the restaurant. A foggy mist hung over the fields, and the sun had given up trying to burn it off. The air was warm and sticky, salt-laced, and thick. Penny's figure was obscured by the fog, but when Regina called out to her, she turned and came back. She looked awful.

"Would you like to talk?" Regina asked. "Sometimes it helps." *Poor kid,* she thought. *She's no match for Don Drummond.*

Penny sniffed and wiped her cheeks with the back of her hand as they walked down the path toward the main lounge together, two lonely figures in a sea of gauze.

"I don't want to bother you with my troubles," Penny said.

"Don can be extremely difficult," Regina offered.

And Penny turned to study her, a blue-eyed fawn in flight. She needed to unburden herself, but Regina couldn't prod; only stand by, willing to hear, as the forest stands and protects its soft, delicate underbelly from the fierce onslaughts of nature. Don could be fierce, too. But Regina feared it was too late to protect Penny. Lightning had already struck.

"I've made a terrible mistake," Penny began. "I'd give anything for it not to have happened."

Regina placed a hand on her thin child's arm. "Don't make confessions to me, Penny. I don't deserve them. And besides I already know about you and Don."

Penny stared at her in astonishment. With all of the life those eyes had seen, Regina marveled that they could be freshly surprised. "How do you know?"

"I told you, I'm not a saint."

"How many others know about us?" Penny asked. Her shoulders visibly sagged as though shame pressed them down.

Regina so wanted to lighten her load. "Only the ones who are concerned enough to observe. Probably no one else in a place like this."

Penny shivered and pulled her sweater more snugly around her body. "I've broken off with Don. But he doesn't want to accept my decision." She gave her head a toss, and her straight flaxen hair rippled with the movement. "I don't care what he says; it's over."

"Don must be devastated at the thought of losing a conquest. He has a well-cultivated, enormous ego."

Penny glanced at her and saw a look of amusement in Regina's eyes, and then she smiled.

Regina smiled back, and they both giggled.

"I guess I've really done it, haven't I?" Penny asked.

"I guess you have," Regina laughed.

But their mirth was short-lived when Penny sighed. "I don't know what I'm going to tell Beau."

"Does he know?"

"Oh, no! That would be terrible."

Regina's eyes strained to make out the shapes of trees and bushes in the shifting mists. Their shrouded majesty lent an air of gloom to an already gloomy subject. She understood Penny's reluctance only too well. "You're not planning to tell your husband about Don, are you?"

"Would you?"

"No. I can't imagine anything more foolish or unnecessarily cruel."

"And yet it would show him that I've really finished with Don, that I have no intention of ever going back."

"Are you certain of that?"

Penny sighed again. "Most of the time."

Regina understood. It was amazing to her how much she had in common with this girl. "If you tell your husband you've broken off with Don and he didn't know about it at all, then you'd be hurting him in the guise of helping him."

"Yes," Penny argued, "but if he suspects, then I'd be reassuring him."

"They always suspect, don't they?" Regina commented.

Penny looked at her from under a fringe of lowered lashes, as though the brightness of Regina had to be taken in small doses like the sun. "What are you going to do about Cord?" she asked.

Now it was Regina's turn to be astonished. For a moment she didn't know what to say, and the unanswered question hung between them. Until Penny said, "I guess I was concerned enough to observe." And Regina laughed, a deep, rich laugh.

"My God, we're such fools, aren't we? What have we been looking for? Why are we doing this?"

"I've thought a great deal about that," Penny said. "And I realized that for me, a girl from Oregon who's been as low as I have been, an affair with Don Drummond was the most exciting thing that ever happened to me. My husband has been very . . . distant lately. I started to believe that he didn't love me . . . that he didn't want me. And to prove that I'm still desirable, still worthy, I did the one thing which makes me the most unworthy. Don was like a narcotic to me. A crutch I used to escape from reality. But there are terrible consequences one pays when trying to escape from reality." Suddenly her face contorted with pain. "Beau is the only person who's ever loved me in my life, and look at the way I've treated him."

Regina put her arms around the girl, holding her as she would her own daughter. She didn't know what to say. She was certainly no one to give advice. "Perhaps we hurt the ones we love, because they've hurt us."

Penny reached into the pocket of her dress. Don's handkerchief was still there and she used it. "Beau has hurt me, but that's no excuse."

"I wouldn't be so hard on myself if I were in your place," Regina said. And then she realized that she was exactly in Penny's place. With one important difference: Penny had told Don good-bye, but she hadn't broken off with Cord. She hadn't even thought about doing it. And yet she must. How had this frail child found the strength to stay away from her narcotic? What was the secret?

Regina prayed she could find a way. But Cord was so much a part of her; or was he merely a part of her past? The most wonderful part. Did she love him with the total absorption she believed or was she merely playing a role, the modern woman having an affair? And wasn't there a bit of anger against Mike underlying it all? *A bit,* she thought, *more like a ton of it.* But when Mike was the way he had been lately, there was no need for other men. No need at all. Yet she had wanted this affair. She'd fantasized about it, dreamed about it, longed for Cord with her entire being. Then why the hell didn't she enjoy it?

Maybe she didn't know how to enjoy anything.

The fame that she had achieved within the first year of Majesty's formation had come immediately. There had been no gradual buildup. She'd never really struggled, not the way others had for years and years. And once she had arrived, it was a terrible fight to stay there. Each album was harder to do than the one preceding it; each new song, more difficult. She'd worry, What if her current work wasn't as good as her past, would she still retain her place in the circle of glory? And the pressures were intense; long hours on the road, screaming fans, massive crowds, and photographers snapping shots of her in every place, every position. Nothing was safe; nothing sacred. Someone once had photographed her by telephoto lens sitting on the john. Regina Williams belonged to the world, not to herself. And there'd been no time to reach maturity, or place to do it, only the stage or quiet moments in bed with Cord. Through him she felt tied to her childhood as though he held the key to her very self. As though only he could unlock the adult that lurked inside her, longing to come out. When Gene died and Cord left, she'd wanted to die too. To be so abandoned again after losing her family, she'd used coke to keep her wired, keep her from feeling the terrible loss and awful guilt. What a devastating time it was.

Regina noticed the fog that lay on the ground had slowly lifted, revealing the enormous root system of the nearby redwood trees. And she was struck by a new perspective, a new insight, as though she'd been shrouded like the forest, covered over with a blanket of mist, never taking time to look, really look, at herself. Emotion welled up inside, and as she turned toward Penny, her composure broke. She felt raw and exposed and needy. Penny's arms went around her as she cried, the child comforting the parent. She cried with so much sorrow, so much pain. She cried for Gene, and for Cord, and for their lost love. She knew it was lost. They could never recapture it. It died when Cord left her, when the group broke up in anger and resentment. Her life was with Mike now, she realized it freely, completely, and with even a touch of hope.

Penny handed her Don's soggy handkerchief.

"You know what, Penny," she said. "You and I are going to get through this.." And for the first time in a long time she believed it in her heart.

CHAPTER
37

The fog held on, refusing to burn off or blow away, and by midafternoon the air grew chilly with a damp biting cold. Everyone bundled up in sweaters and parkas and flannels. Beau played his own compositions on the keyboard for the group and Louise was impressed with his potential, though she could sense an almost paralyzing panic in the young man, a fearfulness that was nearly palpable. His eyes darted from face to face searching for something. *What was it?* she wondered; *approval, acceptance, or merely tolerance?*

For the second night in a row the coyotes howled until dawn. This time they kept Don awake. "Damned animals," he cursed hour after hour. At breakfast Fideo came up to him.

"How is the princess?" he asked. "I haven't seen her for days. Is she getting her supply somewhere else?"

"She left two days ago. She was so tiresome I asked her to leave."

Fideo seemed surprised. "How did she leave? No one took her to the plane, and she didn't ask for a car."

"Well, she's gone. Just up and left. Maybe one of your boys took her to the airport and didn't tell you."

"I'll check," he promised, hurrying away.

Don was surprised. How did she get to the airport, certainly not by hitchhiking? Come to think of it, it was strange that she hadn't sent for her clothes yet. All her belongings were still in his room. He went back to his cabin to see if he could figure out what was missing.

Fideo knocked on his door ten minutes later. "No one on my staff has seen her for days, and none of them took her to the bus or the train or the plane. She wouldn't have walked out of here, would she? She was in a very unstable condition."

Don regarded the disgusting little man in front of him. "Unstable, my ass. She was hooked on the poisons you gave her, and if anything's happened to her, it's your fault!"

Fideo sucked in his breath. "Don't start with me, Drummond. You'll find I'm a dirty fighter!" He went over to the phone to call the highway patrol and the forest rangers.

The fog hampered the search. Visibility was only ten yards. Those waiting at the Inn could hear the voices of the rescue teams calling Sonia's name, their lights shining now and then in the mist. But a pall of gloom had settled on them all.

Regina's anger with Don grew at every minute. "What was the last thing you said to Sonia, Don? What kind of mood was she in?"

He didn't reply, remembering.

"How could you not know she was missing?" Cord said. "Where are your brains, man?"

But no one wanted to pursue it. Not until they had some news.

Penny finally asked, "Has anybody heard the wolves howling at night?"

"They're coyotes," Fideo told her, and she shivered.

Beau felt scared and lonely. He identified with the lost woman, knew how she was feeling, so cold and abandoned, surrounded by gloom. Every noise would be terrifying. But not as bad as the feeling of rejection that must have sent her out there in the first place.

The bloodhounds bayed in the distance, sounding sometimes as though they were right on the meadow with the anxious group, other times like they were Cerebus guarding the gates of hell.

"Do you think she's really out there?" Regina whispered to Cord. But he wouldn't answer her and kept his eyes averted, finally disappearing into the fog.

Fideo joined them.

"Is it dangerous out there?" Regina asked.

"Yes," he replied gruffly. He was annoyed with this turn of events.

"The press is going to have their pound of flesh about this," Regina said. "Even if we keep it quiet for a while. God, I hope she's all right."

"We all do," Louise said.

Regina noticed the tight lines of worry around Louise's eyes. Louise was genuinely concerned. And Regina realized that the animosity she'd felt toward Louise had begun to dissipate in direct relation to her change of heart about Cord. She could almost regard the woman objectively, noting her superior qualities without too much jealousy. Regina knew she was more beautiful than Louise, more talented, and certainly more vibrant. But Louise did have a kind of hard-earned perfection about her. She had class, Regina decided. Perhaps it was only Louise's superior education that irritated her.

She tried to see ahead into the fog which stopped at the edge of the patio like a curtain, but it was impenetrable. She wondered how long Cord would be gone. And then, after some time she became aware that Louise was studying her too, as though she wanted to talk but was unsure of the reception she'd receive.

Regina spoke first. "I'm worried about Mike. He's driving down the coast in this fog."

"How did he make out with Lubow?" Louise asked, responding to the tentative offer of a truce. Regina wasn't offering friendship, but it wasn't resentment either.

"You mean has he gotten his name on the marquee?" Regina asked.

"No. The money Mike owes him."

Regina looked at her without comprehension. "What money? What are you talking about?"

But before Louise could answer, Cord reappeared out of the mist carrying a lantern and wearing a volunteer insignia pinned to his windbreaker. "If anybody wants to assist, Sergeant McKinzie says they could use us. The perimeters of the search are getting too wide."

"I'll join you," Louise offered, anxious to get away from Regina. She realized she'd said something she shouldn't have.

"I'm coming too," Don said.

"That's the least you can do," Regina commented. She watched as the three of them were swallowed by the thick gray night. What the hell had Louise been talking about, she wondered, reaching into her pocket for a cigarette and lighter.

It annoyed her to think that Louise might know something about her husband that she didn't know. And if there *was* anything to know and he hadn't told her, she'd kill him; she'd absolutely kill him!

She could hear Sonia's name echoing over the ravines as the searchers called out to her. The echoes bounced off the redwoods and floated through the fog; a lonely sound.

"Why doesn't she answer?" Penny asked.

"Lord, that poor frightened girl," Florie said. She had been in to kiss the children good night and she joined Penny and Regina on the patio. "It's col' here, ladies. You best be gettin' inside by the fire." And she hustled the two women indoors, leaving Fideo and Beau standing on the patio.

"Come inside with us, Beau," Penny asked, but he didn't follow her.

The comfort and warmth of the lobby filled with the scent of fresh coffee made a glaring contrast to the drama being played out in the shrouded night.

"Sonia's out there somewhere," Regina said, fighting the desire to be lulled by the pleasant surroundings.

"They's gonna find her," Florie insisted. But she sounded fearful too, alternately hugging her body with her rounded arms and squeezing her hands together in an attitude of prayer. She leaned over to Regina. "You don't think those same men who was bothering Mike could have taken the princess, do you? Maybe they thought she was you!" The moment she said it she was sorry, but now that awful thought hovered in their minds.

"I know that's not it, darling," Regina assured her, but now the fear had taken root. What if someone had meant to harm her instead of the princess? And where was Mike? Was he safe too? She forced herself to smile for Florie's sake. It wasn't good for Florie to worry. Florie felt responsible enough for their troubles as it was. Regina took Florie's hand and held it.

"Why would a lovely-looking girl like that fill herself full of drugs and wander off in the woods all alone?" Regina asked.

Penny stared into the fire. "Because sometimes the demons inside make you do it. You get so crazy that you'd rather be out there with the snakes and the insects and the cold weather than be with those demons any longer. Sometimes you'd even rather be dead."

A look passed between Regina and Florie. "I'm gonna pray they find that girl," Florie said, and she closed her eyes. But Regina could feel Florie's body trembling; she was still so afraid.

CHAPTER
38

The terrain was difficult to cover. There were few paths or trails, hardly any open fields, and the fog hampered every effort. An area which had been carefully searched could still hold the unconscious body of a young woman, invisible to the searchers. It was tedious, tiresome work; the volunteers held heavy-beamed lights or wore them on their heads, and the radio equipment and the loudspeakers were cumbersome too.

Mike arrived around three in the morning, but before Regina could show him how happy she was to see him, he had kissed her and gone out to assist the volunteers. It was certainly not the time to question him about Louise's comment, but it was on her mind. He looked tired. His plane from New York had circled San Francisco for three hours, and then he'd had a long drive down the coast.

Shortly after dawn the fog began to lift and the forest was revealed, green and fresh in the early light. Fern, wildflower, weeds, and bushes seemed innocent in daylight, where before they had held ominous mystery.

At five forty-five in the morning a call came over the walkie-talkie that they'd found her. "We need someone to make an identification." The searcher's voice cracked over the small microphone.

Cord looked at Don. "Identification? That means she's unable to tell them who she is."

"Thank God they've found her," Mike sighed. He was so exhausted that he didn't know if his relief came from the success of the search or the anticipation of sleep.

Cord described their position in relation to the search. "Stay there," the voice instructed. "Someone will come for you."

About ten minutes later Sergeant McKinzie, who was in charge of the search team, appeared, followed by other officers. "Which one of you is Mr. Drummond?" he asked.

"I am," Don replied, suddenly shaken by the look on McKinzie's face. "Is she all right?"

"Come with me," he said.

"We'd better all go," Mike insisted.

Don was the first to see her. The whole right side of her face and shoulder had been torn away, and there were gaping holes in her flesh that exposed jaw and teeth and bone. "She's been mauled by a mountain lion," McKinzie said.

"Oh my God," Don whispered. He could feel the sickness building inside of him. There was blood all over what was left of the white chiffon negligee. His stomach heaved and he turned away.

McKinzie pointed to animal tracks leading off into the woods. "Our search party frightened the animal or he'd never have left his catch. She must have been hurt already or perhaps unconscious; the cats seldom attack humans."

Mike reached the body and took a look at her. "Oh Jesus!" The thought that his children had played among these redwoods made him weak.

McKinzie covered the body. "What the hell was she doing out here anyway and in these clothes?" He looked at Don and Mike accusingly.

Cord came up to them right behind Louise and only got a glimpse of Sonia's body through the group of men before McKinzie covered her, but it was enough! He turned and lunged at Don. "You son of a bitch. You sent her out here to die!" Don tried to evade him, but Cord grabbed at him again. Cord's hands were around Don's throat, and he shoved Don backward into a tree, slamming him into the trunk again and again. Don was too stunned to fight back. At this moment he didn't blame Cord for the way he felt.

Cord felt Don go slack and he let go. "You're disgusting, Drummond! You're the most selfish bastard that has ever walked this earth. There should be criminal charges against you. And I'm not going to stop until I see you publicly ruined."

"No you won't," Don shouted, regaining his temper. "Because if you do, you'll be the one to pay." He glanced at Mike pointedly.

Mike didn't see the look. This tragedy would give the reunion a horrible taint, he realized. The papers would use every stinking detail. And Lubow would be furious. If he had been here all along, maybe this wouldn't have happened. Cord was taking Sonia's death very hard.

Someone brought a stretcher, and they loaded the body onto it. Then McKinzie gave a nod, and they all headed back toward the lodge.

Suddenly Cord stopped and turned to stare at them, a wounded bull ready to charge again. "I'm quitting!" he announced. "I've had it!"

Oh, shit, Mike thought.

"I won't continue working with Don. I refuse to appear on the same stage with him."

"Wait, Cord," Louise said. "Give it some time. We're all upset."

"She's right," Mike said. "And besides you can't quit! We're all counting on you; your fans are counting on you."

"I don't give a damn!" Cord insisted. "And Regina won't do the concert either when she hears what has happened."

"Regina won't want to, but she'll still do the concert," Mike said. "I know this is a terrible shock, Cord. But we have to go on. Regina will feel that way too."

"You think so!" Cord said.

"Yes!" Mike insisted. "She's my wife and I know her."

"You don't know shit!" Cord told him. He pushed away from the group and ran ahead to find Regina first. He'd convince her to give up the concert.

Cord pushed past the people milling around outside the main lobby waiting for news. Regina was inside with Florie, who had fallen asleep. He was out of breath as he grabbed Regina's wrist and pulled her up from the sofa. "I've got to talk to you."

Florie awoke with a start. "What's happening?" she asked, sitting up abruptly.

"Did they find Sonia?" Regina asked.

"They found her," he growled. "She's dead. She was killed by wild animals."

"Oh, God," Regina exclaimed.

"Lord keep her soul," Florie said, clutching at Regina, and then she cried out, a loud, keening sound halfway between a lamentation and a wail.

Regina turned to soothe her, but Cord pulled her away. "Come with me," he said, yanking her across the room. They nearly collided with Fideo, who was standing outside the door.

"Cord, stop, wait!" Regina begged, trying to hold back while he kept pulling her along. She was terribly worried about Florie. Florie shouldn't be left alone right now.

Cord half dragged, half pulled her across the porch, across the lawn, and around the side of the building until he reached a spot he thought would be secluded enough to talk before Mike and the rest of them got back.

"Cord, let me go. I have to go back to Florie," she insisted.

But he took her shoulders in his hands, pressing his fingers into the flesh. "No. There's something I've got to discuss with you."

She stared at him. "What is it?"

"I've told your husband that I'm quitting. I'm not going to do the concert. I said you wouldn't do it either."

"But why?"

"How could you even ask? If you'd seen Sonia's body you'd know. It was horrible. She'd been torn apart, her flesh, her body." His chest heaved from tension and exertion.

"Oh, God, how terrible!"

"It was Don's fault. He let her wander off. No, worse than that; he told her to get out and she did. She was loaded on drugs. She didn't know where she was. But he told her to get out, and now she's dead."

"That poor thing," Regina said, shuddering. "I can't believe it. And you told them I wouldn't do the concert either? But why? Why did you speak for me?"

His fingers dug into her shoulders. "Mike said you would react like this, but I told him he was wrong. I told him you had integrity."

"I do have integrity. What has that got to do with the concert?"

"Don't you see? Another person is dead because of Don. Someone he abused the way he abused my brother."

She looked at him in shock as though she'd never really seen him before. He was obsessed by this need to blame someone for his brother's death. It was insane. "Cord. The Princess's accident had nothing to do with Gene's death. She was drugged all the time, practically a Zombie. You can't blame Don for that. Don't you see? You can't protect people from themselves."

Her words weren't getting through to him. He looked stricken, as though she'd touched an unknown part of him, revealed an infected aspect of his soul.

"Cord," she said, more softly, frightened by his reaction. "This would have happened no matter who the woman was involved with. For all you know Don may have kept her alive longer than anyone else. He might have even made her happy."

"You can't believe that!" he shouted.

"All right, so I don't believe it."

"Don't you care about her? She's dead! *She's dead!*"

"Yes, I care. It's horrible!"

"Then why are you defending him? He's a no good shitheel." He looked at her with disgust. "I didn't want to believe this of you, but you're as bad as he is." He let go of her, pushing her away.

"And you're so tied up in the past you'll never get free," she cried, wanting to dig her fingernails into him and hold on, wanting to do anything within her power to wipe the look of scorn off his face. He was leaving her again. For a moment the pain was so intense she thought she just couldn't stand it, and then suddenly it was gone, and she felt great relief. Perhaps he too had been looking for an excuse all along?

"Cord, whatever you think of me, don't quit!" she pleaded. "Don made a terrible mistake with Sonia, but I know he never meant for this to happen."

"You just don't see, do you, how destructive his selfishness is."

"I see how your hatred of him is destroying you. Don't let it. Please Cord, don't."

They heard someone coming and turned toward

the footsteps. It was Mike. Regina started guiltily, assessing how the two of them looked together.

"Well, what did she say?" Mike asked.

"She's your wife," Cord answered bitterly and turned away toward his cabin.

"What are you going to do?" she called after him.

"I'm quitting!" he said. "I'm through."

"No," she cried and then turned to Mike. "He can't do it. He just can't. Don't let him."

"I'll talk to him, baby, don't worry," he said. She looked exhausted. "Don't worry." He put his arm around her shoulder and led her back.

But just as they reached the main building, they heard a commotion. Suddenly the door flew open and Fideo ran toward them, beckoning and waving.

"It's Florie! We've called an ambulance. I think it's her heart."

CHAPTER 39

It was forty-five minutes before the ambulance and the paramedics arrived. Forty-five agonizing minutes while Regina stood helplessly by watching Florie suffer excruciating pain. There was very little they could do for her, except to give her first aid, until the medical team got there. Regina could only hold Florie's hand and wipe her forehead while she writhed with the horrible compression in her chest and perspired until she was soaking wet. And then she vomited from the pain, begging God to take her and put her out of her misery.

"No!" Regina cried. "You've got to live. Just hold on. God doesn't need you as much as I do."

"If she survives the initial attack, she might pull through," someone said.

Regina barely heard it. All she could focus on was that her beloved Florie was dying. She went with Florie in the ambulance to a nearby hospital in Monterey and then waited while they wired Florie up to the cardiac care unit and medicated her. They would only allow Regina to see her for five minutes on the hour; so she sat and waited, hour after hour, for those precious visits, alternating between tears, and sobbing, and hope, and despair. *If only she'll be all right. Please, let her be all right.* Everyone from Antelope kept calling, but there was no change. Florie was barely holding her own.

Mike offered to take her place at the vigil, but Regina declined. She wouldn't leave Florie's side. Mike sounded terribly pressured on the phone, but Regina couldn't help him. Only Florie mattered. She didn't give a thought to Cord's quitting the reunion. If anything happened to Florie, she wouldn't have the heart to go on herself.

Exhaustion, strain, and fear finally took their toll, and she fell asleep on the sofa in the waiting room of the hospital, her cheek sticking to the vinyl, her knees pulled up and cramped beneath her. It was the only sleep she'd had in twenty-four hours.

By eight o'clock that night the crisis had abated, but the next few days would be critical. Regina was still terrified that Florie wouldn't live till morning. She felt that by staying at the hospital and being nearby, merely by her presence, she was keeping Florie alive. But finally she agreed to go back to Antelope and get some rest.

She found Mike packed and ready to leave.

"Where are you going?" she asked, nearly at the edge of her strength.

"I've got to go and find Cord, talk him into coming back."

"Cord is really gone? How could he leave at a time like this? Doesn't he know about Florie? Doesn't he care?"

"Cord has always been totally self-involved. He and Louise left this morning."

"Mike, I don't want you to go. Send someone else. I need you to be with me."

He was touched by her words. She seldom asked for his help, but this was one time he couldn't give it. At least not directly. But by bringing Cord back he would be doing her a much greater service in the long run than by just staying to hold her hand. "I'm the one who's responsible, Regina. I've got to do this. Cord wouldn't listen to Don, and besides Don has accompanied Sonia's body to Austria and won't be back until after the funeral. I'm the only one who can convince Cord to return, so Lubow says."

"Did you talk to Lubow?"

"He was here. Flew in by helicopter with Stylwickji."

"The man from New York?" she asked, her voice losing its strength with the question. He nodded.

"Did they threaten you again?"

Mike averted his eyes. He couldn't tell her what Lubow had made him do or how Lubow had threatened to hurt both of them if the concert was cancelled.

"Lubow was very insistent that I bring off this event. There's a great deal at stake now for all of us. He made that clear."

"But there was no more talk of Choo Choo?"

"No," he assured her. "That never came up."

"How are the children?"

"They're bewildered and frightened. They've heard some awful rumors about Sonia, and then when Florie got sick and you left, they didn't know what to think. They really need you right now."

She started to cry. "I really need them too. They're all I've got."

He put his arms around her for a brief moment and then he was out the door.

She remembered something she'd been meaning to ask him and called out, "Mike!" His van was driving away. "Do you owe Lubow any money?"

She could barely hear his reply.

"It's nothing," he called back. "A few hundred dollars. I'll tell you about it when I get back." And the van rounded the bend in the road.

* * *

How many days without sleep? Mike had stopped counting. He'd grabbed a few hours on the plane from California to New York, but it wasn't nearly enough. And the one question that gave him no rest was Regina's last one. How had she found out about the money he owed Lubow? She'd caught him completely by surprise. And that was one subject he didn't care to discuss with her, *ever*. In fact he'd go to extremes to avoid it.

Cord must have wanted to be found or he wouldn't have gone to Louise Carlin's apartment. Louise opened the door and ushered Mike into the living room where Cord was waiting in his perennial blue jeans.

They circled each other warily, two wrestlers looking for an opening. "I'll leave you alone," Louise said after offering coffee.

Cord looked like he had slept, but they were each wrung out, stretched taut, harboring thin membranes over deep injuries.

Mike dropped into a flowered-print chair. The room felt like a fresh English country garden, and he realized that he was out of place here. His face itched from indecent neglect, and he smelled inside his suit. But he'd rather smell and be alive than clean and dead. He could still hear Stylwickji's voice saying if he failed this time, it would mean his life, Regina's life, and their children's lives. Every time he thought about that, his control went down the drain, and panic flushed through him.

"You've got to come back," he began. Cord had a way of thrusting his jaw forward when he was being defiant that Mike found petulant and annoying.

"I don't *have* to do anything."

Mike rubbed his eyes, they were grainy and bloodshot from seeing too many problems. *The producer's life,* he thought ironically, *is to be scared shitless.*

He hadn't had a bowel movement in three days. "I know how you feel, Cord."

"Don't give me that bull!" Cord shouted, immediately out of control, his eyes were round and wild like a cornered animal. *That's what we all are,* Mike thought. *Cornered like Sonia was when she was attacked by another stronger beast. We think every friend is an enemy, and every enemy is a friend.*

"Can we talk about this civilly?"

Cord's muscles were tight, as though he were ready to pounce as he waited for his adversary's thrust. But Mike was too tired to even parry. He waved his hand for Cord to calm down. Cord unclenched his fists and relaxed his body. It was as if a ramrod had gone slack.

"What would I have to do to get you to come back? What is it? Anything? Ask me. Go on, ask me."

Cord just stared at him, and then he shook his head. "If I came back, I might kill Don."

Mike nodded. "What else?"

"That's not a condition; it's a fact of life."

"What else?"

"There's no way, Mike."

"More money? I could get you another five hundred thousand, maybe a million." He calculated rapidly. He would give Cord a half a million of his own share and hit Lubow up for another half. If it saved the reunion, Lubow would have to do it.

"The money would help, but I'm not coming back."

"You want first billing?"

"You haven't been listening!"

Mike squeezed his hands together, fighting for control. For a moment he considered falling on his knees and begging. "I'm listening. What do you want?"

"There's nothing that could make me work again."

"Yes, there is."

"What?" Cord was curious.

"Regina. She needs you to do this for her. You heard about Florie?"

Cord nodded. A mirrored table between them that held a collection of exotic memorabilia gleamed and sparkled in the delicate manner of brilliant colored objects. The collection made Cord look awkward and ungainly with his long legs and jutting elbows. Ungainly but never insecure.

"I'm sorry about Florie. She's a helluva woman. I know what she means to Regina, but . . ."

Mike held up his hand. "Hear me out. Regina has to do this reunion concert for many reasons. But the most important one is to bury her past, to prove to herself that she made the right choices in her life."

"You mean that she was right to choose you?"

"Yes."

"Well, suppose I don't think she was right. Suppose I think she shouldn't have married you. She should have married me."

"You didn't ask her."

"What if I did now?"

Mike hadn't thought there was any part of him left that could feel more fear than he had felt before, but he was wrong. Cord's question chilled him in a place deep within, in the well of his secret fears where Regina resided. That part of him that was her. He took a deep breath. "Come back and do the concert, and afterwards when it's all over, I won't stand in your way."

"Jesus!" Cord exploded. "You're disgusting. What a worm you are. You'd sell your wife to keep your share of the profits."

"I'm not selling my wife because I know she wouldn't accept your offer. And because there's more at stake here than my pride." How he prayed he was right.

"What other stakes?"

Mike weighed his next statement. He'd hoped it wouldn't come to this. What would Cord do with this information? How badly did he want Regina. If Cord used this against him, he'd surely lose Regina. "I'm going to take a chance and trust you, Cord. What I'm about to tell you is confidential." He tried to keep a semblance of calm, but his entire future lay in the hands of his rival. "Lubow has me by the shorts and he's pulling hard. I got into the promotion of this concert in the first place because I owed Lubow three hundred thousand dollars. Due to a bad investment I lost the collateral for that loan. And Lubow just forced another one out of me."

Louise appeared at the living room door and stood there listening. Mike had suspected her presence within earshot, and now he beckoned to her. "You might as well hear this too." He hoped she would be on his side and help him convince Cord.

She sat on the floor at Cord's feet.

"The way my corporation with Regina is set up for tax purposes, Regina is on an employment contract of five-year increments with our jointly owned company. That way I can deduct my managerial fees separately from our income. Lubow has forced me to sign over Regina's five-year employment contract to him in lieu of the debt I owe him. If the concert takes place, I'll have enough money to pay Lubow back and recover the contract. If not, Regina will be owned by Lubow for the next five years, and when she finds out, she'll divorce me."

A series of expressions crossed Cord's face. But the one that finally took hold was sympathy. He wanted Regina, but he didn't want to have her by default. "Lubow is a worse shitheel than Don Drummond," he said.

Louise shook her head. "That's really rotten."

If they only knew about the threats of violence, Mike thought. "For God's sake, don't tell Lubow that I've told you," he said, praying that they wouldn't. That would really endanger him and Regina.

He pushed himself up and out of the chair. His legs were on someone else's body; his head felt light and dizzy; but he held on. "Will you come back?"

Cord paused for what seemed like an eternity, weighing Mike's offer. Finally he looked up with eyes as redshot as Mike's own. This had been a hard struggle for him too. "I'll come back for Regina's sake."

Mike was almost too tired to feel relief, but he did feel grateful. At least he'd protected himself and his loved ones. He started toward the door. But Cord's voice stopped him.

"There's one condition."

Mike turned back. "What?"

"I'd like you to stay away from Antelope until after the concert. And don't tell Regina what we've discussed."

Mike stared at him, then nodded once and walked to the door. There was only one small advantage to Cord's request. At least he could avoid any discussion with Regina about the debt. He didn't want to keep compounding a lie with other lies. His head felt so heavy that it nearly rested on his chest. "It's two weeks to New Orleans, nearly three until the concert. I'll stay away until you leave for the Superdome. Will you watch out for Regina for me?"

Cord nodded.

And Mike closed the door behind him.

Louise waited until the door closed and then she got up from the floor. "Well, which one of us is it now?" she asked Cord.

He leaned back in the chair and closed his eyes. He didn't answer.

"I think you should get your things together and

leave now." There was pain in her eyes. "I'll join you tomorrow."

He stood up and walked past her into the bedroom.

"And Cord, don't come to me again the next time Regina turns you down. Because I won't be here."

CHAPTER 40

Mike flew to Austria and took Don's place with Sonia's family. It was a difficult task to explain to Sonia's arthritic mother and younger brother how their only living relative had been eaten by a mountain lion. Once Don and Cord had returned to Antelope, rehearsals got underway again. All the musical arrangements had been completed and they had laid the main voice tracks for the album, but outside of the recording studio neither of them spoke to each other. Penny's rosy complexion had lost its bloom and she grew morose, eating chocolates and showing a belly where none had been before. And Beau was as depressed as ever. But no one had the ability to cheer him, least of all Penny, though she made a valiant effort. But all of her attempts went unheeded.

Fideo picked up the telephone on the first ring. He hardly left his office lately because of all the problems he'd had. His nerves were constantly jumping. A couple of Quaaludes mellowed him out, but he still had to juggle the press and the temperaments of the artists under his care. And tension was high. So high you could almost feel it leaping from person to person. A lot of that tension was being aimed at Beau. He would be glad when the Majesty group was gone.

"Fideo, here," he answered.

"How's our boy doin'?" It was Choo Choo.

"Shooting a packet a day and still holding on, barely," Fideo told him. "How's your aunt feeling?"

"I'm callin' from the hospital where she's at," Choo Choo said. "She been here a week an' that bitch Regina didn't even tell me she'd took sick. My aunt had the nurse to call me."

"Regina's had a lot on her mind," Fideo conceded. Even Regina couldn't have been expected to remember about Choo Choo with the reunion almost cancelled and Florie so ill.

"Yeah? Well, someday I'm gonna pay her back."

Fideo could just imagine what that meant.

Regina approached Florie's room on tiptoe until she heard voices coming from inside. Florie wasn't asleep. She had a visitor. Regina stopped a minute in the hall to listen. She would know the hated sound of Choo Choo's voice anywhere.

So he'd found her.

Well, at least she hadn't been the one to tell him. His presence would only endanger Florie. He should be barred from the hospital.

She walked back down the hall to wait until she saw Choo Choo leave and then she slipped into Florie's room. Florie had lost so much weight during her ordeal that the flesh on her arms and under her chin was soft and loose, giving her the appearance of someone who was melting inside her skin. Florie's full-cheeked, robust look was gone, and Regina's heart wrenched anew with each daily visit.

"How are you doing, sweetheart?" she asked.

Florie smiled at her and reached out her hand. The IV was attached to her wrist, and her forearm above the bandage was swollen and distended where the IV had infiltrated the flesh.

"I'm better now that you're here. You know who come to see me all the way from New York?"

"Yes. I didn't want to interrupt your visit, so I waited until he left. I hope you don't mind."

"Lord, no. I'm always glad to see Lionel, but I know how you feel."

"I'm sorry, darling," Regina said. "You know whatever makes you happy is fine with me." But just having Choo Choo nearby worried her. He was ignorant, and so volatile, and mean. He might do something just to get at her and in the process hurt Florie. Choo Choo was dangerous if you pressed him, but she had no intention of doing that.

"Have you seen my doctor?" Florie asked.

Regina shook her head. "No. Hasn't he been here yet?"

"I been waitin', but not so far. He's supposed to give me the damages today."

It was time now to assess what Florie's future would be like.

"How's my babies doin'?"

"They went horseback riding this morning and to the beach this afternoon. They're as brown as can be, and they love Melissa, the college girl who's taking care of them."

"Lord bless them. And how's their mama?"

"I miss you." She fought the tears again. "And I miss Michael. He hasn't come back to Antelope yet even though Cord is here and he hasn't called in days; or when he does telephone, I'm always unavailable."

"He's just doin' his job, sugar."

"No. I think he's avoiding me and I don't know why. He knows how much I need him right now."

"Maybe he don't want to come back and see you with Cord."

"I'm not with Cord. We've barely been civil to each other. No. I think Mike is avoiding me or punishing me, or both. But for the life of me I can't figure out why, unless . . ." She suddenly remembered about Louise's comment. Perhaps Mike's debt to Lubow was larger than he'd admitted. Was that why he was avoiding her?

"Unless what?" Florie asked. "Unless he knows how you been carryin' on with another man."

"Florie, come on now. I don't want to talk about me. It's you we have to plan for. When you come home, I'm going to get you a nurse, full time, and you're going on a special diet. Should have been on one long ago."

"Quit fussin', now. Hear? I been lyin' in this bed a long time thinkin' about you and what you're doin' with your life. And I want to talk about it whiles I still can. You got a good man, honey. Why you fixin' to bother your own life that way?"

Here it was again. That same question.

"You know, when I'm with Cord, life is like a circus. But when I'm with Mike, sometimes it's like a roast beef sandwich on white bread."

Florie chuckled. "I never heard it that way before. But don't you know what it is you're sayin', honey? Roast beef and bread will sustain you; those are the staples of life. But a circus can only entertain. Yessir, Cord is an exciting man. Even a woman of my age can see that. Why if I was a bit younger myself, I might even give him a tumble."

Regina threw back her head and laughed. "You old teaser!" she exclaimed. And Florie laughed with her. "Honey, Cord is your prince on the black stallion."

"That's a white stallion," Regina corrected.

"Mind if I change it a little?"

Regina grinned, "You mean he's my fantasy?"

"That's right. But he's never gonna be there when you need him. Not like Mike."

"Then where is Mike right now? I need him, but

he isn't here. And Mike makes so many mistakes, Florie. He doesn't always tell me the truth."

"But he loves you, baby. And he loves those girls."

"Yes, he does that," she agreed.

"Why don't you find him, and you ask him to come back?"

Florie was right. It was time for her to stop being afraid, to stop avoiding a commitment to Mike. She'd do it. She'd insist that he come back to Antelope and be with her. But first she'd have to settle things with Cord.

Just then Dr. White came in to examine Florie and asked Regina to step into the hall. He was with her only a few minutes before he came out and joined her.

"May I have a word with you, Miss Williams?" he asked, indicating for her to follow him into a nearby waiting room. He was a young man, balding and pale-skinned. His face was kind, but he saw tragedies all day long. They seldom belonged to him.

He stared at her through clear-framed glasses. "May I be frank?"

Regina nodded and held onto the edge of a nearby table. A sudden sense of fear had taken hold.

"Your friend Mrs. Trainer is not a well woman. She's suffered a great deal of damage to her heart with this attack. Frankly, I'm surprised that she survived. There's a major blockage stemming the flow of blood to the left ventricle—that's the ventricle that pumps the blood to the body. The angiogram done last year indicates that she is not a candidate for a bypass surgery."

"When did she have an angiogram? I was never informed of that."

"Her records stated that it was done in Alabama last fall. I guess she never told you about it."

"That's just like Florie," Regina said. "She probably didn't want me to worry."

"That's too bad. Perhaps you might have been able to monitor her diet more closely. A woman in her condition should never be as overweight as she is."

"Just what is her condition, Dr. White?"

"It's extremely serious."

"How serious?" Icy fingers clutched at Regina's heart. She wanted to cover her ears and scream to keep from hearing what he was about to tell her. Instead she stared back at the doctor.

"She could have a fatal attack at any time. I'd suggest that you spend as much time as possible with her in the very near future. It may be your last time together."

"How near?" The words came out before she could stop them.

"Weeks, maybe a month. Anytime, really."

"But I have to go to New Orleans in a few days."

"I can only apprise you of the situation, Miss Williams. What you do with it is up to you."

Regina kept a tight hold on herself until she got back to her cabin. And then she threw herself across the bed and sobbed. Oh, God, no. Not again. How could she lose another mother and survive? All the love Florie had given her and all the support. She couldn't bear the pain of this loss. It wrenched her, tearing at her heart. She wanted to die, herself.

She felt little hands touching her back, stroking her hair. "What'samatter, Mommie? Didja have a nightmare?"

Regina wiped at her eyes and turned over. Jamie and Jana were standing there in their blue bathrobes. Jamie's hair was wet from her shampoo and it curled around her face in ringlets. Their cheeks were bright pink from a day in the sun, their eyebrows bleached blond. She took them in her arms, revelling in the sweet softness of her children. Jamie's arms went around her neck, Jana's around her waist, and the three of them hugged each other hard.

"It's all right, Mommie," Jamie said. "We're here."

"I know you are, sweethearts." Regina held her children tightly, but not too tightly.

"Are you crying 'bout Florie?" Jana asked.

"Yes," she said. "Florie is very sick."

"Is she going to die?" Jamie asked.

"Only God knows that," Regina replied.

"If she dies, then could she come back in another body like the man in the movie we saw?" Jana said.

Regina laughed in spite of herself. "Oh, baby," she said, "I'm so glad I've got you two; you mean everything in the world to me."

"And Daddy too," Jana reminded her.

Regina sighed. "And Daddy too," she agreed. But where was Daddy? When was he coming back?

CHAPTER 41

They were winding down. Only a few more days to go. The voice tracks were completed, the act was nearly perfected, and Regina had to grudgingly admit that Louise Carlin had done a brilliant job supervising the final mix and laying down additional instrument tracks. Louise had used very little overdub, wanting the album to sound like their live performance, which had been a particular practice of Majesty's in the past.

The group had been photographed in every vale and glade at Antelope. The documentary film crew was pleased with their footage. Everything was smooth on the surface. But the sense of camaraderie was missing. *We're cold together,* Regina thought. *All of us.* There was nothing she could do to bring Don and Cord closer or Don and Beau, but she and Cord could be friends.

With a fluttering in her stomach she approached his cabin. He was sitting on the porch, leaning back in his chair, feet on the railing, guitar in hand, a toke in an ashtray on the table, a glass of white wine nearby.

"Hi." She perched on the railing next to his boots, her cotton skirt formed a waterfall of raspberry color as it billowed over the edge. The evening was warm, the air so soft it made her want to throw open her arms and gather it in.

Cord was strumming softly. She saw him glance at

the glaze of pink sunburn across her cheeks and forehead, the sprinkle of freckles on her nose. "You've gotten some color."

"Yes, I'll probably peel."

"How's Florie?" he asked.

At the mention of Florie's name that same awful feeling threatened to take over her mood. "Let's not talk about her, all right? It only makes me weep."

He nodded, strumming, changing chords, settling on a melody. It was one of her songs, "Just Friends." The lyric ran through her mind as he played.

Were we just friends,
I'd know you in the quiet of my heart.
Were we just friends,
I'd hold you there beside me.
Were we just friends,
Your smile would light my evenings and my days,
The special afterglow of loving that you bring
Were we just friends,
I'd feel your touch in everything I do,
Though we would pass and nod along the way.
And if we're friends,
I couldn't love you mo-re than I do,
So be my friend
Until my life is through. . . .

He gazed at her as he played the last note of the song. "Is that the way you want it with us, Regina? Just friends?"

"Loving friends?" she said.

"I won't share you."

"I know." She traced her finger along the dusty stitches of his boot, watching the clean leather appear under her touch. She wished she could wipe her life clean as easily. "We've finally grown up, Cord. At least I have. I know what I want. And I can see

what you need. Both alternatives are painful for me."
He tilted his head to the side and stared at her; his eyes were achingly clear, and he seemed to be waiting for her in their depths. "I will always love you," she said. "I love what we had together. I will always want you to love me and only me in some perfect vacuum where everything is pure and I can have anything I want. But I can also see that a woman like Louise is better for you than I am."

"Just as I can see that a man like Mike is better for you than I am."

The words stabbed her with pain for a moment, and she held her breath. But then her heart resumed its normal beating, and the pain faded.

"You know," he said. "This conversation is making me crazy. I want to yell and tear the walls down and bellow NOooo! It's not right! We belong together! But I can't. The goddamned inevitability of it weighs as heavy on me as blocks of granite."

"For someone as stubborn and self-willed as you that must be frustrating."

"You should know."

Her eyes and throat were dry. She took a sip of his wine. He took a drag on his joint, offered it to her; she declined.

"Mike isn't such a bad guy."

"Neither is Louise."

"But it isn't the same," they both said in unison and laughed.

"We can make it different with them, Cord. Different and in many ways better."

"I guess you have grown up, princess," he grinned. And her heart turned over when he called her that, thudding in her chest for just a moment.

She leaned over and touched her lips to his, lightly, fighting the urge to go further. Such soft, velvety fullness. That desire would always be there, but she understood it now, placed it in its proper place. *Great sex does not a relationship make. But it sure helps,* she smiled to herself, *it sure helps.*

He kissed her back, lightly, fondly, friendly. "See ya around," he said as she stepped off the porch.

She waved, blinking back just a touch of wetness, and headed toward her cabin to call Mike.

Regina hurried past Louise's cabin. Her windows were dark, and so she was startled when Louise called out to her.

"How's Florie, Regina?"

She turned quickly, almost guiltily toward the voice, and Louise switched on the porch light. She was leaning over her railing, gazing out on the meadow and the fabulous stars flung above it like chunks of magic sparkle dust. Louise's view of Cord's cabin was unobstructed. She must have seen them together. Regina hoped she hadn't heard, too.

Regina came over to her, looking up to where she was standing. "I didn't know you were there."

"No, I guess you didn't," Louise answered. "How is Florie doing?"

"Not well."

There was an awkward silence.

"Louise," Regina began. "I know there's no great love lost between us, but I want you to know that I greatly admire what you've done with the album. It's top work, and I'm proud to be on it. My songs were handled to perfection. I'm grateful to you."

"Thank you," Louise said, pleased in spite of her animosity.

"And I think you should also know that I'm not going to be seeing Cord anymore except on a professional basis. It's over."

"That's none of my business, Regina," Louise replied.

"I thought I'd tell you anyway." She started to go

down the path and then turned back. "Oh, one more thing. Mike has told me *everything,* about the money he owes Lubow and all."

"Did he?" Louise seemed surprised. "I guess now that the reunion is going ahead he felt he'd have enough money to pay his debt."

Regina nodded, her hands suddenly turning to ice.

"I can imagine how worried you must have been to think of that creep Lubow owning your personal contract, even for a short amount of time."

Regina could barely speak; every muscle in her body was rigid. "But there was a lot of money involved." She was guessing; a wild guess. Louise would say, "Five hundred dollars? A lot of money?" and they'd laugh.

But Louise said, "I can't imagine what it would be like to owe someone three hundred thousand dollars. But I guess in your league that's not unusual."

Regina's feet felt rooted to the ground. She had looked back at Sodom and Gomorrah and been turned into a pillar of salt; bitter, bitter salt.

"No, Louise. In my league it's a lot of money, too. Good night," she mumbled and turned away as quickly as her leaden feet would turn her. My God, what had she done? She'd just killed her options with Cord and committed herself to a liar. A liar. A liar. A liar! *Oh Michael, why?*

She felt burned out, seared from the acid knowledge that ate at her insides, hollow and charred ribs housing the remnants of a burnt heart. *This is what I've always been afraid of,* she thought. *Exactly* this! *This is why I've never committed to him.* How she longed for Florie at this moment. What could she do; where should she turn?

She ran down the path, up the stairs, and into her cabin and tore into the children's room, gathering them up in her arms in a sleepy tumble.

"Mommie, what's the matter?" Jamie asked.

"Shh," she soothed, needing to feel their aliveness in her hands, wanting just to know that they existed, a part of her still true and pure and uncorrupted, unlike their father.

Jana didn't even awaken. She kissed them both and lay them back down. Jamie turned over and fell back to sleep in an instant. And she was left to put out the blazing coals burning inside her.

CHAPTER
42

The day they were to leave for New Orleans, Regina drove up to Monterey to say good-bye to Florie. Cord offered to go with her, but she turned him down. She needed to be alone with Florie, the sadness inside of her was overwhelming.

I won't tell her my troubles and I won't cry, she promised herself. But the minute she saw Florie's brave smile, her resolve deserted her, and her heart ached to be parting from her dearest friend.

"I'd give anything if I didn't have to leave you," Regina said.

Florie's tears spilled over and ran down her own cheeks. "You'll be back, honey. And we'll laugh at these doctors, you and me. I ain't goin' nowheres. I'll be around for a long time." Florie always said that. She opened her arms, and Regina came into her embrace, wanting to stay there forever, loved and protected. But Florie's arms were so much weaker now. Her magic hands patted Regina's cheeks softly. Was it for the last time? Regina noticed how much less there was of Florie than there used to be.

On the way back to Antelope she realized that Florie had tried to spare her, but there was a terrible look of fear in her eyes when Regina left. *I should be with her,* she cried. *I shouldn't have to leave her now. What a price to pay for my work. Please God, keep her safe until I get back.*

She found Mike's suitcases sitting in the living

room of the cabin. He must have driven up from L.A. to go to New Orleans with her. But the sight of those neatly packed bags incensed her. She didn't want him here now. It was too late! She found him in the bedroom.

"What are you doing here?" she demanded. "How can you show your face after the way you've treated me? How could you?" She had to pull herself together. She went into the bathroom and ran the ice water tap, splashing her red blotchy face.

Mike looked at her helplessly. "If I could have been here sooner, I would have."

She turned in exasperation. "Don't give me your excuses." She clutched the wet towel in her hand, itching to throw it at him. "I have something to ask you, and I want a straight answer! Why haven't you called me? What's been going on?"

"Nothing, Regina."

He was lying again. She knew that look on his face. "Do you have any idea what I've been going through? Florie's dying! She's dying!" Horrible spasms gripped her with the realization, and she cried out in agony, clutching herself and rocking back and forth with the pain.

Mike had never seen her like this. He reached out to her, but she pushed him away. Finally the pain eased a bit, and she faced him again. "All right, I want to know! What about Lubow? What about the money you owe him?"

"I don't owe him anything. It's all been taken care of." He stared at her in amazement. How did she find out? Cord had told her. He shouldn't have trusted him.

"Nothing? You call three hundred thousand dollars nothing? Where did you get the money to pay him back?"

"From my share of the advance for the reunion."

"And what did you use for security?"

He just stared at her, unable to reply.

"My contract. You used *my contract,* didn't you?"

His nod was barely perceptible.

So it was true. "And why did you owe him the money?"

"It's nothing, Reg. It's all in the past."

A scream came welling up from deep inside of her, and she let it out all at once. "You're driving me crazy, Michael! Don't you realize what you've done. You've betrayed me. I had to learn about what you've done from strangers. You've killed my love. You've killed what we had between us. And after you swore that you'd told me everything. Now—tell—me—what —you've—done!" The last words were at the highest, strongest pitch her voice would allow.

He looked at her in shock. "Regina, you're going to injure your throat."

"I don't care!" she screamed.

The strain of the last week showed in every muscle of his body. He couldn't hold out against her anymore. He was just too tired. But God, he didn't want to lose her over something that had happened months ago. Not after the way he'd worked to achieve something just to impress her. And not after the torture of the last two weeks. The things he'd imagined while he stayed away. He'd told himself that if it came to a choice between him and Cord, she would choose him. Now he didn't think so. "I borrowed the money from Lubow to pay back a loan from the bank."

"What loan?" Her voice came down an octave.

"Tony Darakjian and I invested in a film. We co-produced it."

"So where is the film?"

"The shooting was completed long ago. It's all in the can. But it's unusable. We've had to write it off."

"What do you mean, unusable?"

"Just take my word for it; it's a total loss."

She was stunned. How had he done all this without her knowledge? She held back another explosion until she'd heard it all. "Where did you get collateral for that kind of a loan?"

He mumbled his reply, trying to light a cigarette. The smoke burned his throat; he hadn't smoked in years.

"Answer me!" she shouted, her body tense and straining.

"I used the house as collateral."

"How? How? HOW could you do that without my signature?"

He just looked at her and then away.

The truth hit her like a fist in the stomach. She could only whisper. "My God, you forged my signature. Didn't you? You forged it. Oh, Mike." The enormity of it was too much. She looked at him with total disbelief. This man she was married to was a complete stranger. Suddenly she felt calmer than she had in weeks. This was it? She was through with him! He would be lucky if she didn't press criminal charges. "Not only have you cheated your own wife, you've cheated yourself. You *had* to get me to do this reunion, didn't you? So that you could fulfill your obligations to that rat Lubow and save your own skin."

"At the bottom of everything I did it for you," he said.

"No, Mike. I won't accept that anymore. You mean to say you cheated me for my own sake? You left me alone here to suffer through one of the worst experiences of my life for my own good? With a friend like you who needs enemies?" She grabbed her linen jacket off the bed and headed for the door.

"My bags are ready. Have someone check under the girls' beds before we leave and be sure to look inside their showers."

"Where are you going?" He seemed terrified. But she wouldn't be in the same room with him another minute. She swept by him without an answer. "I'll see you in New Orleans."

CHAPTER 43

Mike accepted his banishment from Regina, and she went on the Antelope jet to New Orleans, while he took the Continental flight with Penny Morgan. In a way he was grateful for the separation. It would give her time to calm down. He didn't blame her for her reaction. He just wished none of it had ever happened. The most difficult thing he'd ever done in his life had been to stay away from her during the last weeks. And now his sacrifice and his avoidance had completely backfired.

He leaned back in his seat and closed his eyes. Maybe once they got to New Orleans, he could make her see how much he loved her, how different things were going to be from now on.

Penny was relieved that the airplane wasn't full. She took a seat in an empty row across the aisle from Mike. There were empty seats all around her and an emptiness inside, in spite of the baby growing there. How could anything so exciting have turned out so wrong? How could she have been such a fool? She'd hurt Beau, hurt him badly. Now all she wanted to do was make it up to him. If only she didn't feel so rotten and cheap. Not since the time in Oakland before she met Beau had she felt this way.

Don had only used her. And she'd let him. God how she'd let him. Her cheeks burned with the memories of their sexual encounters. She had felt so grown up, so womanly, so special being desired by him. The forest, the beach, the trails, the closets, no place was sacred from their lust, even though he made fun of her, the way she talked, the way she defended Beau, and especially the "little bugger" inside of her, as he called her baby. How crude he'd been. How she hated him now. No. She didn't hate him; sometimes she still wanted him, in spite of her resolve. At first not seeing him had been like the relief that comes after a beating when the absence of pain is exquisite. But then the soreness and the ache began. And dear Lord she was sore. Not only her body, but her heart. She could not forgive herself for what she'd done to Beau in her quest for Don's attention. Beau must know about her and Don by now, though she prayed that he didn't. It would be too terrible.

Mike Shaw was watching her from across the aisle. He came to sit by her.

"Is there anything I can do for you? Aren't you feeling well?"

The look of concern on his face touched her, and she couldn't hold back. "I've made such a mess of everything. There's nobody I can talk to. Beau won't speak to me anymore. I'm so afraid of what is going to happen."

Mike hadn't expected such an outburst. "What kind of mess, Penny?" He put his arm around her awkwardly. Her shoulders were shaking.

"It's not that bad, is it?" he asked. "Why don't you tell me about it."

She tried to calm herself enough to tell him, but she couldn't talk.

"Shall I get you a glass of water?"

She nodded.

If Mike hadn't been walking carefully back down the aisle with a full cup of water, he might not have noticed Stylwickji sitting halfway between Penny's seat and the stewards' station in the center section. He felt his heart fall into the pit of his stomach. Stylwickji's blond hair was neatly parted; his dark three-piece suit, carefully tailored; and that ugly scar on his cheek sent chills down Mike's back. Why was Stylwickji still following him? Just to scare him? Well, he was scared all right. Scared pissless. He'd done what they'd asked of him, fulfilled every obligation. He'd kept the reunion together, kept his mouth shut about Lubow's drug connections, and Regina certainly hadn't said anything either. Lubow must know that. What did they want with him? He stopped in the aisle.

"Why don't you leave me alone?" he asked. His voice shook, revealing the inner terror. The glass of ice water was turning warm in his sweaty hand.

"Just following orders," Stylwickji said. "The boss told me to check up on you now and then. Until the money's paid back." He returned to his magazine.

"Dammit. Lubow owes me much more than I owe him."

Stylwickji looked up with an expression that said, "This is different."

Mike forced himself to walk past. They still didn't trust him. But why? Fuck Lubow. He'd lost everything that mattered to him because of that bastard. The thought filled him with despair. He handed the water to Penny and sat down.

She thanked him. "I'm sorry for my outburst, but I've got to talk to someone."

Mike fastened the seat belt and tried to concentrate on what she was saying, but Stylwickji's presence on the plane was like a beacon of fear to him, a reminder of his precarious safety.

"When we get to New Orleans, will you talk to Beau for me? Tell him that I love him. I don't want to lose him."

"Wouldn't it be far more meaningful coming from you?" he asked.

"Believe me, I've tried. He just won't listen."

"Okay," he promised. "I'll have a talk with Beau the first chance I get."

She smiled gratefully.

But Mike's eyes were irresistibly drawn to the blond man with the glasses, though Stylwickji never once turned around to look back. It didn't matter. Mike knew he had eyes in the back of his head.

CHAPTER 44

The day of the concert dawned clear and hot. The weather bureau predicted a scorcher, and by eight A.M. the air that hung over New Orleans was heavy with expectancy. Even the humidity was high, at eighty-six percent. Crowds had begun lining the parking lots of the Superdome days before the concert was scheduled, and there were incidents of violence reported all over the country between fans who had missed out on concert tickets and those who had bought them. Countless theaters and stadiums in various U.S. cities were carrying simultaneous broadcasts of the concert. The reunion of Majesty was bigger than the resurrection of Elvis Presley. And in a way it was a resurrection of the past, of an era of greatness remembered, which could only be surpassed by the originals themselves. Half the country thought the concert would be a devastating disappointment; the other half lived in frenzied anticipation of the event. Majesty's fans were like refugees from displaced countries as they poured into New Orleans by plane and train, in their vans and trailers, wagons and campers, buses and cars. Hawkers sold authorized Majesty memorabilia; posters, albums, tapes, souvenirs, and books. Black marketeers sold pirate copies, and everyone was raking in a fortune.

Everything was timed to peak at 8:00 P.M. daylight saving time. By the time the opening drum roll announced the beginning of the concert tonight with

James Fitzgerald as the lead act, the whole world would be at a fever pitch of expectancy for the biggest, longest, most desired, collective climax in history.

Mike's work was cut out for him. Everybody had a complaint or a problem. Regina didn't like the location of her dressing room at the Superdome; it was at the wrong end of the corridor. And she had insisted that the members of Majesty stay at different hotels to avoid the crush of fans. Setting everyone up at different hotels was very difficult. The crew were all quartered at the Hyatt next to the Superdome, which would have been more convenient for everyone. Things were terribly strained between Regina and Mike. She hardly spoke to him. Over the past four days if Mike tried to apologize or explain, she'd just nod and then go about her business. But he decided not to press her. Once the reunion was behind them, he'd make her understand.

Don hated the photograph chosen for the album cover and wanted it reshot. He was grabbing strangers in hallways and asking their opinions. But it was impossible to change it, since the albums were ready for release and the distributors were awaiting the go-ahead to begin their promotions in Europe and then around the globe.

"This Superdome is a fucking barn," Cord complained. Concert fever had gotten to him too.

Jerry Lubow was in conference with the director of the documentary, Marsh Wallace. Mike hadn't seen Marsh since he finished filming with the group at Antelope. But the rushes were good, and Mike was anxious to tell him.

Mike spotted Lubow talking with a group of men including Stylwickji, and his heart reacted to the sight of the man. *Should I go and speak to Lubow,* he wondered. *Tell him to call off his watchdog? What could I say? I promise not to tell the Feds on you, you gangster. Sure. I'd be dead in no time.* He waved to

Lubow, who ignored him. Then he remembered he hadn't checked on the marquee. Nobody had said anything to him about it. There was very little chance he'd be on it. But the marquee wasn't set up yet. The forty-foot figures of Majesty hadn't arrived from L.A. Mike called the freight yard and screamed at five people before he got a promise that they'd be there within the hour.

"They should have been here a week already," he yelled, slamming down the phone.

Louise beckoned to him as he passed by the sound booth. He stuck his head in the door.

"Should we do anything about Don's complaint?" she asked.

"There's nothing we can do," he said.

She nodded. "Where's Beau? I haven't spoken to him, have you?"

Mike recalled his conversation with Penny. In these past few days he hadn't had time to keep his promise to her. "Beau's staying at the Charles, isn't he?"

"No, he's not. Cord's at the Charles. Beau's at the Pierre; Regina's at the Pavillion; Don's at the Royal. It sounds like a Noel Coward number."

"I'm going over there now to talk to him. Be back in an hour or less."

"Don't take too long," Louise called after him. "We need you here."

Lubow looked up from the floor of the Superdome and noticed Mike's departure. "Where's he going?" he asked Stylwickji.

Stylwickji shrugged.

Lubow nodded after Mike. "Keep an eye on him. I don't need any surprises."

Regina could never remember feeling as isolated as she did now. All around her was the pressing frenzy of reunion fever while her private world was cold and subnormal. Without Florie and Mike nearby to bolster and support her, she had to muster every inner resource just to function. Her days were only slightly more tolerable than her nightmare dreams, though the demands of the children continued no matter what the condition of her state of mind and forced her into a semblance of normalcy. And she grabbed at the children's daily routine as a thread of sanity, focusing on them as an avoidance of her own turmoil.

But it had to be faced. Mike's treachery. And her own contribution, if any, to the circumstances in which she found herself, alone on the most important day of her life. She didn't know which aspect made her sadder, the acts of financial stupidity Mike had committed or the loss of hope for their marriage. How tragic it was to have finally made such a crucial decision and find it flung back in her face like pollutant from an exhaust. The acrid taste of failure filled her mouth with bitterness. Was there anything left to salvage? Could she forgive him? Did she even want to?

She had learned from Tony Darakjian and her banker that Mike had told her the truth. His losses on the film were primarily due to bad luck. "He had been desperate to prove to you that he could succeed on his own," Tony told her when she called him. It helped to soften some of Regina's anger. It had been criminally wrong of him to forge her signature. But perhaps she had been wrong to give him an unconditional no on any more independent projects. At least she would have known what he was doing, and the loss might have been prevented.

And what of her own lies and treacheries? Her affair with Cord certainly hadn't brought her closer to Mike. She had been pushing Mike away for years. Hadn't her own lying equalled his?"

But it's different! she insisted to those stubborn

voices judging the weight of each lie, one against the other. *No, it isn't,* they replied. *A lie is a lie. A breach of trust in any form is just as deadly.* She and Mike had ingested the poisons of their own making, cyanide pellets of self-indulgence.

But he'd sold her personal contract to Lubow!

What else could he do? They might have threatened his life again, possibly yours.

Did they, Michael? Is that what happened?

Oh, for the wisdom of an impartial jury. Who is right? she wondered, wanting to be very badly. *But suppose I'm not right. Would he forgive me?*

She had paid him back for his acts before the fact. They'd each had their turn at the dart board and scored bullseyes of painful thrusts. *Clever skills, haven't we,* she thought. *Good shots, both of us.*

She remembered the expression on his face when she'd accused him. He'd been hurting. She remembered his words, "Everything I've done, I've done for you." Could that be true?

No.

It was his need to be important that motivated him, his need to be successful in some world judged by bullshitters as "the way to go." But what was wrong with that? Didn't she have those same needs? My God, yes. But Mike tried to achieve his mark in the wrong way, the easy way. There was no easy way to success in life; that's what he couldn't seem to learn.

But during the preconcert activities she'd watched him handling the various problems with expertise. And there had been some tough ones. (She had caused a few herself.) Scores of people turned to him, relied on him, and he was in total control under the most trying circumstances. She had to admit she'd been proud. Perhaps all his failings had taken place in the past, and she was only looking at the residue now, at the remnants of former mistakes. Maybe he had changed.

She didn't know; she just didn't know.

But one thing was certain: they had to talk. And without the pain of betrayal clouding the issues. He was still the man she'd chosen after all, and he deserved a forum, a chance to explain.

A fleet of cars had been rented for members of the concert, some with drivers, some without. Mike asked for a red Buick compact. Beau's hotel wasn't too far away, through the west end of town, around Robert E. Lee's Circle, and down St. Charles Street. As he pulled into the hotel garage, he noticed another Buick just like his, only gray, parked across the street from the hotel. And Stylwickji was behind the wheel.

Damn! They knew where he was going before he got there. What did they think he was planning to do? Sabotage his own concert? The parking attendant gave him a ticket and told him where to park.

The corridor leading to Beau's room was long and narrow. Even with a recent remodeling the hotel had a look of age about it. Beau's door was ajar, and as Mike knocked, it swung open. But Beau was not alone. There were two men with him. One of them was Choo Choo Trainer, and the other was his bodyguard Largo.

"What are you two doing here?" Mike asked, trying to push his way past Largo who stood in his way. Choo Choo always turned up in the damndest places.

"I'm jes here visitin' mah frien' Beau," Choo Choo said.

And then Mike noticed Beau was sitting on the edge of the bed with his sleeve rolled up. A tourniquet squeezed the flesh of his upper arm, and he was about to shoot himself with a hypodermic.

"Beau!" Mike lunged toward the bed. "Don't do that, man. Don't do it!" But Choo Choo and Largo kept him back.

Beau's hands were shaking so badly he could hardly hold the hypodermic steady. Mike tried to get past Choo Choo, but Largo grabbed hold of both his arms and held him.

"Beau," he pleaded. "Not that shit. Penny is worried about you. She loves you."

But Beau paid no attention. He was trying to steady his hand so he could inject himself.

It made Mike sick to watch. He tried to squirm out of the grip of the big man behind him, and suddenly it all seemed too familiar. He remembered how he had felt that time in New York when other men had held him and beaten him. He tried to concentrate on Beau. "Penny asked me to talk to you, Beau. She loves you; she can't get along without you."

"She wants Don," Beau answered. "I'm no good for her. She'd hate me if she knew about this." He injected himself and lay back on the bed to wait for his rush.

"She'd understand, Beau. You're wrong about her."

"If she knew, she'd hate me for sure." His speech was slurring.

"But you can break the habit again. You can get off. You did it before." Choo Choo's bodyguard let go of him, and Mike went over to Beau.

"I never got off before," Beau mumbled. "She only thinks I did."

"I can help you. I've got friends, therapists who know about these things. They've gotten good results helping addicts."

"Leave him alone, man!" Choo Choo said. "He's doin' jes fine."

Beau was almost in another world. "You're a good guy, Mike. I appreciate what you're trying to do. As soon as the concert is over I'm going to get my head straight . . . I promise. . . . You tell Penny for me, okay?" He drifted off.

Mike was alarmed. He turned to Choo Choo. "Man,

you must be crazy giving him that kind of dose. You're gonna screw up the concert! He's got to go on in a few hours. Lubow has thirty million bucks riding on this, and if you fuck up his drummer, he'll have your hide. It's not my ass, or Beau's ass, it's yours, baby, all yours! He'll put Stylwickji on you!"

Choo Choo's normally nervous body began twitching with an electric energy, and he stared at Mike with a wild look in his eyes. Mike immediately regretted that he'd said anything.

"So. Mr. Lubow ain't gonna like it, hey? Or Mr. Stylwickji? Well, ain't that too bad!" Choo Choo was laughing! He nodded to the big man, who pulled a gun out of a holster under his jacket and pointed it at Mike.

"Now wait a minute," Mike said.

"What you think, Mr. Producer? You gonna be the one who tells 'im? No, you ain't." He shook his head. "You ain't gonna tell nobody, and he ain't gonna find out. Largo!" he commanded, and Largo shoved the gun into Mike's ribs, grabbing him and pulling him backwards toward the door.

Beau raised his head up just long enough to see what they were doing to Mike. "Hey man, leave him alone." He tried to get up, but Choo Choo shoved him down again.

"Stay on your cloud, punk, if you wants what I gives ya, or you'll be hurtin' real bad."

Beau's eyes couldn't focus on Mike. He just lay there.

Choo Choo motioned to Largo, and the two of them pulled Mike out of the room.

Only that time in New York had Mike been this frightened. "Hey, Choo Choo. You know *me*," he tried. "I'm not going to say anything."

"Yo damn right you won't!" Choo Choo insisted, giving him a push from behind.

The three of them walked closely together down

the hall to the service exit and waited for the elevator. "I wants him in the car fas'l" Choo Choo said to Largo.

They were each gripping Mike's arms tightly. "I've got to stay with Beau! I've got to take care of him so he can play tonight. Have a heart, Choo Choo," Mike pleaded.

"Shut yo mouth," Largo said with a push for emphasis.

The elevator arrived, and the three of them got in. Mike prayed that someone would get in with them and give him a chance to escape. But no one did. He couldn't believe this was happening to him. He had to think of something! Where were they taking him? What were they going to do with him? His mind could only imagine the worst.

CHAPTER
45

The excitement and frenzy of the concert was exactly the way Regina remembered it, only better. It had been a long time since she'd aroused a reaction like this from the public. She never thought she'd feel this elated by it, but she did. Wild confusion reigned as her limousine pulled up to the special entrance to the Superdome. She could actually feel the pulsing and the clamoring of the fans from inside the car. But what really gave her a shock was the marquee.

Michael Shaw & Jerry Lubow Present CAMIL Records's Production of Majesty's Reunion.

What do you know, she thought. *Michael did it.* Maybe his luck was changing.

Regina's driver handed a special pass to the police officer, the first in a row of security guards lining the red carpeted area, and she and her secretary got out of the car while hysterical fans screamed and shouted, trying to push their way through the barriers to adore her up close. How Florie would have loved this, she thought, making a mental note to describe it to her later in detail.

Inside the Superdome the tension was so high the huge auditorium fairly crackled with electricity. Worker ants didn't scurry about with as much purpose as the hundreds of technicians and television crew members and roadies and hangers-on. She hadn't seen such superhype in a long time.

She pushed and shoved her way through the debris of advanced technology looking for Mike. They hadn't spoken since yesterday, and he deserved her congratulations. But nobody knew where he was. Finally she found Louise and Jerry Lubow.

"Regina!" Lubow said, kissing her. "Have you seen the marquee? We took care of your boy, didn't we?"

Regina would have liked to throttle him. Her *boy!* No wonder Mike had to try so hard. "Why did you give it to him, Jerry? Was it the debt or my contract?"

"No," he smiled expansively. "Mike earned it. He's worked his tail off for months, and he was the one who convinced Cord to return after he'd quit."

Mike had really talked Cord into coming back? She hadn't known that for certain until now; but then she'd been so involved with Florie, how could she have known? She wondered what Mike had said to Cord to convince him.

"Where is my husband?" she asked. "What did he say when he saw the marquee?"

"The creep hasn't even thanked me yet," Lubow said. "He took off hours ago."

"Mike went over to Beau's hotel," Louise said. "But he must be back by now. Why don't you wait in your dressing room, Regina. I'll find him."

The elevator opened in the garage, and Choo Choo stepped ahead of them to look around. There was nobody in sight.

"Come on," he motioned to Largo, and the three of them moved into the garage. Mike tried to hang back, but they pulled him along, the gun jammed into his ribs.

"We better take his car, boss," Largo said.

"Yeah." Choo Choo reached into Mike's pockets, looking for his keys. "Which car is yours?"

I won't tell him, Mike thought. But the license number was attached to the key ring. Largo pressed the gun harder into his side. "It's the red Buick compact," he said.

Choo Choo's hand closed around the keys, but as he pulled them out, they fell to the floor with a clatter. Largo bent to pick them up and Mike saw his chance! He jerked his arm away from Choo Choo, shoved Largo from behind so that he lost his balance, and dashed between two nearby cars, ducking down out of sight.

"He's over there!" Choo Choo shouted. "Get 'im." He pulled Largo to his feet.

Mike crawled the length of his hiding place and skirted around the next car.

Voices. People were coming. From where he was crouched he could see an old woman and a little boy getting off the elevator. They saw him too and stopped and stared. He motioned to them frantically and mouthed the words, "Go away." But they just stood there staring. *Where was the parking attendant?* he wondered. He could hear Largo and Choo Choo hurrying between the cars. They were getting closer. Mike stuck his head up, and they saw him.

"Do something fas'!" Choo Choo hissed, and Largo raised his gun, but the old woman was between Mike and Largo.

"Watch out!" Choo Choo yelled. "We don't want the cops."

Mike ducked down and ran away from where he was hiding. Choo Choo ran after him.

"What are they doing, Grandma?" the boy asked.

"Hush, Billy. None of our business."

Mike ran from row to row, keeping down, ducking between the cars, and trying to keep sight of Largo's and Choo Choo's feet as they moved in a circle to box him in. His heart was pounding, and there were shivers of fear in his guts. God, they would kill him!

He worked his way in an arc, trying to keep away from them and get to the exit. The old woman had moved toward her car, and he was right behind her. "Get down!" he whispered to her, but she just stared at him and began to shake.

Choo Choo was behind him; Mike could hear the movement of his body against the cars. The little boy broke away from his grandmother's grasp and ran out of the garage shouting, "Police! Police!"

Largo fired at the boy, and the grandmother screamed, "No!"

Mike crawled around the end of three more cars and reached the safety of a pillar where he could catch his breath. The boy's voice carried to them from outside the garage. Largo had missed. Mike could see Largo's feet between him and the exit. He peered around the pillar and saw that Largo's gun was still drawn, and he was looking in Mike's direction. Mike ducked back. Choo Choo was climbing over the tops of the cars on his left, getting closer every second. The woman was huddled down somewhere off to his right. His back was to the wall; he'd have to get past the woman on his right and get out. He began to crawl out of his place when another shot rang out! The bullet whizzed right past him, and he nearly fainted. Largo fired again!

"Don't shoot!" Choo Choo cautioned, "till you see 'im."

The woman screamed for help. She was crying now, and her terrified cries echoed in the cavernous garage. Mike crawled under the three remaining cars to where he'd left her and tried to comfort her. But when she saw him, she screamed even louder. "Get away from me! He's here. Over here!"

"No, no. Be quiet!" he begged, but it was too late.

Largo was on him in a minute with the gun pointed at his head.

They shoved the woman aside, and Choo Choo grabbed Mike by the collar, yanking him up. Largo slammed him in the kidneys and the stomach and the chest with his fists. Over and over the blows came until he was a mass of pain. A knee to his groin took his breath away, and he doubled over in agony. Largo raised one enormous hand and brought it down on his neck; and then nothing.

Stylwickji was tired of keeping tabs on Mike Shaw. Shaw was a boring guy, never did anything unusual. Mr. Lubow's fears about him were proving unfounded. But Stylwickji had been told to stick with him like glue, so glue he would be. You never could tell with these things. You watched a guy for weeks, sometimes months, and then one day the thing you never thought would happen happens, and you nail him good.

Stylwickji had been parked by the Charles Hotel for about twenty minutes when he heard a commotion and a boy came running out of the garage, crying and shouting for the police. Stylwickji looked around, but no one stopped or came to the boy's aid. *People,* he thought. *Never want to help their fellow man.* He left his motor running and crossed the street to the boy.

"What's going on, son? Why do you want the police?"

"Mister, you gotta do something." He stared at Stylwickji's scar. He was very frightened. "There's two black men with guns in there chasing a white man. And my Grandma is in there too." Tears were running down his cheeks.

Southern retribution, Stylwickji thought, but just then he heard the sound of a car roaring up the ramp. A black Cadillac came tearing out of the garage, screeching as it flew by. Stylwickji thought he recognized the driver. It looked like Choo Choo's man, Largo. The Cadillac was followed immediately by Mike Shaw's red Buick compact, only Choo Choo Trainer was driving! As Mike's car sped by, Stylwickji noticed a piece of Mike's jacket hanging out of the trunk.

Without a second's hesitation he ran back across the street, jumped into his own car, and took off after them.

CHAPTER
46

Nobody knew where Mike was. Louise called Beau's hotel, but there was no answer in his room. Neither Don nor Cord, nor even James Fitzgerald had seen Mike all afternoon, and it was getting close to concert time. Louise was detained from finding Mike while she arranged a few technical details for James, who had generously agreed to be one of their opening acts. And then finally the only place she hadn't looked for Mike was in Beau's dressing room.

She found Penny outside Beau's door, pacing back and forth. "He still won't talk to me," she told Louise. "Please ask him to let me in. Tell him I'm so sorry . . ."

The poor girl looked desperate.

"Is Mike Shaw in there with him?"

Penny shook her head. "I think he's alone."

Louise knocked sharply. "Beau, it's me. Louise."

She heard the door unlock and she went in.

One look at Beau and her heart sank. His eyes were horribly red and swollen from crying, and he was staring straight ahead with a glassy expression. He moved back to the corner of the room. His shoulders were hunched forward, and all his pretense was gone. He was so loaded that he was barely conscious of her presence.

She came over to him and touched his arm. He flinched as though he'd been struck and began to whimper.

"Beau, it's all right. It's me, Louise." She led him over to the studio couch against the opposite wall and helped him to sit down. "Beau, you've got to pull yourself together. "You have to go on very soon." *My God,* she thought, *how did this happen?*

"I'm all right," Beau said, his words barely audible.

"Penny's outside. She wants to see you."

He was exhausted, defeated. "Not like this. Not now."

"What should I tell her?" Louise looked around the room for some way to sober Beau up. There was nothing.

Beau clutched at her clothes. "Tell her Mike was my friend. But I couldn't do anything."

Louise's pulse began to pound. "What do you mean Mike *was* your friend? Where is Mike? Have you seen him?"

"I didn't see anything." His watery eyes pleaded with her not to press. Beau was slipping further and further into desperation. Louise didn't know what to do.

She put both hands on Beau's shoulders. "What didn't you see, Beau? Tell me. Was it the marquee with Mike's name? Is that what you're talking about?"

Beau dropped his head to his chest in misery. "I don't know where Mike is. He tried to help me. He didn't want me to shoot up. But I couldn't help it." He looked pitiful. "He said I could lick it, but I can't. I never have. Please! Don't tell Penny."

Louise took Beau's face in her hands, trying to make him focus. "Beau, where is Mike?"

"Choo Choo and another man took him away. They had a gun." Tears were pouring from his eyes; he wiped at his nose.

"Where did they take him?"

"He only wanted to help me," Beau repeated. "I don't know where they took him."

"Jesus!" Louise swore, resisting the urge to shake

Beau. In his drugged state he had no conception of time. Mike might have been gone for hours. He could be in terrible danger.

She left Beau and ran out into the hall. "Stay here," she said to Penny. "I've got to find Mike. I'm afraid something might have happened to him."

"What is it?" Penny asked.

"Beau told me that Mike has disappeared. Choo Choo Trainer and his baboon Largo took him at gunpoint. I'm going to report it to the police."

"What was Choo Choo Trainer doing with Beau?" Penny's voice sounded small and scared.

"Just stay here," Louise insisted. "I'll be back as soon as I can." And she ran down the corridor to the elevator.

There was a security guard with a walkie-talkie, but he couldn't locate Jerry Lubow. She made her way to the main floor, pushing and shoving a path through the excited throngs to where she'd seen Jerry earlier, but he wasn't there. Just as she was about to go back to the dressing rooms again, she spotted him.

"Jerry!" she screamed, and he turned, catching sight of her. She ran to him, pushing through crowds of jostling people.

Breathlessly she told him what Beau had said.

"I'm sure Mike's all right," Jerry assured her. "Stylwickji was keeping an eye on him."

"Then why isn't he here? He wouldn't stay away from this place unless he was in trouble! You know how invested he is in this damn concert. God, I wish I'd never heard of it. You should see Beau. He's an absolute basket case. I'm going to look for Stylwickji. Maybe he knows what happened."

Jerry grabbed her arm and pulled her back. "He's not here. And I don't want you involved in anything to do with Choo Choo Trainer."

"Then *you* do something, big man!" she shouted. All around her the frenzy and revelry were at a furious pitch, but inside she felt sick and cold with fear.

"There's nothing I can do, baby," he pleaded. "Whatever has happened to Mike, neither of us can help him now. Leave it alone."

"If anything has happened to Mike Shaw," Louise said to Jerry through clenched teeth, "I'm holding you personally responsible."

"I got him the fucking marquee," Jerry yelled to her as she hurried away. "What do you want from me?"

She cornered a Louisiana policeman and frantically explained to him that Regina Williams's husband was missing.

"He's the producer of this reunion; he's been working on this show for months and he'd be here unless something has happened to him." She gave the officer a description of Mike and Choo Choo and Largo, and told him what happened. The officer promised he'd make inquiries, but Louise had a desperate feeling of frustration. There was so much she still had to do before curtain, which was rapidly approaching. Only two hours more. The thousands of chores would keep her busy, keep her mind off her fears. But someone had to tell Regina. Where was Mike? She prayed everything would be all right. But something told her it wouldn't be.

"Bertie!" Regina called from the bathroom. "Make a note to order me a half-dozen peachglow eye shadows from Boyd's Chemists." She studied her newly applied makeup with satisfaction. "And be sure they're packed against breakage. I hate using flaky eye shadow."

Bertie's reply from the next room was muffled. Regina's makeup was something that Florie always took care of. *Don't think about Florie now,* she cautioned herself. She missed Florie terribly. Tonight especially. And where the hell was Mike? Gone again! He knew what she went through before a performance. Why wasn't he here? She might have to get used to being without Mike. The idea made her throat constrict.

Somebody was knocking on the door. She could hear Bertie on the phone. "Can you get the door?" she called. She heard Bertie hang up the phone and go to the door and then voices. Was it Mike? She heard Bertie cry out and she was instantly alert. Oh God, what now? Was it Florie? She ran to the doorway.

Louise Carlin was standing in the dressing room with a terrible expression on her face. And Bertie was crying.

"What is it?" Regina gasped. "Is it Florie?" She looked from one to the other. Oh, please God, don't let it be. Not now! Not yet!

"Florie's all right," Bertie said. "I was just on the phone with her."

Sick terror grabbed Regina with a sudden jolt. "Then it's the children! Is it the children?"

Bertie shook her head. "No. It's Mike. Louise thinks he's been kidnaped. He was trying to keep Beau from shooting heroin, and Choo Choo Trainer took him away at gunpoint."

"Beau's an addict?" she whispered. *It can't be. Not again.* Regina just stared at Louise. "I've always been afraid that something like this would happen." She could feel the hysteria welling up, feel the color draining from her face. Suddenly her knees wouldn't hold her up. Bertie grabbed her as she was about to fall. She held onto Bertie in desperation. "Tell me everything you know, Louise. I want to know everything. What about my children? Are they safe?" She was squeezing her fist so tightly that her nails dug into her palm. Bertie helped her to a chair. Mike hadn't been kidnaped! It wasn't true. He would walk through that door any moment.

"The children are safe," Bertie assured her.

"They're with Mrs. Briggs at the hotel. She's bringing them over just before curtain."

Regina nodded. Everything seemed unreal to her. Mike? Kidnaped? *MIKE.* She needed him. He was always here! Especially before a performance. "I want him!" she cried. *"Please!"*

Bertie ran into the bathroom to find Regina's tranquilizers. Regina's eyes pleaded with Louise. "Mike is going to be all right. They probably want money. They'll contact us. And we'll pay the money. I've thought about this many times. I'm not going to make any examples where my loved ones are concerned. I'll pay anything they ask. Anything. Anything." She was shaking all over. The enormity of the invasion was more than she could take. First Florie nearly dying, and now this.

She was eleven years old. She was on the bus coming back from a weekend in Brussels. The bus pulled into the school yard and all the parents were there, waiting. She looked around for Mama and Mitchell, but she didn't see them. And then she saw Mrs. Wogen. She was wearing a black dress and coat and hat. She looked religious, like the sisters at the Catholic church. But Mrs. Wogen was married. She wasn't a nun. Mr. Van Eyke made her stay on the bus until all the other children got off. Why? What had she done? And then he took her by the hand and helped her down the stairs to Mrs. Wogen. Mrs. Wogen hardly had to lean over to talk to her, and Regina realized how much she'd grown lately. Mrs. Wogen used to be so tall. "Where's my Mama?" she asked. Mrs. Wogen had been crying.

"Regina-Marie," she said, "I've some bad news for you."

Regina screamed, "Mike."

Bertie grabbed her hands and forced a pill between her teeth. She swallowed but it stuck in her throat. She was so dry. Someone handed her a cup of water.

God, she wanted to cry. But she couldn't cry. It was less than an hour to curtain. If she cried she wouldn't have time to redo her makeup. She still had to get dressed. Mike always fastened the last buttons and hooks on her costume for good luck. She couldn't go on and do a performance now. They would have to cancel the show. But they couldn't cancel! It was too late. There would be a riot!

"Is it too late?" she whispered.

They stared at her, not understanding.

"We'll find him, Regina," Louise said.

She tried to smile, but her face was frozen. *Please God*, she prayed. *I'll do anything you ask. Anything!*

CHAPTER 47

Stylwickji ran two red lights before he realized he couldn't keep such a close distance behind the two cars ahead or they'd see him. But neither could he risk losing them. Luckily, a few blocks from the hotel both cars slowed down and began observing the traffic laws. They didn't want to be stopped by the cops either. Stylwickji wished he could phone for help, but that wasn't possible. At least he wouldn't lose them now, since Largo was waiting at each signal for Choo Choo's Buick to catch up with him.

The Cadillac and the Buick wound through the streets of the city, and Stylwickji followed. They seemed to be as unfamiliar with its layout as he was. This abduction was obviously spontaneous and poorly planned. But then Choo Choo's brains had always been in his ass.

They reached the industrial part of the city with its factories, huge storage yards, shipping and loading docks, and freight yards piled high with building materials. The Cadillac pulled over to the side of the street, and Largo got out. Choo Choo pulled up behind him, and Stylwickji hung back a block and waited. The two men seemed to be arguing about what to do. Choo Choo reached into the glove compartment and pulled out a map. Then they argued some more about where they were. Stylwickji strained to hear them, but he couldn't distinguish their words.

It was getting late. Mr. Lubow would be wondering where he was, why he hadn't checked in. The stadium must be a madhouse by now.

The two men found something on the map they were looking for, because Largo got back into his car and pulled it up the street to a parking zone and locked it. Stylwickji thought that was amusing. Then Largo got into Mike's rental with Choo Choo driving. The traffic was light, so Stylwickji stayed a discreet distance behind. Neither of them had noticed he was there. He followed them another half mile until Choo Choo made a right turn. When Stylwickji turned the same corner, the red car had disappeared! Damn, he thought. They must have spotted him after all. He sped up, trying to find which way they had gone.

The street ahead turned into a dirt road which inclined downward and ended right at the river's edge. They couldn't have gone that way. But there was nowhere else to go. He noticed a set of tire tracks off to the left. They must be somewhere up ahead. He pulled his car over to the side, left the keys in the ignition, and went ahead on foot.

He moved quietly, sticking to the side, crouching down into the low brush by the tire tracks, trying to find cover among all the debris that was strewn around on the banks of the river. He looked around. He was behind an abandoned freight yard; the place was completely deserted.

From time to time he stopped to listen, but all he could hear was the lapping of the water and the sound of boats going by on the river. A slight breeze rustled the weeds around him. And then he heard the sound of a car motor off to the left. He crouched low and crept ahead until he came to a cleared area. There was Mike's car! Choo Choo was standing off to the side of the clearing with his arms folded around his slight body as he watched Largo drive the car away from him. And then Largo threw the car into reverse and backed up at a high speed, heading directly towards a pile of cement pillars.

He was going to crush the back of the car. *Shaw is in that trunk*, Stylwickji thought. Jesus. Lubow didn't want him dead. Stylwickji reached for his gun, but it wouldn't do him any good at this point. The car was screeching backwards. If he shot Largo, the car would still crash in reverse. Suddenly the car swerved, skidding on the debris of smaller cement fragments that lay about in front of the larger pillars, and as it reached the point of impact, it slid to the side, crushing the left rear instead of hitting squarely on the trunk. Largo wasn't even shaken by the impact and he threw the car forward again for another go at it.

"Wait a minute," Choo Choo yelled. "Clear some of that crap outta there so's you can get it right on!"

"Okay," Largo agreed and he jumped out of the car, leaving the door open and the engine running. He ran around behind the car and began to clear a path directly in front of the cement pillars. Choo Choo stood by, directing his labor.

This was Stylwickji's chance. Creeping low, he moved around behind them, keeping in front of the car so they wouldn't see him or his shadow. The sun was low in the sky behind him, and purple and brown colors darkened the twisted and rusted shapes of metal sidings, cement blocks, and iron scrap that lay about.

Stylwickji moved quickly toward the open car door, crouching low as he moved, but in his haste he didn't see a piece of curved metal siding, punctuated by sharp multiple prongs until he had stepped on it. The piece of metal flipped up and jammed its jagged prongs deeply into his calf. An intense pain shot up his leg, and he bit his lip to keep from crying out. He fell to his knees and pulled the vicious thing from his leg. Blood spurted out of the wound. But there was nothing he could do at the moment. He pressed against the wound and crawled the rest of the way, pulling himself painfully into the driver's seat. He kept his head down and carefully reached for the gear shift. But just as he was about to put it into gear, Largo turned and saw him. "Hey!" Largo yelled as he tore around the other side of the car and leaped into the passenger seat, grabbing Stylwickji around the neck.

At the same moment Stylwickji pressed his foot on the gas, and the car shot forward. Largo held him fast and grabbed for the wheel as the car turned in a circle. They struggled desperately for control, grunting and thrashing. Stylwickji's leg felt like white hot irons were searing it. As the car swung wildly to the left and Largo's door slammed shut, the door on Stylwickji's side followed with a loud bang. Largo jerked the wheel in the other direction.

The two men were locked in a deadly embrace, but Largo had the advantage because Stylwickji could barely maneuver with the wheel in front of him and the pain throbbing in his leg. The fabric of his trousers was sticking to him where the blood oozed steadily. Largo let go of the wheel and used his other arm around Stylwickji's neck. He squeezed tighter and tighter, pressing on Stylwickji's windpipe. Stylwickji jammed his elbow into Largo's ribs, trying to break his hold. Again and again they fought for control of the gears. Largo kept trying to shove them in reverse while Stylwickji kept his right hand in an iron grip; all the while the car careened crazily around the yard, bursting forward with sudden thrusts of speed.

Stylwickji couldn't let go long enough to reach his gun. He could barely breathe. If only he could reach his knife. But it was strapped to his injured leg. He tried to lift it, but he couldn't raise the leg for the steering wheel and the pain in his calf. He was losing ground. He had to get a breath of air or he would pass out. In another few moments his neck wouldn't be able to hold out. Already he could barely see where he was going. He gave the wheel a sudden sharp turn to the left and at the same time he yanked with his upper arm slamming it into Largo's face. For a second he had broken Largo's hold, and he gasped as the air filled his lungs. The car was heading straight for Choo Choo, who was yelling and running back and forth, trying to dodge the oncoming car. Largo regained his balance and grabbed Stylwickji again, throwing Stylwickji's head back against the head rest with such a force that the head rest snapped off. Stylwickji used all his remaining strength to stiffen his upper body and keep his neck from being broken by the incredible strength of his foe.

Ahead of him he could see a cement pillar; the car was heading for it, but Choo Choo was in the way. If he could only make it a few more seconds. With one final thrust of strength he jammed his foot on the throttle, and the car rammed directly into the cement post, crushing Choo Choo on impact. Stylwickji had known the crash was coming and he held onto the steering wheel, but the unexpected impact threw Largo forward, and his head went flying through the windshield. As the car settled back, Largo slumped forward, impaled on the glass, bleeding onto the dashboard. Choo Choo's dying screams and cries of agony from beneath the car rent the air as Stylwickji climbed out and dragged his injured leg away from the wreck. If Shaw hadn't been in the trunk, he would have fired into the gas tank and put Choo Choo out of his misery. *Shaw must be dead by now,* Stylwickji thought, noticing the way the left rear end of the car was smashed in. He could barely walk. His shoe was filled with blood; the metal prong that punctuated his calf must have hit an artery. His neck burned from where Largo had choked him, and his body ached from all the blows he'd received.

He was halfway across the clearing when the sound of shredding glass made him turn. Largo was standing outside the car pulling pieces of the windshield from his bleeding head. *My God,* Stylwickji thought, *the man is indestructible.* And then he saw Largo's gun.

Stylwickji reached into his jacket for his gun, but Largo fired. Stylwickji felt the bullet rip through his side. His gun went flying, and he was thrown backwards to the ground in shock and terror. He lay there in disbelief, cursing himself for his stupidity. *Why didn't I shoot him?* he wondered. *I thought he was dead. Those niggers have bones where their brains should be.* The pain in his side blended with the pain in his leg, and he screamed. And then another bullet hit him in the hip. He moaned and rolled to the right away from the shots, trying to find cover. He pulled himself a few more inches before he couldn't go any further. The next two shots missed him. But he knew if he didn't get out of there he was going to die.

The misshapen form of Largo came stumbling toward him, gun in hand. His face was a mass of glass splinters and blood. One of his eyes had been torn from its socket, and his lip was cut in two and hanging down on his chin, revealing a horrible skeletal grin. He stood over Stylwickji and raised his gun, but his strength began to fail and he sank to his knees. The gun wavered at Stylwickji's head.

Stylwickji reached his hand frantically around for his gun. But he wasn't close enough to where he'd dropped it after that first bullet. He couldn't reach his knife because he couldn't lift his leg. Largo's hand shook as he tried to hold the gun steady. His ghoulish appearance added to Stylwickji's terror. The barrel righted itself again, and Stylwickji searched the ground around him as he waited for death.

Suddenly he felt something! His hand closed around the piece of metal siding that had punctured his leg. He pulled it toward him. With his last remaining ounce of strength he swung it at Largo's head. The metal siding pierced the side of Largo's temple just as Largo fired at Stylwickji, right on target.

CHAPTER 48

Penny stood before the open door of Beau's dressing room afraid to move. Louise had run off to find Mike Shaw, leaving her on the edge of disaster. Something was terribly wrong. She could hear Beau in the dressing room. The sounds he was making wrenched at her. After waiting a very long time for Louise to come back, she stepped forward and walked into the room. One look was all she needed for every horrible memory of her past to engulf her. She remembered the scabs and sores on her body that wouldn't heal, the constant nausea when she didn't have drugs, the degradation, the hypodermic tracks, the frantic search for pills and the money to buy them. And the highs. Even those came rushing back. She could never forget that feeling. Once an addict, always an addict. The child within kicked as though in protest to her thoughts, but in spite of the baby she had an overwhelming desire to join Beau in his state of forgetfulness. Anything not to have to face what was staring at her from the sofa. Only that child kicking inside of her made her hesitate from grabbing the hypodermic that lay on the table and jabbing it into her vein. And suddenly she knew that hell was this dressing room in the Superdome in New Orleans, Louisiana and that she was in it.

"Beau," she cried. "Did I do this to you?"

Beau's body seemed drained of all its vitality. He

tried to focus on Penny and keep control, but he couldn't do it. All he could do was shake his head in stupefying uncertainty.

Penny took a step toward him and reached to take him in her arms when someone grabbed her from behind.

"I've been looking for you." It was Don. He took in the room at a glance and gave Beau a look of sheer disgust. And then he pulled Penny back toward the door.

She looked from Beau to Don, rooted between them. If only Beau would call her back. She wanted him to very much. She was certain now that he knew about her and Don. He had chosen drugs to deal with the pain.

"You're going to screw it up out there today, aren't you, turkey?" Don sneered. "I dunno what you ever saw in him." He pulled Penny with him toward the door.

But she resisted, waiting for Beau to stop her, waiting for him to call her, to want her again. *Please, Beau,* she prayed. But he turned his head away.

It was like a knife in her heart. She stumbled into the hall after Don and fell against him, unable to stand the pain.

Mike was squeezed into a black womb of pain. Excruciating jabs pierced him with every breath, terrifying him more than the darkness of his cramped, coffinlike space. Silence surrounded him, wet sticky silence. A gasoline leak dampened his clothes and filled the trunk with nauseating fumes, sickening him more with every moment. There was a cut in his head that oozed blood down his face into a sticky puddle under his cheek. His head had been cut during one of the car crashes. Which one he didn't know. Neither did he know how long he'd been here. He'd lost all sense of time as the car careened over streets and curbs and ruts, shaking him, bruising him, injuring him more than he already was. And then there were the crashes; first in the back and then the front. And then he heard the screams of someone dying. Those screams still echoed in his head, horrible, agonizing death screams. He cried out with each cry of the tortured man, whoever he was. And then gunshots! He didn't know who was shooting or whether they were coming to shoot him. It seemed like he was waiting forever just to die.

He could barely move in the cramped space. Each time he tried, another pain ripped through him. In his mind he saw his own broken ribs waiting to jab their pointed ends into his lungs, saw his lungs fill with blood as he drowned on his own fluids. His head throbbed with every beat of his heart, and he could taste the salt from the blood that ran down his head and into his mouth.

He lay on his left side where they had thrown him, his back to the opening; he was unable to move in either direction or turn over.

Where had they gone? he wondered. Were they waiting out there for him to make a sound so they could shoot him right through the metal of the car? Would a bullet pierce the trunk accurately? He could feel it happening at any second. *Get hold of yourself, Shaw! Don't lose yourself.* But the confines of the space and the pain made him want to scream and kick and claw his way out. If he did that, he could kill himself in a fit of temper. He clamped his teeth together to keep them from chattering.

Could anybody out there hear him? Cautiously he tapped on the inside of the trunk and held his breath as he waited. There was no reply. He tapped again. If he only knew Morse code. Two dots and a dash. Every movement sent a burning pulse up and down his back, so that he cried out in pain. Why didn't they kill him? What were they waiting for? They'd already killed some poor bastard who was pressed under the car. Who was it? A policeman come to help him? He'd never get out. He'd never get out!

Something was pressing into his leg. He moved his leg up a few inches, but the pain shot through him again. He moved again, more cautiously this time. It was a piece of metal, some kind of tool. Probably part of the jack. He tried to drag it close enough to reach with his hand, but the jolt of pain was so terrible he gasped and then tried to muffle his sounds. If anyone was out there, they were leaving him alone. Alone to suffocate, he realized. He had to get out of here! Already it was difficult to breathe. He reached for the tool under his leg, stretching almost beyond his endurance until finally his hand closed around it. But he wasn't facing the door. He had his back to it and he would have to move forward in a circle in order to get a clear shot at the trunk latch.

Carefully he ducked his head toward his chest, trying not to increase the bleeding from the wound in his head. He had to fight to keep from fainting as the pain radiated through his body. Slowly he began his turn.

The air in the trunk was very close. How much longer would it last before he suffocated or died of toxic fumes? He could only move himself an inch at a time as he pushed his body forward in a tight ball. The inside of the trunk scraped and gouged his skin and tore at his clothes. Progress was minuscule, and with every move a fresh jab of pain set him gasping as his ribs pushed against his lungs. Every other minute he was forced to stop and rest in spite of the mounting fear and panic that engulfed him. His strength was weakening with every second, and he was still losing blood. *Hold on, Shaw,* he told himself, *keep going!* At the halfway mark he found his knees pressed tightly against his chest, and the pain was so intense that he passed out. When he came to, he had to force himself to keep going forward in his tight circle. And then finally a piece of luck. His shoulder touched upon another metal tool. The lug wrench, round at one end to fit over the wheel bolts and smooth and narrow at the other to pry off the hubcap. Gratefully he grasped it in his left hand and continued his maneuver until he was in position to fit the blessed tool into the space between the trunk and the latch. Slowly he began to pry it open.

Beau heard voices outside his door as though they were coming through a funnel whose apex was placed directly inside his ear. The voices sounded hollow and tinny, but every syllable was achingly clear. And through it all Penny's wrenching sobs played a counterpoint to the conversation.

He wondered why she was crying. Don kept telling her how much better off she'd be without him. That was true, wasn't it? Beau knew the truth of that better than anybody. He heard Regina's voice.

"Why is Penny crying?" Regina asked. "*Her* husband hasn't been abducted."

"She found out her weak-livered husband has been shooting up again."

Regina came to the doorway and stared at him. "Do you realize what you have done? My husband might be dead right now because of you. And you did nothing to help him. And I want him! Please, God, find him!" There was an awful pain in Regina's voice. Beau knew the sound of it well.

Penny was staring at him from the open doorway. He could tell she thought he was disgusting too.

"Just remember who it was that didn't want him in the first place," Don said. His voice sent needles into Beau's brain. "But all of you were so goddamned stubborn. The man's a joke. A stupid joke."

"What's going on?" Cord shouldered his way past Penny and Don. He noticed that Regina had a wild look on her face as she turned from one to the other helplessly, and then she began to hyperventilate, breathing rapidly, beyond control.

"Stop it!" Cord said. "You're making yourself sick, Regina. Calm down. This won't do any good, and it won't bring Mike back."

"The way Mike brought you back when you quit. *You* would have let everybody down, but not Mike. He saved the reunion," she gasped. "Like he tried to save Beau, and look where it got him. It's Beau's fault," she insisted, close to hysteria.

Inside his dressing room Beau cried silently.

Cord stared at her angrily. "Come on, Regina," he said, taking her arm. "Come away from here. Leave Beau alone."

She hung back defiantly. "I'm not leaving! I'm not."

"Jesus Christ! Don't you people ever learn? What the hell's the matter with you?"

"Why won't you admit it?" she cried. "He's no good; he's weak! He's an addict just like your brother!"

Regina saw it coming but there was nothing she could do. The sound of Cord's slap echoed in the hall. Penny gasped. And Regina just stood there stunned while the white imprints of Cord's fingers on her cheek grew redder and redder.

"I hate you!" she said, regaining her control. And then she turned and ran toward her dressing room.

"Well, loverboy. You've really done it this time," Don said. "And she's right. Beau was a shitty choice right from the start. We should have replaced him in the beginning."

Shitty choice . . . shitty choice . . . The words pounded in Beau's heart.

But Cord didn't even respond to Don. He was too shocked at what he'd done to Regina. He turned and went back to his own dressing room.

Finally Beau was alone. He knew they were right about him. He was no good. Slowly he got up from the bed and went to find his kit. He had to have something to stop this feeling of misery and fear.

CHAPTER 49

The old terror was back. Only this time with valid cause. She was all alone. As alone as she had been the first time she came to California after the death of her mother and brother. She had almost lost Florie, and Mike, and now Cord. The extreme emotions that assailed her alternated between strength and despair. *I'll survive!* she told herself, gaining a moment of courage. And then the claustrophobia would press in on her, and the walls of her dressing room would enclose her.

When Cord slapped her, it had done something besides shock and infuriate her. It had brought everything into sharp focus. Every last vestige of desire she'd felt for him was gone. She didn't want Cord anymore. Not now, not ever. The reality of Mike, flawed and imperfect, was more valuable than the fantasy of Cord. If only she'd have the chance to tell him so. *Oh, please be safe, Mike,* she prayed.

"Forty minutes to curtain," someone called. The opening acts were well into their performances. After James there would be an intermission; and then Majesty. She never came to the wings until the last possible moment, but tonight she needed the diversion, the crush, the people, something to hang on to in this sea of insanity. She opened the door of her dressing room and stepped into the hall, meeting everyone's gaze, all their questioning eyes, with her head held high.

A roadie came to escort her to the elevator, and Cord was standing there. She looked at him calmly, objectively. He was beautiful and appealing, but not for her. For a moment in Beau's dressing room she had wanted to kill him, but now he aroused nothing in her at all.

Cord reached for her arm, and she brushed him away. "I'm sorry Regina," he said. "I lost my temper."

The elevator opened just as Don came out of his dressing room and joined them. "You going to be all right?" he asked Regina.

She nodded, grateful for his concern, and they stepped into the elevator.

But when the doors opened on the first floor and a surge of people surrounded her, she felt the iron fist of panic grab her throat, squeezing tightly. She'd never be able to sing tonight. She noticed a cinematographer off to the side recording her every reaction.

Vultures.

She forced herself to smile for the camera, but she wanted to smash the lens. She wanted to have a screaming, hysterical, heel-kicking fit! The press hadn't heard about Mike's disappearance, but they knew something was in the wind.

She turned to Don. "You've got to help me; I'm not going to make it." She started to shake again.

He pulled her aside. "You will because you have to. How much of this is guilt over your relationship with Cord, and how much is concern about Mike?"

"I don't feel guilty about Cord anymore," she told him. "It's over."

"It's about time," he answered.

The cinematographer followed her, keeping her tightly in his view. When she turned around, she realized that Cord had heard what she said to Don. She gazed into his eyes until he looked away.

The elevator door opened behind her, and she heard someone call her name. Bertie came rushing up to her. "I just got a call from the police! They've found him. They've found Mike. He's all right! He's alive!"

"Where is he?" Don asked.

"I don't know. But he's safe," Bertie said.

"Is he really all right?" Regina asked.

Bertie squeezed her hands. "Yes, it's true."

Regina moaned with relief. "Thank God."

The cinematographer never stopped filming. "Who's alive?" someone asked, and Regina thought, *My husband is alive!*

All during James's performance she waited anxiously for reports. First she heard Mike was in the hospital; then someone said he was on his way to the Superdome. As James neared the end of his act, she got word that Mike's car had arrived, that he was inside the building, that he was being brought to her.

And then she saw him.

People stepped aside and she ran to him.

There was a bandage on his head and a crutch under one arm; the other arm was in a sling. But he was alive!

She kissed his face, smoothed his chest with her hands, holding him, touching him, unaware of her costume or her makeup. "Oh, Mike," she said. "I love you.

Mike tried to stroke her hair, but everything hurt. "It's okay, baby. I made it, I made it."

"You sure as hell did," she said. "You even got your marquee."

"How about that?" he grinned. "They couldn't stop me from being with my girl."

He would never forget this night. Especially the moment when that crowbar finally released the trunk lid and the warm Louisiana air rushed in around him, liberating him from suffocation. That had been the highlight of his life until the moment he held Regina in his arms.

"Are the children all right?" he asked.

She nodded. "They aren't aware of what's been going on."

"I'm glad," he said. "I'll sit with them during the show.

She hugged him tighter. "What you must have been through."

"I don't know if I'll ever be able to describe it," he said while she stroked his cheek. "Are you all right?" He was referring to her usual preshow panic.

"I am now." It amazed her how much she meant that.

Mike looked at Cord watching them. Louise was standing next to Cord, and he was holding her hand. She smiled at Mike and gave him a high sign. He noticed Penny standing nearby. "How's Beau?" he asked her. In all that had happened, he'd forgotten about Beau.

"He's in terrible shape," she said. "He's still up in his dressing room. I don't think he can make it down here by himself."

"I'd better go get him," Mike said.

"You can't do that," Regina insisted. "You're badly injured. Let someone else go."

"No. I want to see him," he told her.

"I'll go with you," Louise said, and she helped Mike to hobble over to the elevator.

"Intermission. Twenty minutes to curtain," someone called.

Regina watched the elevator close on Mike and Louise and she realized she was too nervous to stand here waiting. "I'm going too," she announced and pushed the other elevator button. Cord and Don and Penny all got into the second elevator with her.

* * *

When Mike opened the door to Beau's dressing room, his worst fears were realized. Beau was curled up on the floor with his knees pulled up against his chest like a baby. He looked very innocent and peaceful, but he wasn't asleep. He was dead.

Mike felt so helpless. He could barely bend down to see if there was any sign of life. Louise stepped forward and reached for Beau's pulse. She had tears in her eyes as she shook her head.

Just then the rest of the group arrived, and Penny broke through the crowd at the door. She saw her husband lying on the floor. "Beau, you have to wake up." She turned to Mike. "Tell him to get up." But Mike's expression told her it was too late. "Do something!" she screamed. "Help him. Help him! Please help him! He said you would help him." Her anguished sobs seemed to be crying for everyone. "No, no, no, no," she cried.

Regina pushed Don aside and looked into the room. "Oh God, not again," she said. Cord was right behind her, but she was afraid to look at him. She could feel his eyes boring into her with disgust and loathing.

And then he roared, "NOOOOO!" The sound of his voice echoed down the corridor to mingle with the screams of the excited fans.

"Five minutes to curtain," came the call.

"Is he dead?" Don asked.

Mike nodded.

"Should we cancel?" Regina whispered.

There was a commotion in the hall as Jerry Lubow came running and pushed into the crowded room. One look told him what he had heard was true.

"Mike!" he said. "Glad you're all right. Drummond! Get hold of John Lawson."

Don looked as though he didn't understand. This was one thing he had never expected.

"*Now*, Drummond!" Lubow shook him. "Where's Lawson?"

"I suppose he's in my dressing room," Don answered.

Lubow gave him a push. "Then go get him!" He stepped around the room and began pulling people out of their shocked immobility. He put his arm around an hysterical Penny and moved her forcefully away from the body. "Sit down, Louise," he ordered. "You're about to faint."

Mike looked at Cord. His face was a sickening shade of yellow. His mouth worked in a tight movement, opening and closing as though his rage was about to explode again. Finally it happened. "If you think I'm going on a stage with you animals, you're all fucked!" he shouted.

Lubow jumped up and grabbed him by the shirt. "You're going on, Crocker! You're a performer! You've got a contract, and you're not going to disappoint millions of people. Save your hatred for later. Because right now *you're going to sing!*" They glared at one another while Cord fought for control. Lubow let go of him. "We're all sorry about this, Cord," he said softly.

Penny still sobbed as though her heart was dying along with her husband. Regina sat down next to her and put her arms around her. "Shh, darling. Be careful of the baby."

"Beau, Beau, Beau . . ." Penny sobbed. "Oh, I'm so sorry. I'm so sorry. Please don't die. Don't die."

Don returned with John Lawson.

"Two minutes to curtain! On stage everyone!"

The announcer's voice over the loudspeaker system penetrated the inner sanctum of the corridors and dressing rooms. A roar went up from the crowd that filled everyone with shattering tension.

Regina was sick from Penny's grief. *How will Penny survive,* she wondered. *How can we go on after this?*

She looked at Mike questioningly, and he said quietly, "Knock 'em dead, sweetheart!" She turned then and walked out of the room with Mike's arm around her.

Louise and Penny were crying, but not Cord. He was a pillar of control as he stared at the body on the floor and clenched and unclenched his fists. His jaw was clamped together, and his eyes burned with hatred. "After tonight never again," he whispered, and then he strode out of the room.

Penny got up from the bed and went to put a pillow under Beau's head. Then she took the cover from the bed and pulled it over her husband up to his chin. "Sleep in peace, my darling," she said. And then she sat down next to him and began to rock the baby in her womb.

They waited backstage in darkness. Their emotions would have to be put aside for the next two hours. John Lawson joined them. He'd managed to squeeze into Beau's costume; the legs of the pants were rolled up. Regina swallowed hard, forcing a surge of sourness back into her stomach. Don cleared his throat. Cord took a deep breath, fighting the knives of pain that twisted inside of him. He let the air out slowly as the voice came over the lourspeaker:

> Ladies and gentlemen . . . The moment you've all been waiting for . . . the Reunion of Majesty. . . .

And they came out onto the stage amidst worldwide frenzy, each of their faces an impenetrable mask.

Dell Bestsellers

- [ ] TO LOVE AGAIN by Danielle Steel $2.50 (18631-5)
- [ ] SECOND GENERATION by Howard Fast $2.75 (17892-4)
- [ ] EVERGREEN by Belva Plain $2.75 (13294-0)
- [ ] AMERICAN CAESAR by William Manchester . . . $3.50 (10413-0)
- [ ] THERE SHOULD HAVE BEEN CASTLES
  by Herman Raucher $2.75 (18500-9)
- [ ] THE FAR ARENA by Richard Ben Sapir $2.75 (12671-1)
- [ ] THE SAVIOR by Marvin Werlin and Mark Werlin . $2.75 (17748-0)
- [ ] SUMMER'S END by Danielle Steel $2.50 (18418-5)
- [ ] SHARKY'S MACHINE by William Diehl $2.50 (18292-1)
- [ ] DOWNRIVER by Peter Collier $2.75 (11830-1)
- [ ] CRY FOR THE STRANGERS by John Saul $2.50 (11869-7)
- [ ] BITTER EDEN by Sharon Salvato $2.75 (10771-7)
- [ ] WILD TIMES by Brian Garfield $2.50 (19457-1)
- [ ] 1407 BROADWAY by Joel Gross $2.50 (12819-6)
- [ ] A SPARROW FALLS by Wilbur Smith $2.75 (17707-3)
- [ ] FOR LOVE AND HONOR by Antonia Van-Loon . . $2.50 (12574-X)
- [ ] COLD IS THE SEA by Edward L. Beach $2.50 (11045-9)
- [ ] TROCADERO by Leslie Waller $2.50 (18613-7)
- [ ] THE BURNING LAND by Emma Drummond $2.50 (10274-X)
- [ ] HOUSE OF GOD by Samuel Shem, M.D. $2.50 (13371-8)
- [ ] SMALL TOWN by Sloan Wilson $2.50 (17474-0)

At your local bookstore or use this handy coupon for ordering:

Dell DELL BOOKS
P.O. BOX 1000, PINEBROOK, N.J. 07058

Please send me the books I have checked above. I am enclosing $_____
(please add 75¢ per copy to cover postage and handling). Send check or money order—no cash or C.O.D.'s. Please allow up to 8 weeks for shipment.

Mr/Mrs/Miss _____

Address _____

City _____ State/Zip _____

**Sometimes you have to lose
everything before you can begin**

To Love Again

Danielle Steel

Author of *The Promise* and
Summer's End

Isabella and Amadeo lived in an elegant and beautiful world where they shared their brightest treasure—their boundless, enduring love. Suddenly, their enchantment ended and Amadeo vanished forever. With all her proud courage could she release the past to embrace her future? Would she ever dare TO LOVE AGAIN?

A Dell Book $2.50 (18631-5)

At your local bookstore or use this handy coupon for ordering:

Dell	**DELL BOOKS** **P.O. BOX 1000, PINEBROOK, N.J. 07058**	To Love Again $2.50 (18631-5)

Please send me the above title. I am enclosing $ _____
(please add 75¢ per copy to cover postage and handling). Send check or money order—no cash or C.O.D.'s. Please allow up to 8 weeks for shipment.

Mr/Mrs/Miss _____

Address _____

City _____ State/Zip _____

THE PASSING BELLS

by

PHILLIP ROCK

A story you'll wish would go on forever.

Here is the vivid story of the Grevilles, a titled British family, and their servants—men and women who knew their place, upstairs and down, until England went to war and the whole fabric of British society began to unravel and change.

"Well-written, exciting. Echoes of Hemingway, Graves and *Upstairs, Downstairs*."—*Library Journal*

"Every twenty-five years or so, we are blessed with a war novel, outstanding in that it depicts not only the history of a time but also its soul."—*West Coast Review of Books*.

"Vivid and enthralling."—*The Philadelphia Inquirer*

A Dell Book $2.75   (16837-6)

At your local bookstore or use this handy coupon for ordering:

| Dell | DELL BOOKS   THE PASSING BELLS $2.75   (16837-6)
P.O. BOX 1000, PINEBROOK, N.J. 07058 |

Please send me the above title. I am enclosing $ _____
(please add 75¢ per copy to cover postage and handling). Send check or money order—no cash or C.O.D.'s. Please allow up to 8 weeks for shipment.

Mr/Mrs/Miss _____

Address _____

City _____ State/Zip _____

A beautiful woman at the pinnacle of power can commit many sins. Only one counts—getting caught.

INDISCRETIONS

by
EVELYN KONRAD

"Sizzling."—*Columbus Dispatch-Journal*

"The Street" is Wall Street—where brains and bodies are tradeable commodities and power brokers play big politics against bigger business. At stake is a $500 million deal, the careers of three men sworn to destroy each other, the future of an oil-rich desert kingdom—and the survival of beautiful Francesca Currey, a brilliant woman in a man's world of finance and power, whose only mistakes are her *Indiscretions*.

A Dell Book $2.50   (14079-X)

At your local bookstore or use this handy coupon for ordering:

Dell	**DELL BOOKS** INDISCRETIONS $2.50 (14079-X)
	P.O. BOX 1000, PINEBROOK, N.J. 07058

Please send me the above title. I am enclosing $ _____
(please add 75¢ per copy to cover postage and handling). Send check or money order—no cash or C.O.D.'s. Please allow up to 8 weeks for shipment.

Mr/Mrs/Miss _____

Address _____

City _____ State/Zip _____

SHARON SALVATO
co-author of *The Black Swan*

Bitter Eden

**He taught her what
it means to live
She taught him what it means to love**

Peter Berean rode across the raging landscape of a countryside in flames. Callie Dawson, scorched by shame, no longer believed in love—until she met Peter's strong, tender gaze. From that moment they were bound by an unforgettable promise stronger than his stormy passions and wilder than her desperate dreams. Together they would taste the rich, forbidden fruit of a *Bitter Eden*.

A Dell Book $2.75 (10771-7)

At your local bookstore or use this handy coupon for ordering:

Dell	DELL BOOKS P.O. BOX 1000, PINEBROOK, N.J. 07058	Bitter Eden $2.75 (10771-7)

Please send me the above title. I am enclosing $ _____
(please add 75¢ per copy to cover postage and handling). Send check or money order—no cash or C.O.D.'s. Please allow up to 8 weeks for shipment.

Mr/Mrs/Miss _____

Address _____

City _____ State/Zip _____